TO THE LAST
BREATH

Cover art: Blue Bridge over St. Marys River © 2022 by Michael K. Zimmerli
Interior Design: Michael K. Zimmerli
Hardcover ISBN: 979-8-9872713-8-4
Paperback ISBN: 979-8-9872713-7-7
Ebook ISBN: 979-8-9872713-6-0
First Printing: 2023
Printed in the United States of America

MARSHGRASS PUBLISHING
ST. MARYS, GA

Contents

Dedication

This novel is dedicated to the memory of my mother, Dagny Zimmerli, who instilled a love in me for the written word, and to my father, Jacob Wesley Zimmerli, who became a published author at age 96. It's never too late.

Acknowledgments

Once again, it takes a village—or in my case, a small city—to produce a story.

Robert Nicholson – a friend since 2005, has been an invaluable resource for weapons and automobiles, plots and their holes, editing and proofreading, hints, helps, and more. He is also a big encourager.

And my thanks to Robert's daughter, Sarah Nicholson, for getting the first Blue Bridge Mystery book for your dad and for sharing your nursing expertise with him and me so the hospital and medical scenes can be correct.

Jimmy Street – thank you for letting me pick your brain about small planes. I'm glad you enjoyed the first two books, and hopefully, you'll find the third one a pleasure to read and maybe even contain an extra twist you weren't expecting.

Roberto Pepé Perez – thank you again for letting me borrow your name and for your encouragement. Thank you for giving me your insights about firearms, the police, the

Navy and security—some of the things "normal" people don't have a need for or access to.

To two of my boyhood friends – Tim Ryan and Eric Larson – thanks for letting me borrow your names. It's very small notoriety, but it's some notoriety. I may have found an untapped source for names of characters: the people I grew up with! At our age, it's kind of fun to suddenly find your name in a book, and not the Memories book at the funeral home! I borrow from my own childhood in Redwood Falls, and I know you both remember Young's Hut out on the east edge of town. I changed the owners' names because, honestly, I couldn't remember who had it!

To my beta-readers: Trisa & Keith Chancey, Lana Beck, Chris Kessler, Paula Veno, and Karen Perez – thank you, thank you, thank you! You're the first readers and the last eyes to see the manuscript before I publish.

To all who have cheered me on and encouraged me to keep writing stories, and to all who have asked me when the next book is coming out: this is for you.

And to my wife, Mary, who encourages me and pushes me forward to be better: I think each book gets a little better. Just like each year that we have been married.

A BLUE BRIDGE MYSTERY

TO THE LAST BREATH

MICHAEL K. ZIMMERLI

Marshgrass Publishing
St. Marys, GA

Prologue

There was a time when saying the word polio could bring instant fear and despair to the hearts of parents with young children. As if it wasn't enough to survive two world wars and a flu pandemic, American parents between 1916 and 1955 were consumed with the fear of their children catching the polio virus. In the 1950s, polio ranked only second behind the atomic bomb as the thing Americans feared the most.

The disease's full name is poliomyelitis, and it is not new. It is a disturbingly easy-to-transmit virus that has regularly affected humanity throughout recorded history, especially in the first half of the twentieth century.

Even though polio was not a guaranteed death sentence, it killed often, usually those most at risk. The disease attacks the nervous system, causing varying degrees of paralysis that can last weeks, months, or entire lifetimes. For the unluckiest, which were often the youngest victims, polio viciously cut short their lives.

The first major polio epidemic in the United States occurred in Vermont in the summer of 1894. By 1952, nearly 60,000 were infected in that one year. Places people loved to commune and congregate, like movie theaters and municipal swimming pools, were considered breeding grounds for the disease. Many of young people's favorite places were often closed in an attempt to quell the spread of polio during the summer when kids were out of school.

Children—especially infants—were affected most, but adults were also frequently afflicted. Future president Franklin D. Roosevelt was stricken with polio in 1921 and essentially lost the use of his legs. He was 39, twelve years before his first presidential term. Roosevelt later transformed his estate in Warm Springs, Georgia, into a recovery retreat for polio victims. He was instrumental in raising funds for polio-related research and treatment.

For years, that treatment was limited to quarantines and hope. By 1928, the infamous "iron lung," a metal coffin-like contraption that aided respiration, was being employed as a treatment. By the early 1950s, researchers had zeroed in on a successful vaccine. A colossal field trial in 1954 showed Dr. Jonas Salk's pioneering jab to be up to ninety percent effective against polio. Researchers called Salk's inactivated polio vaccine (IPV) "safe, effective, and potent." Newspapers picked up on the phrase, and headlines crowed, "Salk Polio Vaccine Safe and Effective" and "Polio Vaccine Nearly Perfect." Journalists breathlessly greeted the announcement, writing that polio was on the way out. The new vaccine was hailed as a miracle drug, capable of vanquishing the dreaded illness that was indiscriminately killing and paralyzing the nation's children.

Jonas Salk was soon a household name. An entire generation hailed him as a hero, and Presidents and other world leaders praised his accomplishment. Fan letters arrived from far-flung corners of the world, and schoolchildren sent him thank-you notes for including them in his polio vaccine tests. An unprecedented 1.8 million people, including hundreds of thousands of schoolchildren, joined Salk in his testing, proudly displaying their POLIO PIONEER button and registration card. The deployment of the new vaccine and later ones virtually eradicated the disease. However, becoming a polio-free world would not be without setbacks and difficulties.

Bernice E. Eddy, a celebrated virologist and epidemiologist, was initially known for her work with the flu vaccine during WWII. In 1954, Eddy was responsible for examining samples submitted by companies planning to make and distribute the new polio vaccine. It was part of her job at the National Institutes of Health in Bethesda, Maryland.

As she checked a sample from Cutter Laboratories in Berkeley, California, she noticed that instead of protecting against the disease, the flawed vaccine had *given* polio to a test monkey. Rather than dead viruses, the Cutter Laboratories sample contained live, infectious viruses. Something was very wrong.

"There's going to be a disaster," Bernice told a friend.

Instead of being proclaimed a hero, however, Eddy was dismissed from polio research at the National Institutes of

Health and reassigned to testing flu vaccines again. The flawed polio vaccine she had discovered was licensed and *approved* for public use.

A few months later, in the spring of 1955, hospitals across the country saw a sudden spike in polio cases, something not unexpected. Most polio outbreaks happened during the summer when kids got out of school and congregated together; the pattern was a familiar one. What happened next, however, was demoralizing for a country that had just loudly heralded a victory against the disease.

More than 200,000 children in five Western and mid-Western states received a polio vaccine, including doses from Cutter Laboratories. It's estimated that 120,000 children were injected with the Cutter vaccine. Within days there were reports of paralysis, which was not supposed to happen after the employment of Salk's vaccine. Within a month, the first mass vaccination program against polio had to be abandoned.

At 10:38 a.m. on April 27, 1955, a telegram was dispatched from the offices of Cutter Laboratories in Berkeley, California, to health departments and drug stores across the American West and Midwest. The telegram read: "URGENT. NO FURTHER INJECTIONS OF CUTTER POLIO VACCINE ARE TO BE MADE. IMMEDIATELY ADVISE YOUR PHYSICIANS."

In their haste to rush the vaccine to the public, the federal government had not provided proper supervision of the major drug companies contracted by the March of Dimes to produce nine million doses of the vaccine for 1955. Despite the Surgeon General ordering a temporary halt to all polio inoculations, such was their fear of polio and belief in the new vaccine that Americans continued vaccinating themselves and their children. To Salk's credit, outside of the Cutter incident, not a single case of polio in the United States was ever attributed to the Salk vaccine.

Investigations conducted later revealed that the Cutter vaccine was responsible for up to 40,000 polio cases, or one in every three who received the Cutter vaccine. Despite lawsuits, Cutter Laboratories successfully expanded its business, purchasing four other companies by 1960 before ultimately being purchased themselves in 1974.

Of the 40,000 polio cases the Cutter vaccine caused, nearly 200 children experienced varying degrees of paralysis. Ten children directly connected to the vaccine batch died, among them five-year-old Gary Middleton from San Francisco.

Gary Middleton developed paralytic poliomyelitis, usually characterized by spinal cord inflammation and resulting in varying degrees of muscle weakness or paralysis. The paralysis could be partial and temporary, involving just one limb, or it could be permanent, attacking multiple limbs or paralyzing the victim's breathing, potentially resulting in death.

Gary first exhibited fever and muscle aches, but only a day later, he experienced trouble breathing. Rushed to the hospital, Gary died just sixty-one hours later, cradled in his father's arms.

Three days after Gary's funeral, his older sister Carolyn, age eight, was diagnosed with polio. Carolyn contracted polio from exposure to her brother, not the Cutter vaccine.

And unlike Gary, Carolyn was immediately admitted to the hospital and placed in an iron lung.

After a month "on the inside," Carolyn recovered enough to be discharged and live a mostly normal life. At the time, it seemed like Carolyn had beaten polio. She eventually went to college and later married David Henry Dawson.

When she was twenty, she and her husband, David, had a baby boy they named after the younger brother Carolyn had lost to polio. They called their baby boy Gary Henry Dawson after Carolyn's brother, Gary Middleton. They nicknamed their baby Little Hank after his father.

Introduction

THE DARKENED BEDROOM flared with another flash of lightning. She counted the seconds until the thunder rumbled. *One-one thousand, two-one thousand, three-one thousand ...* She continued counting until *ten-one thousand* was interrupted by the grinding rumble of thunder. Sound travels a mile every five seconds, which meant the lightning was two miles away.

The woman had been counting seconds and mentally tracking the storm's march up the coast for nearly an hour. The time between flashes and thunderclaps was decreasing rapidly now.

Hurricane Nicole had landed in central Florida about 250 miles south of her location, its wind and rain slashing at the Sunshine State's Atlantic Coast. After pushing across the state and swinging out over the Gulf of Mexico, the storm had turned northward, hugging the Gulf coast. As Nicole crept north, the storm's eastern side continued to pummel Florida's Atlantic coast. Even though the eye hovered over the Gulf coast, the storm's rotation dragged moisture and winds in from the east. That was why meteorologists say the eastern side of the hurricane is often the worst side to be located on.

The woman was alone in the big house looking out over the marsh, and the main power had failed as the storm's winds had arrived in advance of the bulk of the storm. The backup generator had operated as expected, kicking in automatically when the main power stopped. The lightning flashes were all she had to gauge the storm's advance.

The lightning flashed again. *One-one thousand, two-one thousand … five-one thousand …* a sharper crash this time. Only a mile away.

Most backup generators were powered by gasoline, but this one was powered by propane, with a five-hundred-gallon tank in the backyard. Unfortunately, the tank had been neglected as the hurricane season wound down and was now woefully shy of the fuel needed for an extended outage. There had been too many bad thunderstorms during the summer and fall, coupled with an electrical infrastructure strained by local businesses, home growth, and increased demands. The combined disruptions had caused the generator to run more often than usual during the season, drawing down the tank's propane level.

Technically, the hurricane season ran through the *end* of November, but nobody expected a heavy storm this late in the season, let alone so late in the year. Nobody could remember a hurricane making landfall this late in the past umpteen years. As it turned out, Hurricane Nicole was the first hurricane to make a November landfall on a Florida coast in thirty-seven years.

Another lightning flash. She didn't even reach three-one thousand before a sharp crack of thunder shook the house, rattling windows. The bulk of the storm assailing her location was now less than a mile away. She couldn't tell if it would pass directly over her or just nearby. A miss could be as bad as a hit because hurricanes often brought tornadoes and strong, dangerous thunderstorms exacerbated by the storm's rotation.

Ordinarily, a power outage was no big thing, but Carolyn Dawson was not like other people riding out the storm on Florida's First Coast. For that matter, she was not like most people in the *world*. Carolyn was one of the last three people in the United States still confined to an iron lung machine. Without power, the 700-pound machine couldn't breathe for Carolyn. Without power, she couldn't sleep because she had to consciously inhale if the device wasn't helping her breathe. Sleeping switched off her brain, the same as being unconscious. Although she could breathe without the machine, it required a conscious effort.

Rain pelted the side of the house in waves; it was impossible to tell the storm's direction. Another thundercrack, simultaneous with a flash, shook the entire house, rattling the windows harder than previously. Carolyn jumped at the loud noise and bright flare, but her machine's tight collar kept her imprisoned. The device was both a savior and a potential executioner.

She listened to the sounds around her. The motor on the iron lung was still running. After all these years, its sound was like a comforting white noise, a masking tool that helped her sleep. It was far more concerning when she *couldn't* hear it.

The dim nightlights around the room flickered, then steadied.

Not tonight, she thought. *Not yet.*

Carolyn wasn't totally dependent on the iron lung, even at night. It was more of an insurance for her than a necessity. As long as she was awake, she was fine—even during sleep many times. But on those rare occasions when breathing became challenging, she could still do "frog breathing." She gave a tiny smile at the funny name for the lifesaving technique. Polio victims in the 1950s were taught it soon after being consigned to an iron lung for an extended period.

In a Los Angeles hospital in 1948, Dr. Clarence W. Dail noticed that one of his polio patients, a young man with almost completely paralyzed breathing muscles, had unconsciously developed a substitute way to breathe without the machine. The technique's technical name was glossopharyngeal breathing, but everyone involved called it "frog breathing" because it resembled how frogs gulp down air. The doctors in charge believed other patients could be taught the same technique.

By 1953, two years before Carolyn was diagnosed with polio, the National Foundation for Infantile Paralysis was teaching the method to partially paralyzed patients at all its centers. The technique increased patients' time outside the iron lung from minutes to hours. For those young patients, it felt like the doors of their jail cells had been flung open.

Many polio patients lost the ability to breathe independently when the virus paralyzed muscle groups in the chest; death was frequent at this stage. However, those who survived usually recovered much or almost all of their former strength. Some went on to live completely normal lives with no visible scars from their ordeal. Others were confined to the breathing machines indefinitely or permanently. The latter ones were usually the patients paralyzed from the neck down.

Carolyn was one of the lucky survivors. In 1955, she was eight and spent a month in an iron lung. She didn't even miss any school. She was much more fortunate than her little brother, Gary.

Another simultaneous flash and crash of thunder brought her back to the present. She could see the radar in her mind's eye, the storm's angry red and orange blotches passing directly above her location.

Flash-boom! Amelia Island was north of where the hurricane was crossing Florida, but it was also on the eastern side of the storm, the wettest and windiest place to be. As the storm rotated, it drew moisture off the ocean and fueled strong thunderstorms, dropping multiple inches of rain each hour. Carolyn had seen storms associated with hurricanes drop five, six, or even eight inches of rain in an hour.

There had been a time when a power outage could have been fatal for Carolyn, but that was sixty-seven years ago when doctors diagnosed her with polio. They had incarcerated her in a metal tube to keep air moving in and out of her eight-year-old lungs. These days, she only needed the machine at night for sleeping, and that was only because she didn't like how her CPAP forced air unnaturally into her lungs.

CPAP machines and most respirators pushed air in and out of the lungs, while an iron lung used negative pressure to let the lungs inflate and deflate on their own.

Carolyn had been able to breathe on her own as her health improved and she grew into adulthood, but it still occasionally required conscious effort. The older she got, the more frequent those times became.

This could be one of those times.

Since entering her mid-seventies, Carolyn sometimes used a small, portable oxygen pack to aid her breathing. She could use it now, too, except for one thing: she was alone in the house, and it took another person's help to get into and out of the iron lung. She was trapped inside until someone arrived to help her get out.

Even a power outage wasn't a guaranteed death sentence. As often happened during summer thunderstorms, the power might fail, and the generator would take over until the power company came back online. The two electrical sources repeatedly passed the baton back and forth during particular nasty storms. Like this one.

Another flash-boom! lit up the room, shaking the windows. The nightlights along the bottom third of the wall flickered, dimmed, flickered again, and then went out. The sound of the motor in the iron lung faltered, but only for a second. The nightlights flared again, and the iron lung's motor filled the room with its comforting white noise as the generator obediently took over the job from the power company again.

Listening to the sound of the outside generator sucking up the propane, Carolyn Dawson's thoughts kept returning to the probability that the propane would run out. The idea of being without any breathing machine reminded her of the night her little brother died in a hospital in California.

Her father had held the small bundle that was his five-year-old boy as he struggled to breathe with lungs that couldn't respond. The awful irony was that the boy's lungs themselves were healthy enough. The polio virus caused them to fail by paralyzing the muscles that exchanged the oxygen necessary to sustain life.

That was what the iron lung did for its inhabitants: it helped the paralyzed lungs push and pull oxygen in and out because they no longer worked. The iron lung was designed so that, in the event of a power outage, a nurse or family member could manually keep the apparatus breathing for the patient by pulling and pushing the handle at the rear of the machine.

In Gary Middleton's case, it wasn't a power outage that took his life. The disease had raced through his body like a wildfire feeding on dry prairie grass, crushing his defenses and destroying the brain cells that told his lungs how to breathe. Poliomyelitis strikes the gray matter of the brain stem and destroys nerve cells. The paralysis usually occurs after two to three weeks but sometimes takes only days. The suffocation was the most terrible part of all. Death came for Gary Middleton when the paralysis reached his respiratory tract. His otherwise healthy body could no longer move air in and out independently.

At 12:43 a.m. on May 12, 1955, Gary Middleton died. His father held him as he quietly suffocated, neither father nor son able to articulate the horror and the pain. If Gary's father could have, he would have traded places with his son in a heartbeat; no thinking or bargaining required. But no one offered him that option.

Another flash of lightning followed by an immediate crash brought Carolyn's thoughts back to the present. Her mind knew she would be fine as long as the generator kept working. Even if it quit, she should be okay since she was conscious and could breathe on her own for a while. And someone would come home soon, wouldn't they?

Carolyn's son, Hank – at 55, no longer "little"– had lived with her all his life. Hank's father had died two years before Hank graduated from high school, and Hank had taken his responsibilities as the man of the house seriously. He eschewed the usual things teenage boys on the cusp of manhood did, staying home to ensure his mother could get into the iron lung each night. The two-person job (minimum) took about an hour each time.

Hank went to a college close enough for him to commute to, ensuring he was home every night. While other young men were going on dates and learning firsthand about the birds and bees, Hank was helping his mother lie flat on a cot inside the iron lung, adjusting the snug collar around her neck and making sure everything was joined together correctly to let the machine to do its job.

Carolyn and David's house was on a spit of land where the Amelia River and Kingsley Creek meet, almost a half-mile of marsh between the house and the open water.

Although called Piney Island, it was more of a peninsula than an island. Situated on the landside of Amelia Island, the house afforded the small family the best of both worlds: waterfront and deep water access while providing a barrier from storms with names. Others had built in the same area, but David had been smart enough to buy extra land as a buffer against the suburban subdivision living.

David built the house for Carolyn soon after they married. Although located on the eastern side of Florida, it was tucked into a little "armpit" on the Atlantic shore, nestled against the coast, and usually ignored by all but the most determined wayward hurricanes. Even a nearly direct hit from Hurricane Matthew in 2016 and the strange confluence of three hurricanes during the 2004 hurricane season failed to do much damage.

The house faced the river and the vast, grassy marsh that hid the river from sight during long tidal stretches during the day. David had built it on sturdy pilings, each sunk deep into the ground, affording the house extra protection from storms and subsequent floods. Little Hank had been born and raised in the house, his father had died nearby when Hank was sixteen, and it was where his mother had grieved two major losses in her life.

In 1987, when Hank was twenty, his mother published her first book, a mystery about a private detective named Nick Steele. That first book, *Cold Steele*, introduced the world to the Steele Detective Agency: private detective Nick Steele and his female partner, Diana. Nick had the moves, rugged good looks, and the snappy repartee, but Diana was the brains of the outfit. Diana figured out who killed whom and why they did it as she guided the duo on the hunt for their quarry.

In real life, Carolyn was the intellectual creator behind Nick Steele, "the brains of the outfit," but Hank quickly became the face, attending book launchings and signing books in his mother's stead. It was only fitting since the pseudonym she published under was her son's name: Gary Dawson, an homage to her little brother, Gary, and her husband, David Dawson.

Chapter 1

The windows shook from the wind and sounded like someone was throwing handfuls of pebbles against them. The torrential rain tried its best, but repeated attempts to invade the condo's interior were unsuccessful. Jimmy and Wendi stood inside, side-by-side by the windows that faced the ocean, watching the rain blow sideways in sheets. The power had blinked on and off several times during the night, but thanks to underground utilities, it stayed on most of the time.

Standing where they were in the living room of Wendi's condo in Fernandina Beach, Florida, Jimmy could see a reflection of Wendi in the window. She was wearing denim capri pants and a white oxford-style shirt with the sleeves rolled up to the elbows. The shirttails were knotted in front across her flat, trim stomach. Her feet were bare. The window acted as a mirror for her blonde hair. She was petite, about 5-foot-3, and in Jimmy's mind, the quintessential Florida beach bunny.

Wendi had grown up on Florida's First Coast, and Jimmy had lived there since 2010. He had been through a dozen hurricane seasons counting this one but couldn't recall ever seeing a hurricane so late in the season. Wendi had considerably more experience with tropical weather but couldn't remember the last time it had happened either. She agreed it was a rare occurrence.

"How did you deal with hurricanes when you first moved here?" Wendi asked Jimmy, still looking outside at the slashing rain. Through the window, it looked more like they were in a car wash than in Wendi's home.

"Honestly, when I first moved here, I had no idea what to expect or how to prepare," Jimmy answered. "I knew about tornadoes – which, by the way, you can't prepare for since they just pop up without much warning, and there's no rhyme or reason to where they go. And I also knew about blizzards. Surprisingly, my years of experience with blizzards prepared me more for hurricanes than anything else."

"Blizzards? You're kidding."

"I am absolutely serious," Jimmy said, making an X over his heart. "When I first moved here, I couldn't understand why people left a week or more before a hurricane arrived. They boarded up their windows and hightailed it north. The weather was still beautiful, but people were running away like it was the tornado from *The Wizard of Oz* bearing down on her aunt and uncle's little Kansas farm." Wendi grinned because it was true, and Jimmy continued.

"That first year, because I moved here after hurricane season was already underway, I didn't have the benefit of seeing the Hurricane Preparation Kits that all the TV meteorologists hawked, and I never saw the lists you could pick up at Walmart before the season started in June."

"So, what did you end up doing that first season?" Wendi wanted to know. "Was it exciting or scary, or …?"

"I did what I usually do: research. I watched a lot of TV weather and spent hours poking around on the National Hurricane Center's website. And, honestly, it still makes no sense to me. It's kind of like how I'm always surprised by the saltiness of the ocean, the brackish water in the St. Marys river near my house, and the fact that the water levels rise and fall several feet a couple of times a day," Jimmy said.

"Where I grew up," he continued, "the water didn't change levels unless there was rain or drought, and it was fresh, not salty. There are lakes in northern Minnesota and Canada where the water is as pure as tap water. On a clear, sunny day, you can look over the side of a boat and see down ten feet below the surface. Get a little thirsty while fishing? Scoop up a handful of water. It's cold and clear, and some lakes have better water than some towns and better than a lot of metropolitan areas. Of course, you do have to watch out for beaver fever: giardia."

"You're making that up," Wendi laughed. "Beaver fever?"

"Stick a needle in my eye. Giardia is an infection caused by a parasite. It causes stomach aches and diarrhea for a lot of people. The first time it was called beaver fever was up in Canada. There was an outbreak of giardia at Banff National Park. A group of hikers became sick from drinking water from a stream contaminated with the giardia parasite from beavers peeing in the stream. Hence, beaver fever. True story."

The winds outside continued to howl, and several strong gusts slammed impotently against the windows. The windows were hurricane windows, designed for storms like this. Much stronger than windows made with standard glass, hurricane impact glass features a strong polymer layer sandwiched between the glass panes. Most of the condo owners in Wendi's building had upgraded several years earlier. They all felt they got their money's worth in just one season. Besides the extra protection from unpredictable winds, the windows also block UV rays, provide noise insulation, and increase home security. Plus, insurance companies often reward policy owners with hurricane windows. *Winner, winner, chicken dinner!*

"So, what is it about hurricanes you don't understand?" Wendi asked, keeping one eye on the storm outside, hurricane windows or not.

"Okay, since you asked," Jimmy replied. "You've got this big storm *possibly* coming at you, and you track its path for a week or more ahead of time, right? But people always seem surprised when it comes to town. That's what I don't get. Up north, if a blizzard was coming, we got ready. Maybe because there was no place to go. You can get out of a hurricane's way, but not a blizzard—unless you fly to the Bahamas. Short of flying somewhere tropical, you have to just hunker down and prepare for the worst. If you don't, you stand a good chance of freezing to death."

"And with a hurricane, you have a good chance of drowning or being crushed by a fallen tree or hit by flying debris," Wendi responded. "None of those are very pleasant ways to die, I imagine. Actually, I prefer not to imagine."

"I'll agree with you there," Jimmy replied, watching palm fronds and other detritus fly past the condo's windows.

Since Jimmy had finished his recent case with Lyst Publishing, he and Wendi had been seeing a lot of each other. In the case, he had saved Wendi and her father-in-law, Hillary, several thousand dollars in extortion, untold amounts of bad publicity from losing a potentially best-selling manuscript, and put them back on the path to seeing big profits when the recovered manuscript becomes published. Hillary had farmed the manuscript out to a private editor, which was fine with Jimmy as it freed up Wendi's time and allowed her and Jimmy to get to know each other better.

Near the end of the missing manuscript case, Jimmy did something he should have done from the beginning: a deep background check on both of the Lysts, not just Mr. Lyst. Initially, he erroneously thought Wendi was 'just a secretary,' so he hadn't dug into her background. Big mistake. And because he failed to do his due diligence, Jimmy spent a week believing Wendi was married to his client, Hillary Lyst, in a May-December relationship, or at least an August-late-November one. It was a miserable week for Jimmy, feeling guilty about being attracted to another man's wife. The truth finally came to light when Wendi asked Jimmy to join her and Mr. Lyst for Thanksgiving at *her* house, not *their* house.

That Thanksgiving get-together was still a couple of weeks away, but Jimmy was making up for that week when he had wrestled with his conscience, and his conscience won.

Jimmy was not an oversexed horndog; he was an ordinary man captivated by an attractive *single* woman who reciprocated his feelings and attentions. Both parties were interested in discovering where the relationship was going.

Jimmy had stayed here at Wendi's the previous night. Neither of them had slept, but not for the reason most people would think. They were up all night watching the Weather Channel and local news coverage of Hurricane Nicole's arrival. The local meteorologists were happier than pigs in slop. TV weathermen (and women) live for weather alerts and weather disasters. They become downright giddy tracking a potential tropical system "traveling on a vector across the Atlantic" that might bring the storm close to the First Coast of Florida and Georgia.

One side of Jimmy was pleased that Hurricane Nicole was making travel difficult. He didn't relish driving home from Fernandina Beach in ripping winds and slashing rain. He planned to cook brunch for them and check on the weather again in a couple of hours. On the other hand, Jimmy was nervous about overstaying his welcome, in large part because he didn't want to come across like a teenager on prom night.

If he did, he knew Wendi could literally toss him out on his ear anytime she chose. He had snuck up behind her one day to reveal that he had discovered the truth about her marital status, and he found out the hard way that she had been trained in self-defense and martial arts. Remembering the recent incident, his hand involuntarily went to his throat, feeling the spot where Wendi's jab had utterly neutralized him to the point he even briefly fell unconscious. But, in a

Snow White reversal of sorts, Wendi brought Jimmy back to the land of living with a kiss, or more accurately, CPR.

Wendi was beautiful and intelligent and seemed genuinely attracted to Jimmy. Even better, she didn't seem put off by his jokes or fascination with obscure facts and minutia. It had been years since Jimmy had experienced such strong feelings for someone, and he didn't want to mess it up.

"Speaking of horrible ways to die," Jimmy said, picking up where they had left off, "I read that one of the worst ways to go—"

His impromptu lecture was interrupted by Wendi's cell phone ringing. She held up a finger to signal him to hold that thought.

"Hello?" she answered. She listened for a moment. Her brows became furrowed, drawing her perfectly-shaped eyebrows close together.

"Carolyn? Are you telling me you're at home alone? In this storm?" Wendi said to her caller. There was another pause as she listened to the reply.

"Are you sure? I thought Hank always took care of that. He did what? Wait. Where's Aleesha?" Jimmy stepped away from the window and sat down in one of the chairs strategically positioned for maximum ocean viewing.

Wendi caught Jimmy's eye and motioned for him to get up. He didn't want to hear Wendi say what he thought she was suggesting. But she did.

"Don't worry, Carolyn. Jimmy and I will come over and sit with you or help you with whatever you need. It's not a bother. We'll take my Jeep, so we'll be there soon. Don't worry. We're on our way. What? Who's who? Jimmy? Well, Jimmy is. …?" She paused.

Jimmy looked at Wendi, lifted his shoulders, and raised his hands, palms up, as though to say, "Yes, who *is* this Jimmy you speak of?" But he kept his mouth shut, waiting attentively.

In his mind's eye, Jimmy pictured the white and black spotted dog with his head cocked sideways, hearing his master's voice emanating from an RCA Victrola record player. He may not be a horndog, but he was definitely smitten. Wendi smiled and waved Jimmy off.

"Jimmy is a friend. I'll—*we'll* be there soon." Wendi clicked off the phone, turned, and walked across the room. When she looked over her shoulder and saw Jimmy had not moved from where she had left him, she stopped, turned toward him, and placed her hands on her hips. *Uh-oh.*

"Do you need an engraved invitation?" she asked.

"Invitation, no. A little information might be nice, though," Jimmy answered. "Like, who's Carolyn, who are Hank and Aleesha, and where are we going during a hurricane? Because, in case you've forgotten, Hurricane Nicole made landfall earlier this morning about 250 miles south of here and is churning its way northward toward us as we speak."

She waved a hand in the air dismissively, then motioned for Jimmy to come along, and he reluctantly placed one foot in front of the other like a pouty kid. "It's only a tropical storm now, Jimmy. I'm sure you've been through worse storms running through a sprinkler in your yard."

"My sprinkler never took the siding off my house or branches from the trees …" Jimmy's voice trailed off because he knew he would follow this woman wherever she asked him to go. But also because she was no longer listening to his excuses.

Grabbing their jackets, they descended the stairs to the parking garage in the condominium complex. Chances were good that the elevator would have worked just fine, but why tempt fate?

Of course, Jimmy could think of far worse people to be stranded with in an elevator when the power went out. Unless Wendi harbored a secret fear of tiny, dark enclosed places, in which case he didn't want to be too near her martial arts-trained hands.

Walking through the parking garage, Wendi told Jimmy, "I'll drive. I know where we're going, I know all the quirks and eccentricities of my Jeep, and besides, I doubt you'd want to be seen driving it."

Jimmy looked at her quizzically.

She stepped up to a vehicle in the garage, motioned like a TV model showing off a prize package on *The Price Is Right*, and giggled as she announced, "It's *pink*!"

Chapter 2

WENDI'S JEEP WASN'T a soft, girly pink. It was a shade of pink that *screamed* for attention. It was like a commercial for Pepto Bismol mounted on four knobby tires.

"Let me guess," Jimmy said as he climbed in on the passenger side. "You made a fortune in Mary Kay?"

Wendi shook her head as she pulled her seatbelt across and buckled it. "No, I wanted it to be unappealing to my husband."

Her late ex-husband, Jimmy added inside his head to assuage his own feelings.

Wendi continued, "If it had been a regular color, he would have assimilated it for his own. I figured there was no way he would let his buddies see him driving this."

"I can see his point. A guy driving around in this would be like wearing the pink rabbit costume Ralphie wore in *The Christmas Story.* It would invite abuse and ridicule."

"Oh, come on. It's not *that* bad," Wendi replied, backing up and heading for the exit from the parking garage. She paused briefly to make sure her lights were on and all the windows were up before leaving the garage and braving the storm.

Jimmy was distracted by a row of rubber ducks – mostly pink ones, but also in all the other colors of the rainbow and a few more – spread across the dash at the bottom of the windshield. He had noticed other Jeeps displaying the tiny flotation devices before but had never asked anyone for an explanation. He opted to hang onto that question until later. You never knew when you might need a safe but unique topic for conversation.

She feathered the gas pedal with her toe, and they rolled slowly of the parking garage. Jimmy's world turned white.

The wipers were going as fast as they could, but the rain was falling so hard it was impossible to see. Wendi immediately let off the gas, and they rolled to a stop. It truly was like being inside a car wash.

"I'm going to try something," Wendi hollered, trying to be heard over the racket the rain was making on the Jeep's soft-top roof. She switched off the wipers. Instantly, their vision improved. The rain was coming down more like a solid wave than droplets. It wasn't perfect, but they could see. They started forward tentatively.

Wendi played with various wiper speeds and intervals, finally settling on a slower rate with longer interludes than usual for a hard rain. Driving slowly and letting the rain roll off in sheets made visibility possible, but it was still far from ideal. They made steady progress, though, mainly because very few people had ventured out yet. There were a few looky-loos out, but for the most part, people weren't ready to examine their houses and yards for damage yet, let alone drive around town in this wicked downpour.

Jimmy nearly wet his pants when a palm frond slapped against the windshield and stayed there for a few seconds. Wendi flipped the wipers, and with the help of the wind and rain, the frond sailed on its way. Jimmy tried to carry on a normal conversation, hoping to bring a sense of normalcy to this abnormal situation. As they crept slowly and cautiously along, he asked his safari guide, "I know I've asked this before, but who is Carolyn?"

Wendi was gripping the steering wheel tightly with both hands but not uneasily. She carefully piloted the vehicle as they avoided branches and patio furniture the winds had set free. Jimmy did his best to help from the passenger seat, but his options were limited, with no steering wheel, brake, or gas pedal at his disposal. When the road became fairly clear of debris, she answered Jimmy's question.

"Carolyn is Carolyn Dawson," Wendi replied, her gaze fixed out over the Jeep's front. That hot pink hood was about all Jimmy could see at times.

Jimmy waited a reasonable length of time before asking, "You get five points for a partial answer. Now for five more, who is Carolyn Dawson? A mahjongg or pickleball partner? Someone you met at a quilting club or while shopping at Publix?"

Wendi kept her hands on the wheel but took a couple of quick glances at Jimmy; her incredulity was evident on her face.

"What?" Jimmy asked. "Why are you looking at me that way?"

"You don't know who Carolyn Dawson is? Do you know who Gary Dawson is?"

"Yeah. Gary Dawson writes some detective books, but I haven't read any of them. Are Gary and Carolyn related?"

Wendi grinned broadly. "In a way," she said. "Gary Dawson is Carolyn's nom de plume, her pseudonym, her pen name. But it's also her son's name, and he does the book signings for her. Most people have no idea that Gary Dawson is a woman."

"So, what's the deal with her son handling her book signings? Is she shy? Afraid to go out in public? Too busy cranking out the detective books?"

Wendi shook her head. "She has a medical condition that makes it hard for her to go out and meet her public, but it's not agoraphobia. The big book signings are one part of being an author she doesn't care for, so her son does it. They're a team."

They had just passed Lyst Publishing and were on A1A. Stoplights were blinking red in all directions, the hanging lights blowing wildly in the wind. The blinking stoplights indicated that the intersections should be treated as four-way stops if anyone felt they absolutely *had* to go out. Jimmy knew they'd be over the short causeway in a few minutes.

"What kind of medical condition does she have? And why do you know so much about her?"

"Duh! She's an *author* Jimmy, and my father-in-law and I run what kind of business? A publishing company!" She briefly let go of the steering wheel with one hand to smack Jimmy's forehead lightly to emphasize that he wasn't connecting the dots today.

Hands back on the wheel, she continued. "Carolyn Dawson, aka Gary Dawson, kept Lyst Publishing afloat during the early years and some other lean times. We've gotten to know her and her son, Hank, very well since we published her first book thirty-five years ago. I haven't known her that long, but Hillary has."

"So, what kind of a medical condition does she have, the investigator asked his beautiful partner again?" Jimmy hoped a little flattery would earn him an answer.

"Carolyn Dawson, successful author and mother, is one of three people left in the United States who still rely on an iron lung to stay alive."

Wendi let her statement sink in.

Jimmy sat and stared out the windshield, trying to come up with a response to what Wendi had revealed. Unable to find other words that worked, he turned and looked at her and said, "What?"

Wendi smiled and breathed deeply, keeping her eyes on the causeway as they climbed the man-made concrete, steel, and asphalt hill that carried them up and across the Amelia River. The river was the body of water separating Amelia Island from the mainland. She knew they'd need extra diligence locating the turnoff for Piney Island with their vision compromised by the rain. At least the causeway had thick concrete walls that would prevent them from going over and falling into the river below.

"Carolyn Dawson is one of the last three people in the United States—maybe in the world—still using an iron lung. She's a polio survivor," Wendi clarified for her passenger.

"Wait a minute," Jimmy responded. "Wasn't polio back in the thirties and forties and went away by the early 1960s? Why would someone still be using an iron lung today? An iron lung looks like a miniature hyperbaric chamber for divers after a long, deep dive; they need to spend time in it to avoid getting the bends. Even if they were still impacted by polio nearly seventy years later, aren't there new technologies to help them breathe? I see people all the time with little oxygen packs and tubes that go to their noses. Won't that work for someone who's had polio?"

"From what I understand from conversations I've had over the years with Carolyn, the oxygen canisters people carry around don't force air into their lungs like the iron lungs. They're more of a supplement rather than a breathing machine. Portable ventilators *push* air into the lungs but often stretch the lung tissue too much. An iron lung is actually better for the patient because it acts more like their natural lungs instead of forcing air in and out."

"How so?" Jimmy asked, always interested in adding to his mental storehouse of information.

"It's more like pulling air into their lungs than pushing. An iron lung pumps air *out* of the chamber, which makes a small vacuum inside where the patient lies," Wendi explained patiently. "That vacuum expands the person's chest and abdomen, drawing air into the lungs through their nose and mouth, just like breathing. Then the motor puts air back into the chamber, creating the right amount of pressure inside it to let the air escape their lungs through their nose and mouth, like exhaling. And besides, Carolyn hasn't been in the iron lung all her life. There was a long time when she hardly used it at all. But she told me that many people in their seventies who had polio as a kid back in the 1950s are experiencing relapses now."

"I thought polio made people unable to breathe? I mean, didn't everyone who caught polio have to be in an iron lung?" Jimmy asked, a little embarrassed by his lack of knowledge on the subject.

Wendi shook her head. "No, mm-mm. Polio doesn't always affect the lungs. Think about FDR—President Franklin Roosevelt. He lost the use of his legs to polio in the 1920s. There was—or is, actually— two main types of polio, *paralytic* polio and *non*-paralytic. *Non*-paralytic polio had flu-like symptoms and often only lasted about ten days. In people who had *paralytic* polio and survived, up to half of them can have some symptoms again forty-plus years later. It can cause sleep apnea, muscle weakness, and trouble breathing and swallowing. That's Carolyn. For some years now, she has been using the iron lung nearly every night to help her breathe while she sleeps. Kind of hard to take one of those on a book-signing tour, don't you think?"

Wendi carefully angled the Jeep to the right, expertly making the turn onto Piney Island Road. When she turned, the rain came at them from a different angle, and they could suddenly see much better. With her vision improved, Wendi increased her speed as they continued on their way to see the author in the iron lung.

Chapter 3

THE PRIVATE ROAD sign was hard for them to see in the driving downpour, but Wendi knew where it was without needing to see it. She left the Little Piney Island main road and the housing subdivision behind, driving into an area mostly populated with pine trees but interspersed with occasional palms and live oaks. Jimmy was comfortable being in the trees, having grown up in the forests of Ontario, Canada. Later, he gained his U.S. citizenship while sojourning at a chain of newspapers scattered throughout the pine and birch forests of northern Minnesota and Wisconsin.

After driving the equivalent of a couple of city blocks, the private road emptied out into a wide yard in front of an attractive three-story house on stilts. It seemed designed to take advantage of the views in all directions. *Are we in the front or the back of the house?* Jimmy wondered. *Does the front face the marsh or the driveway?*

The house looked like a three-story house, but the bottom was parking and garage, the sides mostly open. Wendi pulled up under the house and parked. Both were glad to be out of the rain's direct impact. Jimmy jumped out of the Jeep, landing in a puddle and splashing the bottom of his jeans. Jimmy looked around quickly. Wendi's Jeep was the only vehicle parked in the garage. The storm still spat rain at them even though they were under the house. Luckily, the garage sheltered them from the storm's main force.

Wendi walked over to a door that obviously led to a stairway. "C'mon, Jimmy. No time for playing in puddles." She smiled as she said it, her smile giving Jimmy a warm feeling inside. Wendi located a key on her keyring and unlocked the door. Jimmy placed a hand on her arm as she went to turn the door knob.

"You have a key to this place?" he asked, looking questioningly into Wendi's eyes.

"I told you, we—Lyst Publishing—have gotten to know Carolyn and Hank very well over the years. With her … *condition*, we all felt it was best to have someone outside the family with a key for emergencies. I have a key, and so does Hillary. I don't know if anyone else does, but I'm the one she called, so that's all that counts." Wendi finished explaining, opened the door, and stepped inside. As expected, Jimmy saw a staircase leading up.

He followed, shutting the door tightly behind him against the weather. He stood still for a second, amazed at the difference in sound volume between the inside and the outside. Wendi was already mounting the stairs, not waiting for Jimmy to decide to follow. She seemed to know where she was going, so Jimmy followed her without asking questions. *For now.*

At the top of the single flight of stairs, Wendi opened a door and stepped into the entryway leading to the main part of the house. Jimmy was right behind, closing the door and following the former Mrs. Lyst.

He still thought of her that way sometimes—Mrs. Lyst—but quickly reminded himself that when they first met, she had allowed him to believe she was Hillary's new, younger trophy wife. Mr. Lyst's wife of forty years had died in the same auto accident that took their son, Charles, Wendi's husband at the time. Wendi explained to Jimmy that she and Charles had been separated for several years when the accident took his and his mother's lives. A divorce decree arrived within a few weeks after his death. Playing Hillary's replacement wife at the office kept the riff-raff at bay, she explained to Jimmy. When he asked if she still thought of him as riff-raff, she sidestepped his question by saying she didn't know him when they met. If she had originally ID'd him as riff-raff, her opinion of him had drastically changed in the period since.

Wendi and Jimmy exited the entryway and walked through a comfortable living room with large floor-to-ceiling windows that afforded a spectacular view of the marsh and river. At least, it did on most days, those days when a hurricane was *not* passing nearby.

Wendi hissed at Jimmy and signaled him to follow her as she went through an open doorway on the other end of the living room. Jimmy guessed it was a bedroom, but as he entered, he scratched his head because it was like no bedroom he had ever seen.

A large metal tube—*an iron lung!*—monopolized the bulk of the room's space, looking more like a meat smoker than anything else Jimmy had ever experienced. He had friends who had converted large, 500-gallon, whole-house propane tanks into meat smokers. The iron lung wasn't painted black like the BBQ smokers he had seen, but it was still roughly the same size. There was one other thing, though: Jimmy had never seen a smoker with a woman's head sticking out of one end.

*

Wendi walked around to the other side of the iron lung and smiled at the white-haired lady's head protruding from the breathing machine.

"Are you okay, Carolyn?" Wendi asked the author.

"I will be if you can help me get out of this blasted contraption. Thank you so much for coming out, Wendi."

Carolyn shifted her eyes in the mirror mounted above her head on the iron lung to make eye contact with Jimmy.

"You must be Jimmy. Please excuse how I'm dressed. I'm Carolyn Dawson. I'd shake your hand, but... Although, if you *really* want to, there's a port on the side of the machine. You can reach in and shake my hand. Assuming you can find my hand." Carolyn winked at Jimmy. He looked at Wendi, who shook her head slightly. Jimmy took the hint.

"It's nice to meet you, Miss Carolyn, but I'll wait until we get you out of there to shake anything."

The woman laughed, and Jimmy smiled, relieved that he had made the right decision. Laughter made any situation better.

"This monstrosity is a relief to get into at night and a relief to get out of in the morning," Carolyn said to Jimmy. "But I am so grateful to have it. They don't make them anymore. The last one was made in 1977, and parts are becoming very hard to track down."

"How long does it take to get in or out of it?" Jimmy asked curiously.

"Well, as you can probably see, it's not a one-person operation since after you lie down on the little mattress bed inside and poke your head out of your shell like a turtle, someone else has to roll the halves together and seal you up inside. To get out again, we just do everything in reverse. But no one ever figured out that sometimes, a person needs to get out of it by themselves. Like now! If you two would please help me get out of here, I need to pee."

Jimmy's head snapped up, and he looked at Wendi, who stifled a laugh. She let loose a girlish giggle and said, "Come on, Jimmy. Let's get going. You heard her. The woman needs to pee!"

With Carolyn's guidance, they extricated her from the breathing apparatus in less than fifteen minutes. She was not wholly dependent on the machine for oxygen, and with no paralysis, she could help her saviors get her off the cot inside.

When they rolled the two parts of the machine apart – Jimmy couldn't help but think it was like separating a turtle head from its body – he saw that Carolyn was covered with a pink blanket. Two bare feet with red painted toenails poked out from underneath.

"Jimmy?" Carolyn addressed him. "I'm going to ask you to leave the room while I finish getting off here and take care of business. Even an old bird like me needs her privacy and an opportunity to make herself presentable for callers, especially male callers."

"Yes, ma'am," Jimmy replied. Looking to Wendi for support, he asked, "Where …?"

Carolyn answered first, saying, "Go back through the doorway to the living room. You'll see the entryway for the kitchen. Go make us some coffee. Now get out before I burst!"

Jimmy scurried from the room and followed Miss Carolyn's directions. He quickly found himself in a well-appointed kitchen. It had a Keurig for making single cups of coffee and a Bunn for making a whole pot.

The Bunn coffeemaker reminded him of the Grand Rapids, Minnesota, newspaper break room down the hall from his office. The breakroom housed a similar coffeemaker, but the pressmen had desecrated it. Instead of using only water when making coffee, the pressmen would pour the day-old coffee back through the tank to give it an extra kick. Jimmy had seen them make coffee once, and he immediately went out and bought a Mister Coffee for his office.

Since there were three of them, Jimmy decided to make a full pot in the Bunn if he could find the grounds and filters. If not, he saw individual K-pods for the Keurig.

Jimmy opened several cupboard doors and drawers before locating what he needed. He scooped the coffee into the filter, placed the loaded filter in the basket, and filled the carafe with water from the sink. He poured it into the top of the coffeemaker, flipped a switch, and closed the lid on top.

Since Wendi and Carolyn had not come out of the bedroom, Jimmy watched the coffee brewing. The hot brown elixir of life, he called it. He watched as it filled the carafe and then continued filling, overflowing the pot and onto the counter and the floor. The coffee just kept coming out, even though the decanter was full. Jimmy was scrambling, grabbing paper towels, washcloths, and dish towels. At last, the stream of coffee slowed to a drip and quit.

Jimmy looked down at the pile of soaked paper towels, washcloths, and towels around his feet. The coffee was coffee in name only; it looked more like very weak tea. Jimmy couldn't figure out what had gone wrong. It was how he had made coffee in other Bunn brewers.

"Who are you? And why are you spilling coffee all over the kitchen?" a gruff male voice said behind Jimmy.

Jimmy whirled around and came face to face with a book cover.

Not only was Hank Dawson the virtual face of author Gary Dawson, but he was apparently the model for the fictitious detective Nick Steele on the covers of Carolyn's books. Assuming this person was Hank and not a live-in book cover model, that is. Wendi had enlightened Jimmy briefly about the Dawson family on the drive over, but he was still putting the pieces and faces together.

The man facing Jimmy looked to be somewhere in his fifties. He had a handsome face with strong lines, solid bone structure, gunmetal-blue eyes, salt and pepper hair, and a well-trimmed matching beard. The hair and beard shouted of regular trips to a barber—no, check that: a *"stylist."* The guy stood about five-ten or eleven, with broad shoulders, wearing a long-sleeved shirt that seemed red and blue at the same time, denim blue jeans, and tan Minnetonka classic driving moccasins that Jimmy recognized from his years in northern Minnesota.

At first glance, the newcomer seemed fit, but as Jimmy continued to regard him, he became aware of his slightly thickened waist, heavy chest, and shoulders that sloped a little more than they would if he was active or engaged regularly in manual labor. His hands were clean and smooth, and his fingernails had a shine to them that wasn't natural. He wasn't all hard angles and muscles, *but who is when they reach their fifties?* Jimmy thought.

Jimmy decided to play it friendly. Extending a hand, he introduced himself. "Hi! I'm Jimmy Favreaux. I'm a friend of Wendi Lyst. She's in with Carolyn right now. They sent me out to make coffee, and somehow it ran over. I only poured one carafe of water in—"

"You don't pour water in that coffeemaker," the book cover man said, ignoring Jimmy's hand. "It's hooked into the house plumbing. You just push the switch after you put the basket and grounds in place. It automatically measures the right amount of water and makes the coffee. If you pour water in, you get liquid for *two* pots. And, obviously, a big mess."

Hank waved his hand to indicate the wet chaos around Jimmy's feet, making the same Big Reveal motion as Wendi had when she introduced Jimmy to her hot pink Jeep Wrangler.

"Hank! Don't be that way!" The voice came from a solidly-built brunette. "Not everybody hooks their coffeemakers up to the kitchen plumbing. He didn't do anything wrong, and at least he mopped it up rather than letting it sit in a giant brown pool on the floor."

The brunette extended her hand to Jimmy, saying, "Hi. I'm sorry this happened to you. I'm Aleesha Dawson, Hank's wife." She chinned at the book cover. "Carolyn is my mother-in-law. I used to be her caregiver before Hank and I got together. I still do a lot of the same things for her, but now she doesn't have to pay me!" Aleesha cackled. Her voice rose two octaves in pitch and went from about 55 to 80 decibels – just below yelling and about the same level as a lawnmower needing a tune-up.

Jimmy had shaken her hand when she offered it. Her grip was firm and strong, more like a man's handshake than a woman's. But if she was used to lifting people in and out of iron lungs and maybe bathtubs and beds, her physical strength should come as no surprise.

Hank was still picking up washcloths and dish towels and wringing them out in the sink. Aleesha bent to pick up the stray paper towels. She got rid of the weak 'coffee' and set about making a fresh pot.

"Hank? Aleesha?" Carolyn's voice came from the bedroom.

"Yes, Mother!" Hank called back. "It's us. We're back in town."

"Please come in here, Hank." Carolyn's voice was not harsh, but there was no mistaking her motherly tone that didn't allow for refusal.

Jimmy guessed Hank to be in his mid-fifties, and Carolyn had to be in her seventies since she caught polio during the 1950s. *Once a mother, always a mother,* Jimmy thought silently.

Hank let out a small, annoyed sigh, dumped the wet towels and cloths in the sink, pulled out a dry one from a drawer for his hands, and then walked to his mother's bedroom.

Aleesha took over at the sink, gathering the towels and washcloths to take to the laundry room. She leaned near Jimmy so her voice wouldn't carry to the bedroom.

"I'm sorry you got involved in this. We left last night after Miss Carolyn went to bed, but we couldn't get back home until just now because of the storm."

Aleesha was several inches taller than Jimmy. Her face was round, and her brunette hair was cut short for ease of care. She wore minimal makeup, just a little eye shadow and eyebrow pencil to accent her dark brown eyes, and simple, neutral lipstick. She wore Vans on her feet, jeans, and a loose t-shirt showing a little cartoon dog in pajamas. The caption on the shirt said, "Breathe. The universe is taking care of everything else."

How apropos, Jimmy thought.

The second pot of coffee worked much better than the first. Aleesha gestured for Jimmy to climb up on one of the bar stools by the pass-through counter between the kitchen and living room. She placed a filled and steaming cup in front of him, then held out a container of liquid hazelnut creamer and a bowl containing a pastel-colored riot of pink, blue, yellow, and green sugar substitute packets. Jimmy pointed at the hazelnut creamer, and she set it in front of him.

After pouring the creamer into his coffee and taking a sip, he announced, "I'm Jimmy, by the way. Jimmy <u>Favreaux</u>, that is, not 'Jimmy By The Way.'"

He smiled at his own joke but refrained from laughing.

Not Aleesha. She screamed a laugh that Jimmy was sure the neighbors would have heard – if there were any.

When she finished laughing, Aleesha came around to where Jimmy was seated and asked, "Do you mind if I join you?"

"Su casa su casa," Jimmy answered, eliciting more raucous laughter. Jimmy wasn't sure what she was on, but he wanted some.

Aleesha slid onto the stool next to Jimmy, who watched her doctor her coffee with hazelnut creamer and a couple of sweetener packets. She had just taken her first sip when Wendi came out of the bedroom.

Wendi made a beeline for Aleesha, who rose and gave Wendi a big hug.

"I'm so glad to see you here," Wendi said. "You've been such a fixture in this house for the past several years. It wouldn't be the same if you chose to do something else."

"What, just because I married Hank? Like I told Jimmy here, I still do a lot of the same things for Miss Carolyn; I just don't get paid for it anymore!" This comment was followed by her room-filling laugh.

"I heard you laughing out here from clear back in the bedroom," Wendi replied, laughing a little herself. "We need some laughter on a stormy day like this."

"Well, there's no mistaking when I'm around," Aleesha chuckled.

Jimmy decided he liked the girl. She was funny, sarcastic, able to poke fun at herself, could look on the bright side of bad situations, made good coffee, and laughed at Jimmy's lame jokes. Best of all, she didn't label his jokes as lame, dad-joke retreads.

"What's Her Majesty talking to Hank about?" Aleesha asked Wendi, who was pouring a cup of coffee for herself.

Wendi lowered her eyes, keeping them on her coffee. Either she didn't want to participate in the name-calling or was embarrassed because she usually *did* join in, and she didn't want Aleesha to notice she was holding back today. Wendi lifted her cup to her lips and took a sip, buying herself a little respite before needing to provide an answer. Jimmy's natural nosiness rescued her.

"Why 'Her Majesty?'" Jimmy asked. "She seemed nice enough to me, the little bit that I talked with her."

Wendi answered, "You think every woman that flirts with you is nice."

Aleesha giggled and asked, "Did she try to get him to put his hand in the iron lung port and find hers?"

Wendi nodded and took another sip of coffee.

"And did he do it?" Aleesha wanted to know.

"I think he was tempted," Wendi answered, her smile taking over her whole face. "He's pretty easy—"

"Hey!" Jimmy interjected, his face turning a bright red. "I'm right here!"

Wendi and Aleesha both erupted with laughter, and a second or two later, Jimmy joined them.

"At least Miss Carolyn didn't have to punch me in the throat to get me to kiss her," Jimmy added, still laughing.

"What? Oh no, you didn't!" Wendi yelped playfully, shoving Jimmy's shoulder back and raising her hands in a Hai Karate pose. Aleesha's laughter filled the kitchen and living room over their exchange.

After a minute or two, the hooting and laughing subsided. All three focused on their coffees. It was Aleesha who asked again, "So, what *did* she want to talk to Hank about?"

Wendi set her cup on the counter in front of her and shook her head. "I don't know. I was cleaning up in the bathroom, and their voices were too low to hear what they were discussing. When I came out, they stopped talking and waited until I left the room before starting again."

Aleesha waved a hand in dismissal. "I'm sure it's nothing. She just has too much time to think when she's in the can."

In the can? The bathroom...? Jimmy wondered before deciding she meant the iron lung.

"It's too bad nobody designed an iron lung with an emergency release like they have in car trunks. Then she could get out by herself," Aleesha continued.

"Of course," she added, "having an inside release handle would put a lot of people out of work. Oh, wait—no, it wouldn't!"

Jimmy looked at her curiously.

"You know, all *three* of us!" she added, looking at Jimmy questioningly. He wasn't getting the joke.

Aleesha finally explained that only three people in the United States were still using iron lungs, so there weren't many caregivers for them. Jimmy had forgotten that Wendi had told him something similar. Of the remaining three survivors, only one – Paul Alexander – was confined to his iron lung all the time.

Paul had been six when he caught polio in July 1952, three years before Carolyn. Unlike Carolyn, Paul was completely paralyzed, and it was years before he could escape his life-saving prison, and then for only a handful of hours at a time.

With occasional oxygen support when outside her iron lung, Carolyn could lead a remarkably normal life. But she preferred to trust her sleeping hours to the unthinking, unblinking, one-trick pony that was her iron lung. Unfortunately, getting in and out was a two-person job, hence the situation Jimmy and Wendi discovered themselves in.

"It sounds like a party out here."

It was Hank. Apparently, his conference with his mother was over. He walked past the trio at the counter and poured the last cup of coffee from the pot Aleesha had made.

"We were just getting acquainted," Aleesha replied.

"Well, you already knew Wendi. And what did you say your name was?" Hank addressed Jimmy.

Jimmy rose and went over to the kitchen island where Hank stood. He set his coffee cup on the island and extended a hand toward Hank.

"Hi, again. I'm Jimmy Favreaux. I'm a friend of Wendi's. I was at her condo when your mom called her."

Hank shook Jimmy's hand and smiled, but his well-practiced smile didn't reach his eyes. "Pleased to meet you, Jimmy." He released Jimmy's hand and said, "I appreciate you and Wendi coming over, but it really wasn't necessary. I'm sorry you had to become involved."

Become involved? Jimmy said to himself. It wasn't like we were part of one of Carolyn's books.

"It wasn't a big thing," Jimmy answered Hank. "I wanted to get outside and see what kind of damage the storm had done anyway. Coming out here gave us an excuse to get a little fresh air, you know, even though most of it blew right by us!"

Hank took a drink of his coffee and remained mute.

Tough audience! Jimmy thought.

From a sideways glance, Jimmy saw Aleesha staring into her coffee cup. She didn't seem enthused about Hank's social skills at the moment. She also seemed smaller somehow, like she didn't want to be noticed. She hadn't laughed or joked since Hank had joined them, either.

Jimmy noticed Wendi watching him. He leaned over, placed his elbows on the kitchen island, and hunched his shoulders in a tiny shrug, letting her know he didn't think they'd be double-dating with Hank and Aleesha anytime soon.

Chapter 4

A VOICE CAME from the living room. "I smell testosterone. Wendi? Aleesha? Are these two boys trying to figure out who the alpha male is? Because I'm the only alpha-anything in this house."

Carolyn was slowly making her way from the living room to the kitchen, apparently angling for a special seat near the windows overlooking the marsh. She was using a walker, but she was using it for a cart to bring her portable oxygenator. Jimmy saw that she wasn't attached to the machine. *Just a precaution,* he guessed.

"Good morning, Miss Carolyn," Aleesha chirped, as cheerful as any bird Jimmy had ever heard greeting the morning. "I'd be glad to make another pot of coffee if you'd like."

"Thank you, no. I want some green tea this morning." The information was not delivered as a request; no "please," "if it's no trouble," or "would you, dear?"

Jimmy didn't see any change in Aleesha's facial expression as she went to start the tea kettle and make the older woman's tea, but he felt the temperature in the room drop a few degrees.

Hank pushed off from the kitchen island he had been leaning against and went over to stand next to his mother. His tennis shoes squeaked slightly on the tiled floor. He was wearing blue jeans and an untucked, button-down, long-sleeved shirt that looked solid blue from a distance but, up close, revealed itself as a plaid comprised of tiny boxes of red, blue, and green.

"We were just getting to know each other when you came in, Mother. I told Wendi and Jimmy they didn't need to come out in a tropical storm. Aleesha and I were simply slightly delayed by the weather and the stupid cops who close off roads whenever there's a storm with a name passing nearby."

"If I had been able to get ahold of you *myself*, there would have been no need for them to come," Carolyn replied. "But as I told you before, I tried for hours to get through to let you know the situation here. Every call went straight to voicemail. I left several messages asking you to call me, but you never did."

"And I told you in the bedroom, *Mother*, that my phone ran out of juice and there was something wrong with the charger cable," Hank responded through lips stretched tautly over gritted teeth.

"Yes, well, I needed to get out of my can to *go* to the can. Wendi was nice enough to come and rescue me, and she brought a man with her in case anything was wrong."

Jimmy wondered if there was something veiled in that last statement, as though Carolyn was questioning Hank's manliness.

The teakettle suddenly began whistling, and Aleesha turned the switch off and picked up the kettle, pouring the boiling water into a cup with a tag on a string hanging out of it. A green box proclaiming GREEN TEA sat nearby on the counter.

"Hank, it was no big deal for Jimmy and me to come out," Wendi interjected into the discussion. "You know how long I've known you and Carolyn, and Hillary has known you even longer, so it's not like your mom called some stranger for help. I don't see what the big deal is."

"The big deal is," Hank said as he walked around the kitchen aimlessly, coffee cup in hand, "I've been her caregiver for nearly forty years, ever since my dad died. I have always been there—been here!—for her. I gave up having a normal life to take care of her. And I have done it gladly." Jimmy could tell from his tone that he hadn't always done it as gladly as he asserted.

"Here we go again – Hank the Martyr," Carolyn responded icily to Hank's comments. "I never asked you to give up your life for mine. I never—"

"—Exactly! You never ask. You expect people to do things for you. Let me ask you a question, and I'd like an honest answer." Hank waited, staring at his mother.

After a moment, she replied, "Well? Ask!"

"Did you *ask* Aleesha to make you a cup of tea?"

Aleesha was in the process of squeezing the teabag with the spoon against the cup's side but froze in place at the sound of her name. She went rigid for a heartbeat, then placed the cup in front of Carolyn. There was another slight pause before Aleesha stepped back and away from the center of the conflict.

As though to answer Hank's question, Carolyn lifted her cup in a mock toast to Hank, then took a quick, noisy sip of the hot liquid.

"Well?" Hank asked again. "Did you ask Aleesha to make you a cup of tea?"

"Obviously, I must have," Carolyn answered. "It's right here."

Hank glared at Wendi and then at Jimmy. Wendi looked down at her coffee while Jimmy held Hank's gaze but felt confused, wondering what Hank wanted from his guests.

Jimmy got the feeling he was witnessing the latest episode in an ongoing drama.

"Even you don't pay attention to what you say or do, do you know that?" Hank threw at his mother. "And I guess if *you* don't pay attention to what you say or do, we couldn't expect you to pay attention to anyone else, now could we?" Hank's face had turned pink, and his ears were red. Aleesha was over by the open refrigerator, looking inside for a hiding place or cooling off; Jimmy couldn't tell which.

"I don't understand what you're asking from me, Hank," Carolyn replied.

Hank remained where he stood and crossed his arms. "I'm asking for common courtesy, Mother. To Aleesha, to Wendi and, … and, what's-his-name."

"Jimmy …" Jimmy interjected, which earned him a nudge in the ribs from Wendi's elbow.

Hank still wasn't done. "And some courtesy to *me*. Not all the time, but even occasionally would be nice."

Carolyn said nothing; she simply took another sip of tea, her face remaining stonily neutral.

"Did it ever occur to you that we might have had trouble getting home? For all you knew, we could have been lying in a ditch, dead in a car wreck …" Hank stopped.

He looked at Wendi, and his face turned beet red. His eyes opened wide.

"I'm s-sorry, Wendi," he mumbled. "That was insensitive of me."

"It's all right," Wendi said quietly.

The pause in the conversation seemed incredibly loud to Jimmy. Carolyn filled it.

"See? I'm not the only one. *You* put your foot in your mouth with that one," she threw back at her son.

"But there's a difference, Mom! I stopped and apologized. You still treat Aleesha as though she works for you. But Aleesha's my wife, Mom. She's not your caregiver or nurse or servant. She's my wife. If she chooses to wait on you hand and foot, that's her choice. But I wish you would take notice and appreciate even *some* of the many things she does for you."

He turned his back on his mother and faced the kitchen island. Aleesha was at the counter next to the refrigerator, not looking at anyone, just quietly arranging meat, cheese, and bread on a plate. Jimmy hadn't noticed her getting the food from the refrigerator. She was avoiding the eye of the storm and had apparently been here before.

Jimmy started to clear his throat, but Wendi placed a hand on his arm and squeezed.

Carolyn noticed Wendi's move, though, and said, "I'm sorry you two had to witness my son's little tantrum."

Wham! Hank's hand slammed down on the island with a bang that resounded throughout the house.

"What?" Carolyn barked crossly. "I was just telling them I was sorry. I thought that's what you wanted me to do. Show some common courtesy. Isn't that what you said?"

Mommie Dearest! Jimmy thought. *It's like a scene out of that movie about Joan Crawford!* He looked around as unobtrusively as he could to make sure no wire hangers were nearby. His movement earned him another arm squeeze from Wendi.

"That's just fine, Mom," Hank said, infuriated. "They don't even know what's going on here."

"What *is* going on here, Hank?" Carolyn asked her son.

"Do you want to know exactly where we were last night, Mom? Do you?"

Carolyn simply stared back at Hank. Jimmy thought it felt like they were caught recreating roles from when Hank was a teenager wanting the car on a Friday night.

"Well, I'll tell you anyway. We were looking at a house. One for just the two of us, meaning me and Aleesha. Down in Orange Park. Far enough away so we can have a life of our own."

Jimmy stole a look at Aleesha and saw that the color had drained from her face, and her mouth was drawn into a single, tight line. She noticed Jimmy's eyes on her and quickly turned back to her lunch preparations.

Hank kept talking, his voice filling the house.

"And we couldn't get back when the storm hit, so we checked into a hotel. We didn't even try to call. We just looked out for ourselves. That's how it's supposed to be with a married couple: they look out for themselves."

With his words hanging in the air, Hank walked out of the room and over to the stairway leading down to the carport below the house.

Aleesha quietly continued her meal prep, and Wendi looked at Jimmy. He shrugged as if saying, *What can you do?*

After a few heartbeats, Carolyn cleared her throat. "I guess you probably know that every family has their little flareups. I'm sorry you had to witness one of ours."

From the floor-to-ceiling windows, Jimmy saw a figure in a bright yellow poncho walking across the yard in the rain. The rain wasn't pouring down quite as hard as earlier. Hurricanes, tropical storms, and depressions dropped their rains in bands. The current band of rain must be petering out, and they might get a short break before the next one rotated through their area.

"Aleesha?" Carolyn said without turning around. "Can you bring me … *May* I please have a toasted bagel with cream cheese?"

"Yes, ma'am," came the mousy reply. Aleesha's meek answer was nothing like the raucous laughter she had unleashed in the room earlier.

Carolyn took another sip of tea, then, as an afterthought, added, "Thank you."

Wendi tugged at Jimmy's arm, and they rose from their stools by the counter, and she led him to another room off the living room. It was a tidy office, with a fairly new-looking iMac on the desk, a large window that would ordinarily fill the space with sunshine, and a wall with built-in bookshelves. Like Hillary Lyst's office, the shelves were loaded with books, but with one big difference: these books were all by the same author: Gary Dawson, Carolyn Dawson's *nom de plume*.

"Whoa," Jimmy said. "I had no idea there were so many books in the series."

"There are fifteen titles going back to 1987; there's her first one: *Cold Steele*. Since 2008, she has had one new book every two years, like clockwork. Her newest—number sixteen—is due out in a few weeks for the Christmas season: *Refined Steele*."

Jimmy was looking at the titles of the books on the shelves. Paperbacks and hardcovers were mixed together, but they were all sorted by title. Some of them were in multiple languages – English, French, German, Italian, and Spanish, and some in Asian languages. Jimmy had no idea if some were in Japanese and others in Vietnamese—if they even were!

"And these are all about Remington Steel?"

"*Nick* Steele, you dope, and the Steele Detective Agency," Wendi corrected him. "Yes, they are all about Nick and Diana Steele. Nick has the looks and witty dialogue, but Diana is the one who really orchestrates solving the crimes."

"Just the opposite of us!" Jimmy replied. Wendi ignored his comment.

There was a tentative rap on the doorframe behind them. They turned together and saw Aleesha standing there, her eyes fixed on the floor.

"Miss Carolyn was wondering if you'd please stay and have a simple lunch with us. It's still raining and blowing outside, and since you came out and helped her get out of her iron lung… well, she—*we all* would like for you to stay."

"We don't want you to go to any trouble for us," Wendi replied.

"Oh, it's no trouble. I was making some sandwich fixings, and we have Cokes in the fridge, chips in the pantry, and I made a nanner puddin' yesterday before we left."

Before Wendi or Jimmy could respond, Aleesha stepped across the room quickly and quietly. In a voice that was almost a whisper, she said, "I hate it when they fight, so I would count it as a personal favor if you'd stay."

Wendi looked Aleesha in the eye for a moment, then smiled and announced in a voice that carried to the kitchen, "We'd love to stay. We don't have anywhere to be since the storm is passing through. Maybe we can play Rummikub or something after lunch."

Jimmy knew Carolyn could hear Wendi's acceptance of the lunch invitation in the kitchen. He was sure Wendi intended it that way.

The change in Aleesha's demeanor was marked. Her face lit up, and she was back to the boisterous person Jimmy had met after his coffeemaker debacle. Meek and mousy Aleesha was back in hiding, replaced by the loud jokester.

The three of them returned to the kitchen, Aleesha leading the way. Carolyn was still in the same place: sitting in front of a tall window in the breakfast nook area, staring through the glass at the dwindling rain, the trees and marsh grasses standing much straighter. Jimmy caught an occasional flash of yellow rain slicker outside as Hank moved around, checking the property for storm damage.

Carolyn gave no hint that she saw anything outside, but Jimmy was sure her eyes were taking in everything within their range. Jimmy was also sure she was mulling over Hank's announcement that he and Aleesha were looking for a house of their own.

It was neither Jimmy's nor Wendi's business, but he was pretty sure it would be the number one topic in the Dawson house after they left that afternoon.

Aleesha announced, "Grab a paper plate and make a sandwich. We've got a couple of types of bread, ham, turkey, roast beef, and sliced cheese, too. There are corn chips, pretzels, and potato chips, and I put out bowls for the nanner puddin.' We have plenty, so don't be shy."

Chapter 5

THEY ATE LUNCH without Hank. No one even suggested they call him in.

It must be a regular occurrence, Jimmy thought.

Jimmy remembered eating supper at Albert Hoppman's when they were about nine. Albert—later just Al when they became teenagers—and his mom lived across town, clear on the other side of the bridge. His mom was a nurse at a nursing home and a single mom before it was fashionable. Jimmy never asked Albert where his dad was. Divorce was not something people talked about back then, so Jimmy assumed Albert's dad had died in a horrible car wreck or a similarly gruesome tragedy. Marriage vows were supposed to be 'until death us do part,' so it only stood to reason that Albert's dad was dead.

Albert's mom made them pancakes, which should have been a treat: breakfast for supper. But they didn't smell the same as the pancakes Jimmy's mom made, and there wasn't any pancake syrup. Instead, Albert's mom had plain, white (clear) Karo syrup for the boys to use.

For some unknown reason, Jimmy had no appetite that night. That never happened at home, but he was in unfamiliar surroundings with food that wasn't the same as at home and people who weren't his family. Jimmy tried, but he couldn't eat more than a couple of pancakes. He could usually put away at least six and once had eaten ten in a single sitting. On the other hand, Albert had no problem eating all the pancakes his mom placed in front of him. It was his house and his food, after all.

Jimmy looked at the spread that Aleesha had laid out for them. Various loaves of bread: white, whole wheat, even pumpernickel rye bread. There was bright orange cheddar cheese, cream-colored Muenster with an orange edge, baby Swiss cheese with holes, and Colby-Jack that blended white and orange together. There was even a panini press on the counter if someone wanted their sandwich toasted and squished together.

There were jars of Duke's mayonnaise, yellow mustard, brown stoneground mustard, horseradish, and ketchup. Just past the condiments, Aleesha had placed a crudité tray on the counter filled with baby carrots, celery sticks, sweet pepper rings in green, red, orange, and yellow varieties, and a bowl of ranch dressing that took up the middle of the tray.

At the end of this feast for "a little lunch" was a white 9x13 glass pan filled to the rim with banana pudding — nanner puddin,' as the locals called it. Layers of pudding, banana slices, and 'nilla wafers, like a sweet, semi-tropical lasagna, and all topped with meringue. This was a Southern delight Jimmy had fallen in love with when he arrived in the area more than a decade earlier. Aleesha said it was "slap your mama good!"

Some cooks wimp out and top their nanner puddin' with whipped cream, but Aleesha had gone all out, topping the dessert with meringue and carefully toasting it a golden brown under the broiler.

Luckily for Jimmy, there was no repeat of the Albert Hoppman incident, and he crafted sandwiches that would have made Dagwood jealous. He filled a bowl so full of nanner puddin' that Aleesha squealed and laughed as Jimmy took scoop after scoop.

Wendi's plate was less calorific and much more healthy—no doubt—but Jimmy's was the kind cooks liked to see. Wendi ate as Jimmy expected, a single sandwich made with whole wheat, a little mayo, lettuce, a slice of Swiss cheese, and some paper-thin, deli-sliced turkey. She had a few chips, a large helping of veggies from the crudité platter, a bottle of water, and a small bowl with about three bites of pudding. Jimmy was pretty sure Wendi took the dessert simply to be polite.

Many cooks view food as an expression of love or an art form, not just fuel for the body. Whatever. Jimmy saw Aleesha's nanner puddin' as an art form, and he appreciated it.

*

Hank eventually came back in and ate some lunch. Alone. He put together his sandwich and sides, got something to drink, and went to the living room to eat. His plate looked more like Wendi's than Jimmy's.

Jimmy could see that Aleesha was disappointed that her husband chose to alienate himself from the others in their little impromptu, storm-driven clan, but there was nothing anyone could do about it. A – Jimmy was here with Wendi and B – Aleesha was Hank's wife. Jimmy had just met them, so overstepping would be extremely easy and could swiftly become messy or even violent. Jimmy could tell Hank had an angry streak, and he had no desire to discover how deep it ran.

Jimmy soon discovered his eyes had been much larger than his stomach when he scooped Aleesha's pudding into his bowl. It was fun to hear her squeal and cheer him on, but after consuming his sandwiches and chips, he struggled to get it all eaten. Right now, Jimmy only wanted to sit back and let his stomach settle. He hoped it wouldn't be too rude to snatch a quick nap.

"Jimmy."

It was Carolyn. So much for napping.

"Jimmy." The woman obviously had no respect for an after-lunch nap.

He pushed himself up into a more attentive-looking, less-slumping position and replied, "Yes, ma'am?"

"Wendi tells me you're a private investigator. Is that true?"

"Yes, ma'am, I am. A finder of people, places, and things. Licensed for all of Florida."

"Then how is it that I haven't heard of you? I have extensively researched investigations and investigative techniques while writing my books; your name has never come up. Have you been in this area long?" Carolyn asked.

"Over ten years," Jimmy responded, wishing he could go back to slouching and alleviate some of the pressure on his puddin'-filled stomach.

Why did I eat so much? he moaned inwardly.

"Your answer tells me how long you've been here but not why I haven't heard of you before."

Wendi jumped in to rescue him. "Jimmy likes to stay below the radar. It's kind of like undercover cops: they do heroic deeds but can't be acknowledged publicly because it would blow their cover or put their loved ones at risk."

Wendi looked at Jimmy for corroboration, but he could only smile weakly and put a hand over his mouth as a burp threatened to work its way up through the pudding.

"Do you?" Carolyn asked, ignoring Jimmy's post-meal discomfort. After all, no one had forced him to eat so much. "Do you have loved ones around here?"

Jimmy didn't know if she was asking about family or surreptitiously asking Wendi about her relationship with Jimmy.

"Actually—" he started to answer, but Wendi jumped in again.

"Jimmy doesn't have any *family* here – if you mean blood relatives – but he has people here who are *like* family. His partner, Pepé ..." and she trailed off, unable to come up with anyone else on his list. But it was enough.

"And Wendi and Hillary," Jimmy added. "I'm actually going to spend Thanksgiving with them, assuming it's not canceled by a hurricane, flood, or pestilence."

"Ahh," Carolyn replied. "I see."

Jimmy wasn't sure she did. He figured she was asking because Jimmy was at Wendi's when Carolyn called for someone to rescue her that morning. Most people leap to the canoodling conclusion when two people are together early in the morning. Honestly, he would assume the same thing if he were not the one who had been up all night talking with Wendi while the hurricane abused the Florida coast.

There was just something about Wendi. They never ran out of things to talk about when they were together.

Since Jimmy's case with the Lysts had ended a week earlier, they had been nearly inseparable. The fee they had paid Jimmy gave him some breathing room financially, so he was pretending he was independently wealthy and not actively seeking work. Wendi made him feel whole, like an essential part of him had been missing but was now in place. He would have to get together with Pepé and see if this is how he felt with Gwynn.

He wasn't sure how he would approach the topic. Guys didn't usually talk about things like that. Pepé was different, though. Despite his competence with weapons and ability to recognize potential dangers, he had a tender heart. Pepé was a warrior but not a brawler. He was a protector, one who stood in the gap between the people he had been charged with protecting and the danger they were facing. If evil was going to reach them, it would have to go through Pepé first. It was one of the reasons he was on the security team at his church. Jimmy didn't know if Pepé had always been that way or if it came from his years in Navy security and law enforcement. "To Serve and Protect."

Jimmy realized Carolyn had asked him something, and he had missed it, thinking about spending time with Wendi and needing to talk to Pepé. Mostly thinking about being with Wendi.

"I'm sorry, Miss Carolyn. I didn't catch what you were asking," Jimmy said. "We were up all night watching the weather and talking. I guess I'm a little tired now, and all those carbs in my lunch have made me a little groggy."

"I was asking how long you and Wendi have known each other," the mystery writer replied.

Wendi answered. "We've only known each other a few weeks, but it seems a lot longer. Honestly, there are times I feel like a teenager, sending texts and pictures—"

"Clean ones!" Jimmy interjected. There was no need to give their host more ideas than she already had.

"Of course, clean ones!" Wendi responded, her face turning a brilliant shade of red. "Sunsets, plates of food, waves on the shore, birds, squirrels, flowers, and things like that." Wendi paused briefly before continuing.

"You remember what it's like when you just want to share every little thing with someone special, Carolyn," Wendi added.

"Indeed, I do," Carolyn answered. "I still remember when David and I were dating in college, even though it was nearly sixty years ago. I know what it's like to say goodnight and go into the house alone. And when I was that age, my breathing wasn't quite so much of an issue. But as I got older, especially after I had Hank, the polio slowly reasserted itself in my body. It wasn't too bad in my twenties, but it became a real issue when I hit my forties. I don't know if it was the stress of losing David when Hank was sixteen or the pressure of providing a life for the two of us here on Piney Island. Or, most likely, it was just what it was: a delayed consequence of having polio when I was eight."

"I've read that many people who had polio as children have symptoms and issues later in life," Jimmy added, and Carolyn nodded in mute agreement. Jimmy continued, "I knew a guy up in northern Minnesota, Gene, who had polio in the 50s when he was a kid. When Gene turned 55, it was like someone threw a switch, and he started having trouble with his legs again. He didn't have trouble breathing when he was a kid; he couldn't walk. But like you, Carolyn, Gene got better when he was a kid. He wore braces to help him walk, but just for a while. The last time I saw him, I noticed he was wearing braces on his legs again. That was over ten years ago now. I don't even know if Gene is still around anymore."

Carolyn nodded. "I know what you're talking about. It's called post-polio syndrome. There was a long stretch when I didn't need to use my metal 'bedroom' more than once a week, sometimes less. But then, one day, it was like my lungs forgot how to breathe. It required more and more conscious thought and effort."

"And yet, despite your physical struggles and other hardships—" Wendi started.

"Other hardships?" Carolyn broke in.

"Losing David, of course," Wendi continued, "but being unable to carry Tammy to full-term was hard on you, too."

"Tammy?" Jimmy asked, looking from face to face for an explanation.

Wendi made brief eye contact with Carolyn, who grimaced slightly but then pasted her smile back on and forged ahead. Jimmy got the feeling that she didn't relish revealing whatever was coming, but she had done it before, so she knew she could do it again.

"When Hank was two, I got pregnant again. I was so happy. David was, too. We wanted to have at least two children and were hoping for a little girl to round out our family. Things were fine in the first part of my pregnancy, but at about six months, things took a turn. I was spotting—sorry for the graphic picture, but it was what it was—and they tried bed rest to see if they could settle things down. Sure. 'Bed rest' with a two-year-old boy running around! David had a new job with an architectural firm that was taking him out of town more than either of us liked, and—long story short—I lost the baby. A little girl, just like we wanted. I had already named her Tammy."

Carolyn sniffled and reached for a tissue. Wendi followed suit. They both dabbed at their eyes. Jimmy decided it was best to stay quiet.

"For a year afterward, I barely got out of bed. I was clinically depressed, drowning in grief over losing my baby girl …" Carolyn paused and took a deeper breath. It was clear to Jimmy that she was struggling to tell this personal story, one quite different from her crime and mystery books.

Carolyn picked up the story again. "It was during that time that I started writing, mostly poetry, writing my way through the pain. Things I couldn't talk about flowed out of my fingers onto the page. Most of it had no commercial value, but a few pieces were accepted by some women's magazines. It was the early 70s, and women were burning their bras and marching for their rights. The country was still deeply enmeshed in Vietnam, and then we were forced to endure Watergate. Everyone was so much angrier than in the late 60s when 'love was all you need,' and people danced and sang under the moon at places like Woodstock and San Francisco. People smoked weed, dropped acid, and had sex with whoever was nearby and willing. I was already a mom by then, though, so I didn't get involved in any of that. My life revolved around caring for our little boy, keeping my husband happy, and being pregnant. We were more like Ozzie and Harriet in a three-bedroom ranch house than Moon Child and Rebel Wolf, living out of a VW Microbus."

Jimmy nearly laughed out loud. As a teenager, he had gone through a phase when he wanted to be nicknamed Wolf, but most of his friends called him Nerd instead. Instead of laughing, he asked, "And you lived here? If you were born and raised in California and married there, how did you end up clear over here on the opposite side of the country?"

"David was in the Navy when we married, stationed in San Diego. They reassigned him to Mayport Naval Station after our wedding. The Navy moved us across the country. One of the first things he did was build this house. It was finished about the same time Hank was born. It's the only home he has known." She looked away as she said this.

"And that's why it hurts that he wants to move away, right?" Wendi pressed.

"Yes," Carolyn answered, then sniffled a bit and wiped her eyes again. "I should have expected it, though. After all, as soon as I got married, we moved across the country, far away from everything and everyone I had ever known growing up. Hank and Aleesha have barely been married a year, and they're talking about moving. I don't know why. They have complete freedom here, and it'll all be theirs when I'm gone, which may not be long. Polio survivors don't usually have the longevity other people enjoy. I'm seventy-five, and there are days when my lungs tell me loud and clear that they've done all the breathing they want to do. I have to coax them along almost like I have to baby that machine I sleep inside in my bedroom."

"Really?" Jimmy asked. "It shouldn't be that hard to maintain, should it? There must be somewhere you can get parts, right?"

"You'd think so," Carolyn responded, "but the truth is, no one is making the specialized parts for these old dinosaurs. And when I say dinosaurs, I'm referring to the iron lungs, not me or the two other people still using them."

Jimmy held up a hand like a traffic cop to jump into the conversation.

"Aleesha and Wendi both said the same thing, that there are only three people using iron lungs now," he said. "Excuse me, but how can that be?"

Carolyn gave a slight shake of her head and let out a sad laugh with no mirth inside. "As I said, Jimmy, I'm seventy-five, and the other two people are even older. Polio comes back to bully us and show us it's still the king of the playground. People have passed away, and even though there are other polio survivors, they have other weaknesses and issues rather than breathing troubles. The vaccines have almost completely eradicated polio, but there's still one strain that's resistant to being killed once and for all. Polio is a real bastard, Jimmy, pardon my French."

Wendi slid into the conversation, asking, "You say Hank and Aleesha have complete freedom here, Carolyn. Where do they stay? I've only seen your bedroom and the living room and kitchen."

Carolyn pointed a finger straight up toward the ceiling. "They have the upstairs all to themselves. I'm not going up there unless Jimmy carries me!" She laughed.

"You've never asked to come upstairs," a tiny voice said from the kitchen.

They had forgotten that Aleesha was still in the kitchen, taking care of the cleanup after lunch. Hank had disappeared, but Aleesha was like any good servant: invisible and mute, part of the furniture in the background.

"Aleesha! I'm so glad you're still down here. I was wanting another cup of tea but didn't want to get up and make it. But since you're here, you can get it for me." Carolyn announced to her former caregiver-cum-daughter-in-law.

Aleesha came over to where the trio was sitting. She said nothing, reached out, took the cup from Carolyn's hand, and walked back toward the kitchen sink. Carolyn was talking to Wendi again, but Jimmy couldn't catch what she said because he was focused on watching Aleesha.

She walked to the sink, set the cup down, turned, and quietly left the room. Jimmy saw her go to a door he hadn't noticed in the living room when they arrived. When she opened the door, he saw a set of stairs. Aleesha went in and closed the door behind her. He heard her quiet footsteps creaking on the steps as she went upstairs.

For the time being, there would be no more tea.

Chapter 6

BY MID-AFTERNOON, the rain had slacked off. Jimmy and Wendi said goodbye to Carolyn and went downstairs to the carport, where Wendi's hot pink Jeep waited. Jimmy took note of a white Subaru Outback – Hank's car – that had joined Wendi's Jeep in the space under the house. Jimmy carried a Tupperware-style container with generous amounts of banana pudding, another container with veggies for Wendi, and a zippered gallon bag with sandwiches for whomsoever would. Jimmy would later. Wendi might, but probably not.

Driving back to Wendi's condo, she decided to take a side trip to see if there was flooding or damage from the tropical storm. They were nearing Fernandina's historic downtown. All its streets were named for trees alphabetically—Ash, Beech, Cedar, Date, Fir, Gum, Hickory, etc. Suddenly, Jimmy's phone dinged with a text. He thought it might be Pepé, so he dragged it out of his pocket and looked. The message read,

Stay out of Dawson business

Jimmy thumbed a quick reply, half-expecting the brusque text had come from Hank.

Who is this?

The reply came just as quickly.

It's 7 O'clock, Jimmy.

Le Bonhomme Sept-Heures! Or at least that was what Jimmy's gut said.

It was an immediate, unthinking reaction from hearing the name as a boy. It was the Canadian equivalent of the boogeyman: the Seven O'clock Man. Kids knew they had to be home before seven o'clock to avoid being taken by the Seven O'clock Man. Some said he ate the children he caught, and others said he kept them caged for a while before killing them. The legend was so ingrained in Jimmy's mind that he still got nervous if he was out walking at dusk and the street lights came on. *I gotta get home!* his heart told him.

In Jimmy's rational mind, he knew there was no real *Le Bonhomme Sept-Heures,* but he had already had a conversation with the man on the other end of the phone recently, and he had claimed to be the stuff of nightmares. Indeed, The Man had made nightmares for several people Jimmy had crossed paths with. One was dead, while two others were still recovering from beatings a few weeks ago.

What Jimmy knew so far was that The Man was the boss of a small gang of thugs who preyed upon those weaker and smaller than them – like most crooks of that ilk. Jimmy had outsmarted one of them three times, a big brute named Gabriel, who had turned out to be less than the sharpest crayon in the box. Like in baseball, three strikes meant you were out because Gabriel ended up in a jail cell at the Nassau County Sheriff's Office and somehow died there.

The two men who received beatings were involved in the theft of a manuscript, and neither had played their part very well. When Jimmy got close to figuring out what was happening with the manuscript, the first man was sent to the hospital after three of The Man's goons used him for a hacky sack for not revealing its hiding place. And after the money for the manuscript slipped through the hands of the second man, the same goon squad paid Jimmy a visit that was neither pleasant nor social, looking for the rest of the money they had hoped to get for the manuscript.

Jimmy knew about all three men because The Man had called and taunted him, gloating about his ability to act with impunity, beating and even killing those who disappointed him. And he did it right under the local law enforcement's nose.

"Jimmy? What is it? Is it Pepé?" Wendi asked.

"What? No. It's not Pepé."

"Is it bad news?"

"Huh? Oh, no. Everything's fine," Jimmy tried to lighten his tone. "My, uh, mom has texted me on her birthday every year since I've been down here. Then I text her a happy birthday, and we're both happy." Which was true. *Except I haven't gotten a text from her for five years since she passed away.*

"All right, if you say so, but you had a funny look on your face," Wendi replied.

Jimmy wanted to say, "How would you feel if you opened a closet door and discovered your worst childhood fear was real? And it was standing in front of you?"

Instead, he answered, "Did you see how much nanner puddin' I ate? I am <u>way</u> too full. I hope I can keep it all down because it was too good to waste."

"Yeah, now you're being kind of gross," she said. "Let's drive down to the marina. I want to see if everything is okay down there."

Jimmy nodded mutely, still upset by the text.

A large tree had split and fallen at the corner of Beech and Eighth, damaging the white picket fence that corralled the old house, but at least it had fallen away from the Victorian-style house that was home to the Beech Street Grill. Most of the branches had stayed on the lot; just a few ended up in the street. Wendi turned the Jeep left and headed toward the waterfront.

Surprisingly, there was very little storm impact on this side of the island. Earlier in the morning, they had watched numerous reports on TV about the devastation the hurricane had done to the beaches and roads along the coast by Daytona Beach and Volusia County. Some of the beach homes were falling into the surf, while others stood on spindly-looking "legs," their beachfront patios dangling nearly twenty feet in the air above the waves and sand. The storm surge had washed away the beach, the dunes, and backyards from the homes, destabilizing the structures and eliminating the prospects of rehab for many. For them, their recovery would be accomplished by bulldozing the lot flat and starting over, that is, if the owners had enough insurance and liquid equity.

Even if they did, they couldn't rebuild that close to the water again because the beach was now fifty to a hundred feet closer to the street behind the houses. Nicole had washed away so much beach that some homes that used to be on the "wrong side" of the road were now oceanfront properties.

But the damage was minimal here in Fernandina on the island's leeward side. The river had risen and invaded Front Street down by the marina, as evidenced by a debris line on the east side of the street. Big puddles were all that remained to show where the water had been. This was the kind of impact the locals were used to. Businesses on Centre Street had sandbags stacked across their storefronts and in front of their doors. In a few hours, the sandbags would be stacked to dry and get stored for the next storm. Most of the businesses probably had minimal water encroachment inside, in part because they had all been able to plan for the storm and prepare. That was one advantage a hurricane had over a tornado: you could prepare in advance for a hurricane. Tornados drop out of nowhere and coldcock you.

Seeing the Centre Street sign struck a melancholic chord in Jimmy. Thoughts about childhood boogeymen, his neighborhood while growing up, and his mom all tugged at his heart. He was uncharacteristically quiet, and Wendi told him so.

"I guess you really did overdo it on the pudding, didn't you? Are you sure you're all right, Jimmy?" she asked.

"I'll be fine," he answered. He was slouched down in the passenger seat. "I just may not eat until tomorrow. Possibly not until the day after."

Wendi smiled and laughed at this, and Jimmy felt better immediately. Seven O'clock Man or not, she was good for what ailed him.

They drove around the waterfront area for a few blocks and then neared some public restrooms. Wendi pulled over and stopped.

"Need it?" she asked.

He answered, "My dad always said to use it whenever the opportunity arose. So, yes."

They each grabbed an umbrella from the backseat and hopped out. Wendi beeped the key fob to lock the Jeep, even though no people were walking around downtown.

"Meet you back here in a few," she told him, running toward the ladies' room. Jimmy jogged to the men's room, but only partway. Jogging made his stomach feel worse.

Once inside the bathroom and his business complete, he pulled out his phone and typed a short text.

 What's it to you?

He pushed the send button. A few seconds later, the reply came.

  Stay out of Dawson business
 I don't know if I can
  Nothing in it for you
 The joke's on you. I'm not in it.
  Stay out of Dawson business.
  Or else!
 Or else what?
  If your hand offends you, cut it
  off. An eye for an eye.

There were no other texts. Jimmy put the phone away, stepped out of the bathroom, opened the umbrella, and walked back to the Jeep, keeping to the sidewalk, and avoiding the soggy lawn. Wendi was already in the vehicle.

"Feel better?" she asked.

"Yes, I think I do," he replied.

"Good. Let's go back over by my place and see if I have a beach left."

"Sounds like a deal," Jimmy answered.

He was curious why The Man was interested in Carolyn and her family and why he didn't want Jimmy involved. For that matter, involved in what? What business? The text said to "stay out of Dawson business." Jimmy had a strong feeling he was going to get to know the Dawsons a lot better in the near future.

*

Driving through town and seeing barely any other vehicles was a bit weird. All in all, there wasn't nearly as much damage as people had planned for. It sounded rather pessimistic, but when you prepare for your roof to blow away, all your trees to be uprooted, or for three feet of water throughout your house, anything less than that bad is good. Plan for the worst; you'll always be relieved when it's not as extensive as you feared.

They drove through the parking lot past Publix, Staples, and Lyst Publishing. Everything was closed up, but nothing looked damaged. Wendi pulled back out onto Sadler Road and headed toward the beaches.

When they left that morning to help Carolyn, it was raining so hard that they couldn't see more than a few feet from the Jeep in any direction. Now they were between rain bands, and although there were some weird colors and streaks of clouds in the sky, there were also a few patches of blue sky overhead where the sun even tried to peek through.

Driving slower than usual and avoiding large stretches of standing water gave them more time to discuss their recent experience with the Dawson household.

"Let me ask you a question," Jimmy posed. "Was that the usual vibe at the Dawson house, or was that special?"

"Oh, that was definitely special," Wendi replied. "I've never seen Carolyn and Hank argue and fight like that. I've known them since I started working for Mr. Lyst, and that's nearly twenty years."

"So, this was a new look for Hank?"

"It was new for Carolyn, too," Wendi responded.

She slowed down the Jeep and maneuvered around some puddles of unknown depth and bedraggled palm fronds the wind had separated from their tree. Once past the detritus in the road, she continued her answer.

"I haven't seen them much since Hank and Aleesha got married about a year ago. I wouldn't have expected such a venomous exchange between Hank and his mom, but it's definitely a new vibe around there since Aleesha quit working for Carolyn and became part of the family."

"I was wondering about that," Jimmy answered. "How long did she work there before they got married?"

"I think about two years, and they've been married a year. So, I guess I've known Aleesha for about three years. She can be a lot of fun – and loud! I'm not sure what the mousy, servile attitude was today. When she was just working for

Carolyn, she was much more bubbly – like she was before Hank and Carolyn started picking at each other today. Whoo! Once those two started sniping at each other, Aleesha tried to blend into the woodwork. That was something new, too."

"Maybe it's not just Hank and Carolyn arguing. Maybe Aleesha and Hank have been arguing, too, and so when he argues with his mother, it gets too much for Aleesha," Jimmy said. He was quiet for a bit, watching the road and seeing more branches and debris as they neared the beaches. "What was your takeaway from that tea thing?"

Wendi answered, "You mean when Carolyn asked for more tea, and Aleesha took her cup, put it in the sink, and went upstairs to the apartment? Yeah. I didn't see that coming. There are obviously some strong emotions flying around in that house."

"What about Hank's announcement that he and Aleesha are trying to find a place down south of Jacksonville in Orange Park?" Jimmy asked.

"Seriously? You could have knocked me over with a feather. Hank has lived in that house his entire life. I mean, literally, since he was born. And he's been the visible face of Carolyn's books for years and has done the book tours in her place. Not that she couldn't do them herself, but she doesn't like to do that stuff, and I think Hank does. He's living through her author-persona, vicariously taking the bows and collecting the kudos. And I think she likes for him to do it. Usually, the introvert or home-bound person lives vicariously through the outgoing, mobile person, but this is like they're living out a fabricated life together. If I were a shrink, I'd probably say there was some kind of symbiotic relationship going on where they both get something out of it."

Jimmy thought for a second and then asked, "Do they collaborate on the books?"

Now it was Wendi's turn to be quiet, as though she was weighing her words carefully.

"I think Carolyn tried, but I don't think Hank's ideas meshed with hers. The books they worked on together did not sell nearly as well as the ones she wrote alone. Of the fifteen books – check that – *sixteen* books she'll have published by the end of December – they only worked together on *Plated Steele* and *Hardened Steele*. When those books didn't catch fire with the fans, Hank wasn't interested in doing more, and that was fine with his mother."

"So, they settled back into the roles where they were comfortable? She writes the books, and he goes to the book tours and signings, playing the author at the meet and greets with the adoring public?" Jimmy asked.

Wendi nodded. "That's about it."

"What does he do the rest of the time?" Jimmy asked curiously.

"I guess he putters around the homestead. Isn't that what 'kept men' do?"

"I've never been one, so I can't speak from experience. But it's usually a wife doing the keeping, not a mom. Gotta give him credit, though: he's living The Dream. He's in his mid-fifties and still living with his mom."

They both laughed at Jimmy's comment.

"What can you tell me about Aleesha?" Jimmy asked.

Wendi ticked off some quick bio bullets. "Local girl. Graduated from Fernandina Beach High School. Played softball in school. Went to Coastal Georgia College in Kingsland for some kind of nursing degree. I think that helped her get the job with Carolyn."

"How much younger is she than Hank?" Jimmy wanted to know.

"He's fifty-five; she's thirty-five."

Jimmy whistled. "Twenty years. Can you say daddy issues?"

Wendi laughed, her sweet melodic laughter filling the Jeep. It was a sound Jimmy was coming to love.

He didn't get the answer to his last question. They arrived back at Wendi's condo and pulled into the parking garage that substituted for a first floor. Wendi parked the Jeep, turned off the ignition, leaned over, and kissed Jimmy. Not long or passionate, but a kiss nonetheless. *Always leave them wanting more!* he thought.

"Thanks for not making a fuss about going along to Carolyn's. It means a lot that you were willing to drop everything and help someone who needed us," she said, putting her hand on his. She looked into his eyes, and he waited for her to say something else. Instead, she kissed him again, even more quickly this time, opened the door, and jumped out.

Chapter 7

Jimmy and Wendi exited the Mary-Kay-pink Jeep and walked over to the east end of the garage, where some slit windows between the support columns gave them a view of the beach.

"It's still there," Wendi said excitedly. "The beach is still there!" She turned and threw her arms around Jimmy, hugging him and giving him another kiss. *I could get used to this!* went through his mind.

Wendi was practically dancing a jig as she looked toward the ocean and the debris-strewn beach. "I'm so happy the beach didn't get washed away. All those news stories from Daytona Beach this morning showing big stretches of highway washed out, houses falling into the ocean, and the beaches simply washed away ... I didn't know what to expect here. But it's all still there!"

Jimmy had also been saddened to see the damage in Volusia County and Daytona Beach, but part of him thought, *They knew the risks when they built there.* He would not say that aloud, though, because he liked having Wendi happy and spontaneously kissing him. Keeping her happy made Jimmy happy.

Jimmy was pragmatic, not insensitive. Sometimes he was so sensitive it got him into trouble when he let people off the hook after hearing their sad stories. Pepé constantly reminded him that not every case has a happy ending and, despite what people want to believe, there are consequences for actions.

Jimmy was not immune to the sadness caused by acts of nature. He understood the grief produced when a house burned down after being struck by lightning, trees were toppled by a tornado's winds, a beach was washed away by a hurricane, or a house full of memories tumbled into the ocean. Like many people living in this part of the world, Jimmy chose this location because he believed hurricanes would either skip this area or weaken before arriving. The worst storms tended to shy away from it, but Jimmy knew not to say the words out loud lest he jinx himself.

The pragmatic side of Jimmy wanted to tell people who lost their homes and belongings to hurricanes, "You *chose* to live there. You know hurricanes are a real possibility from June through November every year. That's half of the year. As my mom used to say, if you can't stand the heat, stay out of the sauna."

But Jimmy had a good thing going with Wendi, so rather than open a can of worms about personal responsibility and living next to a beach that was wide open to hurricanes for most of the year, he let it slide. Instead, he took Wendi's hand, and they walked out of the parking garage and up to where the beach access boardwalk began. Yellow caution tape was strung across the entrance, not unusual after a big storm.

"Do you think this tape still needs to be here?" Wendi asked him.

Jimmy did a quick head swivel to check for cops or lifeguards, then pulled the tape off the wooden posts, wrapped it up, and shoved it in his pocket. "I don't see any tape," he replied with a grin. "Besides, this is private access, isn't it?" They walked ahead.

It was still breezy as they walked on the boardwalk, down through a valley between the dunes and up the other side, catching glimpses of the dark green ocean and white-capped surf. They came out at an opening between the dunes and waving sea oats that marked an entrance onto the beach. They could only go out about ten feet onto the beach, though; the waves were stronger than normal. The waves swooshed up to where Jimmy and Wendi had stopped to gaze out at the ocean. The combination of tide, wind, and storm surge had brought the water, foam, and storm debris farther up on the shore than ordinary.

"Hi, kids!" A voice hailed them from behind, and they turned their backs on the seashore. Jimmy wondered if they were about to be dinged for going past the yellow tape. He reached into his pocket and felt the ball of tape.

"Hi, Mr. Lancôme!" Wendi replied cheerfully. "We came down to see if the beach was still here, and it is!"

"Yes, ma'am, it is. There was a lot of rough surf and a butt-load of foam, but the ocean stayed on the right side of the barrier dune," Mr. Lancôme responded. The man was wearing a tan and purple windbreaker with the hood up over his head, the strings tied securely under his chin. He wore khaki pants and Crocs with no socks, a good footwear choice since the waves were still trying to get past the sandy hill he called the barrier dune. Jimmy speculated that he lived in the same building where Wendi lived.

Lancôme had called the sand hills that rose up in miniature mountain ranges between the oceanfront property and the ocean "barrier dunes." Before moving here, Jimmy had seen manmade breakwater barriers along Lake Superior's North Shore, which extended from Duluth northward to Thunder Bay, Ontario. Some of the towns along the giant inland sea possessed long, stone-block barriers that protected their marinas from the storms that could produce ship-swamping waves. Grand Marais sprang to mind, with its long, dark breakwaters protecting the harbor. No longer in use by iron ore boats, the harbor had become a recreation area for boating, fishing, and (allegedly) swimming. How anyone could get in that cold water, Jimmy didn't know.

Thinking about Lake Superior and the waves caused Jimmy to think of the Gordon Lightfoot classic, "The Wreck of the Edmund Fitzgerald." He hummed the opening as the words ran through his mind.

> *The legend lives on from the Chippewa on down*
> *Of the big lake they called Gitche Gumee*
> *The lake, it is said, never gives up her dead*
> *When the skies of November turn gloomy.*

Jimmy had been only a kid when the Edmund Fitzgerald sank in Lake Superior on November 10, 1975. After he grew up, he visited the Duluth, Minnesota, waterfront museum several times, looking at relics recovered from the doomed ship of musical fame.

The winds and the waves on Amelia Island weren't nearly as cold as those on Lake Superior. Most of the year, the waters around Amelia Island felt like bathwater, with temps reaching the middle eighties, sometimes flirting with ninety! After moving here, he discovered that water temperatures over eighty were a big factor in developing hurricanes, the evaporating water fueling the cyclonic activity.

Jimmy heard that the Gulf of Mexico's waters typically rise into the nineties from the summer heat, which is why storms that have weakened often restrengthen into hurricanes once they get out over the Gulf waters. Numerous storms in recent history had done just that, intensifying over the Gulf before slamming into the shoreline from New Orleans east to the Florida panhandle.

The current storm, Hurricane Nicole, came across the Bahamas, pausing long enough to suck up moisture and energy before assaulting Florida's Atlantic coast as a Category One hurricane. Nicole made landfall on Florida twice: first on the Atlantic side south of Vero Beach and then, after swinging out briefly over the Gulf of Mexico, landing again northwest of Mexico Beach on the panhandle. That westward swing had put Amelia Island and Fernandina on the eastern side of the storm, the wet side.

In 2019, Hurricane Dorian paused over the Bahamas before grinding up the eastern coast of the U.S. for two days, staying parallel with the coastline. Along the way, it dropped 3-5 inches of rain in the Jacksonville area.

Although TV meteorologists and locals said it was business as usual after Dorian turned eastward away from the coast, it was anything but typical for Hillary and Wendi Lyst, as the rains from Dorian greased the road Charles and Elly Lyst were traveling, causing their car to hydroplane, ultimately taking their lives. Hillary lost his wife of forty-five years and his forty-year-old son. Wendi lost her husband of seventeen years, although they had been separated for the last two years and were waiting on a final divorce decree.

Jimmy watched absentmindedly as Wendi chatted with Mr. Lancôme for a few minutes before she skipped down the boardwalk toward the beach. He wondered if hurricanes reminded her of that day during Dorian or if she had made her peace with the caprices of nature's storms.

"Jimmy! Come and see what the storm washed up!" Wendi was calling him from just over the dune walk. He shook off his lethargy from being up all night, followed by the "excitement" at the Dawson's, all topped off with the too-large meal. He was also trying to avoid thinking about the message from The Man to 'stay out of Dawson business.'

Catching up with Wendi, Jimmy saw her squatting near the edge of the sand. She was holding a stick and poking something. Jimmy knew whatever she was investigating could be literally anything. Hurricanes blew things loose from oceanside homes, hurled detritus from ships and boats trying to ride out the storm in a safe harbor, sometimes dredged things up from the ocean bottom, and sometimes uncovered 'treasure' from under the dunes when it washed the sand away.

As he approached Wendi, Jimmy suddenly stopped. He had seen many uncommon and odd things washed up after storms, but it was the first time he had seen a human hand. That is, it was the first time he had seen a human hand in the sand not still attached to its human.

Suddenly, his recent text conversation with The Man leaped into Jimmy's mind.

> If your hand offends you, cut it
> off.

"Wendi!" Jimmy's voice was urgent, with a touch of panic. Wendi heard the alarmed tone and turned her head his way.

"Back away from it, Wendi! Don't touch it anymore. We've got to call the cops!"

"I didn't move it," Wendi responded, sounding slightly indignant that he would suggest that she had. Jimmy was digging his phone out of his pocket.

"That's good," he said, trying to sound calmer than he felt. "But now we have to let the pros come and take care of it. Unless you see someone wandering around the dunes with a bloody stump, this is not something we need to be involved with today."

Today? How about ANY day? Jimmy thought to himself.

Wendi came over to where Jimmy now stood. "I was just looking to see if it was a clean cut or ragged," she said. She didn't look pale or horrified, which both surprised and worried Jimmy. A girl who can keep her head in difficult times is a good thing, but a person who isn't bothered by evidence of extreme violence is another thing.

"9-1-1. What's your emergency?" the voice on the phone was asking him.

"We're down near the main beach in Fernandina, looking at the storm damage, and we just found a human hand in the sand," Jimmy said, doing his best to sound as flat and professional as he could.

"Excuse me, did you say a human hand?" the emergency operator asked.

"Yes, ma'am. A human hand." He looked at it and held out his right hand for comparison. "The left one," he added.

"Yes, sir. Have you seen any signs of a person who could have lost it or signs of other people walking around near there either looking for it or who might have tossed it into the surf?"

Good questions, Jimmy thought. He took a deep breath and started looking around the area with an investigator's eye instead of as an innocent bystander.

"There are no signs of a lot of blood like you'd expect if it was done here. But if it was done during the storm, it could have all washed away, and we'd never know," Jimmy told her.

While Jimmy spoke with the 9-1-1 operator, Wendi was walking along the surf line at the edge of the dunes. She was looking from side to side, looking with the eyes of someone who knew this specific area, who walked along here nearly every day for … well, Jimmy didn't know how long Wendi had lived here.

"Thank you, sir. You haven't picked the hand up, have you?" the emergency operator asked him.

"No," he assured her. "It's in situ."

"Are you with law enforcement, sir?" she asked. Jimmy figured it was from his use of the term 'in situ.' He wasn't about to tell her he learned it from watching CSI.

"I'm a private investigator," he answered. "Are the cops on their way?"

"Yes, sir. They've been busy since the main storm moved away, but they're on their way. It should only be a few minutes. You may hear the sirens any minute."

Wendi nodded at Jimmy, tilting her head to one side. Apparently, her hearing was better than his. After about ten seconds of hard listening, Jimmy heard the sirens, too.

"I hear the sirens now, ma'am," he told her.

"Okay, thank you, sir," she answered. Then, almost as an afterthought, she asked, "Are you okay, sir, or would you like me to stay on the line until they arrive?"

Jimmy thought briefly about his answer before assuring her, "I'm fine. There's no threat here."

The emergency operator asked, "I forgot to ask your name. Can I get that for my log?"

"It's Jimmy Favreaux. F-A-V-R-E-A-U-X. I live over by the blue bridge on Highway 17."

"Oh, hi, Jimmy! It's Sarah from the Fernandina Police Department. I'm picking up some of the excess calls after the storm."

Sarah ... Sarah ... oh, yeah. Jimmy remembered now. Kind of short, cute, with brownish hair tied in a single ponytail. Married with two children. Two boys?

"Hi, Sarah. Yeah, I haven't talked to you for a long time. You sounded so professional on the 9-1-1 line. You did a great job. Well, your guys are here. I guess I'll talk to you later. Thanks again." Jimmy clicked off his phone.

"Sarah?" Wendi had sidled over and was listening.

"Married with two little boys," Jimmy replied.

"Is she cute?" Wendi asked as they turned and took a few steps toward the cops approaching on the boardwalk.

"Nope. She's married," Jimmy answered without making eye contact.

"Uh-huh. Because married women can't be attractive."

"That's right," Jimmy replied.

"You thought I was married," she said coyly.

"Hey, guys! Over here," Jimmy hollered, raising one hand in the air, avoiding answering her veiled accusation. He snuck a sideways glance and noticed she was watching him and smirking. She was having fun making him uncomfortable.

Jimmy led the police officers to The Hand, as he now thought of it.

"Yup. That's a hand," the older-appearing of the two said. The nameplate above his right breast pocket said GARCIA. The younger cop's shirt said JENSON.

Jimmy had seen the older one. Luis Garcia. Tall and Hispanic, with a goatee and a shaved head. The back of his head had a wicked-looking scar that hair might have hidden, but his shaved skull spotlighted it instead. Jimmy had never spent enough time with Luis to ask him the story behind it.

Jenson was nearly as tall as Luis but not as solid. Blonde, slight build, about six feet tall, and sporting the Nordic looks Jimmy had seen so many times in northern Minnesota. *You could drop him up on the Minnesota Iron Range, and he'd blend right in,* Jimmy thought.

Jimmy quickly shook hands with both officers. He and Officer Garcia nodded a silent greeting as they shook. The younger officer offered his name with his hand.

"Officer Jenson. Conrad Jenson. Nice to meet you, Mr. Favreaux. Did you find the hand?"

"It was me. I did," Wendi answered for Jimmy. And just like that, nobody cared about Jimmy anymore or what he thought.

Both officers turned to her. Jimmy was sure they noticed her model-like good looks, but both were professional enough to not show it.

They asked Wendi the expected questions: Was the hand where she found it? Yes. Had she touched it? No. Had she moved it? No. Was it buried or out in the open? Just like it is now; I didn't move it. Did she have any idea whose hand it was? No, sir. Had she been home during the storm? Yes, all night long. Had she heard anything outside? Only the storm, officer.

Officer Garcia took several pictures on his cell phone, using an ink pen for size comparison. Then he took a zippered plastic bag out of his pocket, turned it inside out, put it over the hand, and picked up the detached appendage, turning the bag right-side out and capturing the hand inside without touching it. Jimmy had seen a lot of dog walkers do the same trick when picking up their dog's deposits on the boulevard.

Officer Jenson told Jimmy and Wendi that there was no way to know where it came from at that point. They'd be turning it over to forensics in Jacksonville to check the prints and see if they could figure out who it belonged to. Officer Garcia thought it could have come from a shrimp boat mishap or a tragic meeting between a swimmer and a boat propeller. It could have been lost any time in the last day or so and been washed up on the beach by the storm. But they wouldn't really know anything until after forensics looked at it. And, just as quickly as they had come, the cops and the hand were gone.

Alone again, Wendi took Jimmy's hand in hers and they walked along the beach. "That hand was not in the water very long, if at all, Jimmy."

Jimmy stopped and looked at her. He raised his eyebrows, a tacit question that wordlessly asked, "How do you know?"

"It was a smooth cut, not ragged. Nobody had been nibbling on it. Even a smooth cut in the water with the fish and sharks along the beach here would have gotten shredded quickly. I looked; there were no bites out of it," she said.

"Do fish eat when there's a storm?" Jimmy asked.

"The storm is above the water, not below," she answered him. "If this thing came from a boating or shrimp boat accident, it would have been chewed on out in the water before making it to shore, IF it ever made it to shore. Even if it eventually washed up on the sand, it would be minus a lot of bite-sized chunks. Once you go down in the water to a certain depth, the waves cease to have much impact. And yes, fish eat during storms. Especially a fresh, bloody hand floating in the current. I believe that hand was tossed where I found it, Jimmy."

"We need to find out who lost their hand and who needs a citation for littering on the beach," Jimmy replied.

Chapter 8

Dᴇᴄɪᴅɪɴɢ ᴛʜᴇʏ ʜᴀᴅ been out in the wind and rain enough for one day, Jimmy and Wendi went back to her condo. It was getting toward late afternoon, and the long previous night without sleep was taking its toll on them. That, and the excitement at the Carolyn Dawson's, followed by their discovery on the beach.

"Are you going to be hungry in an hour or two?" Wendi asked Jimmy, who had claimed her recliner as his new favorite place to kick back and relax.

"I don't think I'm going to be hungry for at least a week," he replied. He was now fully reclined and flipping through the channels on Wendi's TV. In the end, he settled on one of the local Jacksonville channels. The meteorological team Jimmy and Wendi had watched all night was still working, relaying information to their viewers, showing numerous videos of the storm surge, and tracking Hurricane-cum-Tropical-Storm Nicole. The television station team had upped their game and now featured slick, custom graphics and a dramatic hurricane-report theme song.

Wendi stretched out on the couch while Jimmy watched the meteorologists try to share old information in new ways to try and keep it fresh. The men had rolled their sleeves up to let people know they were working, while the weather team's female staff members remained as perky as ever, hair immaculate and makeup flawless. Jimmy wondered if the station had a giant coffee urn or a fifty-gallon drum of Mountain Dew brought in for hurricanes.

A slight noise caught his attention. It was like distant thunder but softer and closer. *Closer?* Jimmy muted the TV and listened. He soon traced the low rumble's source to the couch, where Wendi was napping, purring softly. Just like everything else about her, it fit perfectly. If she was going to snore, it had to be like this, not big and noisy like Jimmy's grandpa had snored or screeching and squealing like a balloon when you pinch the mouthpiece as the air escapes. Jimmy recalled his Aunt Nelda snoring like that.

One of Jimmy's previous girlfriends from Minnesota had never heard herself snore and flatly denied that she ever had. She said there was no way to prove otherwise. Always willing to answer a challenge, Jimmy got a small, personal digital recorder from Radio Shack and recorded her snoring. She denied it was her. Jimmy thought about getting a video camera to capture her in the act but eventually decided it was easier and cheaper to move on to a more self-enlightened member of the dating pool.

But Wendi's snoring was perfect. It wasn't getting loud, ragged, or invasive. It was like a tiny motor running in another room, providing a sort of white noise. It was actually comforting. And, as the TV meteorologists droned on and Wendi purred, Jimmy soon found himself responding to his body's need for sleep.

The private investigator's sleep deficit dropped him directly into REM sleep—the dream stage. It was like getting the Monopoly Chance card that says GO DIRECTLY TO JAIL. DO NOT PASS GO, DO NOT COLLECT $200. Jimmy wasn't stair-stepping through the different sleep stages, he performed a swan dive directly into a deep slumber teeming with dark, disturbing dreams.

In his dreams, Jimmy felt like he couldn't breathe. It seemed like his lungs wouldn't do what his brain told them. His lungs were screaming for air, but they were powerless to suck any oxygen in or out. He opened his eyes and saw a mirror above his head, showing him an upside-down, backward view of the room he was in. It was like looking into a camera and seeing an inverted image instead of the true picture. Gasping for air, he strained to move his arms and legs and crane his head around to see the rest of his surroundings, but nothing worked. He determined the mirror was attached to a large metal container, and he was inside the container. He sensed pressure under his chin and felt a collar secured tightly around his neck. Jimmy quickly realized he was in an iron lung like Miss Carolyn's.

Only Jimmy's head protruded from the humongous metal tube encasing his body. His lungs were still unresponsive. He occasionally got a sip of air, the difference between life and death. He was powerless to escape the metal coffin. He felt feverish and had a horrible headache. Fever, headache, and paralysis added up to the dreaded killer of the 1950s. He had polio!

But that was ridiculous. Jimmy had gotten a polio vaccine as a boy. Nobody contracted polio anymore, did they? How could this happen to him?

He heard a chuckle from somewhere in the empty room. It started low and then escalated into all-out laughter. It wasn't the peal of happy laughter – this was an evil laugh from someone reveling in Jimmy's helplessness.

Without oxygen, Jimmy couldn't speak to ask who was in the room or how he had contracted the previously eradicated disease. Without oxygen, he couldn't ask the laughing person to help him escape the iron lung that held him prisoner.

Jimmy heard a slight scuffing noise, the kind a leather-soled shoe makes when walking across a wooden floor, almost like sandpaper on leather. He sensed movement in the room and saw shifting shadows in the mirror over his head. Jimmy realized his mouth was opening and closing like a fish or a frog, trying to capture the air his lungs and brain desperately needed. That's where the sips of air were coming from.

He saw dress shoes in the mirror; he recognized them as wingtips like his dad used to wear. The shoes were attached to legs draped in dark slacks, the kind men wore in the 1950s. Jimmy's mind flashed on *Father Knows Best, The Donna Reed Show,* and *Ozzie and Harriet.* The men on those shows wore dress slacks even after work while relaxing at home.

He heard another sound and recognized the sound of a chair being dragged across the floor. The out-of-sight man was pulling a chair over to sit on, an old-style grey chair with square cushions and shiny button feet at the ends of the legs.

Jimmy saw the chair in the mirror. He remembered chairs like that from Dr. Madsen's office when he was a kid in the 1960s. The chairs were already old, but they were solidly constructed, with thick seat cushions covered in fake leather and a matching back cushion. Those chairs seemed impervious to the assaults of small children, and the fake leather cushions cleaned up easily after unfortunate mishaps of the kind only a doctor's office would see.

Jimmy could see the chair's legs, the man's legs and shoes, and the man's upper torso, but he couldn't see his face. The man's dark slacks were part of a suit, one with a pattern. At first, Jimmy thought it was pin-stripes or herringbone, but then his vision focused, and he saw the design was made up of hundreds or thousands of tiny number 7s. The man was sporting an exceptionally oversized wristwatch that protruded from the end of his suitcoat sleeve. As if realizing that Jimmy could see the watch and the suit pattern, the man laughed again, deep, guttural, and wet, like someone who had smoked for many years.

The man leaned forward and stretched his arm out so the giant wristwatch extended even further from his sleeve. The man rotated his wrist, and Jimmy saw what time the watch revealed: only a few minutes before seven. It was nearly seven o'clock!

Jimmy felt like someone had jerked him backward through time nearly fifty years. He had to be home at seven!

Bad boys that weren't home by seven could get trapped by Le Bonhomme Sept-Heures – the Seven O'clock Man! That's who was in the room with him! He was here, and it was nearly seven, and Jimmy couldn't move, escape, or run home!

The man got up and moved around to the side of the iron lung, his head and face still hidden in the shadows; he was still unrecognizable. He flipped some catches on the metal tube, separating it into two parts. The man swiveled the mirror above Jimmy's head, and he could suddenly see himself lying on a small table inside the iron lung. But instead of his mature body, Jimmy had the body and legs of a six or seven-year-old boy. And all the while, Jimmy felt his mouth opening and closing almost involuntarily, gulping at air, trying to retrieve more sips of oxygen.

Suddenly, Jimmy felt the man's head next to his, even though he hadn't seen him move. With the mirror swiveled to show Jimmy his childlike body trapped in the tube, Jimmy couldn't see the man's face, but he didn't need to see the face to hear the voice.

"It's almost time, Jimmy. Almost time."

The man held his gigantic watch in front of Jimmy's face. The second hand showed it was only about thirty seconds until seven o'clock, and Jimmy wasn't home!

"Jimmy."

Jimmy tried to make his little boy's body move, to get up and run, but it wouldn't respond. All he could do was lie there and swallow air like a frog.

"Jimmy!" The voice was more insistent. "Wake up! You're dreaming."

Suddenly Jimmy's body broke free of the paralysis, and he swung an arm wide, knocking someone aside—the man?—and jumped up, freeing himself from the table where he had been imprisoned.

Jimmy's eyes flew open, and he stared at Wendi, who was sitting on the floor, staring back at him with huge, surprised eyes.

"Well, you are nothing if not unpredictable," Wendi said. She laughed and stood up, taking Jimmy's hand as he automatically extended it to help her rise.

"Wendi, I'm so sorry. I-I didn't know it was you. I thought you were The Man." Jimmy was breathing hard, relishing the oxygen that filled his lungs but still feeling the effects of the adrenaline released in his veins by the dream. Fight or flight was an automatic response, and the brain dumped adrenaline into the bloodstream regardless of your choice.

"Which man?" she asked. She continued holding his hand.

"Le Bonhomme Sept-Heures. The Seven O'clock Man. I think I told you about him while I was trying to figure out the stolen manuscript mess." The words flooded out of Jimmy's mouth.

"Le Bon-who? No, you haven't told me about anybody with a long moniker like that. The Seven O'clock Man? Who is that?" Wendi asked, letting go of his hand and moving over to the couch, patting the seat next to her to encourage him to sit with her. Jimmy shook his head, choosing to remain standing. He needed to feel his legs under him. After the dream, he was ecstatic that his legs and his lungs worked again! He needed to be on his feet for a few minutes until the adrenaline rush subsided.

"The Seven O'clock Man is a name from my childhood in Winnipeg," he explained. "He's the Canadian equivalent of the bogeyman. Don't laugh. We were all scared of him. Every kid knew about someone who had been taken by him. He's the reason our parents told us to be home by seven o'clock," Jimmy explained, feeling his heart settling down and enjoying the full, deep breaths of air flowing into his lungs.

"Go on," Wendi prompted, a sober expression on her face. Jimmy had been afraid she would laugh at him, but she was listening, not judging.

"Legend—and by legend, I mean parents and older siblings—said he was an old man with a big hat and coat who carried a sack. It wasn't a big sack when it was empty, but apparently, it expanded to hold various-sized kids. When kids stayed out after dark – seven o'clock specifically – the old man would catch them and stuff them in his sack. My friend, Eric Larson, said the man ate the kids he caught, but Tim Ryan said his dad told him that the Seven O'clock Man kept the kids he caught locked up underground forever. But Tim also said, "Forever, or until he got hungry again.""

"Well, that sounds perfectly ghastly. It sounds like a vile mix of Hannibal Lecter and Rumpelstiltskin," Wendi said in response to his explanation. "And you didn't see through the legend?"

"How old were you when you quit believing in a flesh-and-blood Santa Claus or Easter Bunny?" Jimmy asked in return.

"Okay, fair point. But I'm pretty sure neither Santa nor Peter Cottontail would stuff me in a sack and eat me for supper. That's horrible, you know. Forcing children to come home by threatening them with a gruesome death or imprisonment by an evil old man. Why seven o'clock, by the way?" Wendi asked.

"You know, be home by dark. Back in my childhood, we were the princes of the kingdom, if not the kings. We had the run of the neighborhood after school until supper. We left home on Saturday mornings and played all day, stopping only for lunch and supper. During summer break, we did it all day, *every* day, plus we took off again after supper for as long as possible. We would have stayed out all night if we could," Jimmy said, sitting on the sofa cushion next to Wendi. He was feeling more calm, his pulse and breathing slowing to normal.

"Our parents knew we would've stayed out all night, too, so they put an arbitrary time on us of seven o'clock," Jimmy explained.

"You mean you never stayed out after seven p.m. when you were a kid?" Wendi interjected.

"Eventually, of course," Jimmy replied. "And we did if we were with our parents or other grownups. But when we were between six and ten years old, we didn't dare push that envelope on our own. You didn't *want* to believe it was true, but you couldn't take the chance, just in case. Like I said, everybody knew about 'some kid' who got snatched and never came back."

Jimmy made air quotes around 'some kid.'

"Like who? Did you know somebody who was taken?" Wendi was gently prompting Jimmy to face his old fear.

Jimmy felt his face get hot. "Not personally, but I heard about a kid from across the Assiniboine River. His name was Russ Leikvold. He just disappeared and was never heard from again."

"Was it on the news? Or in the papers?" Wendi asked.

"I didn't pay that much attention to the news on TV, and I only read the comics in the paper," Jimmy answered rather sheepishly.

"Could this Leikvold boy's family have simply moved? And since you weren't close friends, in your young boy's mind, you *assumed* he just disappeared one day?" Wendi pressed Jimmy to face the holes in his memories.

"I had friends from school that I never saw during summer break," she continued. "At the end of the school semester, we'd promise to see each other in the fall when school was back in. There were almost always some girls who moved away over the summer, and I never saw them again or heard from them or about them. They just vanished, too, don't you see? But it wasn't scary, spooky, or blamed on a serial killer."

Jimmy said nothing momentarily, then conceded, "I suppose some of the kids who disappeared could have moved. Families moved around in Canada, too."

"Okay, good. I just saved you several hundred dollars on a therapist's couch. Now let's think about supper," Wendi said. She scooted forward to the edge of the couch to get up.

Supper? What time is it? Jimmy thought. He was afraid to look at his watch in case it showed nearly seven o'clock like in his dream. He stretched an arm across Wendi's lap to hold her on the couch. "Before we discuss supper plans, let me tell you about the other disturbing part of my dream."

"There's more?" she asked.

Jimmy nodded and started unpacking the details.

"I was in an iron lung, just like Carolyn Dawson's. Only I couldn't breathe. I don't think the machine was working right. I just kept gulping like a fish out of water or a frog, trying to get air in. And sometimes I think I got some air, but not enough to talk or yell. Plus, my body was paralyzed, so I couldn't move. Then Le Bonhomme—the Seven O'clock Man—came into the room where I was, and he laughed at me because I couldn't do anything but lie there. Then he opened the iron lung, and I could see my body in the mirror, only it was a little boy's body, not mine. Le Bonhomme showed me his wristwatch, and it was just a few seconds before seven, and he whispered in my ear, 'It's almost time, Jimmy.' Then you woke me up, and suddenly, I could move again. That's why I knocked you to the floor. I was trying to get away from him."

"But it was all just a dream, wasn't it?" Wendi sounded like Jimmy's mom when he was a boy and used to tell her about his nightmares.

"I guess," he responded. "But I usually find that my dreams are my subconscious working overtime, trying to help me make sense of things I'm wrestling with. Like when I dreamt about the doctor on the container ship and figured out the name thing that had been eluding me."

"So, what does this dream mean?" Wendi asked, surprisingly patient.

"I haven't figured it out yet," Jimmy replied.

"Okay. Well, let me know when the stars align," Wendi said and stood up. "Remember that I didn't eat myself into next week like someone else in the room. Speaking of, are you hungry at all? And if not, do you mind if I make a little supper for myself?"

"I'll come and watch. I might nibble on a carrot or a piece of celery, assuming you have carrots and celery," Jimmy added.

"It just so happens that I do. I brought some home from that crudité platter that Aleesha made."

Taking their conversation into the kitchen, Jimmy leaned on the counter while Wendi tore up lettuce and added chopped carrots and celery, a little diced ham, a hardboiled egg from the fridge, and some oil and vinaigrette, followed by freshly grated parmesan. The woman knew how to make a good salad.

Jimmy grabbed a few carrots and celery sticks and followed her to the table. He was nibbling on them while she ate her salad with her usual gusto. Jimmy had no room in his stomach for any gusto, hence the nibbling.

"Can I tell you something more about Le Bonhomme Sept-Heures?" he asked.

"You're not going to tell me how the Seven O'clock Man had a side salad with his roasted children, are you?" Wendi replied with a smirk.

Jimmy laughed and shook his head. "No, nothing like that."

He took a deep breath and forged ahead.

"I talked to The Man before the end of the last case."

"The Man?" Wendi said, her forkful of salad poised halfway between her salad bowl and her mouth.

"It's a guy here in Fernandina. He's like some kind of gang leader. He sicced those three guys on Oscar Metz and sent them to break into my house. He told them to steal the manuscript from Lyst Publishing."

"And how does he connect to the Seven O'clock Man?" she asked, taking another bite of salad.

Jimmy paused. *In for a penny …* "He told me *he* was Le Bonhomme Sept-Heures." Jimmy let the statement hang in the air over the table where they sat. Wendi chewed her salad slowly and looked at him but said nothing.

The silence was getting uncomfortable for Jimmy. So he stumbled in to fill it.

"He told me his goons call him The Man, but he said he was the Seven O'clock Man, only he used the French Canadian name, Le Bonhomme Sept-Heures. He said it. He knew I was from Canada and knew that name would strike a chord inside me. But I know there's no way he's the real deal," Jimmy said.

"Because the Seven O'clock Man is an imaginary figure made up to ensure kids get home before dark," Wendi added to the end of Jimmy's statement.

"Right." Jimmy paused again and decided to just go all in. "He also texted me today when we were down by the waterfront after we left the Dawson's."

Wendi set her fork down next to her plate, took her napkin, and wiped the corners of her mouth. She smiled at Jimmy, reached over, took his hand, and squeezed it slightly. Then she said, "And…?"

"The text said, 'Stay out of Dawson business.' That's all."

"How do you know it was him?" Wendi asked. "It sounds like something Hank might send, doesn't it? He was cranky today and didn't appreciate us being there. Carolyn was glad we could rescue her, and I think deep down, Aleesha was happy to have us there, too. But Hank definitely was in a sour mood. Could he have sent you the text?"

"How could he? He doesn't have my number, and I didn't leave a card – I don't think. Although, sometimes I leave cards out of habit and don't even realize I did it. But another thing: the phone number was blocked, just like the night I talked to The Man on the phone."

"So you've heard the dangerous Seven O'clock Man and would recognize him if you heard his voice again, right?" Wendi had laid her hand on her fork but refrained from picking it up.

Jimmy shook his head. "Remember when someone called Mr. Lyst to set up returning the manuscript? I think Hillary said you took the call."

Wendi thought for a moment. "I did. It was electronically disguised, like on TV or in a movie."

"Mm-hm," Jimmy agreed. "Mr. Lyst told me the same thing, and it was like that when The Man called me that night, too. And when I tried to see who was calling, all it showed was No Number. That's what it said again today when I got the text: No Number. That's significant because it doesn't say Number Blocked. People can do that in their phone settings. But I don't know how you can make your number completely disappear."

Jimmy got up, went to the fridge, and got a water bottle. Wendi didn't wait for him to ask if she needed one and said, "Yes, please." Jimmy reached back into the fridge and grabbed a second bottle. He retraced his steps to the table and handed Wendi her drink.

"Tell me again what the text said today," Wendi said before taking a big swig of water.

"'Stay out of Dawson business.' That's all it said. I texted back, 'Who is this?' and he sent back, 'The Man.'"

"Is there more?" Wendi asked.

"A little," Jimmy replied.

Wendi held out her hand and said, "Give me your phone." Jimmy complied.

Wendi read the short exchange from earlier in the afternoon.

```
What's it to you?
    Stay out of Dawson business
I don't know if I can
    Nothing in it for you
The joke's on you. I'm not in it.
    Stay out of Dawson business.
    Or else.
Or else what?
    If your hand offends you, cut it
    off. An eye for an eye.
```

"Well, it seems like he doesn't want you involved in whatever is going on over at Carolyn's house," Wendi said, handing back his phone.

"And that makes me *want* to be involved. Do you have any idea what's going on over at Carolyn's?" he asked.

"I'm not sure, but after what you've said, I'd like to go back over there just to make sure everyone still has all their body parts," she replied.

Jimmy couldn't be a hundred percent sure, but that may have been the moment he fell irretrievably in love with Wendi Lyst. Sassy, smart, and unfazed by random body parts on the beach.

"I've also been wondering about that phrase, 'if your hand offends you, cut it off.' Is that Arabic?" he asked.

Wendi swallowed a bite of salad before answering.

"You're close. It's from the Bible. Jesus said it when He was talking about little children. If I remember from Sunday School right, He said if your hand or foot causes you to sin, cut it off. It's better to enter Heaven with one hand or one foot than be thrown into Hell with both of your hands and feet. It's in Matthew or Mark, one of the Gospels."

By the time she had finished, Jimmy had looked it up on his phone.

"It's from Matthew 18. It also says if your eye causes you to sin, gouge it out. It's all kind of weird if you ask me. I'll ask Pepé. He might know. The part about little kids says, 'But if anyone causes one of these little ones who believe in Me to stumble, it would be better for him to have a large millstone hung around his neck and to be drowned in the depths of the sea.' That's Matthew 18:6. I'll ask Pepé about that, too," he finished.

Wendi was eating her salad one-handed, her other hand tapping on her phone and scrolling.

"Hmmm. That phrase is also in the Quran. I'll say this for your bogeyman, Jimmy: he's not illiterate," Wendi added.

Jimmy crunched on a carrot stick and wondered where all the disjointed data was leading them.

Chapter 9

Jimmy hung out at Wendi's until about ten p.m. and then went home to sleep in his own bed. They had only stayed together once: the previous night as the hurricane made landfall 250 miles south of them. There had been no sleeping that night, just lots of talking, listening, staring out the windows, and watching Jacksonville meteorologists update the area on the storm's progress. There was also no canoodling, as Jimmy's mom used to say.

Unlike most people, Jimmy and Wendi didn't need to sleep together to discover their likes and dislikes for each other. Or, as Jimmy preferred to think about Wendi, his likes and *other* likes of her. He hadn't found anything about her that cooled his ardor – a fancy way of saying there was nothing about her that turned him off.

Neither was a newcomer to the event; both had a good idea of how the game was played. Jimmy was in his fifties, and Wendi was ten years younger, maybe a little more than ten years. Jimmy had not come out and asked her how old she was. His mom said it was rude to ask a woman her age, adding, "If she wants you to know, she'll tell you." And he had been a little hesitant to nail down that informational tidbit, allegedly to keep *some* mystery in their relationship.

By the same token, he hadn't told her how old *he* was, mainly because she hadn't asked. He hoped it wouldn't deter her interest in him. Everyone keeps saying age is just a number, usually when two people in a relationship have a significant number of years separating them, like the gap between 89-year-old oil tycoon J. Howard Marshall II and 26-year-old exotic dancer Anna Nicole Smith. Jimmy and Wendi were nowhere near as wide apart in age.

Jimmy knew for a fact that Wendi was forty-three. That was how old her late ex-husband would have been had he not lost his life in a car wreck three years earlier. Before Jimmy ran a background check on her for his previous case with Lyst Publishing, he had estimated her age somewhere within two years on either side of her actual age. He had only hesitated to check in case it was significantly less than his guess. A few years less, and they were heading for fifteen years difference, and Jimmy wasn't sure how she would feel about that.

In the end, he looked. Forty-three. Twelve years his junior. He knew it would come out eventually, but he was in no hurry. *Age is just a number.*

Jimmy knew he had another confession to make to Wendi about the text from The Man warning him to stay out of the Dawson family's business. When Jimmy and Wendi were in the Jeep, he had told her it was a text from his mom. He had already told Wendi about the text—even let her read it—but the lie about who it was from was keeping Jimmy awake just when he badly needed some sleep.

He hadn't told Wendi his mom had passed away several years before, maybe because Jimmy still carried some guilt about not being there when she died. He had seen her a month before she passed away but was back home in Florida when it happened. The distance from Jacksonville to Winnipeg is a tad over fifteen hundred miles as the crow flies, but nineteen hundred miles by car. Either way, it wasn't like running down to Publix for a pint of ice cream.

Jimmy lay in bed, thinking about all the intense conversations he had shared with Wendi, but he kept returning to the one he hadn't had yet. He wasn't sure why he had been so quick to tell her the text was from his mom. Actually, he did know. He hadn't wanted to tell her The Man, a potential threat, was menacing him because he was afraid of worrying her.

But as he lay in his bed, mulling over his decision to withhold the truth from Wendi, he realized there was part of him that wished the text had truly been from his mom. The story he told Wendi about his mom texting him on her own birthday was true, but that wasn't the real text on his phone. Why had he held back? *Have trust issues much, Favreaux?*

Jimmy tossed and turned for a while before relocating to the living room. He figured he was overly tired, but the short nap he took at Wendi's made falling asleep now much more challenging. That, and his brain wouldn't shut off. Circumstances were working against him.

The dream—nightmare—he had at Wendi's was still going through his mind. Thoughts about having polio, being in the iron lung, and having The Man show up when Jimmy was completely helpless were disconcerting. And finding a severed hand on the beach that afternoon! What was *that* about? His mind began turning over the puzzle pieces as he thought about discovering the hand.

Wendi insisted it had not floated in on the tide. She had gotten down on her hands and knees and looked at it more carefully than Officers Garcia and Jenson. She hadn't been squeamish about it in the least. Jimmy felt a little swell of pride about that. If someone had been watching, he would have proudly said, "She's with me." He felt like being with her elevated people's impression of him.

Scenes of the day replayed repeatedly in his mind as he lounged in his darkened living room. He wasn't sure how long Wendi studied the hand before calling him over to share her discovery. When asked, she was adamant that she hadn't touched or moved it, and Jimmy believed her. It looked like it was placed in the sand. *Actually*, he thought, *it looked like Thing from the Addams Family, ready to run around on its fingertips like a ghost crab on the beach.*

Now he wondered if she had taken any pictures of it. Jimmy had been so preoccupied with Sarah from the 9-1-1 emergency services center that he hadn't used his phone to take any shots of the appendage.

The clock said eleven-thirty. If Wendi was asleep, she wouldn't see a text until morning, which would be okay, too. If she *wasn't* sleeping, she could answer his questions, which would be far better than okay. He chanced sending her a short text.

R U up?

He sent the text and sat back. It only took about thirty seconds before Wendi's text pinged in.

Yes, I am. But I shouldn't be.
Can't sleep either?
No.
Did you take any pictures of the hand?
OMG! Yes! My new phone has a micro
setting, and I could zoom way in!
Can you send them to me?
Now?
Are you sleeping?
No. I guess I can.

A minute later, his phone dinged four times in quick succession as Wendi's pictures flew through the night air from her condo to his house, covering the thirty miles in seconds. Jimmy quickly examined the photos on his phone, then decided he needed to see them on a bigger screen. He hurried down the hall to his office and fired up his computer.

Wendi impatiently texted him for updates.

Did you get them?
Yes. They look great. I'm going to look
at them on my computer so I can make
them bigger.
Good idea. I wish I was there.

Jimmy wished so, too. It wasn't the physical aspect of it. They weren't teenagers, but they weren't dead, either. It was a different physical aspect: being physically together was the appeal. Little touches, tiny pats on the back, meeting her eyes with his, her hand gently squeezing his, and the warmth and gentle pressure of her hand on his arm reminding him she was there. That was the physicality that he was finding so appealing. And the occasional kiss, of course!

He wondered if Pepé would understand or ask him if he was taking estrogen pills. Jimmy's phone dinged – another text from Wendi.

> Well?
> I'm just getting to them now. Can't you look on your phone?
> My screen is not big enuf!

Jimmy laughed at her impatience, tapping out, LOL!

He remembered when his mom started using a cell phone and texting and thought LOL meant Lots Of Love. He feared she would use it inappropriately, like if someone's pet died and she was trying to be sympathetic and supportive. He was afraid of getting a text that read:

> I heard Fluffy passed away. LOL.

Jimmy cringed at the thought, then felt a deep twinge of sadness at the memory of his mom. He allowed himself to feel its melancholy sadness swirl and mix with the bittersweet thankfulness that her struggles were over. No more pain or worries. Then he set those thoughts aside to concentrate on the pictures now filling his computer monitor in glorious 5K ultra-high-definition – or hideous, depending on how you felt about severed body parts.

Jimmy could see that there was no puckering of the skin on the fingers. He had washed enough dishes by hand while growing up to be familiar with the phenomenon. The severed hand they found had not been in the water, or if it had, it had been only a very short duration and on the sand again long enough to dry out.

The hand wasn't salty, either; there was no salt film coating it. Jimmy had been in the water off Fernandina enough times to know why you needed the shower stations by the beach changing rooms. If you didn't wash the salt water off, you would feel the dried salt on your skin when you got home; you could even see the white coating on your calf or ankle sometimes.

There was also a lack of fish nibbles on the detached appendage. Wendi said there were no signs of hungry fish taking advantage of the free meal. Jimmy would have attributed it to the storm passing by and the rough surf, but Wendi said no, and she had lived around here a lot longer than Jimmy.

The wind and surface waves were an issue for land dwellers, not fish. With a barometric drop in pressure, Wendi told him, the fish come toward the surface or into shallow water to gorge themselves. If the rain bands accompanying a hurricane were pushed in by a warm wind, the fish continued feeding, but cold northerly winds turned their appetites off.

Jimmy recalled looking at her, his eyebrows raised.

"What?" she had answered. "I read a lot of different things at work. And I grew up here."

Jimmy was not a marine biologist, so he had to take what she said in good faith. From everything he could see on the blown-up pictures on his monitor, there were no signs of fishy foragers, which gave more weight to Wendi's claim that the hand was not in the water.

One thing really puzzling Jimmy was who the hand's previous owner was. Where had the incident—or accident—

happened? Jimmy was pretty sure it had not taken place on the beach because there were no large patches of blood anywhere near the site where they found the hand.

And why was the detached limb on the beach? If it wasn't thrown in the water, why was it on the beach? And why that particular section of the beach? Had someone tossed it there so a specific person would find it? Could it be that whoever relieved the previous owner of his hand was sending signs to someone? Was the sign for the person who *lost* the hand or the person who was supposed to *find* it?

Then another thought occurred to Jimmy: Did the intended person find it?

Wendi was the person who actually found the severed appendage, but she had been with Jimmy at the time. Was it meant for *him* to find? He *was* the investigator, after all. Or was it a sign for Wendi? The latter didn't seem very likely to Jimmy. But how to know for sure? How often do people stumble across a severed hand on the beach? Or anywhere?

And what about The Man's line about cutting off your hand if it offends you? That certainly came along at the right – or wrong – time.

That line of thinking prompted Jimmy to look up "severed hands" on the internet. The first half-dozen hits pointed to someone finding a bloody sack in Siberia in 2018 with fifty-four severed hands inside. The headlines Jimmy viewed onscreen included, "A Bag of 54 Severed Human Hands Was Found in Siberia, And Nobody Knows Why." Experts later concluded that the hands were not a serial killer's work but a lazy forensics lab improperly disposing of biowaste.

Interestingly, Great Britain found more severed body parts than most other places, with giant headlines like "Naked Man Carrying Severed Hand Smashes Through Window To Flee From House."

The search made for grisly web surfing, but it was fascinating nonetheless, even a bit campy in some ways. Jimmy felt most British newspapers were on the same level as the National Enquirer, the Globe, and the National Examiner. He lumped them all together in the tabloid category, meaning they weren't above totally fabricating stories and pictures to sell copies and keep the lights on at the office.

He found websites devoted solely to sharing hundreds of pictures of severed hands: real, fake, cartoon, and even robot ones. There were gothic stories and accompanying websites about warriors with severed hands or who had severed the hands of their enemies. Jimmy wasn't interested in those. He doubted a crazed samurai warrior was running around during a hurricane in Fernandina Beach, Florida, slicing off people's hands.

Jimmy focused on determining whether discovering a severed hand on the beach by your condo could be a personal warning. Searching specifically for that, he found a site for realtors: "What If Someone Gets Injured at Your Open House?" He had to read the bulk of the article before discovering that there was only a single line covering what to do if a prospective buyer severs their hand at your open house.

Jimmy pushed back from his desk to think. He needed to make sense of the recovered hand.

TV shows want you to think it's easy to sever a hand, but the reality is something entirely different. A couple of reasonably strong bones in the wrist will resist being separated from the hand they've known for many years. *They prefer to be inseparable,* he thought, smirking to himself.

Jimmy knew from talking with police investigators and medical examiners that unless the victim was sedated, unconscious, or dead, they would probably fight the process. *Who wouldn't?*

Jimmy looked at his phone. He didn't know exactly how long he had been looking at Wendi's pictures of the severed hand or searching through websites about severed hands, but since there were no more texts from Wendi, he assumed she had gone to sleep.

Just then, Jimmy saw the sweep of headlights across his yard as a car turned into his driveway. The vehicle came in slow and easy, not charging in like a crazed samurai with a vendetta against Jimmy. It approached his house quietly and doused its headlights after turning into the driveway. Jimmy watched through the blinds as the car rolled quietly to a stop. The car's engine switched off, and the night went silent again.

Still looking through the closed blinds, Jimmy saw a flare of light as the driver's door was opened. Rising, Jimmy stood next to his desk and tapped out a quick message to Wendi.

> Someone's here. I have to go.
>> Now? Who is it?
> It's a very dangerous person! Call 9-1-1.
>> I thought you had a fancy security system to do that for you.

Jimmy opened the front door and stepped out into the cool night air. Wendi curled into his side, reaching her arms around him and tilting her head up toward him. Jimmy obliged with a kiss.

"Wanted, huh?" she asked.

"And very, *very* dangerous," he replied. "And especially adept at throat punches."

Wendi lightly punched Jimmy's arm, then turned and pretended to pummel his chest.

"What are you doing here?" Jimmy asked, grabbing her wrists lightly and coiling his arms around her again.

"Why do you think I'm here?" she asked coyly, warm in his embrace and making him even warmer.

Before Jimmy could come up with a smart aleck answer, she said, "I wasn't about to wait until tomorrow to see those pictures blown up on that fancy computer system of yours."

"Well, the joke's on you, Wendi Lyst. Look at the time. It already *is* tomorrow." Giving a little nod toward the east, where the distant sounds of traffic from I95 could be heard, he added, "The sun will be rising from that direction much sooner than either of us want to think about."

Poking a finger into Jimmy's chest, Wendi replied, "The joke's on you, Jimmy Favreaux. According to Mr. Lyst, we won't be open tomorrow, so I don't have to worry about getting home before curfew."

"Curfew?" Jimmy laughed. "It's 2 a.m. Who has a 2 a.m. curfew?"

"Girls who work for their father-in-law. And private investigators. And since it's 2 a.m., we better get inside so we don't get in trouble." Wendi untangled herself from Jimmy's embrace and took his hand, pulling him toward the open door.

"Now, are you going to show me those pictures, or am I going to hack into your computer and do it myself?"

Jimmy held up his hands in surrender. Wendi went inside, and Jimmy followed, giving the security camera doorbell a thumbs-up sign.

The sound of the front door closing was followed by the solid chunk! of a deadbolt being engaged.

Chapter 10

WENDI WAS POINTING at the 5K screen Jimmy called a monitor. "Just look at that!" Wendi exclaimed. "I mean, look at that!"

The screen showed a hand resting in the sand outside her condo. "I can see all the dirt embedded in the lines and wrinkles of the fingers and under the fingernails!" Whoever lost their left hand had a dirty job or a hobby that caused dirty hands. From now on, though, that would be singular – a dirty hand.

Despite Wendi's affectionate actions when she arrived at Jimmy's, the canoodling quotient went way down after she started looking through the pictures sent from her phone being displayed on Jimmy's 5K ultra-high-definition monitor.

Wendi had taken over control of the computer mouse and was zooming in on the back of the hand on the screen. "I can see individual grains of sand! If a fly had been checking out this hand, we'd be able to tell if it was a boy or a girl fly!"

Jimmy chuckled at her comment and excitement at viewing things so clearly and vividly. He'd had the monitor for a few weeks – ever since he'd been paid over ten grand for solving the case of a manuscript that went from missing to ransomed to stolen to fraudulently misappropriated and finally recovered. That case was how Jimmy had met Wendi and her father-in-law, the owners of Lyst Publishing in Fernandina Beach.

What Wendi and Jimmy were doing now was why Jimmy bought the fancy monitor. It cost only half the price of an LCD scanning microscope with a smaller 4K monitor and was far more versatile. A microscope was great for examining things on slides, but Jimmy usually studied pictures of documents, old photographs, and images of things that couldn't ordinarily fit on a microscope slide, like a severed hand. Jimmy didn't need to see the inside of the grains of sand. He needed to see that there was only sand, not salt, and smooth tool marks but no fish or crab bites on the hand.

"What's that in the sand?" Jimmy asked Wendi.

"Where? I see lots of things lying on the sand. I had no idea how gross the clean, white sand by my condo was until I saw it enlarged on your monitor," Wendi said. She leaned in toward the monitor for an even closer 5K look.

"I don't mean something sitting on *top* of the sand. I see an indentation in the damp sand. Nature doesn't usually do straight lines or perfect curves. Some scientists will argue that perfectly straight lines don't actually exist anywhere." Jimmy took the mouse and circled the area he was talking about. "I'm talking about this area right here."

"Okay, so what?" Wendi replied. "What do you think it is?"

"It looks like a shoe print to me," Jimmy answered. He zoomed out from the extreme closeup of the hand they had been looking at. "It's easier to tell farther out than zoomed in. Notice the curve of the front of the sole and then the straight line where the heel is? That's a dress shoe. Who wears dress shoes to the beach? Or, more specifically, who wears dress shoes to the beach right after a hurricane?"

Most people walking on the beach wear flip-flops, sandals, or sneakers—if they wear shoes at all. Mr. Lancôme was wearing Crocs with no socks when they met him. Wingtips would be completely out of character. And they would leave a unique footprint in the wet sand after the hurricane and the storm surge.

Something about the shoe was nagging Jimmy's memory. Someone he had seen recently was wearing old-fashioned wingtip shoes. But for the life of him, he couldn't figure out who.

"Tell me what you're thinking, Mr. P-I," Wendi teased him, her usually well-kept hair looking a bit wild and unkempt. He was pretty confident he was not looking his best, either, but she hadn't said anything. Even with her wild hair and lack of makeup, Wendi still looked beautiful to him. She and Jimmy had been awake almost non-stop for nearly forty-eight hours, with just a short cat nap in the middle.

"I think I saw someone recently wearing a pair of wingtips like my dad used to wear, but I can't figure out where I saw them. Most business guys today don't wear wingtips; they wear smooth-grained leather shoes and don't usually wear leather-soled shoes like on wingtips. That's why this shoe print in the sand is unique. Nobody wears wingtips to the beach. But somebody did, and they wore them right by our severed hand. This is just a guess, but either the person wearing the dress shoes dropped the hand there for us to find or—" Jimmy paused.

"Or?" Wendi replied.

"Or the person wearing the dress shoes stood and watched as someone else did, making sure they did it right," Jimmy said, looking into Wendi's tired, slightly bloodshot eyes. He made a decision.

Jimmy swallowed hard before he spoke, hoping his voice wouldn't crack when he asked the next question.

"Do you want to stay here tonight?"

Before she could answer, he added, "I mean, in the spare bedroom. You saw it once before, the first time you came out here; I gave you the nickel tour, remember?"

"Oh, yeah! I remember," Wendi replied. "There was a pair of girls' pink panties on the floor. You said they belonged to your 'niece.' I didn't know if you were making up a story, but it didn't matter. You were honest enough to admit a girl had stayed here."

"Yes, she did. In *that* bedroom. Not in mine." Jimmy took her hand and said, "And that's all I'm offering you tonight—or what's left of the night. A place to sleep that's more comfortable than a recliner or the couch. A real bed. I would hate to send you home and have you fall asleep on the way and get in a wreck. So, c'mon. Let's get you situated, and then I can go to bed, too, because my eyes are so tired I can barely keep them open."

Wendi patted his hand that was holding one of hers. "Okay. Although I could probably fall asleep right here on this desk."

"I have, many times, and I do not recommend it. I can tell you that you will wake up with a terrible crick in your neck," Jimmy said with a laugh.

"One question, then," Wendi asked.

"Shoot."

"Do you have coffee?"

"Right now?" Jimmy replied. "No, I'm afraid I don't have any made and hadn't planned on making any this late. Or this early. Whichever it is."

Wendi stopped patting his hand and gave it a harder slap. "You know what I mean," she said. "Will you have coffee in the morning?"

"The finest brew you can get from a single-serve maker in under five minutes. Hot, brown, and full of caffeine."

"It sounds delightful," Wendi answered, giggling. They were each so tired that they felt slightly tipsy.

Jimmy closed the picture-viewing program on his computer and put it to sleep. He stood up, held out a hand for Wendi, and pulled her into an embrace when she took it. He kissed her on the forehead and said, "Follow me, madame."

He walked out of the office and down the hall, pointing out the guest bathroom on the left ("there are towels in the linen closet"), and then reached inside the spare bedroom to turn on the light.

"Home sweet home," he told her.

"One more question," she asked. "Toothbrush?"

"In the drawer in the guest bathroom. Brand new in the package. Promise."

"Marvelous. Goodnight, Jimmy."

Jimmy gave her another short kiss.

"There's more where that came from," he said, turning toward his bedroom.

But not tonight, he thought, completely exhausted.

*

Jimmy fell asleep in less than thirty seconds. He had looked at the clock on the bedside table as he crawled between the sheets. *4 a.m.* He closed his eyes and was snoring gently almost immediately.

The revving of a car engine woke Jimmy two hours later. He felt like he'd been run over by a truck, or at least how he imagined he would feel if a truck ran him down. Once again, his body reminded him he wasn't in his twenties, and all-night partying was not a hobby he should take up again. *How rude,* he thought.

Jumping out of bed, he pulled aside the curtains on one side of the window. There were no vehicles or people in the yard. He saw a pair of red tail lights suddenly pop on about an eighth of a mile down the road. He knew Mickey's Tap Room was about a quarter-mile away. The tail lights were about halfway between his house and the derelict bar that was usually frequented by derelicts. Whoever was driving was departing hastily.

Jimmy pulled on a pair of sweatpants and a sweatshirt and went to the front door. Pulling up the security app on his phone, he checked for anyone getting within his motion sensor's range, about seventy-five feet. Nothing. He relaxed slightly.

Jimmy had recently upgraded some of the components in his security system after a break-in by some goons during the stolen manuscript case. His sensors were passive infrared, meaning they detected movement by changes in heat radiating from an object. The motion sensor told the camera to start shooting video of the scene.

But his system assured him no one had gotten close to the porch. Jimmy would have sworn the vehicle sounded like it was right under his bedroom window, but he had been dead to the world at that point, deep in sleep. He decided to go out on the porch and see what he could see. It was still dark, but the sky was beginning to show the faintest signs of an impending sunrise in about forty-five minutes. Standing on his porch, Jimmy faced due east. Highway 17 ran north and south before turning east at Yulee toward Amelia Island and Fernandina Beach. Wendi's Audi was parked near the porch. Jimmy was kind of glad she hadn't brought the hot-pink Jeep.

It was too dark to see, so Jimmy sat on the front steps. He hoped he could fall asleep again once he went back inside. A look at his smartwatch revealed the time – 6:20 a.m.

When he was about ten years old, he was out this early on many summer mornings, delivering newspapers. He didn't have a route of his own, but he made good money filling in for friends when they went on vacation with their families. Plus, Jimmy only *delivered* the papers; he wasn't required to collect subscription money from the customers.

Despite the passage of over forty years, the sad call of mourning doves and a pink and orange sky easily transported his mind back to those days of early morning paper deliveries. The smell of coffee brewing, cigarette smoke, and fresh donuts frying in hot oil completed the sensory trip. The little café was called Young's Hut.

He looked forward to delivering papers to Young's Hut each morning when substituting on the paper route. The café was at the end of his route, a corrugated metal Quonset hut on the edge of town. Jeff and Missy Young ran the small diner, and Missy would give Jimmy a fresh donut every morning he delivered the papers. The Youngs always got a stack of five papers so customers could read the news with their eggs and toast, coffee, and donuts.

Jimmy was reminiscing about Young's Hut when he heard the front door open behind him. He didn't turn around because it could only be Wendi. She sat beside him, and he put an arm around her. She had a small afghan wrapped around her, the one that was usually on Jimmy's recliner in the living room.

"Why are you up?" Jimmy asked.

"I could ask you the same thing," she replied, scootching closer to Jimmy on the steps. "It's chilly," she added, as though she was trying to make excuses for getting closer.

"I heard a car or a truck, and it sounded loud, almost like it was right outside my window," Jimmy explained, tucking the afghan around her a little tighter.

"Mm-hm," she nodded. "I thought I heard it, too, but I wasn't sure."

"I looked on the security app, and nothing was close enough to trip my system. Maybe someone turned around in the driveway. Maybe it was just someone delivering newspapers." He smiled to himself, knowing it was too dark for Wendi to see his expression. He could call up the complex but delightful aroma of Young's Hut at will, with the birds and softening sky acting as a catalyst.

The couple sat some more, neither one speaking, watching the sky slowly blend from black to blue to orange and pink and then back to blue again. Sunrise was at 6:58; Jimmy's watch said it was just a few minutes away.

"What's that?" Wendi asked, poking a slender finger out from under the afghan and pointing toward the road going past Jimmy's house. "Out by the mailbox," she added.

"It looks like trash. Like a fast food bag or the white bag from a bakery," Jimmy answered, thinking about donuts from Young's Hut. It saddened him a little, knowing the metal-clad café was no longer there.

"I'll go toss it in the trash can," he added, getting up from the step.

He walked across the yard, his feet quickly becoming soaked from the dew. It surprised him how cold the morning's moisture was, but it *was* November, he reminded himself. Approaching the bag, he saw the top rolled over and hand-crimped, sealing in whatever was inside.

His feet slipped on the wet grass as he started to lean over to collect the sack, and he went down on one knee, one of his feet kicking the bag as he slipped. The little kick told him the sack was not empty, and the paper bag turned partway over, revealing a red splotch where the bag had been resting. It was too big and dark for ketchup.

"And he's safe!" Wendi called from the porch, pretending to be a baseball umpire making the call on Jimmy's slide.

Jimmy backed away from the bag and pushed himself up to his feet. He reached into his sweatpants pocket and pulled out his phone. Switching on the camera app, Jimmy took a picture of the bag, then zoomed in and took another. He took a few steps to one side and took a few more pictures.

"What are you doing, Jimmy?" Wendi yelled across the dew-covered yard.

"Just stay there, Wendi," he hollered back, trying to keep his voice even and calm.

"Jimmy?" Wendi called again. "Jimmy, what is it?"

He held up a hand to try to keep her on the porch while he put his phone to his ear. He had dialed 9-1-1 after taking the series of pictures.

"9-1-1. What's your emergency?"

"This is Jimmy Favreaux. I'm a private investigator, Florida license number 95736. I live out by the blue bridge on Highway 17. I need you to dispatch a deputy to my house. Someone threw a paper bag in my yard about a half-an-hour ago. I think it contains a body part. It appears to have blood soaking into the bag." Jimmy could hear the emergency operator alerting the Nassau County deputy closest to Jimmy's house in the background as he spoke.

She came back on the line and asked, "Why do you think it's a body part, sir?"

"Because we – Wendi Lyst and I – already found a hand in the sand near her condo in Fernandina yesterday," Jimmy explained.

"Have you looked in the bag, sir?"

"I have not. I took pictures on my phone of the bag where it sat in my yard. The top is folded over like you do to keep everything inside," Jimmy told the girl on the phone.

"Sir? You say you're a private investigator?"

"Yes, ma'am."

"Are you willing to look in the bag?" she asked.

"I'd rather not, but if I need to, I will," he answered, knowing where this was going to go.

"Sir, I wouldn't ask this, except the deputy says he doesn't want to come out that far for a bag of half-eaten hamburgers or chicken nuggets and sweet-and-sour sauce."

Jimmy left the bag on the ground and unrolled the top. Picking up a small stick, he separated the top and lifted one side like peeking under a cooking pot lid.

"It's a hand," Jimmy said to the emergency operator. "It looks like a match to the one we found yesterday."

Jimmy heard the operator talking in the background to the deputy. She came back on the line and said, "Sir? Are you still holding the bag?"

"I never picked it up. I opened the top so I could see inside."

"Okay. The deputy is on his way. He said not to touch the hand or move it."

"Yes, ma'am. You don't have to tell me twice," Jimmy replied.

The operator got some more information from Jimmy. She said she would stay on the line until the deputy arrived, even though Jimmy told her that wasn't necessary. "It's protocol, sir," she answered. "You understand."

Jimmy turned around to see Wendi picking her way carefully across the dew-covered yard. He held up a hand like a traffic cop, but she shook her head and kept coming. He held the phone out to his side and hissed at her, *"Wendi! Stop!"*

She paused about ten feet away and asked, "What is it, Jimmy? Who are you talking to? And what was with all the picture-taking? What's in that bag, Jimmy? Don't make me come over there and look for myself."

"Wendi," Jimmy answered, "don't come over here. The cops are on the way. We can't touch it."

"Jimmy." There was no warmth in her voice. Sternly she said, "What's in the bag? I was nose-to-hand with someone's severed hand yesterday. I'm not going to swoon like a Southern belle. Now tell me, what's in the bag?"

"Another hand," he replied. "And a note."

"A note? Did you read it?" Wendi prompted Jimmy for more information.

He shook his head. "I couldn't read it from where I was at. I was just trying to hold the bag open to see what was inside."

They could hear the siren from the deputy's cruiser approaching in the distance. Jimmy was glad he didn't have many neighbors. In the past month, law enforcement had visited him several times.

Wendi got down on her hands and knees by the bag and said to Jimmy, "Give me the stick." She held out her hand. He passed her the stick, looking down Highway 17 to see if he could see the cruiser's blue and red wig-wag lights. He could.

"Wendi," he hissed again. "They're going to be here in a minute. You need to get up and move away from the bag." He was still holding the phone out to the side. A voice was emanating from the phone. "Sir? Sir? I hear the sirens. Are you still there? The deputy says he's almost to your location."

Wendi stood up and took a few steps backward. Jimmy took the stick and dropped it near the bag. The cruiser's siren was overpowering as the deputy arrived.

The cruiser pulled into the driveway and cut the siren. The deputy didn't drive up to the house but got out where he had stopped and walked over.

Jimmy brought the phone back to his ear. "Ma'am?" he said. "The deputy is here. Thank you for your help." He clicked off the phone without waiting for a response.

The deputy was one of the same ones who had been at Jimmy's the night of the break-in several weeks earlier. He shook Jimmy's hand as he approached the bag. He tipped his hat to Wendi and said, "Ma'am."

Squatting next to the bag, he said, "Let's see what we have here—"

He stopped in mid-sentence as he used his telescoping baton to lift the open end of the bag. It became apparent that there was, indeed, a human hand inside the bag. He stood and put on latex gloves he pulled from his breast pocket.

Picking up the bag, he carefully reached inside and pulled out a piece of paper. He left the hand inside the bag.

He was holding a note written on a blue sticky note. "Does this mean anything to you, Mr. Favreaux?"

"I don't know," Jimmy said. "I didn't do more than look inside the bag to determine there was a hand in there. What does it say?"

The deputy looked at Jimmy, then at Wendi, then back at Jimmy. "It says, 'If we were playing cards, you'd have a pair.' Any idea what that means, Mr. Favreaux?"

"It means whoever left the hand on the beach at Fernandina yesterday left this one, too. And it means neither incident was an accident."

Chapter 11

THERE WAS NO more sleeping going on, mainly because there was no more night. While the original responding deputy on the scene conferred with a second deputy outside, Jimmy and Wendi went inside, prompted by their need for caffeine. Jimmy led Wendi to the kitchen to search for an infusion of liquid motivation. They were not disappointed in their search.

A few minutes after arriving in the well-appointed kitchen, each held a steaming mug of coffee. Jimmy also started a regular pot of coffee for the deputies he knew would soon join them inside after privately discussing their findings outside.

Wendi and Jimmy quietly sipped their coffee while they waited for their houseguests to join them. They sat at a dinette table under a window in the kitchen. Jimmy called it the breakfast nook, but it was just a small table by the window. They were beginning to feel the buzz from their lack of sleep and trying to compensate with too much caffeine. They hoped to pump enough caffeine into their systems to coherently answer the deputies' impending questions, but Jimmy knew from experience that the coffee would only be a temporary fix. They desperately needed real sleep – solid, undisturbed, rejuvenating sleep – but that wasn't an option at the moment, so they had to make do with the coffee.

Staring into his coffee mug, Jimmy broke the silence. "I need to tell you something."

When he didn't immediately continue, Wendi responded, "What is it?"

"It's about my mom," he replied, his eyes remaining locked on the interior of his coffee mug.

"You already told me it wasn't your mom the other day who texted you. It was that Man, you said – the Four O'clock Man—"

"<u>Seven</u> O'clock Man," Jimmy corrected.

"That's the one," Wendi answered, pausing to take another drink of her coffee. She was glad the coffee had cooled enough to switch from little sips to large gulps. When she had asked Jimmy if there would be coffee in the morning, she had no idea what was coming or how badly they would need the caffeine boost.

"Yeah," Jimmy answered slowly. "I told you it was my mom, and then I told you it wasn't. That much is true. What isn't true—and I don't know why I didn't tell you—is that …" Jimmy stopped and tried to gather his scattered thoughts.

"What I'm trying so poorly to say is that my mom passed away a while ago, five years to be exact, so it couldn't have been her who texted. But you didn't know that, and I don't know why I didn't just tell you from the get-go. I guess I was trying to prevent you from worrying. And protect you if this maniac tries to do anything about my involvement with the Dawsons. But mostly, I should have just been straight with you, and I apologize for not laying the truth out for you and letting you deal with it."

"Oh, Jimmy," Wendi said, reaching a hand across the table to his. "I'm sorry about your mom."

"Yeah. Me, too. My mom really did text me on her birthday each year. She didn't want to pressure me, so she always initiated the conversation. I guess you could say she didn't need a lot, but she still needed proof of life," Jimmy explained. He gave Wendi's hand a squeeze. Inside, he relaxed another notch, relieved that he had explained about his lie of omission and Wendi wasn't holding it against him.

They sat shrouded in companionable silence for a few minutes, saving their strength for the forthcoming questions from the sheriff's deputies, each too tired to form cohesive thoughts.

"You know, I can't even tell Mr. Man to back off," Jimmy said after a time. "There's no number for his texts or calls. He's blanked it out somehow, so I have to wait for him to contact me if I want to tell him to leave me alone. When he does contact me, I have limited time to reply. When I've gone back to contact him by replying to his text, it just says No Number Available. So somehow, he's hiding his number and then moving to a new one after some time. I haven't seen anything like it before. I've been thinking it could be some Voice Over IP hack."

Silence settled over them again for a time before Wendi spoke. "I wonder where the hands are from. Are they from the same person? I hope so. I'd hate to think someone is chopping off hands left and right—I'm sorry. I didn't mean to make a pun."

Jimmy stared at her for a moment, uncomprehending what she was saying. Then it hit him. "Left and right." Like the two severed appendages they had found. He began chuckling, and then he couldn't stop. Wendi joined in, giggling at first before their combined laughter grew into full-fledged guffaws. Jimmy knew it was fatigue and stress finding an outlet.

"Somebody's pretty happy in here."

Jimmy and Wendi immediately stopped laughing. It was a Nassau County Sheriff's deputy in his crisp, dark green uniform, leaning against the door jamb between Jimmy's kitchen and living room, a clipboard held against his chest.

"We're sorry, officer ..." Jimmy answered, embarrassed. He wiped the tears from his eyes while Wendi dabbed a tissue at her own eyes.

The deputy walked all the way into the kitchen and took a seat at the table with Jimmy and Wendi. He held out a hand to Jimmy and announced, "Grayson Parker, sir. Nice to see you again." Jimmy shook his hand.

The deputy continued. "You can call me GP. I was here the night your house was broken into. That wasn't that long ago, as I recall."

"It's been a few weeks," Jimmy said, then tried to explain away the laughter. "I guess we're both so tired that we're giddy. We got the giggles, and then we couldn't stop laughing."

Wendi added, "It started because I said people were losing their hands left and right. Get it? Left … and right? Like the hands?"

"Yes, ma'am. And you're name is …?" GP asked.

Wendi held out a hand to the deputy and answered, "Wendi Lyst, from Fernandina Beach. I'm at Lyst Publishing with my father-in-law." She decided it wasn't necessary to go into the story of how Hillary was her *ex-father-in-law* by way of divorce *and* death.

The deputy shook her hand, saying, "It's nice to meet you, ma'am." He laid the clipboard on the table, pulled a pen from his shirt pocket, and clicked it into readiness. He wrote something on the clipboard, probably Wendi's name.

"I just have a few questions to complete our initial investigation. Mr. Favreaux, did you find the severed appendage in the paper sack this morning?"

Jimmy nodded, and the deputy asked, "Can you tell me how you came to discover it?"

Jimmy cleared his throat before saying, "We were sleeping—"

He paused briefly. He didn't think telling the deputy that they were sleeping in separate bedrooms was germane to the investigation.

He continued, "—and about 6 a.m. or a little after, I heard a loud car out by the road. It sounded like they were in my yard, and I heard them rev the engine and then take off. I got up and went to the window and saw their tail lights down the road, heading east and south on Highway 17. I pulled on some clothes—"

I wasn't naked, he filled in for the deputy in his mind.

"—and went out on the porch to see if I could see anything. I couldn't see anything in the yard, so I just sat on the porch to watch the sun come up."

"I came out while he was sitting there," Wendi volunteered.

"Did you hear the vehicle also?" Deputy Parker asked Wendi.

"No. I was in the other bedroom."

The deputy looked from Wendi to Jimmy and wrote something on his clipboard. Jimmy imagined he wrote something like, *"Guy has a great-looking chick stay overnight, and she slept in a spare bedroom. What a loser!"*

"We had both been up for two nights and just really needed to sleep ..." Jimmy trailed off. Wendi covered her mouth with a hand, her eyes crinkling up like she would burst into laughter again. Jimmy suspected she was enjoying his discomfort at explaining the previous night's events to the deputy.

"How did you find the hand?" GP asked.

"When the sun began to light up the sky, I saw a white bag out by the mailbox. It looked like a fast food bag or the kind from a bakery shop," Jimmy responded. "I got up off the porch and walked out to retrieve it and throw it in the trash can. As I got to it, my foot slipped on the wet grass, and I fell on one knee. One foot slid out and kicked the bag, and I could tell it had some weight to it, so I knew it wasn't empty. I thought there was ketchup on the side of it, but something didn't feel right. Maybe because I was so tired, or maybe because we found a severed hand on the beach yesterday after the storm—"

"That was you?" the deputy asked, breaking Jimmy's rhythm.

Wendi lifted one hand halfway, somewhere between a wave and *"Teacher! Teacher! Call on me!"*

GP swiveled to face Wendi. "You found the hand down in Fernandina yesterday?"

"I was just checking to see if the beach was still there or if the storm had washed out the sand. I saw the hand lying on the sand—"

"—and I called 9-1-1," Jimmy jumped in, reclaiming his narrative. "So, when I kicked the bag, I got a slight glimpse inside as the top unrolled a little. It was like someone had crimped the top to make sure nothing came out, you know?"

"I understand," the deputy said, nodding. He had turned back toward Jimmy.

"I got a stick and lifted one side of the bag at the opening, and I saw the hand."

"The hand at the beach was in a bag, too?" the deputy asked Jimmy.

"No. Only the one in my yard. The one at the beach was simply lying there. And we didn't touch it. Wendi just took some pictures while I called 9-1-1," Jimmy explained. "And when I saw that the bag by my mailbox had a hand in it, I called 9-1-1 again. Wendi wanted to come out near the road where I was and look in it, but I told her to stay back and leave it for you guys. And then the first cruiser arrived."

"And when I opened it up with my baton, I could see the note inside, I put on my gloves, retrieved the note, and read it to you. Is that about it?" Deputy Parker asked, looking from Jimmy to Wendi and then back at Jimmy.

"That's about it, except whoever dropped it in my yard has a sick sense of humor. 'You'd have a pair.' That means whoever left the hand in my yard probably dropped the one at the beach by Wendi's condo," Jimmy finished.

"So, you live by the beach?" GP asked Wendi.

"I do," she replied.

"How was the storm?" he asked.

"Like watching a car wash from inside the car. That's why I wanted to see if the beach was still there. Jimmy was at my place the night the hurricane made landfall. We've actually been together for more than forty-eight hours," she added. Jimmy wondered if she was trying to rescue his manhood after the info about sleeping in separate bedrooms. He was grateful.

"All right. Now the big question," GP announced. "Do either of you have any idea why someone would be leaving severed hands around for you to find?"

Jimmy looked across the table at Wendi. The sun was bright in the backyard, visible out the window next to the table. He wondered what time it was. He glanced at his watch and saw it was a little after eight a.m. It had been over an hour and a half since he found the hand, called 9-1-1, and the deputies arrived.

"Jimmy?" It was Wendi this time. "Do you have any idea who might do this? You're the private investigator, and you've had some run-ins lately with what we in the book-publishing industry call *unsavory* characters."

Jimmy rubbed his temples and took another sip of his coffee, which was now cold. *Tell them what? The bogeyman did it? The Man? What could that low-life hope to gain from throwing body parts at me? No, it's not time to involve anyone else. They'd think I was crazy.*

"I honestly can't come up with the name of anyone who would do this," Jimmy fudged. Wendi stared at him but said nothing. "I'm actually quite curious to find out whose hands they are. How long do you think it'll take to get the fingerprints from them?"

"Oh, we've already taken the prints off the one in your yard and sent it to our lab," Deputy Parker replied. "We have Bluetooth fingerprint scanners. They make it a breeze to send the prints in. The hand in your yard matched the one on the beach. They both belonged to a small-time thug named Seth Kremer. Have you ever heard of him?"

Jimmy could honestly say he had not. Wendi shook her head, too.

"I imagine he's either dead or wishing he was," Parker added.

"I imagine so," Jimmy agreed.

He wondered if Seth Kremer was one of the three goons who had hit his and Oscar Metz's houses the same night. Oscar had ended up in the hospital with broken ribs, a concussion, and various cuts, bumps, and bruises. Jimmy only got a black eye.

The memories from that night reminded Jimmy that a second member of the merry band of goons, Gabriel, had died recently. Jimmy felt a sudden odd twinge of guilt that he had never learned Gabriel's last name. Because Jimmy outsmarted Gabriel three times, The Man had Gabriel killed while locked in a holding cell. It had been made to look like suicide, but Jimmy knew it was arranged, especially after The Man had called him and gloated about it.

"Well, that's all I need from the two of you for now. Thank you for your help, Mr. Favreaux, and it was nice meeting you, Miss Lyst?" Deputy Parker was standing as he spoke.

"Mrs.," Wendi replied. Parker's eyebrows rose. Wendi just let the unspoken float in the air between them. Rather than explain, she reached out and slipped her hand into Jimmy's.

"Well, if we need anything else from either of you, we have your contact information," Parker said.

Jimmy was looking at Wendi and thinking how great she looked despite being awake for the better part of two days. *Don't even try, officer. She's mine!*

Jimmy squeezed Wendi's hand before he let it go and stepped over next to the deputy to finish their conversation.

"Thank you, GP. I'll let your department know if I come up with anything connected to this."

Parker reached into his shirt pocket and gave Jimmy his business card. "Thank you, Mr. Favreaux. We would appreciate it. I'll let myself out."

The deputy turned and walked to the front door and left. Jimmy followed him and made sure the door was locked.

Wendi came over to Jimmy and took his hand again, pulled his arm around her, and leaned into his side. They stood like that until Wendi broke the silence.

"Tell me what you're thinking," she said softly.

"I think The Man is involved," he answered.

"Mm-hmm," Wendi murmured, then said, "But I was kind of hoping you were thinking you wanted to kiss me."

Jimmy didn't need to be told twice.

Chapter 12

CAROLYN DAWSON WAS asleep inside her iron lung when it happened. The first sign of a problem was the stillness that had entered the room. The iron lung had stopped.

Like most motors, the machine that helped Carolyn breathe was not noiseless, but its oscillating hum was comforting to her, similar to the white noise machines people buy to help them sleep. The iron lung's motor had a rhythm, and Carolyn immediately noticed its absence. The sudden silence woke her as certainly as a sudden loud noise would have. When you were used to hearing a noise for over sixty years, the sudden vacancy left by its absence was like a jackhammer in the street in front of your house—hard to ignore.

Carolyn could still breathe on her own. She spent long hours—even whole days—outside the iron lung, but in recent years, she preferred sleeping inside. It was easier to sleep knowing the machine was helping her polio-weakened lungs to breathe. The older she got, the more she felt the weakness invading her lungs again.

When the sound had vanished, she woke with a quiet start; she didn't cry out or yell for help. Carolyn used the mirror over her head to check for signs of a power outage. There were two kinds of nightlights in the room, one type tied into the normal house electrical system, the others only activated when the power failed. The regular ones were all functioning as expected, their tiny yellow-orange glow providing comfort and assurance that electrical power was still flowing as expected. So why had the iron lung's motor stopped?

Despite her ability to breathe independently, lying on her back the way she did in the iron lung compressed Carolyn's lungs and made breathing more strenuous. She considered herself fortunate to still have some lung function. One of the other remaining polio victims still using an iron lung— "Polio Paul" from Dallas, Texas—had no lung function. The disease had destroyed that part of his muscle system. If Carolyn had been like Paul – unable to breathe without the machine – she would already be lapsing into unconsciousness and circling death's drain.

She had never forgotten the horrible helplessness she experienced when the polio virus temporarily stole her ability to breathe, even though it was nearly seventy years ago. The doctors and nurses had told her how lucky she was when she was able to cease full-time reliance on the iron lung after only a month. But in 1955, they had no idea that polio would lie patiently like a lion waiting unwearyingly for prey, biding its time until its victims became old, weak, and vulnerable. Back then, doctors and researchers had no idea that after decades of near-normal living, the disease could rear its ugly head and steal a person's independence again.

Now, Carolyn was lying in the iron lung that was usually a comfort, trying to take stock of what was happening in the house. She and Hank had talked about the possibility of the generator failing if the propane ran out, but she knew the liquid gas—although low—was not depleted yet. Since electricity to the rest of the house was still flowing, the generator had not automatically kicked in to provide power for the iron lung. The system thought everything was normal.

The nightlights in her room told her there was no power outage, so her "tin can" should still function. Carolyn wondered if the machine had somehow short-circuited and tripped a circuit breaker.

Troubleshooting the situation was frustrating because it wasn't as if Carolyn could get up to check. It took at least one other person to get her in and out of the machine. That was her son's job for many years after his father died. She hadn't been nearly as dependent on the machine back then. When Hank started helping her, it was rare; once or twice a month was all. The change to nightly use had only occurred in the last seven years or so.

After Hank handled the job every night and morning for several years, they hired Aleesha as Carolyn's caregiver. And after a few years in that position, Aleesha married Hank but still saw to Carolyn's needs. The couple was likely asleep in the upstairs apartment that had been Hank's sanctuary for many years. Originally his dad's office, it became teenage Hank's refuge and now was an oasis for Hank and Aleesha.

Carolyn was in a quandary if no one else noticed the failed machine. Still, she was not without some resources. Carolyn had called Wendi when Hank and Aleesha couldn't make it back from Jacksonville the night before. Carolyn hadn't known why they weren't where they were expected to be, just that they weren't there when she needed them.

That stormy morning, Carolyn had woken up with no way to get out of the iron tube and get to the bathroom. At first, it had only been the desire to get out of the machine. However, as time ticked by and her bladder continued to expand, the need to exit the 800-pound metal behemoth became more imperative.

Although it had happened a few times over the years, she hated when she had "an accident." Part of the reason she so abhorred wetting herself was lying in her own urine, cold, wet, and virtually powerless to do anything about it. Even if she could wriggle out of her nightgown, she'd be naked and wet on a soaked blanket. That was no better.

She hated being helpless. And now, for polio to force her back under its thumb was unacceptable.

Carolyn did not need to relieve herself tonight but was getting a little panicky about moving off her back and out of the machine. Where was Hank? And why hadn't Aleesha come to check on her? Perhaps in their part of the house, up on the next floor, nothing was wrong with the power. They could sleep right on through the night and never know anything was wrong one floor below.

Carolyn suddenly thought she could feel a presence in the room with her and forced herself to become utterly still. Countless hours spent in the machine over sixty-seven years – and fifty years in this room – had made her hearing and other senses hyperaware when she was not alone. Now, without the sound of the motor to cover it up, Carolyn thought she could hear someone breathing somewhere in the room. Unfortunately, thanks to the tight collar fitting around her neck, she couldn't see around the room or swivel her head. However, she could see a few things in the room with the help of the mirror mounted above her head on the machine.

Carolyn had often told people that her hearing had become hypersensitive and had felt vindicated when she read a scientific study that supported her assertions. Several years earlier, she came across a medical journal article detailing research proving the long-held belief that people born blind or who lost their eyesight at an early age had a more heightened sense of hearing. Carolyn had insisted her hearing had sharpened over time as she lay powerless in the machine, listening for sounds that indicated she wasn't alone.

This time, as she lay in the dark, "extending" her hearing outward, she felt a presence; she was certain of it. Apparently, whoever was there didn't want Carolyn to know of their company. She wracked her brain to figure out why someone would hide in the dark from her, or try to, anyway.

Then a scary thought flitted through her head: whoever was in the room may have done something to the machine's motor to incapacitate it. Since the nightlights were functioning normally and the emergency lights installed for outages were not lit, Carolyn knew the problem was with the machine or the electrical service for this room. She was sure the loss of power was intentional. Carolyn was just as certain that someone was hiding out of her sightlines in the darkness, *but why?*

Carolyn remained silent. She wanted to see if she could draw out whoever was hiding in the room. If they were trying to stop her from breathing, she would do her best to make it seem like they were successful.

She held her hands and arms stiffly at her sides inside the metal container, forcing herself to remain utterly still. She didn't want to inadvertently make noises that would alert her listener that she was still alive. She didn't want to even rustle the thin blanket covering her inside the machine.

After what seemed like an hour but was probably closer to fifteen minutes, Carolyn heard it. It sounded like someone weeping nearly soundlessly. Carolyn felt like she could hear the tears rolling down the person's cheeks and falling on the floor.

She knew it wasn't Hank. He couldn't kill his own mother. His way of hurting her was leaving, not physical harm. It could only be Aleesha. Carolyn may not have always treated the girl as family, but she had never done anything to warrant murder! The question that rang repeatedly in her mind was, *Why?*

Carolyn glimpsed a slight change in the darkness reflected in her mirror. She hadn't made out any shapes or seen anyone; it was just a tiny, subtle change in the shadows. Whomever Carolyn's late-night visitor—or saboteur—was, they were on the move. It was impossible to say whether they were moving to another part of the room or leaving. But a few seconds later, the iron lung purred back to life, and commenced its comforting, rhythmic white noise. Carolyn felt the machine prompt her lungs to breathe, the reverse pressure doing what her body alone couldn't – make her breathe.

She tried to determine if the person was still in the room, but all her senses told her she was alone again. The room was empty now. If it was indeed Aleesha, she must have gone back upstairs. Whatever she had done to dismantle the machine, she had also undone.

Carolyn lay quietly, composed calmness replacing the previous feelings of fear. But with the calm came confusion. The nocturnal visitor had to be Aleesha; she was the only logical perpetrator. Hank would have made more noise and certainly wouldn't have wept over his actions. If anything, Carolyn knew Hank would have simply turned off the breaker and gone back to bed. He could have explained his temporary absence from bed by saying he went to check on Carolyn, get something from the kitchen, or the old standby excuse: "I heard something and went to check on it."

In the morning, no one would blame Hank if Carolyn had expired. He could rise early enough to reset the breaker before going to his mother's room. If she died overnight, Hank could claim the mission successful. If not, he could feign ignorance about the machine's failure and sudden resurrection. The device was getting old, and replacement parts *were* becoming a thorny issue.

Another problem with Hank as the perpetrator: if he was mad enough at his mother to try to kill her, she believed he would have turned off the breaker and gone into her room for a ringside seat as she gasped for breath. He had a dark, mean streak most people were unaware of. He would have watched her struggle to the last breath.

It wasn't Hank, Carolyn thought quietly to herself in the middle-of-the-night darkness. *Not this time.*

No, she was sure this was Aleesha's doing, but why? She wouldn't have done it of her own volition. Someone else had prodded her into action. *Who?* That was the glaring, unanswered question. Who had such a strong power over the girl that they could force her to try to kill Carolyn? Did Aleesha have a deep, dark secret that was worth attempting murder? *Perhaps.*

Carolyn immediately began exploring the possibility that Aleesha had a secret she was protecting. Carolyn had written and read so many detective stories over the years that finding a motive came automatically. During her decades of writing about Nick Steele, she had spoken with numerous real-life Nick Steeles, private investigators who did what she could only write about. Hiding and protecting secrets was near the top of the list of motives for murder, but greed took first place.

People will kill to satisfy their greed more than any other impulse. People who are already wealthy or well-off will kill to get richer. Some people kill their families or spouses for life insurance or inheritance money. Others kill their brothers and sisters to eliminate inheritance claims. A quarter of all pre-meditated murders are done for money by contract killers.

The next most common motivation for murder is to avoid humiliation: protecting secrets someone wants to keep buried. And reasons one and two often went together: if a degrading secret were discovered, the perpetrator might lose a fortune. Therefore, murder solved two issues: protecting a secret and getting rich.

That premise could work in her case, except for two things: Carolyn wasn't rich and had no dirty laundry on Aleesha.

Carolyn often woke in the night and, unable to drop back to sleep immediately, turned her mind to plot holes and inconsistencies. This night, much like she had done numerous times before when wrestling with scenarios in her books, her creative writer's brain sifted through clues.

Who would want her dead? Hank? Possibly, but why? He had a good thing going, with no rent and a built-in income from the book royalties Carolyn shared with him. He did the legwork for her, going to book signings and promotions and providing the face of Gary Dawson for his mother's pen name. But there was no real need to hurry the inevitable along. Hank's mother was in her middle seventies and had been struggling with post-polio syndrome for some time, hence the nights in the iron lung. She wouldn't be around forever, and when she died, the house would be his – free and clear. His father had stipulated that in his will, and Carolyn had echoed it in hers.

After Carolyn's death, Hank's situation would improve: he would have the house, all the book royalties, her life insurance benefits, and a cushion to live on until his retirement in about ten years at sixty-five. He could coast into retirement, assuming he played it smart and didn't squander everything immediately after Carolyn's demise.

"Retirement," she thought. If snorting wasn't so much work, she would have punctuated her thought with one. Retirement was for people who had worked. Hank had never worked. He had gone to college but had not excelled, graduating with a liberal arts degree. It wasn't like a Bachelor of Science degree or a Bachelor of Business Administration. In Carolyn's mind, it was like retaking high school.

The college's handbook boasted, "Students who pursue a liberal arts major gain valuable workplace skills such as communication, critical thinking, creativity, and problem-solving—skills they can apply to many jobs. Liberal arts refer to the academic study of literature, sociology, languages, philosophy, history, math, science, and the humanities."

Carolyn had agreed to it because she hoped they could collaborate on future stories. That experiment had failed badly. Hank wasn't creative or disciplined enough to work with Carolyn on the writing end of their collaboration. They decided to do what each did best: Carolyn wrote, and Hank shook hands and signed books.

And for all his talk of moving to Orange Park, he had no idea how the real world worked. Buy a house? And pay for it with what pile of money? No, Hank wasn't the one trying to bump her off. If her head wasn't so immobilized by the collar, she would have shaken it.

Aleesha? Too meek and mousey. Still … Carolyn had felt what she felt and was convinced her daughter-in-law had been huddled in the dark while the machine was inexplicably off. Who could have such a firm grip on the girl as to persuade her to remove Carolyn Dawson from the picture? Not Hank, that was sure.

In her mind, Carolyn made a list of what she knew about her former caregiver.

Aleesha had worked for Carolyn for two years before she and Hank wed a year ago. Although she was a local Fernandina Beach girl, Carolyn hadn't known her before hiring her as a caregiver. Hank and Aleesha probably wouldn't have met if Carolyn had not hired the girl. Twenty years of age separated the two, so their paths weren't likely to cross.

The couple had enjoyed a small wedding at the Clerk of Court's office, with just the happy couple, Carolyn, Wendi, and Hillary attending. None of Aleesha's family came. The newlyweds only took a few days off for a quick honeymoon down the coast at St. Augustine.

Carolyn realized she knew next to nothing about Aleesha's family, or if she even had any. The girl didn't seem inclined to talk about herself or her family. Occasionally she spoke of friends from high school or college, but not often, and she never mentioned her parents. *Maybe they're dead or divorced,* Carolyn thought.

She let her thoughts roll around for a few minutes and then mentally turned the page. That was all she knew of her daughter-in-law. It was not much.

Her mental list of suspects was quite short. Hank and Aleesha were at the top, of course, since they lived there. She tried to think of who else had keys. Hillary and Wendi. The man who filled the propane tank only came when someone was home, guaranteeing he got paid for his load. Hank took care of the landscaping, not someone from offsite, and he and Aleesha handled all the shopping. Carolyn occasionally went along to Harris Teeter when she felt up to it and needed to escape her homemade prison. Online orders from Amazon or Barnes and Noble could be brought up in the dumbwaiter. Carolyn's husband had been farsighted enough to add it when he designed the house. It had come in handy during the COVID-19 pandemic when they had groceries delivered for a while. Now that things were mostly back to normal, the dumbwaiter just waited most of the time.

That was all the suspects she could think of and all the people with keys. Someone was usually at home day or night, and they were very conscientious about locking the doors at night. The road from Yulee to Fernandina had become like a main highway, with traffic at all hours. Other homes in the Little Piney Island subdivision had reported having their cars broken into, which was why the Dawsons had become so strict about locking the house at night.

Carolyn was sure of one main thing: Aleesha had just tried to kill her by turning off the iron lung. But it hadn't worked, and judging by the nearly inaudible weeping Carolyn had heard, Aleesha hadn't wanted it to work.

Despite the failure of the attempt on the author's life, it didn't alter the fact that someone wanted to prematurely erase Carolyn Dawson's character from the story.

Chapter 13

THE BUZZING OF Jimmy's cell phone awakened him. It was lying on the coffee table next to the couch in his living room. Meanwhile, Jimmy was halfway reclining on his couch with Wendi leaning against him, sleeping. She was tucked inside the curve of his arm, her head against his chest. Consequently, he was not going to move any more than was absolutely necessary. He let the call go to voicemail.

Using the arm that wasn't wrapped around Wendi, he slowly reached up and tried to brush her hair from his face. Between the hurricane and the kerfuffle at the Dawson house, they had been awake for the better part of a couple of days. Tacked onto the excitement of a tropical storm and family dynamics was discovering a pair of severed hands, followed by the requisite question and answer period with local law enforcement officers.

Now that he was awake, Jimmy wanted to see who had called. He stretched to reach his phone, just barely snagging it with his fingertips. After retrieving it from the coffee table, he checked the call history. He had missed a call from Pepé, but there was no voicemail message; his partner had left a text instead. Jimmy tapped on the Messages icon to read the text.

> Hey brother! Haven't heard from you
> for a few days and wanted to check
> in to make sure UR ok. Let me know.

Jimmy held the phone out at arms-length after turning on the camera. Smiling, he took a selfie of himself with Wendi asleep on his chest. If his other arm hadn't been occupied cradling Wendi, he would have given a thumbs-up sign for the selfie.

He sent the picture to Pepé.

Wendi turned her head slightly and asked groggily, "What did you just do?"

"I – um, nothing. I mean, I just sent Pepé a text. He wanted to make sure I made it through the storm okay."

She sat up partway, planted one hand against Jimmy's chest, and pushed herself semi-vertical. She turned to face Jimmy.

"You sent him a selfie, didn't you? Of us? Jimmy. My hair's a mess," she said, her voice still thick from sleep. She slid over on the couch, running her hands through her hair before extending one hand toward Jimmy. She curled her fingers into a "gimme" motion. Jimmy gave her a sheepish look but maintained his grip on his phone.

"Show me," Wendi demanded.

Jimmy handed her his phone. She looked at it for a second, then turned her head and raised one eyebrow.

"I look horrible. You don't look much better, but at least you look happy." She handed his phone back.

"What can I say?" Jimmy replied. "*You* make me happy."

His cell phone buzzed again. It was Pepé again.

> Is that Wendi? I hope so! When are
> you going to bring her around so
> Gwynn and I can meet her?

"Pepé wants to know when I'm going to 'bring you around' so he and his wife can meet you," Jimmy told Wendi.

"Bring me around? What am I, a new puppy?" Wendi growled.

"That's not how he meant it. All he means is that he and his wife would like to meet you. Don't get hung up on semantics. They're some of my dearest friends, and I trust Pepé with my life. As a matter of fact, I have many times. And I would trust him with your life, too."

Jimmy rubbed Wendi's back while he tried to explain what texting often hid from the viewer: context, underlying tone, and the texter's feelings.

"Well, it's not going to be today," Wendi replied, somewhat placated by Jimmy's explanation.

Jimmy slid his legs around in front of him and sat up, tapping a reply to his partner.

> We'll get together soon, man. All 4 of
> us. We'll go try a new pizza place I've
> heard about.

Pepé quickly replied, his reply dinging as it came into Jimmy's phone.

> You know I'm always down for pizza,
> dude. Wish we could find some
> authentic New York slices.
> What can I tell you, man? We're in the
> Deep South, not the South Bronx.

Wendi read the exchange on Jimmy's phone, then stood and stretched, leaning forward and backward before reaching down and placing her hands flat on the floor. She worked her way back up, bent from side to side, reached toward the ceiling, and brought her hands down to her head. She tousled her hair.

"I can't do this, Jimmy," she said, not looking at him.

It was as if one of The Man's big goons had punched him in the stomach. Jimmy felt like she had cut him off at the knees.

"W-what do you mean?" he stammered. He thought things were going really well, despite finding severed hands and getting threatening texts from a faceless, nameless underworld figure who wanted Jimmy to believe he was a childhood legend come to life.

"I mean …" Wendi paused and stared out a living room window. Jimmy held his breath, afraid of what she might say. His brain screamed, *I knew it was too good to be true!*

"…not sleeping, eating badly, wearing the same clothes for days, and not showering. I feel so grungy. I'm going to head home in a few minutes, and I'm going to take a shower, and then I'm going to eat a normal meal, and tonight I'm going to sleep in my own bed." She turned to Jimmy, reached over, and clasped his hand, bringing it to her lips and kissing his knuckles.

"That's all I meant," she continued. "We've been up so long without any real sleep, and napping on your couch slumped down in a slouch makes my back sore and stiff."

She saw the remnants of sadness and fear on Jimmy's face and said, "What did you think I meant?"

He stood to his feet and pulled her into his arms. He looked into her eyes and said, "Nothing." But a second later, he confessed, "I thought you meant ... *us*. I thought you were saying you were ... I dunno. Done with me, I guess, what with the severed hands, the Dawsons, the lack of sleep, dealing with the cops, and the rest of the stress."

"Do you have any idea when the last time I went three days wearing the same clothes was?" Wendi asked, putting her arms around the private investigator. He shook his head in reply.

"Me, neither," she answered. "And I can deal with the tension from stray body parts, cops, and all the rest, as long as I can face it with you."

Jimmy thought his mouth might drop open in surprise and made a conscious effort to keep it closed. Wendi continued, "Since you came into my life a few weeks ago when that manuscript went missing, I have felt more alive than I have in the three years since ..." She stopped.

"Since Charles died?" Jimmy filled in for her.

"No ... and yes. Since I had to put my life on hold while helping Hillary deal with the loss of his wife *and* his son. Charles and I were over by then and had been over for some time, but it didn't mean I wanted him dead. The accident was a shock, and his death still saddens me, but so did the end of our marriage. But I didn't have to deal with the same grief as Hillary. I put my life on hold willingly, just so you know." She laid her head on Jimmy's shoulder. She spoke into his neck.

"When I met you, I felt like I woke up from a very long night or suddenly came out of a coma. That was part of why

Charles and I were drifting apart: he was all work and no play. He had no time for me. Not that I wanted our life to be all play and no work, but I wanted a … *partner* is the right word, I guess."

Jimmy remained silent, enjoying holding her close, the faint scent of her shampoo somehow still lingering in her hair after three days. He didn't say anything, afraid of saying something stupid and breaking the spell.

She kept her arms around him and leaned back to look into his eyes. "Do you understand? I want to stay with you and help you figure out these puzzles that your cases are. Not necessarily every time – I still have to help Hillary at Lyst Publishing – but I want to be a part of your life, including this part where you solve mysteries. Besides, Pepé can't always cover you, and I *have* been trained in self-defense, in case you've forgotten." She reached a finger out to his throat and touched his Adam's apple. Jimmy grabbed her finger almost involuntarily and turned it away from his throat.

"I promise I have *not* forgotten," he answered.

Wendi released her hold on Jimmy and let her hands slide down his arms until she was leaning back like some move from *Dirty Dancing*. She held the pose for a second, then snapped upright and said matter-of-factly and brightly, "So, I have to go home and get cleaned up and rested up. I want to discover more about those severed hands and why someone lobbed them at you." She started to turn away but turned back.

"And," she added, "If I'm going to meet Pepé and … Gwynn, was it? Pepé and Gwynn, I want to look better than

I do right now. Call it vanity if you want, but I think you like it when I look my best, too."

Jimmy was still holding onto one of Wendi's hands. He twirled her into his arms, gave her a long kiss, and then twirled her back out to arm's length.

"I told you last night that there was more where that kiss came from. And there's still more if you want," Jimmy said.

"Right now, I need to go. But if you keep kissing me like that, I *won't* want to go, and I need to. You need to shower and clean up, too. And shave. Either choose a beard or none, but halfway in between isn't working for me."

Jimmy felt his three-day-old whiskers and grinned. "You don't like whiskers, either?"

"Either?" Wendi replied with a raised eyebrow. "Who else doesn't like your whiskers?" *Oops!*

"No, not mine. Gwynn and Pepé can't always agree on beards, either. Apparently, she must have agreed to let him grow it out for a while because he's sporting a beard these days. Maybe it got soft enough so she could appreciate it."

Wendi stroked the side of Jimmy's cheek with the back of her hand, giving his stubble a light rub. Looking him directly in the eye, she gently held his face stationary with one hand, appraising it and imagining him with a fuller beard.

"I don't know," she said at last. "I just can't picture you with a beard."

"Not to worry," Jimmy answered. "After I get some sleep, I'll be cleaning up, too, and shaving."

She stepped close and gave him one more kiss, then stepped back and said, "Done. I have to go." She gathered her purse and headed for the front door.

"I'll call you when I'm clean and rested," Wendi said as she turned the doorknob and went outside. Jimmy slowly followed her onto the front porch.

She was already down the steps and getting into her car. Jimmy waved as she started the motor and backed up in a wide arc. She gave a quick wave in return, then drove out onto Highway 17, aiming the car toward Fernandina. Jimmy watched her drive out of sight. Unlike other times he'd watched girls leave—most recently Daani Manyeagles from Wisconsin—he wasn't left with an empty feeling inside this time. *What's that about?* he thought to himself.

Turning back to his front door, he decided to not overthink it. He was going to shower, shave, eat, and get some more rest and sleep. And that's what he did.

Kind of.

*

"Just because you make a good plan doesn't mean that's what's gonna happen." ~Taylor Swift

*

Unfortunately for Jimmy, no one had told the rest of the world about his need for rest and rejuvenation. One of his regular clients called to let him know they had another batch of job applicants and needed Jimmy to validate the applicants' school and employment records. After assuring them he would get right on it, Jimmy tried to get back to sleep, but his brain was awake.

Some people could turn their brains off and put the world on hold while they caught up on sleep, but when Jimmy's brain turned on, he couldn't simply flip an invisible, internal switch and shut everything back down.

When his phone rang the next time, he was half-heartedly watching a documentary on the History channel, trying to trick his mind into giving sleep another chance. He didn't recognize the number, but that wasn't uncommon. His phone was savvy enough to alert him to telemarketers with a "potential spam" designation under their number when they called, but that wasn't the case this time.

He considered letting it go to voicemail. After all, he had talked with one client already and had some work lined up, even if it wasn't exciting, mind-stimulating work. Maybe this would be the latter, and he pushed the button to answer the call.

"This is Jimmy," he said as he answered the call. He waited. He could hear someone on the other end, but they weren't talking. Could it be The Man? Possibly, but Jimmy didn't hear the electrical hum in the background that usually accompanied calls from the person who wanted Jimmy to think he was a real-life legend.

"Oh, you're there. I was waiting for a spiel about leaving my name and number, but you're really there." It was a woman's voice and recognizable, but Jimmy couldn't quite put his finger on just who.

"Yes, I'm here," he responded. "Who's this?" He sat up a little straighter in his chair. Curiosity was winning the battle, stimulating his mind to work, and sleep had dropped off his agenda.

"This is Carolyn, Carolyn Dawson on Piney Island. The author? We met at my house yesterday."

Jimmy listened to her explain who she was, picturing her in his mind's eye. He'd seen her in and out of the iron lung, seen her hospitable side and her unvarnished side when she was arguing with her son, Gary. *Not Gary; he's Hank,* he reminded himself. *Gary Dawson is her alias. His, too?*

"Are you there, Jimmy?" she asked.

He shook his head slightly and answered. "Yes, ma'am. I'm here. It's been three long days, and I'm still a little groggy. But I'm here."

"Is Wendi there, too?" Carolyn asked.

"No, ma'am. She's at home," Jimmy replied. *Unfortunately!* "Were you looking for her?" he asked. He hoped perhaps she was, and then he'd have an excuse to call Wendi.

"No, that's fine. It's you I want to talk to."

"Well, you have me. What can I do for you, Mrs. Dawson?" Jimmy answered, trying to sound more chipper than he felt.

"I want to retain your services, Jimmy," she replied.

When it rains, it pours. First, a client with some tedious but steady work, and now this.

"Okay. What kind of job do you have in mind?" Jimmy asked. "Did you need another model for your book covers?"

The silence on the phone was deafening.

"No, Mr. Favreaux. That position is covered," she answered after a pause. Jimmy was reasonably sure the delay was accompanied by Carolyn Dawson's eyes rolling back into her head at his attempt at levity.

"Just a little joke, Mrs. Dawson," Jimmy replied, trying to regroup.

"Yes. Very little. I need you to do some investigating for me, Jimmy. You *are* an investigator, aren't you?"

"Oh, yes, ma'am. I am a licensed and registered private investigator. I've been doing this for over ten years," Jimmy said, trying to reassure the woman.

"And yet, as I told you yesterday, I've never heard of you, and I write about investigators and their investigations ..." She let the statement hang there.

"I don't know what to tell you, ma'am." Jimmy was starting to sweat a little. $10,000 paydays like the one he received recently from Hillary Lyst were rare occurrences, and he couldn't afford to lose a client. "I'm a finder of people, places, and things, and it doesn't sound like you're looking for any of those. Or maybe we just move in different circles."

Talking to Carolyn about working for her reminded him of The Man's cryptic warning to "Stay out of Dawson business." For Jimmy, telling him not to do something was like waving a red cape in front of an angry bull.

Jimmy started to get nervous, afraid he was blowing it. So, instead of making a flippant remark, he waited for Carolyn Dawson to respond, letting the silence build until he wanted to scream.

"I made a call to Hillary Lyst this morning. He speaks very highly of you, Jimmy," she said at last. *Yes!*

"I did some work for Mr. Lyst a few weeks ago and saved him quite a bit of money," Jimmy answered.

"So he said," Carolyn replied. "He told me you found a stolen manuscript, saved him several thousand dollars in a ransom demand, outsmarted one of the crooks on several occasions, and discovered the true author of the manuscript. The icing on the cake was when he said you put your life at risk on several occasions in the process."

"Yes, well …"

"And you got the girl, too, didn't you?" Carolyn asked.

"Well, I don't know if I'd go that far …."

"Don't kid a kidder, Jimmy. I saw how Wendi looked at you when you were here. What's more, I saw how *you* looked at her. And you were there for her when things were going sideways at my house," she responded to Jimmy's lame attempt at an excuse. "Plus – and this is the big one – you came out to my house without hesitation simply because Wendi asked you to accompany her. You could have been walking into a real hornet's nest, but you just kept walking forward."

Jimmy was starting to feel good about his prior visit to Carolyn's.

"I haven't decided if you're brave, stupid, or naïve," Carolyn concluded her assessment of his post-hurricane outing to her house.

"Which one of my traits did you need for your job?" Jimmy asked, starting to become a little annoyed with the woman's lack of tact.

"The one Hillary said you had in spades: tenacity. He said you're like a kid on the playground who finally gets tired of the bully and just steps up and starts swinging. You don't let a little bloody nose stop you," she explained. "That's what I need. Things can get rough at my house, so I want someone who doesn't roll over and quit at the first sign of trouble."

Jimmy said nothing.

"And ... there's one other reason I want *your* help, Jimmy," she said, pausing.

"And that is ..." he asked.

"You're an unknown factor. None of my little clan knows what to expect from you. I hope you can use that to your advantage, or should I say *our* advantage," Carolyn finished.

"Okay," he answered. "I'm intrigued. What do you need me to do?"

Now it was Carolyn's turn to consider what she was getting into before airing her dirty laundry. To her credit, she didn't wait too long before sorting it for laundering.

"I need you to investigate Aleesha and maybe Hank, too," she responded.

"Investigate your son and his wife? Why?"

Carolyn Dawson, the author of the Nick Steele detective books, a polio survivor, and one of the last people in the world to still use an iron lung, matter-of-factly replied, "Because Aleesha tried to kill me last night while I was sleeping."

Chapter 14

JIMMY HAD TO hold his cell phone away from his ear after telling Wendi what Carolyn had told him.

"She said *what*?!" Wendi yelled into the phone.

"I kid you not. Carolyn told me that, after we left, Aleesha tried to kill her in her sleep."

"Jimmy, that's impossible," Wendi replied, her voice more controlled. "I've known Aleesha since she started working for Carolyn, and I was one of a select few who went to Hank and Aleesha's wedding last year. There is no way I will believe that girl tried to kill Carolyn. She simply doesn't have it in her."

"That's kind of what Carolyn said, too. She told me she could hear Aleesha crying somewhere in the room, but so quietly that Carolyn almost wasn't sure she heard her. She was out of Carolyn's line of sight from inside the iron lung. Aleesha would know that, too, as well as where to hide in the room to be invisible. And one more thing: she knows how to disable the machine without leaving a trace," Jimmy responded.

"How does Carolyn think she did it?" Wendi pressed.

"She's not a hundred percent sure, but she's pretty sure Aleesha went low-tech and just turned off the circuit breaker that powers the iron lung's motor. Easy peasy. Aleesha turns off the power, waits for Miss Carolyn to suffocate, restores the electricity when it's all over but the crying, and returns to bed upstairs. No one's the wiser. In the morning, they find Carolyn dead, and the machine is still working fine." Jimmy waited to see if any reaction or rebuttal was coming from Wendi, then continued his theory.

"Think about it: Carolyn is approaching eighty and was a polio kid. I mean, geez, Wendi, the woman has an iron lung in her bedroom! How many other people do you know that decorate with an iron lung? Any investigation into her death would probably just say her lungs gave out after all these years. Lots of people who never had polio pass away in their late seventies. I'd bet if no one pushed it, the medical examiner's office would probably skip the autopsy. Why bother? She was an older woman with respiratory issues who died in her sleep. Mark the case closed and move on to the next body."

"So?" Wendi replied.

"So?" Jimmy parroted.

"So, why didn't Aleesha go through with it?" Wendi asked. "Why would she start the process and then stop? Was she trying to prove to herself that she could do it? What did they call it in school? A proof theory?"

"Just proving it's feasible, you mean?" Jimmy replied. "It's possible, I suppose. But I don't think that's quite what's going on here."

"Okay. I'm listening," Wendi answered, her voice traveling thirty miles from her condo overlooking the Atlantic Ocean on Fletcher Avenue. Jimmy could picture her sitting on the couch, looking out the windows at the beach and the water.

"I think it's kind of like the proof theory thing, except Aleesha had no idea how hard it would be. Most people have no idea how hard it is to kill another human being, physically or psychologically. And for Aleesha, who trained for and became a caregiver—not a murderer—it goes against everything in her soul," Jimmy summarized.

Wendi picked up where Jimmy left off. "It would be one thing to turn off the oxygen machine for a person you have had no prior contact with, someone ninety years old with dementia and living in a nursing home, or maybe someone in an irreversible coma, but Aleesha was Carolyn's caregiver for over two years. And as far as I know, Carolyn was the only person Aleesha ever worked for as a caregiver."

"My big question is not whether Aleesha tried to kill Carolyn, but why?" Jimmy replied. "Could someone have put her up to it? Hank? Not very likely. Someone else we don't know about? You have a key to their house and a history with the family, not me. What's Aleesha's story? And how about other people she knows?"

Jimmy looked out the window at his front lawn and the mailbox by the road. Less than forty-eight hours had passed since they found a severed hand by the beach outside

Wendi's condo. A day later, they discovered the hand's mate in a fast-food bag near Jimmy's mailbox. That one came with a note saying if they were playing cards, Jimmy now had "a pair." Jimmy thought he had done well not saying anything to Wendi or the deputy about playing the "hand" they'd been dealt.

Deputy Parker had said the hand belonged "to a small-time thug named Seth Kremer." Jimmy had no idea who that was, and Wendi said she didn't know him either. The deputy said Kremer was almost certainly dead, but if he wasn't, Deputy Parker was sure Kremer was probably begging for death to alleviate his misery.

Jimmy knew people could and did survive having their hands, feet, arms, and legs amputated, either accidentally or intentionally. But the cuts to the wrists on the severed hands were so clean and precise that Jimmy couldn't imagine they came from a live person. Who could hold still for such horror?

Jimmy circled back to his questions for Wendi. "Tell me what you know about Aleesha. You said she was a local girl and played softball in high school. After graduation, she went to a local college for nursing and caregiving. Is there more?"

"Like what?" Wendi replied. "That's more than some people's resumé."

"Like, did she always live here? Who are her parents? Who are her friends? That kind of stuff. Those little details we don't think are crucial but often end up being important. It's like building a tower with playing cards. They look steady and strong, but they fall down pretty easily when you pull one out," Jimmy answered.

"I'm not really sure. Let me think about it, and I'll call you back. Maybe we should go and see Carolyn again. She might have some of the answers you're looking for. Or Aleesha might be there, and you can ask her for yourself."

"Maybe we should," Jimmy answered. He knew he would return to Piney Island before very long, but he wanted to have as much information in his back pocket as he could before facing the family. Jimmy decided to switch gears.

"Did you get any sleep?" he asked.

"A little. Not as much as I need, but I got some. I took a hot shower, did my hair and makeup, and put on clean clothes. That made a huge difference in my outlook. Then, I ate some food I made with my own two hands ..." Wendi paused abruptly, and Jimmy knew her mind had flashed on the two severed hands they had found. There was nothing he could do to stop that from happening. It would just take time.

"That's good," he interjected, making the pause less awkward. "Why don't I come and pick you up, and we'll go back to Carolyn's?"

"Without calling first?" she responded.

"Exactly. I prefer to keep people off balance. I don't want anyone to have time to compare notes. We could start with Carolyn, talk to Hank, and finish with Aleesha. That should make Aleesha really nervous. She'll either clam up or spill everything because she thinks the others have turned on her. When we were out there before, I got the feeling that she still feels like one of the hired help. That lends itself to a them-versus-me mindset. How about we stir up a hornet's nest? Sound good to you?" Jimmy asked Wendi.

"It sounds fine, but ..." she paused.

"But what?" Jimmy responded.

"Well, I'd like to ask some of the questions. They know me and might tell me things they won't tell you. Plus, I have some background info on each of them that you don't, so I can tailor the questions to each of them. But you're the private investigator. If I'm off-base here, just say the word."

Jimmy didn't have to think about it too long. "It sounds like a good approach," he replied. "You're right; you have more inroads and history with them than I do. They might see me as an outsider or a cop trying to interrogate them. It probably will go down easier coming from you."

"Did Carolyn say whether Hank knew anything about it?" Wendi asked.

"No. Carolyn didn't indicate that she had said anything to either of her housemates. Let me get going, and I'll come and pick you up. There's no telling whether Carolyn will say anything to them before we meet with her, so we need to get there before it all blows up. Deal?" Jimmy asked. There was a slight pause.

"How about this instead," Wendi replied. "Meet me there. It's halfway between us. We'll save time if you don't have to drive all the way down here and then go back to their house."

It was the better plan, Jimmy agreed. He told Wendi he'd see her in a few minutes and clicked off the call. Pepé once told him that women were better at this sort of thing — logistics. Now Jimmy was finding out for himself.

Wendi's car was already parked by the carport when he arrived. It was no surprise since the house wasn't really halfway – Wendi had ten miles, while Jimmy had twenty. *But at least she left the hot pink Jeep at home.*

Jimmy climbed out of his Nissan SUV and approached Wendi's red Audi A3. She was standing in front of it, leaning on the hood. Wendi definitely looked better than the last time Jimmy saw her, not that she ever looked bad. *Amazing what a shower and a little sleep will do.*

She smiled as he approached. He loved that smile.

"Ready?" Wendi asked, looking way more perky than he felt.

"I could still use a good night's sleep, but I'm ready to beard the lion in its den," Jimmy replied.

Wendy raised one eyebrow. "Have you been talking with Hillary again? That's his kind of phrase."

"No, I've simply been waiting for the right opportunity to use it. You know what it means, right?" Jimmy asked, stepping a little closer and invading her personal space.

"Of course. It means to confront someone or challenge them on their home turf. Kind of like you, standing a little too close." She smiled again, kissed him quickly, stepped back, and said, "Let's go inside. I hear there are lions in there."

Jimmy covered his mouth to stifle his laugh.

*

Just like the first time they had been at the house, they went in through the garage tucked underneath and climbed the stairs to the main level. Wendi led the way, which was okay with Jimmy. She was running point on this operation.

At the top of the stairs, Wendi gave a couple of raps with her knuckles, then opened the door and stepped inside, followed closely by Jimmy.

"Hello?" Wendi called out and waited.

Jimmy heard the sound of shuffling feet from the kitchen on the other side of the living room. Carolyn Dawson poked her head into the doorway, a look of surprise and confusion on her face.

"Wendi? And Jimmy? What are you doing here?" she asked. "Did we set up an appointment, and I forgot it, Jimmy?"

"No, ma'am," he answered. "I just decided not to wait. I have some questions to ask, and, as they say, there's no time like the present. When I was a kid at Christmastime, I used to say, no time like the present for presents."

Wendi looked in his direction with arched eyebrows and gave him a gentle nudge.

"Yeah. Nobody laughed then, either," Jimmy responded. Wendi stepped ahead, literally taking the lead.

"We just want to ask you a few questions, Carolyn," Wendi interjected. "We—I mean, *I* want to ask you about the other night and see if what you told Jimmy might have another explanation."

"Checking up on me to see if the old lady is losing her grip on sanity? Imagining things? Is that it?" Carolyn asked, putting her hands on her hips.

Uh-oh. Jimmy had seen that move before from his mom, and it usually didn't end well for him.

"Not at all," Wendi replied, moving across the living room toward the kitchen and speaking in a steady, calm voice, vocally smoothing Carolyn's ruffled feathers. "You know how men are. I should have said, 'to see if *Jimmy* got the story right.'"

Hey! Jimmy thought, *I'm standing right here; I can hear you, y'know? Geez! Did you want me to change the oil while I'm under this bus?*

"Yes … well … I *do* know how men are. Come into the kitchen, and we'll talk." Carolyn seemed placated.

The three of them headed toward the kitchen. Jimmy gave Wendi a raised eyebrow, and she shrugged her shoulders in silent reply.

Better get used to it, he told himself.

The three of them settled back in the same seats as the first time they had gathered in the kitchen.

Jimmy wondered if everybody did that – gravitate to the same seat they'd previously used. Do people unconsciously mark their territory, announcing to all present that 'this seat is mine?' Or are preordained ranks automatically assumed?

"Jimmy? Wake up," Wendi was saying. "Carolyn asked if we wanted something to drink. A bottle of water for you? Or coffee?"

"Sorry. I guess my mind was wandering," Jimmy answered. "Water would be fine."

"Then will you get them out of the fridge for us?" Wendi asked him, and he realized he must be more tired than he thought. He would have offered to make coffee again, but it had been a big fiasco the last time he tried that in this kitchen.

Jumping up more energetically than he truly felt, Jimmy replied, "Absolutely! Waters all around?" as he walked over to the refrigerator.

"Just you and I," Wendi answered.

Jimmy returned a few seconds later to the kitchen island they had gathered around, each hand holding a sweating water bottle. He handed one to Wendi, cracked open the other, and took a long drink before sitting down.

Wendi opened her water bottle but then screwed the cap back on without taking a drink. She set it on the island, turning her attention to Carolyn Dawson.

"Jimmy told me about your phone call. What happened in the night must have been awful," Wendi said to Carolyn, reaching out and laying her hand upon the older woman's.

"To be honest, it was more surprising than awful or upsetting," Carolyn replied. "I'm a tough old bird; I've had to be tough as a single mother and semi-invalid." She leaned forward slightly and lowered her voice a little. "It was quite out of character for Aleesha, you know? That's the only way I can describe it. It wasn't something I would ever expect her to do or even *attempt* to do. It was like someone else had stepped in and was writing the chapter. The characters were the same, but they weren't acting normally. There are certain things that characters in a story will and won't do, and let me tell you, Aleesha doesn't have it in her to try what she did. I know that's why she couldn't go through with it. Thank the good Lord she didn't, or we might not be having this conversation."

"Oh, my goodness, yes!" Wendi exclaimed. "I just can't imagine what was going through her mind or who could have put an idea like that in her head." She reached for the still-sweaty water bottle and twisted it loosely back and forth in her hands, neither loosening nor tightening the cap.

It was an ordinary motion, but Jimmy thought, right now, it was a prop to make the situation feel more normal. We're just three people talking.

"I couldn't begin to fathom a guess about who might want me dead," Carolyn answered.

Wendi stopped rotating the bottle aimlessly, removed the cap, and took a small drink. Putting the cap back on, she said, "I think we should try. To guess, that is. Let's pool what we know and see if we can brainstorm an answer or a potential one, anyway. I'd hate to think of you lying awake all night again, wondering if you'll see the morning or why the world has turned upside down."

"Aleesha's always been so helpful and is normally very cheerful. Even if I'm having a bad day, she usually cheers me up in no time," Carolyn added.

"How long has she worked for you? Three years or four?" Wendi asked.

"Oh, she only worked for me for two years, and then she and Hank married. I've known her for three years total, I guess. They're just about due for their first anniversary," Carolyn said.

Jimmy listened to the women's conversation while looking out the windows. He tried to be part of the background, just another piece of furniture in the room.

"And before that?" Wendi asked. "Had she worked for anyone else as a caregiver?"

"Not privately, at least, not that I'm aware of," Carolyn replied. "I think she said once that she worked at one of the nursing homes on Amelia Island. I guess it was sort of like a doctor doing his internship working at a hospital."

"Let's see now … she's thirty-five, right?" Wendi asked.

"Mm-hm," Carolyn answered.

"So what did she do for a decade after graduating college?" Wendi posed.

Carolyn looked at her, her expression a mix of surprise and slight confusion. "What do you mean?" she asked Wendi.

"Well, if a person graduates from high school when they're seventeen or eighteen and from college four years later at twenty-one or twenty-two … What did Aleesha do between the time when she was twenty-two and when she was thirty-two and came to work for you?"

"I imagine she did what many young people do," Carolyn answered. "She probably tried to find herself and figure out what she wanted to do with her life. It's not uncommon for people to graduate from college and discover they didn't get a degree that can help them pay the rent. How many people with four-year degrees work at Walmart because a degree in philosophy or general English is not something employers are looking for on a resumé?"

"Do you know what we used to say about girls who didn't have a career goal in mind when they were in college?" Wendi asked Carolyn, her tone and facial expression turning conspiratorial. "We said they were after an MRS degree!

"We said the exact same thing when I was in college," Carolyn replied lightheartedly. "I imagine some said that about me, and they weren't that far wrong. I've always felt that being a wife and mother is a woman's highest calling. I know a lot of women disagree with that, but it's still how I feel. Think about it: only women can bear children. Only women can be wives and mothers, and that's not the same as being a spouse or a parent. Those are generic terms we've come up with to avoid political confrontations. I'm old fashioned enough to still believe the institution of motherhood is noble, and being a wife doesn't make you a servant or a doormat."

"What do you know about Aleesha's parents and background?" Wendi probed gently, the question occurring naturally in the conversation's flow.

"Local girl, graduated from Fernandina Beach High School. Went to Coastal Community College in Kingsland, but it changed to a four-year school while she was there. I don't know what she got her first degree in. I would have to get her information out of the files in my office. I know she returned to Coastal for two years in 2018, maybe in 2017. Since she already had a degree, she could concentrate on her major courses. I think she was already working at the nursing home and decided to get her Associate of Nursing degree. I guess she finally decided on a career path and went after the classes and the degree that could make it happen."

"Okay, but what about family?" Wendi steered Carolyn back to her previous question.

"I believe she's an only child, and her mom died when she was twelve or thirteen, just when a girl really needs her mom," Carolyn replied.

"What about her dad?" Wendi prompted, trying to keep the information flowing.

"I've never heard anything about him," Carolyn said, frowning slightly. "I heard somewhere that Aleesha and her father may have had a bit of a falling out. That happens far too often, don't you think?"

"It does," Wendi replied. Switching gears, she asked, "Do you think you could get the information or maybe the resumé she gave you when she came to work for you? We could have Jimmy look it over for any red flags while we talk about some other things."

Carolyn looked at Wendi momentarily as though trying to see where the plot line was headed in this story. She stood slowly, holding onto the kitchen island, and said, "I'll be right back. I believe I know where it is."

As Carolyn left Wendi and Jimmy in the kitchen, Wendi said quietly to Jimmy, "How am I doing?"

He reached over and took her hand in his and said, "You're doing great, but when are you going to ask her about last night? We need to get more details about the actual attempt."

"We'll get there, trust me. There are some pieces of information about Aleesha I have never known, so I figured it would be good to get all those boxes checked off if I could," Wendi answered, pausing to take a drink from her water bottle.

She continued, "I didn't know Aleesha's mom had died or that she was estranged from her dad. She's never mentioned a sister or brother and what they did together while growing up, so I suspected she was an only child, but I never knew for sure."

"That was smart to ask Carolyn to get Aleesha's resumé. That'll provide some pretty solid background information," Jimmy replied, his head turned slightly away from Wendi as he kept an eye out for Carolyn's return. "I'd still like to know why she did it and if someone pushed her to do it. I know I just met the girl, but I can't see her deciding to make a sudden career change from caregiver to cold-blooded killer."

The sound of Carolyn's voice from the office made Jimmy and Wendi stop talking. They each took a drink from their water bottles in case she was coming back.

"Well, that's funny," Carolyn said from the other room. "I found the resumé, but there's no family or other background information here. I thought for sure there was something listed on here ...."

The older woman's voice trailed off.

Jimmy and Wendi suddenly heard another voice from the other room.

"What are you looking for, Miss Carolyn? Maybe I can help you find it."

Aleesha!

<h1 style="text-align:center">Chapter 15</h1>

IT'S SURPRISING HOW quickly someone can move when a plan blows up. Jimmy and Wendi's strategy had been to talk with Carolyn first and Hank second—they weren't even sure if they needed to speak with Hank—and then question Aleesha last. But with Aleesha's sudden appearance in Carolyn's office, Jimmy and Wendi were forced to reconsider their idea. *Time to improvise!*

They rushed to Carolyn's office and found Aleesha standing just inside the doorway. She smiled at Jimmy and Wendi the same way she always did.

Like last night's escapade never happened, Jimmy thought.

Carolyn stood across the room next to an open file cabinet, a manilla folder in one hand and a printed sheet of paper in the other. Jimmy noticed that Carolyn was on the far side of the file cabinet, its long drawer sticking out. Intentionally or unintentionally, the drawer of the heavy piece of office furniture was positioned between herself and Aleesha. Had Carolyn done it on purpose for protection?

I'm probably overthinking it, Jimmy thought.

As Jimmy and Wendi surveyed the scene for potential drama, Aleesha asked, "What's going on, Miss Carolyn?"

Carolyn looked to Jimmy like an author with writer's block, silently seeking his input, but Wendi spoke first.

"Hi, Aleesha! We drove out to see Miss Carolyn. Jimmy sometimes works for an insurance company vetting people – you know, making sure they are who they say they are and that they really went to the schools they said they attended. You'd be surprised how many people didn't really graduate from college or get the degree they said they did. That kind of thing. It turns out Miss Carolyn's disability insurance is one of those companies Jimmy works for. So Jimmy just needed to see your resumé. It's only a formality since I've known you for several years." Wendi paused for a heartbeat before shrugging and adding, "You know?"

The silence hung awkwardly in the air between them. Suddenly, Carolyn slid the cabinet drawer shut with a loud bang. Everyone jumped and turned to look at her.

"Oh, *that's* why you asked me the questions about Aleesha," Carolyn said, stepping around the cabinet. "I just thought you were being nosy, Jimmy," she added.

Jimmy wasn't sure if Carolyn was reacting to the stress of being alone unexpectedly with Aleesha or was just acting like a crabby old lady. *Or, she's not acting,* he thought. The author moved toward the door, holding out the folder she had pulled from the cabinet.

"Here. This has all the information the insurance people could want, Jimmy." Carolyn handed him the folder, squeezed past the three people occupying the doorway without so much as a 'pardon me,' and returned to the kitchen, leaving the trio staring speechless in her wake.

After a moment, Aleesha asked Wendi, "Why didn't you just ask me?"

"We-uh, we didn't know you were here," Wendi stammered. "We didn't see Hank's vehicle when we drove up, so we assumed it was only Carolyn at home. We just came in like we owned the place and were all chatting in the kitchen before Jimmy remembered what he needed. We certainly could have spoken directly with you if we had known you were here."

Jimmy was mutely amazed and slightly disturbed at how quickly Wendi had fashioned a story out of thin air to cover their tracks. It was close enough to the truth to be a *shade* of truth, just not 'the whole truth and nothing but the truth, so help me, God.'

"Well?" Aleesha asked.

Jimmy and Wendi stared at her.

"Excuse me?" Jimmy replied, confused.

"Has my resumé got everything you need, Mr. Favreaux?" the younger Mrs. Dawson asked. Jimmy thought her smile seemed slightly strained now.

Jimmy opened the folder, stared at the paper inside for a count of three, and then said, "Yes. Yes, I think so—"

"No," Wendi interrupted.

"No?" Jimmy and Aleesha asked simultaneously, swiveling their heads in unison to look at Wendi.

"It doesn't say anything about your family, Aleesha. Carolyn told us your mom died when you were about twelve or thirteen—"

"I was twelve," Aleesha answered quickly.

"Okay," Wendi replied. "And Carolyn said she thought you and your father may have had some kind of a … falling out? Is that right?"

Aleesha stared at Wendi momentarily, then leaned back against the door jamb. "Yes, my father and I were estranged for a long time, but he recently contacted me about trying to make amends and repair our relationship."

"As in, *you* make amends, or your *father* make amends?" Jimmy asked for clarification.

"We both have things we need to work on, but mostly *he* needs to make amends," Aleesha answered Jimmy's question. "However, I can't imagine an insurance company would be quite that interested in my relationship with my father."

"Well, that was more about *us* getting to know *you*," Jimmy replied, wishing Wendi would have fielded that question since she was the one who initially asked Aleesha about it. "Speaking of getting to know you better, where's your other half? Where's Hank?"

"He said he had some errands to do in town, and then he needed to stop at Lowe's," Aleesha answered just before she quickly stepped in very close to Jimmy. He wasn't sure what would happen next, so he didn't know how to prepare to defend himself.

Aleesha reached past Jimmy and pulled the pocket door to close it. Jimmy hadn't even noticed there *was* a pocket door instead of one on the typical hinges. He thought the office didn't have a door, making it slightly more handicap accessible. Aleesha slid the door smoothly and noiselessly across the open space, sealing it into the wall on the other side.

Aleesha turned around to face Jimmy and Wendi. She stood in front of them, her smile gone, her hands behind her back – probably holding the pocket door closed, Jimmy guessed – and, in a whispered voice, asked, "Did Miss Carolyn tell you about last night?"

Jimmy shook his head 'no,' but Wendi nodded and said, "Yes."

Jimmy quickly changed the direction his head was moving. Aleesha either didn't notice his sudden change or ignored it as she continued to look at them expectantly.

When no one answered, Aleesha asked, "What did she tell you?"

Wendi turned her head toward Jimmy, raised one eyebrow, and gave a tiny nod of her head, asking him silently if he was going to just stand there awkwardly or tell Aleesha what Carolyn had said. He took the hint.

Jimmy's words rushed out in a tumble.

"She called and told me she woke up and became aware of the iron lung's sudden motor failure. Miss Carolyn said she also *heard someone* in the room a few moments later. She said it sounded like they were crying. The person *or persons* were out of her line of sight. She said the iron lung's motor started working again a few minutes later."

Aleesha's face had turned red, a fact she tried to hide by hanging her head down. Jimmy and Wendi were unsure what to say, so they said nothing, waiting for Aleesha to continue. They looked at each other, making eye gestures and shrugging their shoulders to express their helplessness.

"I couldn't do it." Aleesha's voice had dropped lower than a whisper, and when she raised her head, her face was still red, but her cheeks were now shiny from fallen tears.

In a voice almost as soft as the younger woman's, Wendi asked, "*What* couldn't you do, Aleesha?"

"I couldn't turn it off and … leave her there. Even if she deserved it—which I don't think she does!—I couldn't do it. I just couldn't do it. That's not who I am. So I turned everything back on and went back to bed. Hank never even noticed I was gone. It took me hours to go back to sleep."

"Did someone tell you to k— I mean, tell you that Carolyn deserved to die ?" Wendi asked. Her voice was still soft, but Jimmy noticed more urgency in it and a slightly rougher edge.

Maybe the urgency was fear that Carolyn might return to find out why they were huddled behind the door instead of sitting in the kitchen with her. Jimmy figured Aleesha's unexpected presence would keep Carolyn out of her office briefly but not forever. The older woman was undeniably wary of her former caregiver today, even though Aleesha had just told them she needn't be.

Wendi rephrased her question more directly. "Who told you to do it, Aleesha? Not Hank, was it?"

Aleesha shook her head vehemently at the accusation, and sparks fairly flew from her eyes as she answered, "No, not Hank. It was my– my father. He said …"

Just as quickly as she had become angry, Aleesha's wrath burned itself out, and she sniffled from a new crop of tears before speaking again.

"He said Miss Carolyn was responsible for a death in our family. He said I should make her pay for what she took from him ... and me. But I couldn't do it."

Wendi stepped forward and wrapped the crying woman in her arms. "Of course, you couldn't do it. That's not who you are. You are a caregiver, a healer, someone who gives life and prolongs life, not someone who takes it away. Just like a doctor, when you finished nursing school, you promised, 'I will do no harm.' You showed me a lamp once you got at school. A Florence Nightingale lamp to remind you of your pledge to do no harm."

Almost no sounds arose from the two women, but Jimmy could tell Aleesha was still crying. After a long thirty seconds, Wendi turned her head toward him and softly said, "Jimmy, I need you to go out and sit with Carolyn. Keep her busy. Tell her stories or jokes or exchange recipes. Better yet, ask her about her books. I need to speak more with Aleesha, so please do that for me."

Jimmy was pretty sure a salute wouldn't go over well, and with the three of them in such close proximity, kissing Wendi was out, too, so he simply stepped around the two women, slid the pocket door open far enough to exit, and stepped out. He swiveled, closed the door, took a deep breath, and set a course for the kitchen.

This should be interesting, he told himself.

He settled back onto a stool in the kitchen. Carolyn had made herself a cup of green tea while they were in the office. Jimmy picked up the water bottle he had abandoned earlier and took a drink. He cleared his throat and tried to think of an appropriate discussion topic but decided another swig of water was in order instead.

"Where are Wendi and Aleesha?" Carolyn asked, removing the onus of speaking first.

Jimmy, water bottle poised at his lips, pointed back the way he had come, directing her attention to the office. Carolyn nodded, picked up her cup of tea, and blew on it to cool the steaming liquid before taking a tentative sip.

Jimmy took a deep breath. *In for a penny…*

"When did you write your first Nick Steele Detective Agency book?" Jimmy asked, surprised that his question sounded halfway intelligent. He had all the words in the correct order and even remembered that it was Nick Steele, not Remington. Maybe he *could* do this.

"Just 'Steele Detective Agency,' not the Nick Steele Detective Agency," Carolyn answered, blowing on her tea again and taking another sip.

Feeling a little chagrinned but knowing that Wendi was counting on him, Jimmy plunged ahead.

"Okay, got it. So when did you start, and how did you choose to write about a detective?" Jimmy asked.

"Didn't I tell you this the other day?" Carolyn asked dispassionately in response.

"You told me about writing poetry after losing Tammy. You didn't explain how you became involved in crime fiction stories with a pair of detectives as lead characters," Jimmy explained. "From what Wendi told me, there are quite a few years between the poetry and the advent of Nick Steele."

"Speaking of Wendi, do you think she and Aleesha are all right in my office?" Carolyn inquired.

Jimmy listened for a minute, his hand cupped to his ear. "Yup. No sounds of breakage, so they must be fine," he answered.

Carolyn gave Jimmy a cautious grin. "You're an odd duck sometimes, Jimmy, but if you have a serious side to go along with that, I can see why Wendi is enamored with you."

Jimmy blushed slightly and said, "You think Wendi is enamored with me?"

"Almost as much as you are with her," Carolyn replied, her grin becoming less guarded and more natural.

"It's that obvious?" Jimmy answered, feeling heat radiate from his face.

"Oh, not at all," Carolyn said sarcastically, giving him another genuine grin. Jimmy took the grin as a positive sign.

"Let's try and stay on track," Jimmy said, pretending to retake control. "How did you get started writing crime fiction with a pair of private detectives for main characters?"

Carolyn gave a small sigh. "Okay, we'll play it your way, Jimmy, although I'm fairly sure that question was answered somewhere in a regional newspaper interview a few years ago. Whenever I drop a new book title, the local paper reprints an old interview, simply inserting the new book's title. It's easier than sending the newest reporter out to interview me – or Hank if they want a picture. That's how they used to do it until some enterprising publisher realized he could save time and a little money by running the old interview with a few tweaks and updates."

Jimmy listened politely, fiddling with his water bottle. Even though she would probably deny it if asked, Carolyn was like most people: their favorite topic of discussion is themselves.

"I wonder if they have my obituary ready," Carolyn continued absently. "Probably. I'm semi-famous, but more semi than famous. I imagine my obit is similar to my new-book interview – my last story is ready to go once someone drops in the date. Unless something exciting happens, the obituary will probably say things like, 'the reclusive author, a polio survivor as a child, detective books,' blah-blah-blah. It'll include the number of books I've written and how many languages they've been translated into. It'll also mention that I'm one of the last polio survivors still using an iron lung. When you add the books, polio, and iron lung thing together, I'll probably get the front half-page below the fold."

When Carolyn paused, Jimmy asked, "So, why don't you want to answer my question – how you started writing detective stories?"

Carolyn gave a big sigh before answering.

"Because it's not new or interesting. Look, we both know you're out here because you're supposed to keep me company while Wendi grills Aleesha about last night, but you're asking the same questions news reporters fresh out of college have asked me dozens of times before," Carolyn answered, taking another sip of tea and staring out the window.

"How did your husband die?" Jimmy asked straight out with no sugar-coating. *Is that new and interesting enough?* he thought.

Jimmy saw Carolyn stiffen ever-so-slightly, but she kept her gaze fixed out the window. He didn't know if she was ignoring his blunt question or if she was reliving the experience. He decided to wait and see which.

"It was 1983. Hank was sixteen and had just finished his sophomore year. David – my husband – was thirty-eight. At the time, it had been fourteen years since we lost Tammy; now, it's almost forty. I had worked through the grief of losing a baby and the depression of finding out I couldn't have another. We were a family, a small one, but a strong, tightly-knit one. Hank was doing well in school, and I had moved on from writing poetry. I was writing some short stories, and a few women's magazines were picking them up. David was thinking about starting his own architectural firm."

Jimmy let Carolyn talk without interrupting.

"Six years before, when Hank was about ten, David bought a small plane. The plane made sense in many ways. David was trained as a Navy pilot, and the travel requirements from his job at the firm kept him away from home, often more than either of us liked. Hank was playing high school football and baseball, and David hated missing his games. About a year before he died, David got his flight teacher certification and started giving flight lessons. He didn't do it for the money so much as to introduce people to the joy of flying. As a matter of fact, that's what he was doing when he died."

Carolyn stopped and took a sip of tea. "This is cold," she said. "Would you mind popping it into the microwave for thirty seconds?"

Jimmy nodded, took the cup across the room to the microwave, opened the door, placed it inside, and pushed the one-touch REHEAT button. When it was done, he brought it back to where they were sitting. He hoped the mood wasn't lost; he wanted Carolyn to continue.

She took a sip and gave Jimmy a rather lopsided, sad smile. "Thank you."

"You said your husband was flying when he died?" Jimmy asked gently to bring the narrative back on track.

"He had taken a young college girl up for an introductory flight. They were hardly in the air ten minutes before the plane dove straight down into the St. Marys River. People living along the river said the plane's tail was all that was sticking out of the water, and it went under soon after. It was only a matter of minutes before it sank. Several local people living along the river jumped into their boats and hurried to the crash site, but no one had come up from the plane, and it was almost entirely underwater before anyone got there. The wreck was long gone before the sheriff's department responded. The county people arrived as quickly as possible, and a couple of the deputies who were a part of the dive and rescue teams jumped in and free-dived the wreck. They eventually brought up their bodies – David and the girl – but they had both died upon impact. There was nothing anyone could do for them."

Carolyn became silent. She looked out the window, her eyes open but not seeing the current world. Her vision was focused on a scene from thirty-nine years before. Jimmy would have allowed her more time for inner reflection, but he needed more information.

"What was the girl's name?" he asked.

Carolyn shifted her gaze from the window to Jimmy, but it didn't seem as though she had seen him yet. "W-what? What did you ask?" she answered, looking surprised to find herself in her kitchen with Jimmy.

"What was the name of the girl who died with David in that crash? The college freshman," Jimmy asked again, trying to keep his voice gentle.

"Her name was Kaycie. Kaycie Abaddon. She graduated from Fernandina Beach High School the year before. She had just finished her first year at UF in Gainesville. She thought it would be fun to learn how to fly. David offered to teach her if her parents okayed it and if they could come up with the money for lessons. That day was her introductory flight. They were going to fly over to the Okefenokee Swamp and back."

Something about the girl's name rang a bell in Jimmy's brain. He knew the name or the word Abaddon from somewhere but couldn't place where.

"Did they figure out what caused the crash?" Jimmy asked. "Did they find the black box?"

"Light planes don't usually have a black box, Jimmy, and certainly not back then," Carolyn answered. "Flight recorders are mainly for commercial carriers, the big planes."

"So, no one ever figured anything out?"

Carolyn shook her head. "Just that two people were dead, and two families would never be the same again."

*

"Aleesha, why would your dad say Miss Carolyn was responsible for someone's death in your family?" Wendi asked the young woman sitting across from her. They had settled into a pair of office chairs and sat knee to knee, their legs even touching at times.

"I honestly don't know. My dad started going on about how Miss Carolyn would try to split up Hank and me, that she was jealous of us and couldn't stand our happiness. He said something about Carolyn's husband dying, and she wanted to get even, or my dad did, or … I don't know. None of it made any sense to me. He just kept hollering at me that Miss Carolyn would try to come between Hank and me to take him away from me. My dad said she had taken someone from him, or her husband had, and we needed to get even. I didn't understand any of that. But when I thought about how nasty Hank and Miss Carolyn were with each other the other day – how they were yelling at each other … well, I started thinking that maybe she *would* try and split us up or come between us. She might try to keep us from moving into our own place. She might cut Hank out of everything – take away his royalties package and stuff. I don't know what he would do if that happened."

"Tell me more," Wendi pressed the younger woman. Aleesha obliged.

"I'm sure you probably already know, but Miss Carolyn controls all the money. Hank has nothing but the portion of the book royalties she gives him. I don't know about that stuff."

Aleesha stopped to take a big breath and wipe her eyes before continuing.

"In my head, I kept hearing Miss Carolyn yelling at Hank, and it was getting all tangled up with my dad shouting that Miss Carolyn took something or someone from him—and me!—and I couldn't get it out of my head. I heard him yelling at me over and over, 'She has to die, or she'll take Hank away from you!' That's why I came down and flipped the circuit breaker."

Wendi stayed quiet, looking at Aleesha sympathetically.

"I thought if I did it, it would help make things better between Hank and me and maybe between me and my dad. Hank wouldn't have to fight with Miss Carolyn anymore, and he'd be happier without her interference in our lives. My dad said I had to be the one to do it. He said it had to be me because no one would suspect me since I had been her caregiver. But I couldn't go through with it. I just couldn't!"

Aleesha started sobbing and sniffling anew, and Wendi grabbed some more tissues and gave them to her. Wendi put her arms around Aleesha and held her until the girl's sobbing settled down.

"Better?" Wendi asked Aleesha after her sobs subsided.

Aleesha nodded her head and blew her nose.

"Okay," Wendi said. "There are some things we need to figure out. First, we need to know why your dad thinks Miss Carolyn should die. We need to understand what he meant by 'she took someone or something' from him. Are you sure he mentioned David, Carolyn's husband?"

"I think so," Aleesha answered, nodding her head. "I'm pretty sure."

"When did you meet with him? Your dad, I mean," Wendi asked.

"Just after the hurricane blew past. Hank and I were down in Jacksonville when it came through, and we couldn't get home. You heard Hank complain about that."

Wendi nodded.

"Well, we were in a hotel room in Jacksonville, and I got a message on my phone to go to the lobby. My dad was sitting there, waiting for me. When we got back, and you and Jimmy were here, Miss Carolyn and Hank argued so hatefully. They fought again that afternoon after you left. I want to run and hide in my room when they get angry like that. It reminds me of how my mom and my dad used to fight. I was little, and they used to yell and scream at each other, call each other horrible things, and he'd slap her, and she'd throw things at him. I guess that's why my dad left. He must have gotten tired of it."

"So, they got a divorce?" Wendi asked.

Aleesha shook her head, her eyes sad and her usual smile gone. "No, he didn't need to. They never got married, so he just left. I was only about five and had just started kindergarten. All that yelling and screaming at home made me want to run away, but there was nowhere to go."

"I'm so sorry you had to go through that, Aleesha," Wendi responded.

"Yeah, well … I guess a lot of people have gone through the same thing," Aleesha replied.

"But most people don't lose their mom when they're twelve. How did she die, if I can ask?" Wendi probed gently.

"She took her own life. She took a bunch of pills and went to sleep; she just never woke up. I guess she got tired of struggling, and … she quit. She quit on life, and she quit on me," Aleesha answered flatly, as though reciting something she had shared so many times that it no longer touched her emotionally.

"How old was she?" Wendi asked, placing a hand gently on Aleesha's arm.

"Thirty. Can you believe it? I'm older than my mom ever was."

"What was her name?" Wendi asked.

There was a tapping on the office's pocket door. It slid open about a foot, and Jimmy stepped sideways into the gap. Wendi held up one finger to let him know she needed another minute.

"Her name was Sonja. Sonja Mortel. Like I said, they never married, so she didn't change her name. She and I were Mortels, and my dad is Doyle Abaddon."

"That's what I was trying to remember," Jimmy exclaimed, opening the door wider and stepping into the office.

"It's Death."

Chapter 16

Jimmy stepped inside the office and shut the pocket door behind him. "Both of those words—Abaddon and Mortel—refer to death. I heard those words when I was a kid living in Canada, especially when people talked about the boogeyman, Le Bonhomme Sept-Heures. It's the influence of our French and British ancestors. Parts of Canada have French as a first language and English as a second. And when I say English, I mean Olde, British-style English."

Wendi started to say something, but Jimmy wasn't quite finished with his linguistics lesson. Before she could stop him, Jimmy continued enlightening his audience.

"*Abaddon* is the Old English word for the devil. Literally, the destroyer, the angel of the bottomless pit. In the Bible, *Abaddon* is the place of ruin set aside for the devil and his angels. Most people call it Hell. And *mortel* is where we get our word mortal. It means deadly. That's why they call a mortal wound deadly; it means it will kill you."

Wendi was staring at Jimmy, taking in everything he was sharing. Aleesha was staring at Jimmy, too, but her eyes had opened wider, and she had paled a few shades since Jimmy began orating about death.

Jimmy looked at the two women staring at him. "What?" he asked generally, then asked Wendi, "Why was Aleesha talking about hell and death?"

"Those are her *family* names, Jimmy," Wendi said, putting one finger to her lips to signal: *'Shut up, Jimmy!'*

"But wait," Jimmy replied, choosing to ignore the signal. "When I was talking with Carolyn, she said one of those names, too, just a few minutes ago. When I came in to see how you were doing and Aleesha mentioned Mortel, both words clicked into place. When I was in the kitchen with Carolyn, she was telling me about Kaycie *Abaddon*, the girl killed in the 1983 plane crash with Carolyn's husband, David."

Aleesha seemed to be shrinking again as Wendi turned back and peppered her with some quick questions. "Aleesha, do you know anything about this Kaycie Abaddon? Isn't that your dad's last name? Was she related? Did you ever meet her? Do you know if your mom knew her?"

Aleesha nodded, gulped hard, and answered tentatively, "I know the *name*, but I never met her. Because, just like Jimmy said, she died in 1983, and I wasn't born until four years later, in 1987. I couldn't have ever talked to her. But technically, I guess you would say she was my half-sister."

Now it was Wendi's turn to be speechless. She hadn't seen that coming. She started turning the new puzzle piece over in her mind, seeking where it fit into the larger picture.

Jimmy leaped into the gap, blurting out questions without thinking, "She was like nineteen years old! That's old enough to become a mom herself. She was probably about the same age as your mom, maybe older! How could you be half-sisters if you weren't born until 1987?"

Aleesha rolled her brown eyes at Jimmy's question. Her color was improving, and she answered him in her typical no-nonsense fashion, "Duh! Half-sisters mean we share one parent. In this case, it's the same dad, but we had different moms."

Wendi replied before Jimmy could take the conversation hostage. "Aleesha, let me make sure I have all the facts. Your dad was married and had a daughter over twenty years before you were born? And that daughter was killed in a plane crash with the husband of the woman who is now your mother-in-law? And the crash was four years before you were born?"

"We're kind of a screwed-up family," Aleesha admitted. "That's part of the reason—no, that *is* the reason I don't usually talk about my family."

Aleesha still held some of the tissues she had used when crying. Now she stood and dropped them into the wastebasket next to the desk. After grabbing a few replacements, she settled into her chair again, dabbed her eyes, and blew her nose.

Jimmy propped himself on the corner of the desk and responded to Aleesha's comment on families. "I think *most* families are kind of screwed up if you start poking around and looking under rocks. But what are the odds you would marry the son of the man who may have killed your sister? Or half-sister, anyway."

The sliding door slid open fast behind Jimmy with a loud noise, revealing Carolyn Dawson, her eyes brimming with angry tears, and her lips curled into a furious snarl. At that moment, Jimmy thought, she looked like she could have held her own against anyone in the room, regardless of her polio history.

"My husband did *not* kill anyone in that crash! They were both victims of a terrible accident. The authorities were never able to find anything specific to lay the blame on, but David did not crash that plane intentionally. He had everything to live for! That's the stupidest thing I have heard in a while. I would appreciate an apology, Mr. Favreaux, and I mean now!"

Jimmy turned bright red at the sound of his name. He quickly stood from his perch on the desk's corner and answered his client, "Absolutely! I am so sorry for my insensitivity. The wrong phrase fell out of my mouth. I wasn't thinking. I didn't mean to say your husband killed her sister; it's just that … well, he was the licensed pilot and in charge of the flight."

Wendi placed herself between Jimmy and Carolyn and said, "I'm so *very* sorry, Carolyn. Jimmy didn't mean anything by what he said. He's just unable to ignore the fact that we suddenly have two supposedly unrelated incidents with commonalities. You've written about that very thing in your books. It's like a big Easter egg that suddenly appears. You know, like the hidden secrets they put into movies, TV shows, and video games."

Wendi put a hand on Jimmy's arm and turned to face him. She reached out a hand and gently covered his mouth before he could say anything else that he shouldn't. "Shh, Jimmy. I know you didn't mean anything ugly, but some things never heal, and sometimes, we can accidentally inflict pain without even trying."

Wendi swung back around toward Carolyn and took a few steps forward, stopping directly in front of the older woman blocking the doorway. Wendi stood toe-to-toe with her, gazing steadily into the woman's eyes for several heartbeats before continuing her corporate apology.

"You know I would never have let him say anything if I had known what he was going to say. If I could sweep up his words and put them back in his mouth, I would. But that's not the way life works. Spoken words are much harder to fix than written words. We don't come with built-in editors and undo buttons. Sometimes words that we later regret escape our mouths. I'm sure Jimmy already regrets what he said, don't you, Jimmy?"

Jimmy nodded in agreement, his eyes riveted to the floor like a schoolboy in the principal's office. Lifting his head, he forced his eyes to meet Carolyn's and said, "I am truly sorry for accidentally implying anything inappropriate in what I said before. I hope you can find it in your heart to forgive me. I thought we were starting to get along pretty well – out in the kitchen – and I would hate to wreck that."

Carolyn looked like she was struggling to maintain the fire of her anger. Her mouth was tight, her lips a thin line. At last, she nodded and said, "It's all right. It just caught me off-guard. After all these many, many years, I thought I was a bit further past it than that."

Carolyn paused before turning to look at her former antagonist and said, "Jimmy?"

He looked at her and waited to see what else she would say. He could see the fury rapidly fading from her eyes. She laid a hand on his arm and said, "Can you help me to a chair? I left my walker in the other room, and my legs suddenly feel very tired and weak."

Jimmy quickly grasped her hand, took her by the elbow, and guided her into the nearest chair. She sat down rather hard and let out a big sigh of relief. All the intensity had vanished, and with it, most of her adrenaline-fueled strength.

Jimmy and Wendi stood together while Aleesha and Carolyn sat, a thick, uncomfortable silence blanketing the room.

Wendi's eyes swiveled back and forth between the two women before remarking, "Who wants to go elephant hunting?"

Jimmy looked at her, confused. Wendi saw his bewilderment.

"There's an elephant in this room, Jimmy," Wendi replied to his perplexed expression. "No one ever wants to talk about the elephant in the room, but everybody knows there is one. This elephant is named Abaddon."

The light bulb in Jimmy's mind was almost visible over his head as he grasped what Wendi was talking about. Carolyn ignored Jimmy's sudden arrival at the impromptu family reunion and faced her daughter-in-law.

"How did we never come across this genealogical nugget, Aleesha?" Carolyn asked. Though her anger had dissipated, her voice was tighter than usual, lacking any fondness or softness. Aleesha's eyes were glued to the wooden floorboards at the prospect of dredging up a potentially-dark part of her family history.

Wendi held out a piece of paper to Carolyn, who took it from her and gave it a cursory glance.

"What am I supposed to see? This is Aleesha's resumé and personal information," Carolyn replied, giving the document a slight wave in the air.

"Look where it asks for parents' names."

Carolyn looked at the paper in her hand again.

"It's blank," Wendi pointed out.

"I think I remember now," Carolyn said, her head turning toward Aleesha. "I asked you about it just before I hired you. You said your mom had died when you were twelve, and your dad had left seven years before that. You said you didn't have any parents to write on that line. When you told me your mom had died when you were a child, I felt so badly for you that I couldn't ask any more questions. I realized you were as well-acquainted with loss as I was. Whenever I've been asked how many children I had, I hate saying 'one. It should have been two. Maybe that's why I hired you: we're kindred spirits, bound together by loss."

Aleesha had yet to break her gaze from the floor. Carolyn reached a hand across the space between them and placed it on her daughter-in-law's knee. She kept it there, waiting.

After a long while, Aleesha briefly placed her hand on Carolyn's but only for the briefest of seconds, quickly withdrawing it.

"It's just … I can't stop thinking about last night," Aleesha said, her head still hanging down. Jimmy saw several large teardrops fall onto Aleesha's jeans, making large, dark circles. She sniffled and pressed a tissue against her eyes, soaking up the liquid threatening to run down her cheeks.

"Yes, *that*," Carolyn responded. She turned to face Wendi but kept her hand fastened to Aleesha's knee. "What did she tell you about that, Wendi?"

Jimmy waited quietly, anxious to hear the answer, too.

Wendi cleared her throat and said, "There wasn't much to tell, Carolyn. Let me start by asking if you knew Aleesha had reconciled with her father."

Carolyn raised her eyebrows as she waited for the rest of Wendi's answer.

"I'll take that as a no," Wendi answered. "It hasn't been a complete reconciliation. Aleesha says he still has to make a lot of amends and changes to get back in her good graces, if he ever really can. Right, Aleesha?"

Aleesha nodded.

Wendi decided to lower the heat a notch on Aleesha and turn it up a little under Carolyn. "Did you ever meet Kaycie before that day in 1983, Carolyn?"

"No," Carolyn answered quickly and definitely.

Jimmy looked at Wendi, and she raised her eyebrows almost imperceptibly, but he caught it. She had noticed, too. *Too swiftly and too surely,* Jimmy thought.

"Was your husband in the habit of taking young college girls up in his plane?" Wendi asked. As she did, she reminded herself to avoid sounding like a police detective interrogating a prisoner.

"Of course not," Carolyn said, a peevish note creeping into her voice.

"But he had received his teaching license for flying lessons, hadn't he? So he was starting to get a little business going on the side, correct? Were all his clients men?"

"Mostly, I'm sure, but I didn't pay that much attention. We were all busy with our individual lives. I was moving into a new career myself, as an author, and Hank was finishing his last high school years," Carolyn answered.

"Was there still enough room in your busy life for your husband?" Wendi asked.

Carolyn narrowed her eyes. "What are you implying, Wendi? Are you accusing David of playing around? Chasing women? Are you insinuating that I was too focused on my new — no, my *first* career? I never had a real career before, and to this day, I have never had a job away from home. To this day! I have always been here for my family."

"I'm just asking if you resented David's mobility, ability—and freedom!—to fly off anywhere at a moment's notice? Maybe you begrudged him the travel his job required? You weren't a best-selling author yet. I didn't know you then, but I know the timeline."

"David's career made life difficult at times, I won't deny it. Especially when Hank was small. But once he was about ten, Hank was big enough to help out at home. I didn't have to worry about him all the time, and David didn't have to worry about me so much," Carolyn replied. She took a breath, and Jimmy noticed how she seemed to struggle to inhale as deeply as she wanted.

Carolyn continued. "I'm not saying it was a good thing or a bad thing. It was just a thing. We were both trying on new identities. Yes, we may have drifted slightly apart from each other, but that happens to almost all couples over time, doesn't it? I have no doubt we would have weathered that little speed bump just fine. But then David didn't come home that day, and our lives were changed forever."

The atmosphere in the room felt more like an interrogation than Jimmy expected. He noticed that Aleesha had grown totally silent, eyes wide and attentive, watching the exchange between the two older women. It reminded him of a few days earlier when Hank and Carolyn had argued, and Aleesha had made herself as small and invisible as possible.

Like a kid when her parents fight, Jimmy thought.

Jimmy had seen it before when a kid's parents fought, verbally and physically. The kids tried to keep the focus off themselves, yes, but also ready to escape if necessary. Jimmy wondered if Wendi had probed Aleesha about her childhood. He had a feeling she was no stranger to abuse.

"So you don't know if David ever talked with Kaycie or met her before?" Wendi prodded Carolyn.

"Why are you trying to taint his memory?" Carolyn shot back.

"As hard as it may be to believe right now, Carolyn, I'm not. I'm simply trying to gather as much information as I can. I'm close to putting some puzzle pieces together and making them fit," Wendi explained. She didn't let Carolyn answer before forging ahead.

"Aleesha's father has been filling her mind with the idea that *you* need to die, Carolyn. It's a matter of family vengeance. According to Aleesha, he mentioned something about you or David taking something from him. He told Aleesha she owed it to him and her mom—even herself—to take care of the situation. She told me he said she could make it look like you died of natural causes. He was adamant at first but quickly became belligerent when she disagreed. He yelled at her that she needed to do it for her family."

Carolyn was quiet for a moment. Her mind was obviously turning over this new information, tumbling it around with things that had bothered her for nearly forty years.

"You're saying Aleesha's father is looking for revenge for *Kaycie's* death?" Carolyn asked. "And since David isn't available, he wants to make *me* pay? With David's death, I think I already paid my portion. But after all these years— why now?"

Wendi was about to speak when Jimmy cleared his throat. She turned his way, and he said, "If I may."

"Have at it, Jimmy," Wendi replied.

"Who stands to profit from Carolyn's death?" Jimmy asked the three women, putting his hands behind his back and pacing in the small office.

"Who's the beneficiary of your estate, Carolyn?" Wendi answered.

"Hank, of course," she replied.

"And by extension, Aleesha," Jimmy added.

"I think you're climbing out on a flimsy limb, Jimmy." Carolyn countered his theory, "I'm comfortable, but I'm not rich."

"But how much would Aleesha and Hank's lives change if you died? Not much at first. Sure, the house would belong to them, but they wouldn't have to split the royalties from the books with you anymore. That alone would be a decent windfall," Jimmy continued.

He continued pacing around the office. All he needed was the deerstalker hat and meerschaum pipe to complete the mental transformation into Sherlock Holmes.

"You say you're comfortable but not rich, but if Hank gets all the royalties, he will become more comfortable than either of you is now, right?" Jimmy posed. "You do have fifteen—make that *sixteen*—books, after all."

"Let's add things up," he continued. "The house, cars, reputation, and royalties, and those royalties are mostly passive income. Granted, royalties are not guaranteed income, but I'll bet they would increase for a while. Dead authors' books and dead artists' paintings usually increase in value for a period right after someone dies. After all, there won't be any new works from them, so people scramble to purchase what they can. People who have only read a few of your stories will buy the whole set. That's another bump up for Hank and, by extension, Aleesha."

"I think I see what you're getting at," Carolyn remarked. "If I die and it looks like a natural death, Hank and Aleesha inherit the house, the whole royalties package, and the life insurance. The potential long-term revenue stream will keep them adequately comfortable for years. They can tack a couple more million onto their package if they sell the house. And if they sell the movie rights to my most popular books? Now we're talking about some significant money. Invest it all the right way, and Hank coasts into retirement without ever working a day in his entire life. It's rather like being royalty, isn't it?"

Wendi stepped back into the middle of their circle. "Which brings us to the other question: what does Aleesha's father get out of it?"

"A clean, freshly laundered conscience," Jimmy replied.

"What?" It was the first word Aleesha had spoken for a while. She looked mystified.

Jimmy focused on her. "Your dad abandoned you when you were five, and your mom died when you were twelve. He can make up for abandoning you with one 'easy' death he's not even involved with directly. You kill Carolyn, and he gets the credit. He can claim he's taking care of you and Hank. How magnanimous!"

"One problem," Carolyn interjected. "What if I don't want to be dead?"

"And what if I don't want to kill her?" Aleesha added, standing to her feet.

Carolyn looked at Aleesha, rolling her last words over in her mind.

Jimmy looked at Wendi for some help. This was why Carolyn had called him to come and investigate the Dawsons. Everyone wanted to know who was pulling the strings for this little puppet show and what the next act held in store.

Wendi bunched up her shoulders and said, "I told you I was *close* to putting all the puzzle pieces together. I didn't say I had *everything* figured out yet!"

Chapter 17

JIMMY, WENDI, AND Aleesha filed out of Carolyn's office; Carolyn brought up the rear, pausing long enough to turn off the lights. The day was moving into late afternoon, but the sun was still high over the horizon. Despite the November sunshine, Jimmy knew darkness would slam shut fast after sundown.

The foursome stepped into the living room, looking at each other as though waiting for someone to take charge and give orders. No one moved toward the kitchen, the garage, or the upstairs apartment. After an awkward moment of inactivity, Jimmy broke the silence.

"Has anyone seen Hank? I didn't see him when we arrived and haven't seen him since. That's been quite a while."

Aleesha was the person who should have known her husband's whereabouts. "The last I saw him, he was getting ready to leave to run some errands. Is his Subaru parked below?"

Wendi shook her head. "It wasn't here when I drove in. That's why I said we didn't think you were here. Jimmy and I came in separate cars, and I got here first. Our cars would be in the way if someone tried to leave."

Jimmy went to a window and looked out. "Our cars are also in the way if someone comes home. Hank's car is out there now, parked behind ours. I didn't hear him come into the house, though, and I didn't see him while I was in the kitchen with Miss Carolyn. I don't see him anywhere outside, but I suppose that's not unusual out here. He could be down by the river, walking in the woods, or just on the other side of the house."

Wendi walked across the room to the windows on the other side. "Nothing out here. We should go outside and see if we can find him."

Aleesha crossed to the door that opened on the stairs leading down to the garage. Wendi followed, and Jimmy came last this time. Carolyn didn't follow them, walking slowly toward the kitchen where her walker was stashed. She explained, "I'll stay in here. Using the chair lift on the other stairs would take me too long. Let me know what you find."

Jimmy hadn't seen another staircase before, but he hadn't looked for one, either. As an able-bodied person, it never occurred to him to wonder how Carolyn got from the garage to the main floor. Some days she might be physically able to climb the stairs, but other days, it might pose a considerable hardship. From the sound of things, though, she didn't leave the house too often. Hank and Aleesha took care of the shopping and most other things that needed to be tended to off-site.

Looking down the stairway in front of him, Jimmy decided a private entrance with a chair lift made sense. The staircase rising from the garage was rather steep and narrow, and a chair lift would block the way if multiple persons attempted to go up or down the stairs. It would certainly be an issue for ambulance personnel, and Jimmy wondered if that had happened before.

Once they arrived in the garage below, the trio fanned out to look for Hank. Garage was a misnomer since it was more like a carport, open on all four sides, exposing the large, solid pillars the house rested upon. Jimmy angled left, and as he headed outside from under the garage's canopy, he noticed the other door. *That must be the stairs with the chair lift.*

He stepped out into the late afternoon sunshine, his eyes surveying the trees and brownish-yellow marsh grasses beyond. Jimmy hoped to see an unnatural color among the greens, browns, tans, reds, and oranges. The synthetic fabrics and patterns of people's clothes were often easy to spot because their manmade colors didn't occur in nature. They simply looked wrong and out of place.

The day Jimmy met Hank, the namesake of Carolyn's books was wearing a blue and red plaid shirt with blue jeans. Jimmy imagined he was dressed similarly today.

He heard Aleesha calling for Hank off to his right. Turning his head to the left, he saw Wendi doing much as he had, scanning the flat land for signs of the man. Without saying so, Jimmy and Wendi both figured Hank should be somewhat noticeable, even if he was lying on the ground. And since they hadn't seen him walking around, paying attention to the ground became more important. He could have had a heart attack and collapsed. He could require medical help.

Aleesha hollered again, a pleading tone in her voice. "Hank! Please come to the house!"

Jimmy walked down toward the river. There were surprisingly few branches and leaves on the ground from the storm, but then, it hadn't been a hurricane when it went through this area. The soil was still muddy from the rain that Tropical Storm Nicole had dropped on them a few days before. Some areas were spongy, hiding their saturation, only revealing their hidden moisture when pressed down by a foot. Other parts were obviously mucky, ready to suck a man's foot deep into the wet earth.

Since moving to the area, Jimmy was always surprised by the ground's capacity to absorb massive rainfall amounts dispensed by passing tropical systems. He knew the high percentage of sand in the soil helped let the water trickle down, and the loose vegetative material from pine straw, marsh grass, reeds, and cattails helped keep the dirt from becoming too compressed. The various native vines all helped keep the soil light and open, but so did the marsh grasses, cattails, and reeds. The sand and vegetative matter were the most abundant components in the soil, not clay, which would have turned the ground into bricks when the hot summer sun baked out the water hidden within. With a high clay content, the marsh would have looked like a parched and cracked creek bed from west Texas during the dry season. The soil was so sandy, Florida was sometimes referred to as the sandbox of the U.S.

The loose, water-filtering soil was quite different from the rich, loamy river bottom dirt stretching across much of Minnesota and into central Canada. That dirt was ideal for growing corn, soybeans, and wheat, and for green pastures for grazing cattle and sheep and letting horses frolic. Farmers loved it; it was like a giant compost heap cooking and evolving over thousands of years. It was the perfect medium for crops, developed and perfected since the glaciers had scraped across the landscape, creating thousands of rivers, lakes, and the Minnesota state slogan, Land of Ten-Thousand Lakes. *And a hundred-thousand taxes!* Jimmy thought.

Jimmy couldn't figure out why the soil near the coast wasn't more like the loamy Upper Midwestern soil. It seemed like this Florida earth should be a giant compost heap, but whenever Jimmy dug a hole on his property near the St. Marys River, the opened cavity always smelled of rotten fish, not the rich aroma of Minnesota river bottom dirt.

Jimmy turned his thoughts back to the matter at hand, finding Hank. His car was here; he should be here *somewhere.*

"Hank!" Jimmy added his shouts to Aleesha's, even though he hadn't heard any replies from anywhere on the property. He briefly flashed on summer days in the municipal swimming pool, playing Marco Polo, and for a second, he was tempted to yell, "Marco!" but he knew that would probably get him in trouble.

"Jimmy!" It was Wendi. She had returned to the end of the driveway where their cars were parked. He looked toward her, and she waved him over. She was holding something for Show and Tell.

It took him only a minute or two to walk from where he had been to where she waited. Aleesha was almost running to join them. Wendi held up a piece of paper as Jimmy approached.

"What is it?" Jimmy asked.

"It's a note addressed to you," Wendi answered.

"Me?" Jimmy asked. "Who is it from?"

"It's not signed. Here," Wendi said as she held it out to him. Jimmy grabbed the paper and quickly scanned it.

```
You were warned to stay out of Dawson
business. I thought the hands would
show you I was serious.
Seth offended me, and he paid the
price. But at least he was useful in
the end. Handy, you could say.
Hank is going to balance the scales,
and there's nothing you can do.
To watch the festivities, go to the
old Chester graveyard. But don't be
slow. Hank's old and soft, just like
the ground at the graveyard.
```

Jimmy turned to Aleesha. "Do you have any idea where the Old Chester Graveyard is?" She stood frozen in place, staring at the words in the note Jimmy held. When she didn't answer, he grabbed her arm and squeezed.

"Ow!" she yelped, but the pain broke the daze she had been in.

"I said, do you know where that cemetery is? Someone has taken Hank, and I'm not sure if we can get there in time. I don't know how long they've had him or how long it'll take us to get there. We were so involved in your history and figuring out why your dad might want Carolyn dead that we didn't notice Hank was missing. And walking around the property looking for him just wasted more time," Jimmy explained bluntly to Aleesha.

"I know where the graveyard is."

Carolyn's voice came from behind them in the garage. She had decided to take the chair lift down after all. She walked slowly toward the group, her walker traded in for a cane, her tired legs and lungs preventing her from moving faster.

"It's at the end of Chester Road, across from the Chester Church of God," Carolyn said, slowly approaching the group. As she reached the trio, she asked, "Who has Hank, and, more importantly, why?"

"Read the note," Jimmy replied. She snatched it from his hand. She read it hurriedly, and her head snapped around, her eyes locking on Jimmy's.

"Who told you to stay out of our family business, Jimmy? And why?" Carolyn shot the words at Jimmy. "It's obvious from today's events that you didn't listen. But what's all this talk about hands?"

Wendi answered, "We found two severed hands. They came from the same person, not two different people. We found one by my condo, and one at Jimmy's house, by his mailbox out by the road. But there was no direct link to your family or anything, really. Then Jimmy received a warning on his phone to 'stay out of Dawson family business,' and it became a little clearer. And now, here we are. Clearly, the people who have Hank are not afraid to inflict severe damage or even death."

Aleesha gasped. This wasn't like the movies or Carolyn's books. Real people—Hank!—could get hurt or worse.

"Now you're starting to scare me," Carolyn responded to Wendi's pronouncement.

"And me!" Aleesha added, a definite tinge of hysteria creeping into her voice.

Jimmy had only thought about Hank as Carolyn's son and almost completely forgot that Hank was also Aleesha's husband. But The Man was threatening to use Hank as a tool for vengeance.

Suddenly, Jimmy felt like someone had cracked him over the head with a 2x4. *The Man!* Aleesha's father, a man with a vendetta, wasn't just 'a man,' he was The Man. The phrase 'unable to see the forest for the trees' came to his mind. He hadn't put two and two together. Maybe he was too close to the situation to objectively analyze it.

They were talking about Aleesha's father, Doyle Abaddon, a man with two daughters twenty years apart by different women. Put that together with the text warning Jimmy to stay out of the Dawson family business and this new note about balancing the scales—Hank's life for Kaycie's, Jimmy was sure—it all pointed to Doyle Abaddon being The Man. Jimmy was sure, wasn't he? But what to do with the information?

Jimmy wondered if Wendi was pulling the threads together and arriving at the same picture. If so, she wasn't giving anything away by her facial expression. *Never play cards with her,* he thought.

What about Aleesha, though? She hadn't given any sign that she knew her dad was an evil mastermind. Maybe she was in denial or too close to see what Jimmy thought was in plain view. But he hadn't seen it right away, either. On the other hand, Aleesha didn't really know her father.

It was nearly thirty years since Abaddon had abandoned Aleesha and her mother. She said she had tried to reconcile with him recently, but Jimmy didn't know whether it was in person or over the phone. Whatever the circumstances, Jimmy was confident the guy was not a candidate for Father of the Year.

Jimmy decided he wouldn't be the one to tell her about her old man, not yet, anyway. Maybe she would figure it out for herself. He would bet Wendi knew but wasn't saying anything. And Carolyn, with all of her experience writing crime fiction, would probably piece things together at lightning speed. Assuming she hadn't already.

Jimmy wondered what it must be like to go through life not seeing conspiracies and schemes at every turn or believing people were basically good. He had seen too much to live that way. Everyone had a past they'd like to keep private, including Jimmy.

He stepped back, simultaneously pulling his cell phone from his pocket. "I'm going to make a call before we move out." Wendi looked at him, and he mouthed, "Pepé."

He walked about ten feet away from the group and hit the speed dial for his partner. He noticed that Wendi had gone about the same distance in the opposite direction. He didn't have time right now to analyze her actions. He just hoped Pepé would pick up.

Unfortunately, Jimmy's call got dumped into voicemail. He was frustrated, but he left a message.

"Pepé, call me as soon as you get this. I need your help. The .38 caliber kind. Maybe larger. *Probably* larger and longer. We're about to head to the Old Chester Graveyard. I'd really love to have you join us for the party. *Really.*"

He walked back to where Carolyn and Aleesha stood back to back, neither speaking. Wendi turned and joined them. She was slipping her cell phone into her pocket as she came.

"Two vehicles?" Wendi asked. Jimmy nodded.

"I'll lead; Carolyn will ride with me," Jimmy replied. "You and Aleesha follow. Let's go get Hank back."

Chapter 18

T HE SUN WAS kissing the far horizon when they reached the intersection in Yulee where Chester Road met Highways A1A and 200. Jimmy hung a right, sneaking through a yellow light, and started down Chester Road. The dash compass told him they were traveling due north. He'd been partway up this road before, but Carolyn told him he'd need to go almost to the end of Chester Road before making another turn.

They quickly left the mattress shops, grocery stores, and fast food places behind. Those were replaced by apartment buildings and single-family dwellings, aka houses. Most of the residences were on the right, while the left side of the road was taken up primarily by pine trees. Jimmy wondered if it was because the trees blocked the setting sun from shining directly into the houses or because a lot of bad weather came from the west, and the trees acted as a windbreak. Or it was just how it was for now, and it would change someday when more apartments and houses were needed.

Most of the houses they passed were single-story affairs with carports on one end. Many had brick façades, but almost all had tall, straight, longleaf pine trees in the front yards. Longleaf pine needles—pine straw in the local vernacular—were often used for mulch. The mulch does an excellent job of keeping weeds at bay in flower beds, and it stymies the grass that vainly tries to grow beneath the tall pines. Its primary benefit is holding in moisture, but Jimmy liked the smell, too. He had come to appreciate the aroma of sunbaked pine needles during July and August's heat. When the pine needles fall, they turn a brownish-orange, and walking on them in summer heat releases their stored-up fragrance.

So far, they had been traveling in silence, but when Jimmy began to ease up on the gas, thinking they were getting close, Carolyn said, "Not yet. We've still got a ways to go before we get there." Jimmy pressed the gas pedal back down, and they continued their northward journey.

Jimmy knew their destination would be near the St. Marys River, and he had already seen a couple of signs by the side of the road advertising shrimp, "Fresh Off the Boat!" There were at least two companies back here in the woods that docked on the river and sold extra shrimp to anyone with a cell phone or Facebook.

Jimmy made a mental note to return to this area and scout out the resources after things settled down again. Everyone in this part of the South needed a reliable source of fresh shrimp. Low-country boils were quite popular and relatively easy to do. The show's star was always the fresh shrimp, and it didn't get much fresher than scooped from a bucket on the boat. Some vendors sold a cheaper, unsized option, the shrimp ranging from extra-small to extra-large, whatever came out of the nets. But Jimmy couldn't plan any seafood get-togethers right now.

Carolyn spoke again. "It's been years since I've been back here. David and I used to drive all over the area just to get out of the house. It was a cheap date."

She spoke so casually that it sounded as though she had entirely forgotten about the situation they were driving toward. The Man was threatening to kill her son.

Despite their circumstances, Jimmy smiled slightly in response to her shared memory. "Cruising" Main Street was the big thing to do on Friday and Saturday nights when he was in his teens. And if you didn't have a Main Street, or your Main Street had too much light, you went off the beaten path to find some privacy. You headed for Make-out Point, Lover's Lane, or whatever name the secluded spot was called in your area. Jimmy still had fond memories of a gravel pit on the west side of town.

He didn't know if anyone still cruised the main drags anymore or went to Lover's Lane. Probably not. Too bad. Cruising, making out, and drive-in movies were all mainstays of time-tested courtship rituals.

Jimmy pulled over when they got to Green Pine Road. There was a big sign on the corner of the lot proclaiming "Green Pine Housing Development," but all he could see was an undeveloped lot covered in pine trees with dark green needles. The name seemed appropriate.

"Why are you stopping?" Carolyn asked, her eyes turning hard and her nostrils flaring.

Jimmy pulled out his cell phone and said, "I need to see if Pepé got back to me. It'll just take a minute. Promise."

His phone showed an unread text message. It was from Pepé. It was a thumbs-up emoji and what appeared to be a green water pistol. Jimmy figured it was probably the only kind of firearm the texting software allowed. The message was clear, though. Pepé would be geared up for the "meet and greet." *If* he got there in time.

Jimmy took advantage of the brief stop to worry about Wendi and Aleesha. Wendi had turned off the highway before Chester Road, and Jimmy wasn't certain where she was.

He pulled up his phone's GPS app, zeroed in on his position with one tap, and then zoomed out. Green Pine Road was about a quarter of a mile long, cutting west to east between Chester Road and Blackrock Road like a ladder rung. He recalled seeing a sign for Blackrock Road about a half mile before the Chester Road turnoff. He figured Wendi was planning on coming in from the opposite direction. He wasn't sure which side Pepé would come from or how soon he would arrive. At the very least, the goon squad would be forced to split their attention between Jimmy in front and Wendi in the back. He didn't know how much of an advantage splitting up would give them—if any—but he was glad for any surprise they could throw at Hank's kidnappers.

Jimmy pulled back onto the road from the grassy shoulder. For a short stretch, there were trees on both sides of the road, then suddenly, it was like they were back in suburbia again, with streets and houses laid out in square blocks. Jimmy drove past a Dollar General and streets named Lee, Miller, Amy, and Chesapeake Road. Jimmy absently wondered if the names belonged to the people who built the first houses or family members of a developer. Except for Chesapeake. Someone must have had a fondness for the iconic bay area that touches Virginia, Maryland, and Delaware. Maybe the St. Marys River's tendrils reminded them of the meandering Chesapeake.

"Well?" Carolyn asked. "Did you figure anything out?" Despite her obvious displeasure at stopping, she had been quiet while Jimmy checked his messages and the map.

Jimmy kept his eyes on the road, even though it was one of the straightest he had been on for some time.

"All I know for sure is that we'll get there. I can't say who the 'we' will be. Wendi apparently took an alternate route down Blackrock Road. Pepé sent me a text indicating he'll be there, too, but I don't know when. He's coming down from St. Marys, so that'll take extra time."

"And in the meantime," Carolyn said, her tone spiked with acid, "*someone* with a misplaced grudge is holding Hank. We can only hope that's *all* they're doing with him."

Jimmy didn't know if she was holding her cards close to the vest and had figured out who the 'someone' was or if she was more focused on what was truly important: Hank's safe return.

Jimmy knew Abaddon's desire for vengeance was ninety-nine percent misplaced, but on the other hand, Jimmy had never lost a child. Both Carolyn and Abaddon shared that experience. And from everything Jimmy had seen in the last month or so, Doyle Abaddon was not a warm, fuzzy, easygoing, live-and-let-live kind of dad.

Whether the man or The Man, he was evil and manipulative, and his previous actions with Gabriel and Seth Kremer revealed his psychopathic leanings. Using the term 'dad' for him was stretching the definition to its breaking point.

Street names and subdivisions continued to fly by on each side of the road as Jimmy drove: Roses Bluff, Bristol, and Tyndale Avenue. Chester Road was lined with small neighborhoods filled with one-story houses with pine trees and oak trees in front, the same as they'd seen the whole trip.

Suddenly they came to the intersection with Blackrock Road. Jimmy had to stand on the brakes to avoid going through the junction. Carolyn's shoulder belt grabbed her and held her in her seat, even as one hand reflexively reached out toward the dash to hold herself in place. Jimmy cranked the steering wheel of his Nissan SUV to the right and immediately saw the Chester Church of God. It was bright yellow with a white spire above the front door.

Jimmy stopped in the middle of the road.

There were three connected buildings, like the Father, Son, and Holy Spirit: three in One, all painted bright yellow. The first building looked like the original church and was evidently the sanctuary. One sign near the front doors read: Chester Church of God, while another proclaimed: "Running Low On Faith? Stop In For A Fill-Up."

The three buildings formed an H. A second two-story building, roughly the same size as the sanctuary and parallel with it, formed the other side of the H, while a single-story building was perpendicular to the other two and placed in the middle, like a crossbar. Jimmy guessed the middle building was the fellowship hall, and the one on the right was probably the education building. The trinity of buildings constituted a small church 'campus,' a term no longer reserved only for large mega-churches.

"There's the cemetery," Carolyn hissed, looking out the passenger window.

Jimmy turned away from the church's bright yellow color that tried to commandeer his attention. The first thing he saw on his right was a chain-link fence erected to keep out gravestone vandals. *That simple fence does a pretty good job*, he thought without cynicism, noting that many of the gravestones were adorned with fresh flowers.

Unlike the houses they had passed on the way, Old Chester Cemetery had none of the tall, straight pines. Instead, it was filled with live oaks, all draped with Spanish moss, guaranteed to give it a spooky look and feel as soon as the sun clocked out for the day. Most of the oaks were not straight or even completely vertical, many leaning right or left, some with limbs hanging all the way to the ground. In another hundred years or so, if the trees survived another century of hurricanes, those bottommost limbs would rest their weight on the ground, helping to hold the trees upright.

Jimmy had seen some giant live oaks at the Hofwyl-Broadfield Plantation near Brunswick. Their lowest branches were as large as some younger full-grown trees and reached down to touch the ground about twenty feet out from the main trunk. The branches extended another thirty or forty feet away from the main trunk after touching the ground, like frozen-in-place octopus tentacles. They were like an above-ground support system, working in tandem with the roots underground.

The small cemetery appeared to be about 250 feet from east to west and probably 150 feet deep. The sun had completely disappeared below the horizon, but the sky still held a hint of blue and yellow overhead, a light pinkish-orange tinge visible in the west to mark the sun's departure. Beneath the spooky, moss-draped oaks in the cemetery, though, darkness already prevailed, the thick canopy of leaves and Spanish moss blocking any remaining shafts of light from reaching the ground.

Jimmy pulled off the road and over to the right, parking on the wide grassy shoulder that stretched the length of the graveyard. This was where cars parked and offloaded mourners for graveside services. He hoped there would be no mourners tonight.

Jimmy was about to tell Carolyn to stay in the car, but she was out of the vehicle before he could get his seatbelt off. Despite her age and infirmities, she walked briskly toward the chain-link fence. As Jimmy's eyes adjusted to the dim light, he noticed a gate in the middle of the fencing. Carolyn was walking toward the gate, one hand lightly resting on the fence for guidance and balance, her other holding onto her cane.

Jimmy watched a pair of headlights approach from the east. They pulled onto the grassy shoulder like Jimmy had done, facing Jimmy's car, leaving about ten feet of space in between. The car's lights went out, and Jimmy could clearly see it was Wendi's red Audi A3. The driver and passenger doors opened simultaneously as Wendi and Aleesha popped out and hurried toward Jimmy and Carolyn.

The group met at the gate, which usually only opened to allow pallbearers to convey a casket to its final destination. There was no padlock and nothing to complicate their entry into the small family graveyard, but they stood outside, waiting.

"Where are they?" Aleesha asked. "Where's Hank?" The three women turned in unison, looking to Jimmy for an answer.

"I've been trying to see some sign that they're in the cemetery, but I haven't seen anything. No lights and no shadows moving between the trees. I haven't heard any sounds coming from in there, either," Jimmy added.

Carolyn reached down, lifted the latch on the gate, and swung it open. "I'm going in," she announced.

"I am, too," Aleesha added, but her voice didn't sound nearly as firm as Carolyn's. The two women moved cautiously into the shadows, united by their personal feelings for the man supposedly being held in this old family graveyard.

Just like the note had said, the ground was soft. Carolyn looked a little unsteady until Aleesha hooked arms with her.

Jimmy looked at Wendi, shrugged, and said quietly, "In for a penny ...."

"In for a pound," she replied. Together, heads and eyes swiveling right and left, they followed the two women in front of them.

The foursome walked south to the back edge of the cemetery, the western sky to their right only marginally lighter. At the end of their short march, they reversed course, faced the church, and walked north toward the road and the gate where they had started.

They had struck out.

They'd seen no one.

No one and nothing.

Just as they were stepping through the gate, two sets of headlights suddenly appeared, one from the west and one from the east. Two large black SUVs with blacked-out windows pulled up and angled in behind Jimmy and Wendi's vehicles, cutting off any chance of them backing up. Meanwhile, a third vehicle, a black sedan with windows tinted as darkly as the others, pulled up in the middle, facing the cemetery and blocking Jimmy's and Wendi's chances of driving forward. There would be no going forward or backward until the newly arrived vehicles left.

Whatever advantage Jimmy thought they might gain by arriving from different directions was negated by the other 'team' doing the same thing. Even worse for Team Jimmy & Wendi, any chance for escape was stymied until the Mob Squad departed or allowed Jimmy and his party to leave.

The trio of black vehicles' headlights were on high and aimed directly at Jimmy and the three women. Involuntarily, the little group raised their hands to try and shield their eyes from the glare. With the lights shining in their faces, even the Chester Church of God across the road was blotted from their sight.

A voice came from the middle car, the one directly facing them. "Thanks for joining us. Sorry we couldn't offer you valet parking, but I don't think anyone will bother your vehicles."

Jimmy couldn't tell if the voice came from the front seat or the back, but the back passenger door opened a second later. Instead of someone stepping out, though, someone fell—or was shoved out, landing on the ground in a heap, making a loud "oof" sound when they landed, then laid still.

A few seconds later, though, the person on the ground groaned loudly.

It was Hank.

Chapter 19

THE HUMAN HEAP on the ground rose slowly, rising painfully and shakily to his feet. Jimmy stepped in front of Carolyn and Aleesha, his arms spread wide to prevent them from trying to rush to Hank's aid.

"We don't know what the play is yet," Jimmy hissed at them. "We have to let them tell us the rules of the game before we do something that might get us tossed out. Permanently."

Aleesha stifled a sob. Carolyn grabbed Jimmy's arm and pushed it away, but to her credit, she stayed where she was. Wendi put her arm around Aleesha.

Jimmy turned around and faced the vehicles. "This is your party," he said in a loud but even voice. "You invited us. Maybe you'd be kind enough to explain what's going on. Some introductions might be nice, too."

There was no response from any of the three vehicles, and Hank took a few unsteady steps from the car toward his would-be rescuers. The driver, dressed all in black and with shiny black dress shoes, suddenly stepped out of the vehicle that had ejected Hank. He walked over to Hank, grabbed one arm, and twisted it behind Hank's back, eliciting a loud yelp followed by a groan.

All vestiges of light in the sky were gone now, but the moon and stars weren't ready to appear. With night's black backdrop behind the cars and the ultra-bright LED headlights shining in his eyes, Jimmy couldn't make a positive ID on the driver, but he thought he looked familiar. He was probably one of the three guys who had broken into his house several weeks earlier, sent to reclaim a manuscript that had already been stolen and ransomed once.

Jimmy didn't peg the driver as The Man, mainly because Aleesha had not reacted to the driver's presence when he stepped out of the vehicle. If Aleesha's recent attempt at reconciling with her father was in person, it should have been enough for her to recognize her father's shape and demeanor, even in the dark.

Aleesha wasn't even looking at the driver. She had eyes only for Hank, who was making painful groans as the driver kept the pressure on Hank's arm. The hold was a very effective means of controlling a person. Jimmy knew that if the driver chose to, he could break Hank's arm or separate his shoulder.

"Stop it!"

Carolyn had used her mom voice, and instinctively, everyone had reacted. The driver eased up on Hank's arm temporarily. Jimmy, Wendi, and Aleesha stood a little straighter, a Pavlovian response to a mother's voice.

"Let him go!" Carolyn yelled, but the spell had already worn off. The driver reacted by lifting Hank's arm higher. Jimmy watched Carolyn's son rise on his tiptoes to escape the pressure and alleviate the pain.

Jimmy took a couple of steps forward but stopped when he heard the SUV's doors open. Shading his eyes against the LED headlights, he saw that the thug on the right was short and slim with hair that stuck straight up. Turning his head to his left to glimpse the third driver, Jimmy recognized him from the house break-in. It was definitely "the big guy" Jimmy had seen on video. Taller than any of the other thugs Jimmy had seen, he probably weighed somewhere between 250 and 275 pounds. In the break-in video, he had placed his foot against Jimmy's front door and leaned his weight against it until the latch warped, and all it took was a "gentle" shove to open the door.

Suddenly, Jimmy was roused from his musings by a voice inside the middle car. It was the same electronically distorted voice he had heard before, the same one Hillary Lyst had said called him demanding a ransom for a stolen manuscript. Jimmy was sure it was coming from the car's sound system, most assuredly connected by cell phone.

"Wheels!" the voice said. "Ease off. Let Mr. Dawson go. He's entitled to see his mother one last time, to tell her goodbye. Even though it's more than I was given."

Despite the electronic camouflage, Jimmy knew it was The Man, aka Doyle Abaddon, aka Aleesha's father. Jimmy also knew The Man was not there in person. 'Never get your hands dirty' was undoubtedly one of his mantras. By never being an eyewitness, he avoided any culpability. That was what subordinates were for. In business, they called it plausible deniability. And they were expendable, as seen in the police reports about Gabriel and Seth Kremer.

'Wheels' let go of Hank's arm and shoved him forward. Whether due to the soft, uneven ground, the unexpected shove, or from whatever physical sufferings they had inflicted on Hank before coming to the graveyard, he fell to the ground, facedown. Aleesha broke away from Wendi's grasp and was at Hank's side in three seconds. She helped him up and supported and steadied him as they walked over to where Carolyn stood behind Jimmy and to his left, all the way back to the fence around the cemetery.

Wheels smirked at the sight. Jimmy made a vow: he would wipe that smirk from Wheels' face if possible.

Carolyn pulled her sweater around herself tighter as Aleesha and Hank huddled together. Jimmy took a few steps in Wheels' direction. Wheels put a hand inside his black sport coat, and Jimmy stopped, raising his hands. Wheels slowly removed his hand from his black sport coat, his fingers wrapped around a 9-millimeter, all black – just like his outfit and heart.

Jimmy knew these goons were serious. He had seen their work before, but never with firearms. The sight of a handgun took this meeting to an entirely different level.

"We don't have to do this," Jimmy said, his voice raised to make sure The Man heard him. He suspected the car had a jacked-up sound system, and The Man should be able to hear him, probably even without Jimmy raising his voice. He was right.

"Oh, but we do have to do this, Jimmy. You know the age-old rule: an eye for an eye. The scales are unbalanced," the electronic voice emanating from the car said. "A debt has been owed to my family for many years and has finally come due."

"About that," Jimmy retorted. "In what twisted way are the scales unbalanced? The way I see it, everybody involved lost, so the scales are perfectly balanced."

The sound from the car crackled slightly with electronic static. The Man answered, "Even your accounting can't be that bad, Favreaux. How can the loss of two equal the loss of one?"

"I know about the people you're referring to. I would bet the second person on your side of the ledger just wanted to forget she had ever been with you. That puts us back at one-for-one, and that was an accident, not intentional," Jimmy replied.

"You don't know what you're talking about, Mr. Favreaux," the voice said. "That all happened while you were still trying to be the class clown in your Canadian high school, trying to get girls to laugh *with* you, not *at* you. Tell me, did you ever find one who didn't laugh at you?"

Jimmy let the taunt wash over him and roll off. His past didn't matter. Wendi was the real deal; he would do anything to convince her to stay with him. The obnoxious robot-like voice from the car kept talking.

"I take it from your silence that you did not. Pity. It seems you had to travel a long way from home to find someone who didn't know your pathetic backstory." The disembodied voice was still searching for a chink in Jimmy's armor. *And doing a pretty good job*, Jimmy thought but tried not to show it.

"Is that all you've got?" Jimmy tossed back at the car with the driver standing in front of it. "I'm comfortable in my own skin. I know I'm not handsome or athletic. I know I'm geeky. I know Wendi could do much better than me, but at least I can face her in person, not through some $9.95 voice modulator from a Radio Shack store closing sale."

No one moved, not Wheels or the other two thugs. They stood like statues. Jimmy figured they couldn't act on their own. They were like puppets, receiving their energy and instructions from the person pulling their strings.

Aleesha and Hank held onto Carolyn, their faces buried in each other's shoulders, not watching the little show playing out in front of the old cemetery. Wendi stood a couple of feet ahead and a few feet to the right. Jimmy kept her within his peripheral vision. He saw her head swivel occasionally, checking right and left, sometimes stealing a quick glance behind her toward the cemetery. Jimmy hoped she was keeping an eye peeled for Pepé and would give Jimmy some kind of a sign when and if she saw him. He guessed no one else noticed, figuring her to be nervous with thugs in front and a boneyard behind.

Meanwhile, The Man's mercenaries stood like sentinels, hands clasped in front of them near their waists, knees lightly flexed, slightly bored expressions on their faces. Except for Wheels. He still sported the smirk Jimmy had seen earlier. Jimmy wanted to remove that sneer with his fists, but not while facing a gun.

He was suddenly struck with a sudden strong sense of déjà vu. Jimmy felt like he was back on the playground in elementary school, surrounded by some bigger boys he'd made look stupid in class. Jimmy tried to stand up to them, to throw the first punch and catch them off guard long enough to run like the wind for home. But his punch was weak and off the mark and only enraged the boy he hit. All three boys piled on Jimmy, hitting and kicking him while he curled into a ball on the ground, arms looped over and around his head to protect himself from getting kicked in the temple. He had read that a blow to the temple could kill you, and he was taking it seriously.

Eventually, the playground version of the Mafia tired of pounding him and wandered off, laughing and tossing jeers over their shoulders. Jimmy huddled on the ground for a long time, partly to make sure they were not returning and partly to make sure the other kids had gone home, too. He didn't want to face anyone, friend or foe.

When he finally uncurled and rolled to his side, he suddenly felt a pair of hands touch his shoulder and arm. It was Vicky Salter, a girl his age who lived a few doors down the street from Jimmy. Jimmy flinched at her touch and curled up again, but she shushed him and said, "They're gone. You're okay. I'll walk home with you."

Jimmy uncurled again, feeling like a turtle coming out of his shell as he exposed his head and limbs again. She took a tissue from somewhere—a pocket, inside one of her books, from the ground—he didn't care. She used it to clean away some dirt and the little dribble of blood from his split lip. His nose hadn't bled, which surprised him. Everybody on

TV and in the movies in a fight always bled profusely from their nose.

Vicky, which Jimmy knew was short for Victoria after the long-dead British queen, handed him his books. She had picked them up from where he had dropped them and kept them with hers.

They didn't talk during the walk home. When they got to Jimmy's house, she unlatched the gate across the sidewalk leading to his house and pushed it open. He didn't look at her. She placed a warm hand on his shoulder, gave him a little pat, and continued to her house. Jimmy watched her go, waiting until she opened her front door and went inside. Only then did he step inside the fence around his house, close the gate, sit down on the ground, and let the tears flow freely, hot and salty, from humiliation more than pain.

Jimmy didn't want to recreate that childhood scene by facing off with the goon squad arrayed in front of their vehicles, but he knew he would if he had to.

Glancing back at Carolyn, Hank, and Aleesha, he saw they were oblivious to events happening near the cars. They were huddled together, heads together, holding each other up, the words of The Man still ringing in their ears: *'He's entitled to see his mother one last time, to tell her goodbye.'*

Jimmy knew the declaration must have shaken the little group; he couldn't blame them. But they didn't know what he knew. Or, at least, *hoped* he knew.

Suddenly, as Jimmy was staring across the dark gulf between him and Wheels, he noticed a small red dot from a laser-sight appear on the left knee of the smirking thug. Jimmy watched it slowly move shakily upward like a bug crawling up a maple tree, following a trail of sweet sap. The dot stopped about three inches below Wheel's chin. *Body mass, dead center.*

Jimmy slowly turned his head to look at Wendi. She gave a small smile and an almost imperceptible nod.

"Wheels!" Jimmy hollered loudly and sharply to get the driver's attention. He wanted the three hoodlums' attention focused on him, so he turned and took a few steps to his left without permission. Jimmy wanted to open up the middle space between him and Wendi and create a clear line of sight to the car Wheels stood next to. He hoped *someone* would take advantage of the clearing.

Just as Jimmy had anticipated, his sharp shout caused Wheels to instinctively reached toward the gun inside his jacket. When no threat manifested before him, he returned his hand to his side, but that was okay. Jimmy wanted the goons looking at him, especially Wheels. The gangster-wannabe lifted his head slightly and locked eyes with Jimmy across the grassy shoulder separating them. The hated smirk flattened slightly, looking more forced and cruel.

To their credit, the other two thugs hadn't moved, standing stiffly straight, one hand clasping the wrist of the other – the classic Secret Service pose. The Man must have been training them to make them look more intimidating or perhaps offering them more money if they looked the part of a security team.

In his black slacks, shoes, shirt, and sport coat, Wheels almost looked the part, but Jimmy recognized him as a garden-variety schoolyard bully.

And schoolyard bullies have cleaned your clock more than once! Jimmy reminded himself, thoughts of Gabriel sucker-punching him several weeks earlier springing unbidden from his memory. *Time to play!* Jimmy said to himself.

"I hope you have your life insurance paid up," Jimmy taunted the man standing across from him.

"Stand down, Wheels." The voice came from the car. "Don't let him get to you. He's all talk and no action. Just ask his girlfriend."

Jimmy felt his face grow warm and wanted more than ever to charge over and wipe the smirk from the driver's face. *But you remember how well that worked in third grade.*

"He's more man than you or any of your goons!" Wendi shouted. Jimmy felt a new flush of heat on his face and was glad it was dark outside.

"D'you need your girlfriend to fight your battles, Mr. Favreaux?" came the expected retort from the car.

Jimmy took a deep breath before answering. "Need? No. But if she doesn't mind getting her hands dirty, I'm happy to hold her purse. Who's going to hold your boys' purses? I can guarantee these mama's boys are no match for her." *She's got a wicked throat punch!* went unsaid.

Wheels slipped the 9-millimeter back into his shoulder holster and let his hands hang loose at his sides. Jimmy could tell he was spoiling for a fight. But it was the guy on Jimmy's left built like a mountain that worried him most. He, too, had dropped his Secret Service stance, arms hanging by his side, fingers as big-around as bratwursts, hands opening and closing into fists repeatedly.

The third guy was still standing his ground, though. Jimmy wanted to rattle the cages of all three.

Turning to his right, Jimmy addressed goon number three. "You're new to this little club, aren't you? I recognize these other two from the viral video of them breaking into my house, but you weren't part of that fiasco. You must be the replacement for Gabriel. Or maybe for Seth Kremer. I hope you keep your hands … or your life … longer than those two bozos did."

The young man in black to Jimmy's right got a confused look.

"Oh, didn't your new playmates tell you? If you disappoint the big boss or – heaven forbid – make him mad, you might find yourself dead by phony suicide or suddenly lacking limbs and appendages you've grown accustomed to. Isn't that right, Wheels? Right, Tiny? You boys know the rules." Jimmy looked back to his left to ensure the other two weren't advancing on him. *One last jab.* "What I find most laughable is that you two are the smart ones!"

Tiny, as Jimmy had called him, took a step forward on his size 17 feet.

Where do you find shoes to fit? Jimmy thought.

"King! Step back," Wheels said. "Stay in line."

The reply from the car was quick. Even with the electronic distortion, Jimmy could hear the anger flowing from The Man. "Kingpin! Wheels! Dimebag! Get yourselves under control. Don't let this buffoon push you off-balance."

Kingpin? Like the comic book thug? And Dimebag? Oh, I gotta know that story, Jimmy thought.

"Dimebag?" Jimmy responded, turning to the thug on his right. "I can understand Kingpin for the big guy, but why did he call you Dimebag? Let me guess, you were always trying to buy a dime bag of pot because you could never come up with more than ten dollars? Or that was how you stayed under the cops' radar – selling too little for them to bother with you?"

Jimmy couldn't see the young man's face very well because of the glare from the headlights aimed his way, but he thought he saw the would-be mafioso's face darken. Jimmy bet the man's face had reddened in embarrassment.

As Kingpin turned slightly toward Wheels, he stopped, pointing a big sausage-like finger at his partner. Kingpin had seen the red laser dot hovering over the other man's heart.

"Wheels!" he rasped out, his voice not the deep bass Jimmy expected. It was surprisingly high, with a definite tenor timbre to it.

He keeps on surprising me, Jimmy thought.

Wheels looked at Kingpin, mouthing a confused 'What?' at the larger mobster. Kingpin pointed a finger toward his own heart, then pointed back at Wheels. The driver looked down, catching a glimpse of the dot in his peripheral vision. His forehead immediately broke out in a sweat.

The smirk was gone. Now it was time for Jimmy to smile.

But then the dot disappeared. Jimmy tried to keep the thugs in sight, but he really wanted to look behind him and glimpse his partner.

In the end, Jimmy kept his eyes forward. He was glad he did. He saw Wheels go into his coat again for the handgun they'd seen just minutes before. Bad move.

From somewhere behind Jimmy and off to his right, he heard the loud report of a firearm. He had never learned how to distinguish guns by their sounds. All he knew was it was loud. Jimmy involuntarily dropped to the ground. He couldn't have stayed standing if he wanted to. The women and Hank had done the same, Aleesha letting out a high-pitched terrified squeal.

At the same time Jimmy hit the ground, he heard what sounded to him like a cannon being fired, and the side mirror on the car behind Wheels exploded into black plastic and glass shards. Wheels looked from his left to his right trying to catch sight of the gun flashes. He held the 9-mil in his hand but never returned fire.

More shots rang out in rapid succession, seemingly coming from two different places behind Jimmy. He was thankful he had stepped over to the side earlier instead of staying in the middle. Even so, he felt like he was on the wrong end of a shooting gallery as he heard the shells whistle overhead. He tucked his head further under his arms, wishing the ground was soft enough to let him dig a foxhole.

The rear driver's-side window blew out, followed in two-second intervals by the rear tire and then the front tire. Wheels crouched down, protectively covering his head with his arms, and the driver's door window exploded into a million safety-glass pebbles.

The disembodied electronic voice from the car roared one word: "GO!!"

Kingpin moved faster than Jimmy thought he could, jumping into the big SUV and slamming it into gear while Wheels jumped in the backseat. In a flash, they were chewing up the sod as their big wheels backed away from the scene. Dimebag – behind the wheel of the other black SUV – performed a mirror-image exit from the other side.

Even as the thugs fled the scene, there was another loud boom – different than the previous group – followed by the metallic clang of a large caliber slug entering the car's radiator. Behind him and to his left, Jimmy heard the unmistakable sound of a shell being racked into a shotgun. Another explosion split the air almost immediately, and the car took another slug to the engine. He heard another shell get racked home, followed by another cannon-like boom. The third slug cleanly pierced the front windshield but blew out the entire back window. The vehicle wheezed once, then fell silent, the shots to the block and motor having struck vital automotive organs, like repeated body blows taking their toll on a boxer. From Jimmy's vantage point on the ground, the front hole in the windshield was precisely where a driver's head would have been.

Almost as quickly as it had started, it was quiet again. The car the gang had abandoned was sending up clouds of steam and a diminishing fountain of antifreeze where the radiator was pierced.

Carolyn, Hank, and Aleesha were all lying on the ground ten feet behind Jimmy, pressed against the chain-link fence circling the cemetery, their eyes wide, the whites visible even in the darkness. A smoky haze spread over the cemetery from the shots fired into the car. Jimmy's ears were ringing, and he knew the others must be experiencing the same thing or worse since they were closer to the graveyard.

Jimmy was still lying on the ground, looking around from his relatively safe place. He could smell the cordite from the gunfire and the sweet smell of the antifreeze from the demolished car. Wendi, however, was already on her feet. Jimmy had seen her drop to the ground when car parts and bullets started flying, but now she was standing in the same place he had last seen her. Jimmy rose and went to her. She held her arms out like a child asking to be picked up. He wrapped his arms around her.

"Are you all right?" he asked, speaking softly into her ear.

She nodded but said nothing at first. Then she whispered, "I think there's something wrong with me."

"Were you hit?" Jimmy asked, his eyes going up and down her body looking for signs of blood.

Wendi shook her head. "No, but I think something must be wrong with me because when all the shooting and things blowing up started … it didn't … scare me. I thought it was … exciting." She tucked her chin into Jimmy's neck.

Jimmy looked over to where the car sat, the one Wheels had driven. It was still sitting in the same spot, but the windows were blown out, two tires were flat, and it was dripping antifreeze and oil.

As Jimmy gazed at the ruined car parked across the road from the Chester Church of God, Pepé walked out of the cemetery behind him. Jimmy turned when he heard Pepé hollering his name. His friend was carrying a laser-scoped Ruger Precision .338 Lapua rifle in his left hand. Pepé had shown it to Jimmy once, explaining that it was for long-range precision shooting. His other hand was empty, but Jimmy saw a Smith & Wesson .357 snugged in a hip holster.

It was the man following closely behind Pepé out of the darkness that blew Jimmy's mind: Hillary Lyst, wearing his usual black slacks and white shirt with rolled-up sleeves. But he had added something to his outfit Jimmy had never seen him wear before—a shoulder holster, the handle of a .38 caliber handgun protruding. The book publisher looked for all the world as though he had been skeet shooting or hunting quail, carrying a Benelli full-choke 12-gauge camouflage shotgun, a tiny wisp of smoke escaping the barrel.

The two men walked over to Jimmy and Wendi.

Pepé spoke first. "I got your call, brother. Sorry I didn't text you back, but you know how the cops frown on texting and driving. And I assume this is Wendi. You look a lot better in person than in the selfie Jimmy sent me."

Wendi's mouth gaped open in surprise, and she elbowed Jimmy good-naturedly before shaking hands with Pepé.

"I was glad I could respond to your call, Wendi," Hillary said to his former daughter-in-law. "You sounded adamant about your need for additional assistance. It seems you were correct in your evaluation."

Pepé jerked his head back toward the cemetery. "We parked on the far side of the graveyard and worked our way through," he said. "We both arrived about the same time. Based on your description of him, Jimmy, I figured this other fella might be your Mr. Lyst."

"Indeed," Hillary responded. "Pepé is quite intuitive and, I dare say, very handy to have in one's corner, as they say in pugilistic situations."

"You're no slouch, either, Professor," Pepé replied. Jimmy quickly glanced over to Mr. Lyst to see if the 'Professor' comment would be challenged, but his concern was greeted with a conspiratorial wink from the publisher.

Wendi moved away from Jimmy and hugged Hillary. Jimmy shook hands with Pepé and clapped him on the back. The four of them walked over to the Dawson family. Jimmy and Hank helped Carolyn rise from where she had knelt beside the fence. Jimmy introduced her to Pepé, and Hillary Lyst stepped close to the author he'd known for decades and put an arm around her shoulders. She leaned her head against his chest, one hand taking hold of his shoulder in a relieved embrace.

"I think we should all head back to your house to compare notes, Miss Carolyn," Jimmy said. "I don't think we want to be waiting around here when the cops arrive."

"Can you give two old duffers and their 'golf clubs' a ride to their cars, Jimmy?" Pepé asked.

"For you, my friends, anything, anytime, anywhere," Jimmy responded, opening the doors of his SUV and popping the hatch.

Chapter 20

Everyone gathered in the living room back at Carolyn's house. There was a brief delay while she rode up the backstairs on her chair lift. During the interlude, Aleesha distributed water bottles and some protein snacks. Jimmy opted for one labeled "Omega-3 Deluxe Mix" despite his fear of getting a mouthful of fish oil. Pepé called the snacks twigs and rocks, but he still grabbed one that proclaimed "Cranberry Health Mix."

"Would anyone like some tea?" Aleesha asked. "I know Miss Carolyn will want some."

Hillary was beginning to raise his hand in reply when Wendi said, "You don't need to do that, Aleesha. The water is fine."

Hillary slowly lowered his hand, but his face showed his disappointment.

"I just feel like I need to do something normal to feel … normal," Aleesha replied. "I don't mind making it; besides, I have to make some for Miss Carolyn."

Hillary lifted his hand again. "Only make it if *you* want to, my dear girl," Hillary responded. "But since you're offering, I would love a cup of green tea."

Jimmy winked at Pepé, who was undoubtedly wondering what his partner had dragged him into: green tea and healthy snacks? Jimmy grinned and took a long drink of cold water from the bottle Aleesha had given him.

Carolyn came into the room, joining the small crowd. She stopped briefly, looked around the room for a seat, and slowly ambled over to an empty recliner.

The author and homeowner announced, "I never sit in this chair. But people say it's quite comfortable." Having declared that she was giving up her usual spot, she allowed herself to slouch and settle in.

Jimmy didn't know if Carolyn's announcement had been her not-so-subtle way of revealing that someone was occupying the queen's throne, but once she landed in the recliner, she seemed fine. He didn't know who was sitting in Carolyn's usual spot but hoped he wasn't the culprit.

After arriving at the house, Hank left the group to clean up in the bathroom. He re-entered the room now, a look of surprise and amusement crossing his face at seeing his mother in the recliner.

He crossed to where she sat and quietly asked, "Are you all right in this chair?"

She shooed him away with a flick of her wrist. He took a slight step backward, eyed her with raised brows, then found a space on the couch and squeezed in, grabbing one of the bottles of water his wife had left on the coffee table.

Aleesha appeared about the same time, carrying a cup and saucer. She was looking at the cup and walking straight toward Pepé. She glanced up, suddenly stopped, looked around the room, and made a beeline for Miss Carolyn, placing the tea on the end table next to her.

Jimmy didn't know if anyone else noticed the sudden course correction, but he did. He could make an educated guess as to who was sitting in Carolyn's usual place.

Aleesha vanished into the kitchen again but appeared a moment later with another cup and saucer, which she set down on the coffee table in front of Mr. Lyst.

"Splendid, my dear," he responded, beaming at her with a big smile. He took her hand, held it between his, and proclaimed, "Thank you for such a kindness to an old man."

Aleesha's face lit up at the simple acknowledgment. She smiled from one ear to the other, then turned bright red and fled back into the kitchen, her safe haven.

Wendi came over and sat on the arm of Jimmy's chair.

Pepé took another snack bag and water bottle from the tray on the coffee table. He tore the snack bag open with his teeth.

Pepé turned his attention to Hillary, who was dunking his tea bag in his cup, and posed a one-word question, "Vietnam?"

Hillary kept his eyes on his tea but gave a slight nod, then deftly lifted his tea bag from his cup with a spoon, wrapped the attached string around it twice, and squeezed it into his cup. He placed the spoon and bag on the side of the saucer, set the saucer on the table, lifted the cup to his lips, blew across the liquid slightly, and took a sip. Every move was smooth, refined, and practiced, the result of drinking several cups every day.

"This is delightful, Aleesha. Thank you again," he said, his voice raised slightly in hopes that she would hear in the kitchen.

Turning back to Pepé, Hillary began the long answer to the one-word question. "It was at the war's end, and we were pulling troops out. I graduated from high school in '71, did a semester in college, and then my number got called. I suppose I could have gotten a deferment, but I chose to serve. My father had reminded me that the government would be more than happy to pay for the rest of my university education when my hitch was up. With the drawdown of troops, I figured I probably wouldn't go in-country. I guessed wrong."

The former newspaperman-turned-book-publisher took another sip of tea and smiled. But then Hillary's face turned serious again as he returned to the topic of his military service.

"In the spring of '72, I was sent in-country. We were supposed to be sending troops home, but the Paris Peace Talks had sputtered out again, and North Vietnam had launched a big offensive—the Easter Offensive—and Nixon retaliated. If I had been a regular GI grunt, I probably would have spent my time stateside cleaning latrines. My big mistake was becoming a journalist. My new job was covering the pullout. Rather ironic, don't you think? Sending people in to report on the withdrawal."

Jimmy had a hard time envisioning the older man as a young man in fatigues, covering the troop drawdown for the

Stars and Stripes or other military publications. But after seeing him emerge from the cemetery with Pepé—shotgun in hand and a .38 caliber revolver in a shoulder holster no less—Jimmy had a newfound respect for the wiry man with a love for words and books.

Hillary continued with his story.

"History books will tell you that all our troops were out by August of '72, but they neglect to mention the asterisk – like with Barry Bonds and the asterisk next to his name in the baseball history books. The entry for August of '72 says, 'The last American ground troops departed Vietnam *leaving only pilots, medical and support personnel.' It turned out that we journalists were support personnel."

"It wasn't until the *following* August that our planes finally stopped making bombing runs over Cambodia," Lyst continued. "Things quieted down considerably after that, and by the end of '74—two years later—the total US military personnel in Vietnam was *supposedly* around 50 men, along with a Marine Corps garrison attached to the US embassy in Saigon."

Pepé nodded. He was in the Navy at the end of the Vietnam War and recalled hearing the same statistics.

"Just one more crumb of information," Hillary said, setting his cup on the saucer. "I came home before the fall of Saigon in April of '75. I watched that news story unfold on television at my parents' house. I had been given the option of staying or going. I looked at the Marine Corporal who gave me the news and said, 'Buddy, good luck finishing the story without me.' I should have known better than to make a prediction like that. That Marine did not make it out. He was one of the last US casualties in Vietnam, struck by shrapnel from a North Vietnamese rocket."

Mr. Lyst picked up his cup again but just stared across it at a place on the floor, his thoughts reviewing events from fifty years ago.

After a minute, Pepé quietly said, "Welcome home, soldier."

Everyone in the room had been listening to the recollections from Mr. Lyst, the last person any of them would have suspected of being a war veteran.

Wendi nudged Jimmy and pointed at Carolyn, who appeared to have succumbed to the comfort of the recliner. Her head was down, her chin resting on her chest. She looked like she was peacefully sleeping.

Hank noticed when Wendi pointed at Carolyn, and turned to look. He smiled briefly, then gave Aleesha a nudge and chinned in Carolyn's direction.

Unlike Wendi, Jimmy, and Hank, Aleesha had a very different reaction to the sight of the family matriarch slumbering in the recliner.

Aleesha quickly jumped up and nearly ran across the room. She looked down at her mother-in-law and turned back toward Hank. "Call 9-1-1, Hank. I think your mother has died!"

Everyone leaped out of their seats and gathered around Aleesha as she picked up Carolyn's wrist and checked for a pulse. Finding no beat, she checked Carolyn's neck, feeling for a pulse in the carotid artery, but there was nothing. Aleesha looked at Hank, her eyes wide.

"Hank?" she said, a hint of panic creeping into her voice. "Do you want me to try CPR? I don't think it'll do any good, but I'll try if you ask me." Without waiting for his answer, she pushed the chair back until the older woman was fully reclined. Aleesha placed her hands on Carolyn's chest, poised over her and ready to begin chest compressions on her mother-in-law. Hank reached out and put a hand on Aleesha's arm.

"No. Don't," Hank replied. "Let her go. She knew this was coming. *We* knew it was coming. It was only a matter of time. Her breathing was getting worse, and she told me she felt like she wasn't getting enough oxygen – even in her machine. So, no, just let her be. She was tired of fighting. Now she can rest. I'll call 9-1-1."

Everyone but Hank and Aleesha went into the kitchen, giving Hank some final moments with his mother even as he pushed the three digits on his phone to call emergency services.

After the 9-1-1 operator answered, Hank told her that his mother had passed, but it was an expected death, there was a nurse present, and there was no emergency. He listened to the operator for a few moments, giving short answers to her questions. When he hung up, he asked Aleesha to get the Do Not Resuscitate order his mother had filled out several years before. While Aleesha went to his mother's bedroom for the DNR, Hank stood beside his mother's body, tenderly holding her hand as she lay in the recliner. The stress on her face had departed, and there was almost a hint of a smile. She looked at peace. Hank bent down and lovingly kissed her forehead.

He was still holding her hand when the flashing lights of the ambulance illuminated the night outside the windows.

*

The EMTs arrived about fifteen minutes after the 9-1-1 call, accompanied by a sheriff's deputy in a separate vehicle. The medical personnel checked for a pulse and respiration, but it was a mere formality. Carolyn had probably been gone for nearly thirty minutes by the time they arrived. From their unofficial standpoint, Carolyn might have accidentally cut off her oxygen supply by sitting in the recliner. She probably felt sleepy and drifted off, letting her head hang down even more. 'Unofficially,' they suggested that her reduced lung capacity was reduced further, and she simply slowly suffocated. They said the doctors could tell Hank more after an autopsy.

One of the EMTs said he had seen it once before with a woman recovering after surgery. Lying in a bed wasn't comfortable for her, so she opted to sleep in a recliner. That was her last night. She, too, had compromised her airway and lung function and slowly suffocated.

"Not a real bad way to go, y'all," he said. "You just fall asleep and don't wake up. That's how I'd like to go."

The sheriff's deputy who responded to the call took Hank into the office to ask him a few questions. Jimmy recognized him – Grayson Parker, the same deputy who had been to Jimmy's house after the discovery of a severed hand near his mailbox. Jimmy stood and followed the deputy to the door when he finished speaking with Hank.

As the deputy stood in the doorway, watching the EMTs carrying Miss Carolyn's body down the stairs, he shook Jimmy's hand. He said, "Trouble seems to follow you around, Mr. Favreaux."

"It's Jimmy," the private investigator reminded the deputy, "and this—" he pointed toward the EMTs carrying Miss Carolyn's body down the stairs, "—was not unexpected. The woman was a polio survivor from the 1950s; she was one of the last people in the world to still use an iron lung. From what I understand from her son and daughter-in-law, she's been slowly going downhill for a while."

"I got the same information from them, too," Deputy Parker replied. He motioned Jimmy to come closer.

In a voice soft enough that only the two of them could hear, he asked Jimmy, "You wouldn't know anything about a shot-up car out by the Old Chester Cemetery, would you? You being a private investigator and all."

"Does this group look like it would be involved in something violent like that?" Jimmy replied.

The deputy gazed at all the people standing in the living room, their median age somewhere north of fifty.

"No, I suppose not. I know the Lysts and the Dawsons – I've even read some of the Steele Detective Agency books. I don't know the other gentleman, and I haven't known you very long, but in the short time since I met you, it seems like you are always nearby when things happen," the deputy said.

GP looked around and motioned Jimmy to step into the office. Once inside, Jimmy slid the pocket door closed.

"Remember we identified those hands as belonging to Seth Kremer?" he asked Jimmy, who nodded.

"His body was found on the shore over by Fort Clinch. He'd been in the water for a few days. Nice clean hole in the middle of his forehead. The medical examiner said probably a 9-mil, but that's not his area of expertise. He said the hands were removed post-mortem, so Mr. Kremer was already beyond caring when they were taken. Why would someone shoot a guy and then cut off his hands?"

Jimmy shrugged, then said, "Strictly hypothetically, perhaps he offended someone, resulting in the bullet to the head. Then waste-not, want-not set in, and the hands were removed to send a message to someone. Strictly hypothetically, of course."

"Uh, huh," Deputy Parker replied. "You know, if it's all right with you, I'd like to go at least a week without seeing you. Strictly hypothetically, of course." Deputy Parker touched the brim of his hat in a friendly salute, slipped out of the office, and descended the staircase.

The sheriff's cruiser and the ambulance drove away, their lights reflecting high in the trees as Miss Carolyn left her home on Piney Island one last time. Jimmy closed the door to the stairway and walked back into the living room.

Aleesha was sitting next to Hank, one arm around his waist. Wendi and Jimmy were sitting together next to them on the couch, and Pepé and Hillary occupied the side chairs. No one was sitting in the recliner where Miss Carolyn had chosen to sit rather than force a guest out of "her" chair. No one was talking, and the feeling in the room was somber.

Hillary stood, assuming the mantel of the elderly leader. "This has been a terribly difficult evening," he said, "and we want you to know you have our complete sympathies, Hank and Aleesha. I have known your mother since she wrote her first Steele Detective Agency book in what, 1987? Thirty-five years ago. She helped Lyst Publishing stay afloat many times and vice versa. We became a substitute family—no, an *extended* family for you, Hank. But you know all this. I'm not telling you anything new. I only mention it to bring everyone else here up to speed."

Hank nodded mutely, and Aleesha dabbed her eyes with a tissue.

"Carolyn Dawson was very pragmatic," Mr. Lyst continued. "She faced death at a young age, and it has been her steady companion ever since. It was always lurking around the edges, watching her, waiting for such a time as today. I trust that when death took her, he took her hand in his and welcomed her gently."

Jimmy leaned over and whispered in Wendi's ear, "Isn't that an old Twilight Zone episode with a young Robert Redford?" She responded by giving Jimmy a quick head butt with the side of her head. It was enough to make him behave.

They heard a rumble of thunder outside, followed by the rhythmic patter of rain on the roof.

"Aww," Aleesha said. "The angels are crying for her."

Pepé caught Jimmy's attention and rolled his eyes but kept his theological thoughts to himself. Jimmy grinned at him and stood up. He addressed the group.

"We got lucky at the cemetery tonight. That meeting could have ended badly in many different ways. People could have been shot or hit with shrapnel from exploding car parts," he shared with the gathering, feeling a little like a coach in the locker room at halftime. "We got lucky, and we brought Hank back. No, scratch that. It wasn't luck. Pepé and Hillary caught the goon squad off-guard through a combination of stealth and expertise. That advantage is now gone. These thugs know we can bring deadly force against them."

"Can you explain what this is all about since I'm the one they wanted to kill today?" Hank asked sternly.

"That's a valid request," Jimmy answered, "and you have a right to know. Absolutely. I just don't know if it's still a possibility."

"Why? Because we shot up a car?" Hank asked, a scowl crossing his face.

"No, because your mother died," Jimmy replied. "When the man behind this mess hears about her death, he might be willing to call off this misguided vendetta. If all he wants is for someone in this family to feel another permanent loss … well, that has happened tonight, and in spades. But if he wants to play the avenging angel and mete out punishment, there's a good chance we'll be looking at another Shootout at the OK Cemetery. His animosity should not be with you and Aleesha but with the previous generation. You were a teenager, and Aleesha wasn't even born when everything happened."

Jimmy thought of the old Mel Gibson movie, *Road Warrior*, and the scene where the leader says, "If you had a contract, it was with him, and it died with him." The Man wanted to hurt Carolyn, but the target of his venomous retribution had died. He couldn't touch her anymore.

"I get all that," Hank said, sounding a little testy. "But what gives this guy the right to try to kill me? What gives him permission to exact his perverted sense of vengeance against me? I don't even know who he is, so how can I know if I've ever done anything to him?"

Wendi tugged at Jimmy's hand, and he sat down. She stood and assumed the leader's spot to address the group. "It's not you, Hank. Trust me, you didn't do anything. I doubt you've ever met the person behind this. But it stems from something that happened thirty-nine years ago – the day you lost your dad."

"What are you talking about?" Hank said, sitting up straighter on the couch. Aleesha tried to put her arm around him again, but he shrugged it off. "What does my dad's death have to do with this?"

"What do you remember about that day, Hank?" Wendi asked.

"I remember everything about that day," Hank answered. "Almost forty years later, and I still dream about it sometimes. In my dream, I'm sixteen again and driving home from town when a sheriff's deputy pulls me over. He says there's been an accident and I need to ride with him. I figured it was something with Mom. I've lived almost my whole life wondering when she was going to die. And now …" He took a breath, dragged a hand across his face, and leaned forward, his forearms on his knees as he continued.

"I had been to town, dropping Dad off at the airport. He was going to take a new potential student on a flight over to the Okefenokee Swamp and back. It was kind of a big deal for me, too, because I had just gotten my license, and he was letting me drive the car home alone. He wanted me to drive back and pick him up again when he got back from the flight."

"Did you know the girl he was taking on the flight?" Wendi asked.

Hank suddenly looked very uncomfortable. His face flushed, and he stood up and grabbed a water bottle from the table.

"Did you know the girl, Hank?" Wendi asked again, watching him, confused by his physical reaction.

"Kaycie Abaddon. Yeah, I knew her. We even went out a couple of times during her senior year. I was only a sophomore, but she said I was more fun than a lot of the other guys. They were always trying to … you know. What teenage guys always try to do."

Aleesha was leaning back and away from Hank, an astonished look on her face as she stared at him.

"You went out with Kaycie? My half-sister?" she asked.

Hank's face turned more crimson, and he rubbed the back of his neck with one hand.

"Yeah, I guess so. But Kaycie wasn't your half-sister then. Remember? You weren't born yet!" Hank answered.

"But you never told me," she replied, her brows furrowing as she rose from the couch to face him.

"I honestly had no idea she was your half-sister until today," Hank continued, trying vainly to explain. "Are you going to hold me responsible for everything I ever did before I met you? How about dreams, too?"

"You've been dreaming about Kaycie, too?" Aleesha asked, taking a few steps to the left to put some distance between them.

"No! I just mean, I can't be held liable for having a life before you, can I?"

Wendi stepped in to try and mediate. "Hank's got a point, Aleesha. He was over fifty when he met you. Hank didn't even know there would *be* a you in his life. He didn't know the two of you would get married. In fact, he waited all those years for you, even though he didn't know who it was he was waiting for. I think it's sweet. Don't you think it's romantic?"

Jimmy saw the fire extinguish in Aleesha's eyes. He looked around the room and saw Hillary and Pepé smiling, their heads nodding slightly. They were guys who had been married a long time and knew how hard staying married could be. Marriages that stood the test of time were based on 'til death us do part.' It took work. It was about serving each other, not seeing how much you could take from your spouse.

Jimmy gave Hank and Aleesha thirty seconds to look into each other's eyes and fall in love again before he brought the group back to earth. He took his place next to Wendi. It felt comfortable; it felt right.

"Hank, do you know who Kaycie's father is?" Jimmy asked.

"As far as I know, I've never met him," Hank answered. "Kaycie told me he wasn't around much when she was growing up. I don't know if she meant he traveled for work like my dad did, or if he didn't get along with her mother, or what exactly she meant. All I know is she didn't talk about him. So, as far as I know, I've never met him, and I couldn't tell you if he's alive or dead."

"His name is Doyle Abaddon," Wendi interjected. "And he's also Aleesha's father, but by a different mother. Aleesha and Kaycie are… or were, half-sisters."

Hank started to say something in reply, but Wendi held up a hand to stop him.

"Yes, even though there's more than twenty years difference between them. Jimmy had trouble with that, too. Kaycie would have been 23 when Aleesha was born," Wendi explained.

"My mom must have been about the same age as Kaycie. I wonder if they knew each other," Aleesha said, mostly to herself.

"What was or is her name?" Hillary asked Aleesha.

"Was," she replied. "Her name was Sonja Mortel. She was 22 when I was born." Aleesha looked at Hank, who was staring at her.

"What?" she asked. "Why are you staring at me?"

"Your m-mom was *Sonja* Mortel?" Hank stammered. "I knew her name was Mortel, but I didn't realize it was Sonja. She was between Kaycie and me in school. I kind of knew who she was, but I never talked to her or went out with her. And now I'm glad because that would be too weird, going out with your wife's mother—your future mother-in-law—when you were in high school!"

Chapter 21

THOUGHTS RAN FAST and furious through Jimmy's head, offbeat as usual. Jimmy decided to go out on a limb and share his thought that it sounded kind of like the Mortels and Abaddons.

"I think there was a Kevin Costner movie where a guy goes out with a girl, her mother, and her grandmother," he blurted out.

"*Rumor Has It*," Pepé volunteered. "It's from 2005 with Jennifer Aniston, Kevin Costner, and Shirley MacLaine. Sarah (played by Jennifer Aniston) hears some gossip that "*The Graduate*" (both the book and the movie) is based on her family."

Jimmy looked at his partner with his mouth open.

"What? Why are you looking at me that way? Gwynn likes those movies. You know that," Pepé explained. Turning to Hillary, Pepé clarified, "Gwynn is my wife. She likes romantic comedies. It doesn't matter if they're old or new. She loves Cary Grant and Kevin Costner equally."

"Thank you, Roger Ebert," Jimmy responded. "I was just thinking about the fact that Hank dated his wife's half-sister and almost dated her mom. But even more, I think we need to talk about the guy who wants Hank dead: The Man. Now that Carolyn has passed, does Doyle Abaddon still want Hank dead? He got his quid pro quo, his eye for an eye, you know? Does it matter that it happened without him pulling the virtual trigger?"

"In my experience, guys that are so fixed on a vendetta that they're willing to wait forty years for the opportunity are not well-balanced, you know?" Pepé replied.

"So you think he's still going to come gunning for Hank, literally and figuratively? If so, I'd lay money down that we'll see his Three Stooges again since The Man never gets his hands dirty. They may have underestimated us the first time," Jimmy answered, "but I doubt they will again."

Wendi and Mr. Lyst edged closer to Jimmy and Pepé. Jimmy knew it wasn't just to hear better – they were going to weigh in on the situation. He realized that he was okay with that.

In the month Jimmy had known them, they had never steered him wrong or left him to face the heat alone. Along the way, he fell in love with one of them and discovered he could trust the other with his life.

"What do you two think?" Jimmy asked, turning to Wendi and Hillary, making an opening to allow their inclusion. Pepé hadn't interacted with the Lysts very much, but he trusted Jimmy's instincts. Even so, he waited to see what their answers were.

"Hillary?" Wendi said, acceding to her boss and former father-in-law.

Just as Jimmy anticipated, Mr. Lyst stroked his white goatee, removed his glasses, pulled a handkerchief from his coat pocket, and cleaned the lenses before putting the glasses back in place. Then, after clearing his throat, he began explaining his feelings on the matter.

"People like this man you're dealing with never give up and never accept compromises. If it's a vendetta he's seeking to fulfill, he won't let anything stop him from completing it." Hillary paused for dramatic effect and made eye contact with all the players before continuing.

"There is only one way to deal with a person like that. If they won't see reason, they need to be put down before they cause more death and destruction. Our country has made deals with insane dictators too often, almost since our country's inception. More recently, our government has finally seen the wisdom in removing some of those dictators from power, directly or indirectly. The CIA has a long history of backstreet meddling, and these days, we use our special forces to clean up politicians' messes. Think of Saddam Hussein and Osama bin Laden. I'm afraid this situation bears similarities. We should try negotiation and diplomacy with The Man first, but he has already shown us that he isn't afraid to employ deadly force."

Jimmy looked at Pepé, but Hillary added a footnote before anyone could respond to what he had said.

"The details of the end of the Vietnam War are still etched indelibly in my mind. On April 30, 1975, the last few Americans still in South Vietnam were airlifted out of the country. At the same time the HELOs lifted off, Saigon fell to communist forces. North Vietnamese Colonel Bui Tin, accepting the surrender of South Vietnam later that day, remarked, 'You have nothing to fear; between Vietnamese, there are no victors and no vanquished. Only the Americans have been defeated.' After decades of fighting and thousands of lives lost, our sacrifices made no difference."

Pepé stepped in to add his two cents.

"Sometimes, you have to put down the wild dog that's been killing your chickens. If you say, 'he's only doing what comes naturally,' soon you'll have no chicken for your table." Pepé looked directly at Hillary, and in a soft but firm voice, said, "We could have won that war, and we should have."

Hillary's eyes glistened behind his glasses, and he clasped arms with Pepé. "And I believe we can win this one, too," Hillary added.

Jimmy realized Hillary and Pepé shared a bond that didn't require months or years to develop. Springing from their shared experiences came an innate knowledge that they were on the same 'team' and could trust each other. Jimmy was glad for their unspoken decision to include Wendi, Hank, Aleesha, and himself in the mission, and he knew the four of them were already under the older, well-trained men's protection.

Jimmy spoke. "So, we're agreed that we need to remove the threat and end this man's vendetta chasing?"

Pepé nodded and added, "But as someone who has taken an oath to keep the peace and has never violated or abandoned that oath, we need to play by the rules, whether our opponents do or not. That's the only reason the three thugs who took Hank are alive tonight. I could have taken all three out before they ever realized something was happening. But as a former peace officer, my oath binds me to a promise to react whenever possible, not striking first unless deadly force is about to be employed against a life I have been charged to protect. I will also respond in kind whenever deadly force is brought to bear."

Jimmy hadn't often heard Pepé make such an impassioned or lengthy speech in all the years he had known him. Mr. Lyst, on the other hand, usually took a paragraph to ask for a cup of tea.

Jimmy replied, "So, to be clear, at what point do we involve the local law enforcement? Before, during, or after all the festivities?"

Pepé looked at Lyst and winked. "I don't think we need to add to their workload, do you, Professor? I think we can bag up the trash and drop it off, so all they have to do is take it to the curb, right?"

Hillary grinned back and said, "Indeed. Excellent use of a metaphor, my friend, inferring that the criminal element is on the same level as rubbish from a five-year-old's birthday party."

Pepé looked at Jimmy, raised his eyebrows, and shrugged. *Close enough.*

*

It was decided that the Dawson group – an unofficial name but the one Jimmy was using in his head – would get together again for an unofficial war council after Carolyn

Dawson's memorial service. Until then, they would lay low and concentrate on caring for their group.

Hank announced to the group that his mother's memorial service would be in four days.

"Are you sure that's enough time?" Wendi asked.

"I agree with Wendi," Hillary added. "You want to allow an adequate period for travel arrangements by family members who live a significant distance away,"

Hank assured everyone that very little of his extended family was left, and those were on the opposite coast in California. He said he had never met any of his relatives from the West Coast, and none of them had ever made the long journey east. Even when his travels for his mother's books took him west, any shoestring relatives remaining failed to avail themselves of his close proximity. Not that his itinerary allowed for a lot of sightseeing between book-signing engagements.

Sometimes Hank flew into a major hub, grabbed his rental car, and spent every other day driving to reach the next site on his tour. Sometimes he finished a signing engagement by midafternoon and then drove until after dark to be in the next town for the following day's 'festivities.' It was not the glamorous life many of Carolyn's readers imagined.

Hank and Aleesha would see to the basic funeral arrangements, but Hillary and Wendi would provide extra support and guidance. The publishing duo's personal experiences with grief were still reasonably fresh from three years earlier when Hillary lost his wife and son – Wendi's ex-husband (*or nearly ex*). Being able to rely on the Lysts' guidance was like being given a basic outline—you just needed to fill in the blanks.

Hillary offered to provide a short eulogy, which Hank and Aleesha accepted. After all, only Hank had known Carolyn longer. Wendi would help ensure all the details were handled promptly and efficiently. She also volunteered to provide a large publicity poster they kept at the office for her rare personal appearances.

While Hank managed most of their engagements, Carolyn did occasional local reading clubs and writers' round tables at the county library.

They told the group that Carolyn had stipulated that she be cremated. Cremation removed the urgency of planning a memorial. It could be in four days or four months. Hank would need to make that call himself as her next of kin.

Jimmy felt a little bit excluded, but he didn't mind. Funerals were not high on his list of not-to-miss events. Hillary was guiding Hank and Aleesha, and Wendi was essentially overseeing all the details, leaving Jimmy free to concentrate on the next potential meeting with The Man's Goon Squad.

Pepé had called Gwynn so she wouldn't worry when he didn't arrive home until later that night, and Aleesha and Wendi were talking in the kitchen. After Pepé checked in with Gwynn, he and Hillary resumed comparing notes and old scars in the living room.

Hank came out of the bathroom, and Jimmy noticed he had cleaned up some more. His face didn't look nearly as rough as it had immediately after the Gang of Three had used him for a hacky sack. Jimmy saw Hank glance around the room before heading for the door leading downstairs to the garage. Jimmy followed and caught up with him halfway down the stairs.

"I – uh, I mean … are you going out for a little fresh air?" Jimmy asked.

Hank turned around on the stairs and looked back at Jimmy. "Yeah," he replied. "It's been a big day. I kinda wanted to step out and regroup, if you know what I mean." Hank turned back around and continued down the steps. Jimmy waited a moment and then followed.

"I hope you don't mind if I come along," Jimmy said.

"Nah. Just don't expect me to talk up a storm. Not feeling super talkative," Hank answered. They walked through the garage area and out into the open.

It was pitch black outside, which slightly surprised Jimmy. They'd been inside for hours, and he had lost track of the time. He looked at his watch and saw that it was after 10:30. When he looked at the sky overhead, he could just make out the dark tree branches silhouetted against the marginally lighter sky. Gazing upward, Jimmy's eyes eventually adjusted to the lack of light, and the sky above the trees seemed to fill with stars.

"No moon tonight," Jimmy observed.

Hank grunted noncommittally.

They walked over to the vehicles parked outside the garage's confines. Hank's car was still parked in the driveway where it had been when they discovered his disappearance late that afternoon. He hadn't been able to park it under the house in the garage because Jimmy and Wendi's vehicles were blocking the entry.

The two men leaned back against Wendi's car and looked up at the night sky. Jimmy wasn't sure what to say, so he kept his silly remarks and usual icebreakers bottled up.

For his part, Hank was just as quiet.

After a while, Jimmy softly said, "I am truly sorry about your mom, Hank."

"Yeah," Hank answered, but it came out, "Yeeaahh," half whisper and half deflating balloon.

After a few more minutes of silence, Jimmy said, "My mom passed away about five years ago up in Canada. I haven't been back since the funeral. I wasn't there when it happened, either."

"Hmmm. Uh-huh," was all Hank said.

Jimmy decided to walk around the perimeter of the property, or at least the developed part, and then go back inside.

"I'm, uh, gonna take a little walk," Jimmy said.

He was about to say goodbye when Hank asked, "Do you mind having a little company? I know I'm not very talkative, but it helps to be around someone else anyway."

"Hey, no, that's fine," Jimmy replied. "This way, if I fall in a hole or step in some quicksand or a bear gets me, you can help. Or go get help."

Hank gave a little chuckle. "You're one screwy fella, you know that?"

"I've heard worse," Jimmy answered, "from family, friends, and clients."

They walked in silence for a bit. They got near the marsh side of the lot, and Hank said, "Better stop here, or your feet'll get wet. You might even find some of that quicksand you mentioned."

"Really?" Jimmy replied, instantly stopping in his tracks.

"No," Hank replied lightly. Jimmy thought it was a good sign.

"When I was growing up," Jimmy said, "I always thought quicksand would be a much bigger problem than it is. It was a huge threat on TV shows when I was a kid, though. Someone was always stepping in it, and they'd be up to their chins before anyone could get a rope to them and tie it to the horn of a horse's saddle or around a tree to winch the person out. I can honestly say I have never, ever seen quicksand."

Hank didn't say anything, so Jimmy shut up. After a couple of minutes, he heard Hank sniffling. Jimmy stayed quiet.

"I'm sure gonna miss that old gal," Hank finally said.

"Yes, you will," Jimmy answered. "But that's okay. The missing helps you remember them."

"I suppose so."

"Tell me about your dad, Hank."

"What's to tell? Navy pilot. Got transferred from California to Mayport after he and Mom got married. Because of her health and a baby boy at home, they said they wouldn't send him to Vietnam. So, he finished his hitch and became an architect. He built this house. It's the only home I've known. He died when I was sixteen. Since then, it's just been me and Mom. Until Aleesha."

"You do have a way of boiling things down to the basics, don't you, Hank?"

"Mom's the one with the gift of putting words together, you know? Or was."

"Yeeaahh." This time it was Jimmy.

They fell silent again, standing in the cool dark night.

You could easily forget what season it was when all you had were hot and not hot. The longer Jimmy lived here, though, the more his blood thinned out, and it seemed like the winters were becoming colder and lasting longer. The night was chilly, and the frogs were already bedded down for winter. It was almost Thanksgiving.

It was hard to believe the coast had been the recipient of a hurricane just a few days earlier, uncharacteristically late in the season. People kept saying how lucky they were because the hurricane had made landfall south of them and weakened to a tropical storm before passing by Fernandina.

Lucky, Jimmy thought. Not so fortunate for the people down the coast who lost houses, roads, and beaches to the two late-season storms that gave Florida a double whammy – Hurricane Ian and Hurricane Nicole.

"You said earlier that you went out with Kaycie Abaddon in high school," Jimmy said.

"So?"

"So, I'm just wondering how you never managed to put that together with Aleesha. I know her maiden name was Mortel, but she must have mentioned her dad's name at some point, especially recently when he was looking to reconnect with her. Didn't she?"

"Let me ask you a question, Mr. Investigator. I know you and Wendi aren't married, but have you told her everything about your past? Anything you're holding back?"

Jimmy was surprised by the sudden turn in the conversation. His thoughts immediately went to a couple of days ago when The Man had called, and Jimmy had lied and told Wendi it was his mom. But he had already confessed that.

Of course, she had never asked him about his years in Canada or Minnesota, but he was sure he could be—would be!—upfront with her about that period in his life. Besides, when people get too hung up on the past, it can have a detrimental effect on their future. Not that he wanted to keep secrets from Wendi, but everyone has embarrassing moments they would just as soon forget.

"I haven't known Wendi long enough to get hung up on her past," Jimmy replied. "But if and when we do get serious, we'll deal with it – my past and hers."

How did I end up on the receiving end of an interrogation? he wondered.

"Well, maybe Aleesha and I never looked through our old Fernandina Beach High School yearbooks to see if we had any crossover. Why would we? I'm twenty years older than she is."

"That's what happens when you rob the cradle," Jimmy replied. They were both mute for a couple of heartbeats.

"You're also not answering my question, Hank. You must have known Aleesha's father's name, and it must have rung some bells for you because of Kaycie," Jimmy pressed, wishing he could see Hank's face.

"Okay, fine. Yes, when we got married, I saw what name she put down on the license application for her parents, and I *wondered* about it, but I didn't spend a lot of time thinking about it. Names are just names. I can't tell you how many times I have met people named Dawson while doing book tours, and they always wonder if we're related, but we never are."

"But Abaddon is rather an unusual name. I wouldn't expect you've run into very many people with that name, have you?"

Hank was quiet for a second before giving in grudgingly.

"No, I haven't. But Aleesha's father's name on the license application didn't have to be Kaycie's dad. It could have been a cousin, a son, or no relation at all. There was no reason for me to be suspicious."

"That's true," Jimmy conceded. He had his own secret about names. No one in this part of the world knew that his birth name was Martin James Favreaux, not James Martin Favreaux. He had started using Jimmy after he left Winnipeg. After he was *asked* to leave Winnipeg, that is.

"But when she told me about her dad trying to reconnect a few weeks ago, and I heard his name again, it made me think about Kaycie and my dad and the crash. And I remembered something I hadn't thought about for years. Something my mother never knew. Only a small handful of first responders and I know about it."

Jimmy waited in the dark, listening to Hank's breathing get a little ragged, like he was getting mad ... or sad, but then he continued explaining.

"When they brought up the bodies from the plane crash, I was there with the two divers and the sheriff on the search and rescue boat. They never said anything about what I saw, and I never said anything to them. I don't even know if they thought anything of it because car wrecks and other violent crashes can do crazy things to the people involved. But when they brought up Kaycie's body, her shirt was off, completely off. I had seen her that day, and she was wearing a pullover shirt. I could see how a crash might tear buttons off or rip open a shirt but not drag a pullover shirt entirely off. You'd expect it to get stuck around the head."

Jimmy stood under the trees and looked out toward the river that he knew was out there but was rendered invisible by the dark. He said nothing.

"I never said anything to my mom about it, and I'm only telling you because mom's not here to get hurt by it," Hank said, sniffling before continuing.

"I think my dad was trying to mess around with Kaycie while they were flying, which could be why they crashed."

Chapter 22

JIMMY STARED INTO the darkness toward the spot where he knew Hank was standing. He couldn't see him or his facial expression, but he knew he was there. He didn't know if Hank had better night vision than he did, but if he did, he could see Jimmy's mouth hanging open and his eye wide in surprise.

If David Dawson was trying to 'mess around' with Kaycie while giving her an inaugural flight, that would unquestionably be a potential cause for the crash. But Jimmy wasn't even sure that could happen in a small two-seater prop plane. *Did little puddle jumpers have automatic pilots?* He'd have to check with a friend in St. Marys.

"What kind of plane did your dad have, Hank?"

"It was a Cessna 152. He said it was the best small plane for flight training and personal use. He got it for both."

If a small plane could be outfitted with an autopilot, then David Dawson could have used his Cessna as an airborne pied-à-terre *(a fancy French word for a love nest)* for an amorous encounter. Not that there was room to walk around—there's barely room to sit in those planes—but where there's a will, there's a way. After all, people have been making cars into no-tell motels for over seventy years, maybe ever since the invention of the mass-produced automobile.

"Do you know if the plane was outfitted with an autopilot?"

There was a brief silence before Hank answered.

"Yeah. There was. I remember once when Dad took me up. He freaked me out. He kept taking his hands off the yoke – the steering wheel – and turning sideways in his seat to talk to me. I would get nervous, and Dad would laugh and say we were a long way above the ground. He said he'd have plenty of time to get it under control. *That* didn't make me feel any better. I just figured it meant we had more time to build up speed before we crashed into the ground. Finally, he confessed that he had engaged the autopilot. It couldn't steer, but it kept the plane at a level altitude. Once I understood, I relaxed."

More good information. Jimmy was putting puzzle pieces together in his mind, and a picture was starting to take shape.

"Earlier, you said when you went out with Kaycie, she told you the other guys were always 'trying stuff,' didn't you?"

"Yeah. Kaycie said she felt like she had a night off when she was out with me."

"A night off?" Jimmy asked.

"From having to fight them off, I always figured. Years later, it occurred to me that Kaycie may have been giving me a signal that I should be making my move. But when you're sixteen, you don't know anything about anything. At the time, I took it as a compliment."

Jimmy had similar memories from high school but chose not to dwell on them. Earlier, when they were at the cemetery, The Man's jibes about Jimmy's adolescence had come awfully close to the bullseye. Jimmy *did* have difficulty finding a girl in high school who would take him seriously. But that was all water under the bridge now.

"What if...?" Jimmy started, then stopped to reorganize his thoughts. *Try again.* He needed to get this right.

"What if it wasn't your dad trying to mess around with Kaycic, but *Kaycic* trying to mess around with your dad, and *she* did something to the plane that made it crash?"

Hank was silent. Jimmy didn't know if he should expect a punch in the nose or a fist to the stomach. He couldn't see enough to avoid either one in the dark.

It was neither.

Hank sniffled again and said, "That's the other thing I never told anyone. It never mattered until now. Kaycie's top was off, but my dad was still fully dressed. Even his belt was still buckled. I just thought he hadn't had time to do anything, you know?"

Jimmy heard another sniffle, and then in a strained, shaky voice, Hank said, "All these years, I've been protecting my mom because I thought my dad was trying to seduce Kaycie, but now I think it may have been the other way around. She was trying to seduce my dad. He was only in his thirties and still trim and handsome, just like when he was in the Navy. He didn't take her shirt off – she took it off herself. She was trying to entice him, to get him to come on to her, but he wouldn't do it, and something happened that made the plane take a nosedive into the river."

"It's certainly plausible, Hank. We'll never know with a hundred percent certainty, but it might restore some faith in your dad and eliminate some guilt you've been carrying around all this time."

"Yeeaahh …" Hank sighed. "Now I wish Mom had lived a little longer so I could tell her. Even though she never lost her complete faith in my dad. She always trusted him to be true to her. I guess I was the one who lost faith in him."

The two men were silent for a minute or two. Jimmy tried to put a hand on Hank's shoulder but only found the branch of a bush. They weren't as close to each other as he thought. *It's hard to judge distances in the dark.*

"One more thing, Hank. Did they ever come up with a reason for the plane crash?"

"No. The plane was in perfect working order. The authorities could never figure out why it went down. And the only two people who might know have been dead for a lifetime – nearly forty years."

Jimmy started to move through the darkened woods toward the house but realized after taking a few steps that Hank wasn't following.

"Hank?"

"I'm here."

"Just checking. I'm going to head in. I think the rest of our group needs to know about our new theory about what caused the plane to crash. It may not make any difference in dealing with Doyle Abaddon, but we never know; it might.

If he realizes Carolyn is gone and that your dad wasn't responsible for the crash, he could back off."

"I–I, uh, think I'll let you tell the guys inside without me, if that's all right with you? It's kind of weird talking about my wife's half-sister trying to make out with my dad. It's bad enough talking about *me* being on a date with her, even if it was over forty years ago. I'm not very comfortable with that. I know I'll have to deal with it eventually, but I'd prefer not to do it right now. I'm going to stay out here for a few more minutes and think about the good times I had with my dad. We spent a lot of time out here enjoying nature. Maybe I can bury the bad thoughts I've had all these years."

*

Nothing had changed in the house while Jimmy was outside. Wendi and Aleesha were still in the kitchen but were hugging. *Some new revelation?* he wondered. More likely just working through the stress of the last couple of days. He'd find out details later.

Pepé and Mr. Lyst still sat where Jimmy had left them in the living room. It didn't sound like they had advanced too far in their autobiographies. Of course, they had a lot of ground to cover, and whenever common ground was discovered, it required extra time to compare notes.

As Jimmy walked through the living room, Hillary caught his eye, holding up a finger to get Jimmy to stop for a bit of conversation.

"Everything all right with Hank outside?"

"Yeah," Jimmy answered. "He needed some alone time to work through some stuff, but I think we may have had a bit of a breakthrough. Actually, a breakthrough which may impact this stupid vendetta Doyle Abaddon is waging."

"Do tell, Jimmy," Hillary replied, turning slightly on the couch to face Jimmy. Pepé perked up, too.

"As I'm sure you know, Mr. Lyst, the authorities never found a mechanical reason for David Dawson's plane crash. It shouldn't have happened. And if it's not mechanical, it must be …?"

"Humanical?" Pepé offered.

Hillary looked at his new friend sitting next to him on the couch, and his face lit up with a huge smile.

"Exactly! What a great word, Pepé! Did you just create that?" Hillary asked.

"What? You mean it's *not* a word?" Pepé responded.

"I've never encountered it in all my days and nights of editing and publishing, nor have I confronted it in a dozen or more dictionaries. However, simply because it's not in a dictionary or a book by some other author doesn't mean it's not a word. It's a new word, Pepé, and we'll treat it carefully, like a newborn babe."

Pepé looked at Jimmy, who shrugged and smiled.

"In other words, Pepé, you just came up with a new word, which a guy like Hillary finds pretty exciting," Jimmy translated.

"Indeed! I find it exhilarating because it simplifies and streamlines the conversation and our hypothesis. Why use multiple words when one will do?"

Yes, indeed! Jimmy thought to himself. Pretty ironic, coming from a walking thesaurus.

Jimmy and Pepé exchanged another glance, then Jimmy continued explaining what he and Hank had uncovered outside.

"Yes, well … the plane had no mechanical problem, which meant it was humanical. It was the human factor on board. In this case, David Dawson and Kaycie Abaddon, either one or both."

Jimmy lowered his voice for the next part, because he didn't want to interrupt the girls in the kitchen or cause Aleesha any bruised feelings. The burden was on Hank to explain the new possible cause of the crash to her.

In a hushed voice, Jimmy continued. "Only the sheriff and two guys from the county search and rescue dive team were there. Those three and sixteen-year-old Hank, watching from shore. He saw when the bodies were brought up. Hank was a teenage kid watching divers retrieve his dad's dead body. That's something no kid should have to experience."

"So where's the epiphany, Jimmy? What new revelation came from backtracking among his recollections after all these years?" Hillary asked, keeping his voice low so just the three of them could be heard.

"Okay, here it is. Hank has never told anyone this, and it's something only three other people saw – the sheriff in the S&R Boat and the two divers. The sheriff has died, but I don't know about either of the divers."

"Get to the point," Pepé pushed.

"Gotcha. Kaycie's shirt was off."

"That's it?" Pepé asked. "When I was on the police force, we saw wrecks that did all kinds of weird things to people. Shoes off, coats off, jewelry found in every nook and cranny of the car. Shoes were the thing that came off most, I think."

"Shoes loosely tied or a pair of loafers might be knocked off by the force of the occupant's movements during impact," Hillary added.

Jimmy shook his head.

"Forget about the shoes. Kaycie's top was completely off. It was a pullover, and it would have left friction burns or serious bruises on her skin if it snagged on something and was torn off. But from what I understand, that's not the case. They crashed in the river and were killed by the force of the crash. Neither had water in their lungs, meaning they didn't drown. Nothing mechanical caused the crash, so we need to look at the humanical."

Pepé smiled proudly at the use of his word. Jimmy chuckled and continued.

"I can only think of two reasons Kaycie's top was off. 1 – David was trying to mess around with her, or 2 – she was trying to mess around with *him*. From Hank's comments about Kaycie, she was no stranger to the amorous advances of teenage boys. Kaycie told Hank it was like a 'night off' when she went out with him. What if she had decided to move up the chain? Move on from boys for a taste of what men had to offer," Jimmy said, pausing to let the seed take root in Pepé and Hillary's minds.

"You're saying the girl was trying to seduce the man; is that correct?" Hillary responded.

"Salomé did the forbidden dance for her stepfather, Herod, and when he said she could have anything, she asked for the head of John the Baptist," Pepé said, providing support from Biblical texts. "And don't forget, the daughters of Lot got him drunk after they were saved from the destruction of Sodom and Gomorrah and slept with him. Both became pregnant, and that's where some of Israel's enemies came from."

"Indeed, Pepé," Hillary replied. "There are other examples in the Holy Scriptures of young women seducing older men, even family members, sometimes for extremely violent ends. But it's important to remember that David and Kaycie are both deceased, and they are the only people who know—or knew—positively what occurred in that plane."

"But let's not forget the other part of the verse about cutting off the hand if it offends you – the first part. I've been thinking about it," Pepé answered Hillary. "Matthew 18:6 says, 'If anyone causes one of these little ones who believe in Me to stumble, it would be better for him to have a large millstone hung around his neck and to be drowned in the depths of the sea.' We usually think about little kids, but what if The Man's thinking about Kaycie? In that case, David Dawson already got his millstone and drowned, didn't he?"

"Indeed, Pepé," Hillary answered. "That would mean there was never a need to seek retribution. But again, I think it goes back to who was seducing who."

Jimmy jumped in, "But maybe we don't need to know everything. Maybe we only need reasonable doubt, like in a court of law."

"Court of law for what?" Wendi asked, and they realized she was standing right next to them, and they were no longer speaking in hushed tones.

Jimmy's voice had risen as he became excited about their theory of the humanical possibilities of the plane crash. Wendi had come to find out why the three men were huddled in the living room, heads together and speaking softly.

"Oops. Hi, Wendi," Jimmy replied, turning a light shade of pink.

She stepped closer, put her arms around him, and nibbled on his lower lip. "Tell me, Jimmy."

He did. He had no other choice.

Hank came in from the garage just as Jimmy told Wendi about the humanical factor and Kaycie's shirt. He stopped and listened as Jimmy concluded their theory.

"So much for keeping things on the down low," Hank said, only slightly to himself. Jimmy turned a deeper shade of red.

"Hank?" Hillary said to the man he'd known for more than thirty years. "Would you care to add anything to what Jimmy said?"

"Yes. I want to apologize to Aleesha in advance because it's going to seem like we're calling her half-sister.... well, kind of a ... a tramp."

He looked at Aleesha, standing in the doorway between the living room and the kitchen. He held out a hand to her, and she took his hand in hers. He pulled her close, his face hidden in her neck. Then he lifted his head, kissed her, and they stepped apart, but still holding hands.

"Jimmy got me thinking," Hank said to Aleesha and the rest of the group. "I've been carrying around a secret for nearly forty years. Kaycie's top was off when they brought her body up from the plane, and I just assumed my dad was trying to seduce her, but it could have been the other way around. If he was putting the moves on her, he would have made sure the autopilot was engaged and that everything was set properly to keep the plane flying. The fact that it crashed tells me that she was trying to tempt him and somehow caused the plane to lose control," Hank continued. "I've been trying to protect my mom all these years, but I should have protected my dad."

He turned to Jimmy and said, "After you came inside, I thought some more about my dad. He was in love with my mom. I never saw him look at another woman. When I was a teenager and starting to notice girls and women, I saw plenty of them looking at him, but he never gave them a second look. So, I have no reason to believe he was trying to put another notch in his bedpost … or whatever. I think Kaycie was the one on maneuvers. And I think she caused the plane to crash."

The room remained quiet after Hank finished.

"Aleesha?" Jimmy broke the silence.

She looked at him, eyebrows raised questioningly.

"Do you think the information you just heard will have any effect on your dad?" Jimmy asked. "That, plus the fact that Miss Carolyn has passed. Maintaining a vendetta is hard when the people you want to hurt are already dead."

"Your guess is as good as mine," she replied. "I don't really know him. I haven't seen him for over twenty years.

Even when he was still with my mom, he wasn't around much." She shrugged.

"It's worth a try," Pepé said, casting his vote for a peaceful resolution.

Chapter 23

Four days later, the Dawson Group—for lack of any better designation—gathered at the funeral home on Atlantic Avenue in Fernandina. It was the oldest and largest funeral home in Fernandina Beach.

According to a brochure Jimmy plucked from a rack in the foyer (pronounced foy-yay), the "magnificent white doubled-galleried Key West Style Mansion on Atlantic Avenue, was officially listed on the National Register of Historic Places on July 3rd, 1986. It is truly remarkable how the integrity of the 1891 structure has been maintained throughout its many usages. Over the decades, it has been a private residence, a hospital, a company accommodation with a cafeteria, a funeral home, and allegedly even a bordello."

Hillary was outfitted in his usual black suit, white shirt, and black tie. *He's always ready for a funeral because he always looks the same,* Jimmy thought. Wendi had arrived with Mr. Lyst, holding his arm as they walked in. She wore a modest black dress that landed just below the knee, a tasteful single strand of pearls, and a white shawl draped over her shoulders to protect against the late November breezes. The contrast between the black dress and her blonde tresses made her hair seem like fine-spun gold. Jimmy wore a charcoal grey suit, a pale blue shirt, and a navy tie. Hillary relinquished Wendi's arm to Jimmy, who was proud to be associated with her.

Pepé looked like ZZ-Top's sharp-dressed man in his black suit, crisply-pressed white shirt, and silver tie that matched his goatee. On one lapel of his coat, he wore a double flag pin – one side a US flag and the other a white flag with a gold star and the letters CPD, for Charleston Police Department, where Pepé had worked in the early 1970s. His other lapel was adorned with a round dark blue pin with a white center and displayed a golden eagle, a ship's anchor clutched in its talons. The blue border of the pin proclaimed United States Navy Veteran.

As Pepé greeted Hillary and they spoke briefly, Jimmy couldn't help but notice how straight they both still stood. It hadn't been too many years since Pepé retired from active service, but it had been decades for Hillary. Despite the elapsed time, Jimmy could still see the soldier in the older man.

The confrontation with The Man's thugs at Old Chester Cemetery had caused Jimmy to reassess his opinion of the publisher. Not that he thought any less of him – Hillary had risen many notches in Jimmy's eyes.

"Everyone looks so nice, don't they?" Wendi said, slipping her arm through Jimmy's. It felt nice.

"They do. I saw Hank and Aleesha. His mom and dad would be proud of him."

"He looks so handsome, and Aleesha looks lovely in her dress. Did you notice she had a little tattoo on her calf?"

"She does? Of what?" Jimmy asked.

"I'm not sure. It's round, though. It might be a face, but I have no idea of what. It's not big, and I couldn't get a good look at it. I didn't want to ask her to show me before the service. I'll wait until another time."

Jimmy asked Pepé where Gwynn was. He had hoped to introduce her to Wendi.

"She had to go to South Carolina to help out our daughter. She'll be back tomorrow evening. She insisted I should come today. I had planned to anyway. My mom used to tell me and my sisters, 'Always go to the funeral. It's for the family, not the person who died.' So I do."

Jimmy thought about what Pepé had said: always going to the funeral meant doing the right thing even when you don't feel like it. Jimmy had seen his partner stand and salute during the national anthem while watching a ballgame on TV. That spoke volumes about Jimmy's partner's commitment to his country and about his character. Jimmy was proud to be seen with Pepé and Wendi.

They moved into the room where the memorial service would be held. Hank and Aleesha were standing next to a large picture of Carolyn. It showed her probably twenty-five years ago, when she was in her late forties or early fifties, with fewer lines and looking much more vital than the woman Jimmy had seen with a walker less than a week earlier.

"That's a nice picture of your mom," Jimmy said to Hank and Aleesha as they shook hands.

"Wendi brought it," Aleesha answered. "It was from a promotion they did with her many years ago, but it still looks like her, just happier."

"That's how I see her in my mind's eye," Hank added. "She was fifty at the time. It was after the fifth book, *Polished Steele,* came out. She was doing a local publicity appearance, and Lyst Publishing paid for a studio portrait."

"It was supposed to be at the library, but so many fans wanted tickets that it was moved to the high school auditorium, and it was still standing room only," Wendi added.

"She couldn't move her right hand for a week afterward," Hank said with a smile. "She signed so many books that she sprained the ligaments in her wrist. I think that was when she decided I could be the permanent public face of the Steele Detective Agency."

Jimmy looked around the room. There were only a few people in the chairs and less than a dozen milling about.

"What time is this supposed to start?" Hank asked.

"Eleven," Aleesha answered.

"That's only about twenty minutes from now," Hank replied. "I was expecting a slightly larger turnout."

"I think there'll be a few more," Aleesha said, looking past Jimmy toward the doorway that opened to a lobby.

"I hope so," Hank said. "It's a twofer today. Two funerals for the price of one: Carolyn Dawson and Gary Dawson. The Nick Steele Agency dies with Mom."

Aleesha prodded Hank in the side with her elbow. "Be nice," she chided.

"About what you just said, Hank," Wendi interjected. "I wonder if we could meet after the memorial to talk with Hillary. He wanted to speak to you about that exact subject. There is one more book coming out next month, remember?"

"Yeah. *Refined Steele.* Number sixteen. It should do well, even if people don't read it. Some fans will buy it just because it's the last one. I assume we'll do the usual publicity tour?"

"Perhaps, but I believe Hillary's been thinking along some different lines."

"Well, if he's thinking about me taking over the franchise and writing more books, forget it. We tried that once – me writing with Mom – and it wasn't good. My part was pretty bad. Even I knew it. Mom had to fix everything I wrote. We could have skipped my involvement, and it would have been the same finished product. It was all her."

"That's not what Hillary was thinking, so you can put your mind to rest about that. But you're right about one thing; we're not quite ready to bury Nick Steele. And Hillary has a plan. All I will say for now is to just keep an open mind, Hank. We'll get together after the service if you're available."

"He's available," Aleesha answered, putting two fingers over her husband's mouth. He looked at her cryptically.

"What?" she said. "You have a wife to take care of, remember?" She took his face in her hands and pulled it down to meet hers for a kiss.

"Let's just get through this assignment first," Hank said.

Jimmy had been watching the lobby and suddenly heard more talking and noise coming from that direction. He was astonished as more and more people began entering the memorial chapel, many carrying copies of Carolyn's books. One face caught Jimmy's attention: Oscar Metz, the freelance ghostwriter he had met on his last case with the missing manuscript. Both Jimmy and Oscar had been roughed up by The Man's mob, but Oscar had received a much worse beating than Jimmy. From across the room, he looked like he was mostly healed, but Jimmy could only see the outside bruises. Metz made eye contact with Jimmy and gave him a small nod before settling into a seat. The available chairs filled quickly, and a man in a black suit and narrow black tie started setting up more chairs. When they were full, people spread around the room's perimeter and stood against the walls.

And then it was time. Hillary Lyst rose from his seat on the 'stage' and went to the small portable dais where he introduced himself.

"I'm Hillary Lyst from Lyst Publishing. On behalf of the family, I'd like to thank each of you for joining us here today. Many of you have seen my company's name in Carolyn Dawson's books over the last thirty-five years. Or you didn't notice because you were so anxious to get into the latest story about Nick Steele, and that's all right, too."

This comment brought a mild chuckle from those in the seats. Hillary paused and continued.

"Carolyn was our client, true, but she was much, much more. She was a friend to us at Lyst Publishing, but she was considerably more than that. Carolyn was the first person at my side when I tragically lost my wife and son several years ago. She was well-acquainted with grief and walked with me through that valley of shadows. Carolyn Dawson became part of our family, and we became part of hers."

Jimmy sat in one of the reserved chairs set up in the front row. The picture of Carolyn had been moved a few minutes before the service started, and an ornate but tasteful urn was on a pedestal next to the portrait – Carolyn's ashes. It seemed so small.

It always astounded him that a living, breathing, walking, talking person could be reduced to a handful of ashes and grit. There's little left when the parts we see and interact with are removed. When a person dies, you quickly realize that the body—these earthen vessels—are only containers for memories. And those memories aren't stored within the body – they are shared with everyone who knew the person. Even though the body has been stilled, switched off if you will, and reduced to its essential elements, the memories remain, so many that a vast auditorium can't contain them all. Jimmy refocused on Hillary.

"Carolyn Dawson loved writing; she lived to write and wrote to live. She wrote for you, each of you. Carolyn wrote because you read her stories, those confessions and desires that flowed from her fingers onto the pages you read. Very few people know how arduous it was for Carolyn to craft her books. That's because most of you don't know that Carolyn Dawson was one of the last people in the world to use an Iron Lung. She had polio when she was only eight but survived thanks to the machine that helped her breathe. She was only confined to it for a month then, but it remained a constant friend—and foe—for the rest of her life."

Hillary continued to share details of Carolyn's story with the attendees. He said only a few words about the death of Carolyn's brother, Gary Middleton, the inspiration for her nom de plume, and very briefly about the premature loss of Carolyn and David's second child before they ever had an opportunity to hold it. He stopped quickly on the accident that claimed David's life in 1983 before moving on to her successes during the years since then. This was a list by Lyst of Carolyn's triumphs and accomplishments.

"During the many hours she spent in the mechanical breathing device, she loosed her mind and allowed it to wander. She gave it free rein to create a new world without polio, pain, weakness, or permanent loss. The Steele Detective Agency eventually took root in her imagination and was birthed out of those creative sessions. You might say everything leading up to that first book was labor – the birth pangs required to bring an idea to life. And we helped her share that idea with you, her readers."

Jimmy thought parts of Mr. Lyst's eulogy were a little thick and self-serving, but overall, it seemed to be what the people wanted to hear.

"Many of you don't know of the heartaches Carolyn Dawson endured before entering the writing world. In addition to suffering from polio as a child in the 1950s, she lost a brother, as I noted previously, to the same disease just weeks before she herself was diagnosed with it. As a married woman, she and her husband lost a baby before it ever had a chance to experience life. And after less than twenty years of marriage, her husband died tragically in a plane crash not far from here in the St. Marys River."

"But the brightest spot in her life was always her son, Gary Henry Dawson, named for her brother, Gary Middleton, who passed away from polio in the summer of 1955, and for her husband, David Henry Dawson. Hank, as they called their son, grew into a fine young man, a graduate of Fernandina Beach High. He lost his father when he was sixteen. Despite that setback, he went to college in Jacksonville and graduated with a liberal arts degree. During that time, Carolyn's polio raised its ugly head again. Hank chose to stay at home, to be his mother's caregiver when necessary, and to help her promote her books. He became the face most of you recognize as Nick Steele and the Steele Detective Agency. He attended the book promotions in Carolyn's place due to the stresses travel took on her health."

Hillary took a breath, wiped his brow with a handkerchief from his inside coat pocket, and continued.

"Carolyn Middleton Dawson died peacefully in her sleep a few days ago, surrounded by loved ones and friends. She was born in 1947 in San Francisco, California, where her father was stationed in the Navy. Growing up with a Navy father, it was no surprise that she fell in love with a Navy man, her beloved David, who moved her here to Amelia Island shortly after their wedding in 1966. Gary Henry Dawson was born a year later in the house he still lives in. He is married to the former Aleesha Mortel, another FBHS graduate. She had been Miss Carolyn's caregiver for several years before she and Hank fell in love. They helped make Carolyn's final years secure and happy, with the sounds of a family filling the house again, especially laughter. She will be missed by her thousands of readers and fans, her many friends, family, and by me, her publisher, editor, and longtime friend. Rest in peace, Mrs. Dawson."

Hillary introduced Hank, who gave a much shorter but more rambling set of remarks, and who looked enormously relieved to sit down again.

After Hank's comments, there was a video song, followed by a non-denominational minister who gave a short sermonette based on Psalm 23 – The Lord is My Shepherd. Another video song played on the large TV screen in the front, and the service ended. The funeral director led the family and their group – Hillary, Wendi, Jimmy, and Pepé – out of the chapel. Pepé and Hillary stopped just inside the chapel doorway, put their heads close together, and then Pepé did a crisp about-face and returned to the front of the chapel and sat in the front row again, just a few feet from the urn containing Miss Carolyn's ashes.

Jimmy stepped near Hillary in the lobby and whispered, "What did you ask Pepé to do?"

"You never know what a fan might do, Jimmy, so I asked him to keep an eye on Mrs. Dawson's ashes. He graciously agreed to my request."

It had never occurred to Jimmy that someone might want to steal something so morbid, but the world is what it is because it takes all kinds of people. He was glad Pepé was willing to guard her remains, weirdly morbid though it may be.

After about a third of the guests departed, Jimmy worked his way back inside the chapel, returned to the front seats, and took a seat beside Pepé.

"Ever guarded a body before?" Jimmy quietly asked his friend.

"Yes," Pepé answered stoically, sitting straight and tall like a proper sentinel.

A few minutes of silence passed. Then Jimmy leaned over and whispered, "Ever guard the remains of a campfire before?"

Pepé pressed his lips together, and Jimmy saw him turn an uncharacteristic shade of dark red. After a moment, Pepé let out a deep breath. He turned and looked Jimmy in the eyes. Jimmy saw a steeliness in his friend's eyes he had never seen before.

"Don't," was all Pepé said. Just "Don't." It wasn't what he said; it was how he said it.

Sufficiently chastised, Jimmy sat quietly. Eventually, much more slowly than they had entered, the people all filed out of the funeral chapel. In his obligatory black suit, white shirt, and narrow black tie, the funeral director came in and somberly walked to the front. He picked up the urn and carefully handed it to Pepé. *Good choice,* Jimmy thought. *I would surely drop it.*

The funeral director handed Jimmy the portrait and took the easel to a side room. He came back, grabbed several of the flower displays, and said to Jimmy, "Please grab the other flowers. They go to the Dawson house. I was told you have a vehicle large enough to transport them?" The statement was presented as a question. Jimmy nodded.

Jimmy picked up the other flowers, and he and Pepé walked out of the funeral home. Jimmy was carrying several large flower displays and a gigantic portrait of Carolyn Dawson, while Pepé soberly carried the urn containing the final remains of one of the last people in the world to use an iron lung.

Chapter 24

AFTER UNLOADING THE flowers, the urn, and the portrait at the house on Piney Island, the group gathered in the living room again. It was already mid-afternoon; they'd all gone out to eat together following the memorial service. Jimmy's suggestion that they go to Culver's for butter burgers was vetoed.

They sat quietly in the spacious living room with its tall, cathedral ceiling, their mood subdued as each came to grips with the realization that the exact group that met here after the confrontation with The Man and his goons at the old cemetery would never meet again. The unexpected loss of Carolyn Dawson changed the group's dynamic.

Even though you know someone will die eventually, and your head knows it will be sooner than later, it still catches your heart off guard. Unless it's a long, lingering disease or a condition with a gradual descent toward death, the timing is always unknown and almost always surprising. No group member harbored any illusions about Carolyn's chances of living another twenty years, but her sudden departure had caught them all flat-footed.

"How are you handling things, Hank?" Jimmy asked.

"As well as can be expected, I suppose."

"It's probably been good to have the memorial service to plan and prepare, to keep yourself busy and occupy your mind," Hillary added, sitting on the sofa next to the home's new owners and sliding into the conversation.

"You're probably right," Hank replied tiredly, sinking further into the couch's cushions, his danger of being consumed by the sofa increasing by the minute.

"And you, Aleesha?" Hillary asked, switching his focus from Carolyn's son to her daughter-in-law.

"It makes me sad when I think about it, and sometimes it catches me off-guard. I'll be in the kitchen, and I'll start to ask Miss Carolyn what she'd like to have for dinner, but then I realize she's not there. And before you know it, I'm crying like a baby. I guess it'll probably take a while to get over her loss."

"When my wife and son were killed," Hillary responded, "I couldn't sleep for weeks. Her side of the bed was so empty, so cold. And when I would finally fall asleep, I'd dream of her. And then I wouldn't want to wake up because she was only in my dreams. The dream world where I could see her seemed better than this real world where she was no longer a part. I struggled greatly. But Carolyn told me it would get better over time, and it did."

Jimmy and Wendi sat together on the living room loveseat while Pepé occupied one of the recliners. The trio was content to listen rather than talk. Wendi was unusually quiet, but it didn't surprise Jimmy. Hillary's son, who had died, had been Wendi's husband, even though they were separated and just waiting for the final paperwork on the divorce. The impending divorce after seventeen years of marriage – fifteen together – did not eliminate the shock and sadness.

"Sometimes," Aleesha said in a timid voice, "I sneak down to Miss Carolyn's bedroom at night. I'm so accustomed to checking on her that I wake up automatically. I come downstairs, go into her bedroom, and sit next to the iron lung, just like I used to. She would often be awake, before … you know … and we'd talk about the day's events or the things scheduled for the coming day."

Aleesha stopped and sniffled a little. She reached over to the coffee table and pulled a couple of tissues from the box. She wiped her eyes and nose before telling the others about her nocturnal visits.

"Sometimes now, I come down and turn on the machine and let it run for a bit while I'm sitting there. It makes everything seem normal again to have the motor noise in the background. It feels like all those times I would come down, and she'd be sleeping. I would just sit and watch her sleep."

She turned to Hank and buried her face in his shoulder. Unlike her raucous laugh, there was no sound when Aleesha cried, but her upper torso rose and fell with the irregular rhythm of weeping. No one said anything to try and make her feel better. No platitudes or words of encouragement that "things will look better tomorrow." They all knew it was something that took time to heal.

After a short pause, Aleesha sat up and wiped her eyes, then blew her nose with a loud honk, making her and everyone in attendance laugh.

Hillary sat forward on the sofa, almost leaning out to occupy the center of the rough circle they had arrayed themselves in.

"Now that the memorial service is complete, I imagine things will calm down and settle back into a normal routine. For you and Aleesha, that is," he said, looking at the couple.

"The upcoming book launch coincides with the December shopping season for Wendi and me. I foresee brisk sales, not merely because many of Carolyn's readers will want her last book. I have been working on a shortened holiday signing tour, and Hank, I think it'll be good for you to take Aleesha with you this time. I have made hotel arrangements and booked a room for two in each city you'll be visiting. She won't need to be here at home helping Carolyn, so I thought she should go along and take care of you. Is that agreeable to the two of you?"

"I don't know about Hank, but I think it's a wonderful idea," Aleesha gushed. "And if Hank doesn't like it, he can stay home, and I'll go. Wendi could come along, and we'd sign those books like they've never been signed!"

"Boy, you've got that right!" Hank hooted with laughter. "But yes, I would love to have Aleesha along for my last tour."

"Don't be too hasty with that 'last tour' business, Hank," Hillary said, sliding back into a more relaxed position on the couch.

Hank looked at Hillary with a puzzled expression.

"There's something you may not have ever realized. Whenever your mother pitched a book to me, she didn't pitch just one. She would give me an outline for at least *three* books each time we met to discuss the franchise's future. Many never saw the light of day; some were shelved until they fit into the series' canon better. Thus, in addition to the book's premiere in December, I have outlines and details for four to six more books."

Hank's eyes were wide, and his mouth hung partway open.

All he managed to utter was, "A half a dozen more books?"

"Yes, at least four more, Hank, and maybe six. That remains to be seen. They just need to be written."

"Wait. We've already tried this, Hillary. I keep telling people I'm not a writer. The two books Mom and I tried together were the worst-selling books in the series. You know that better than anyone else. Despite her talent, it just didn't work. I guess those other books will just sit on the shelf," Hank replied with a note of frustration.

"Have you ever heard of a ghostwriter, Hank?" Hillary questioned.

The other man nodded but didn't reply, unsure where the conversation was going.

"A ghostwriter fleshes out the outline and writes the first draft. I think it's ironic that a ghost – something with no physical body – provides flesh and blood for a project like this. Except, instead of flesh and blood, they provide the words, descriptions, and conversations that bring the story to life. Do you see how this works, Hank?"

Understanding but not agreeing, Hank answered, "But a ghostwriter is never going to write the same way my mother did."

"No, he or she won't. But take a moment and recall who edited every single word your mother wrote for the Steele Detective Agency series."

"You?"

"Yes. I know your mother's style better than she did. She knew that, and she accepted it. What people actually read in her books is a combination of Carolyn Dawson and Hillary Lyst. We made a good team."

Hank looked at Aleesha and then back at Hillary. Jimmy, Wendi, and Pepé continued sitting silently. At the same time, a detective agency everyone figured had died with its creator shook the ashes from its wings and began to rise skyward like a phoenix.

"So you'd write the other books?" Hank asked.

"No."

Hank looked decidedly confused now. Thankfully, Hillary didn't leave him looking that way for long.

"I'll continue to edit the stories as I have since the first Nick Steele book was published. I have someone else in mind to write the books. He's actually a talented writer in his own right, but I recently discovered that he's better as a ghostwriter working from an outline than writing by the seat of his pants. He even won an award recently, albeit second place, but that still makes him an award-winning author, right? And after some recent physical difficulties, I think working on this project will be a great way for him to get his legs under him."

Jimmy looked at Wendi and mouthed, "Oscar Metz?" She nodded her head and smiled.

"Yes, Jimmy," Hillary answered Jimmy's silent question. "Oscar Metz. The same ghostwriter who was pressured into recreating an epic manuscript that had fallen into the hands of a no-talent hack from Jekyll Island. Oscar is still not quite over the injuries provided by Abaddon's bande de trois, two of whom we encountered at the old cemetery a few nights ago. I believe the recent changes to Mr. Metz's life experience will make him a better writer and even more skilled and adept at writing about situations fraught with danger, potential pain, injury, and even death. Those are feelings with which he has recently become intimately familiar. As they say, write what you know!"

"So, Oscar will write the books from Carolyn's outlines, and you'll chisel away the stuff that doesn't look like it came from the pen of the fictitious Gary Dawson?" Jimmy asked.

"Indeed, Jimmy. A sculptor once explained that he simply chiseled away everything from the giant stone block that didn't match his vision. In the same way, I shape and remold the words of the manuscript into the narrative Carolyn and I agreed on. With her outlines and creative inspiration, that arrangement won't change for a number of years to come."

*

Hillary had some other minor details to discuss with Hank and Aleesha, so Wendi asked Jimmy and Pepé to meet her outside to discuss a proposal she wanted to make.

The three gathered in the garage downstairs, then walked out toward the river, stopping at almost the same place Jimmy had paused in the dark a few nights before to talk with Hank. This time, it was mid-afternoon with bright sunshine, though the sun was sliding downward toward the horizon.

The trio stood briefly and absorbed the sunlight dappling the ground while birds warbled softly and car tires sang a mile away on the Fernandina Beach causeway. Jimmy thought to himself, *Piney Island would make a good getaway if it wasn't already occupied.*

Out here in the woods surrounding the house, he could see the marsh created by the confluence of the Amelia River and Kingsley Creek. But the more he looked at it, the less enthralled he became with it. *My house is right next to the St. Marys River. I've got a river, marshland, and trees nearby, and besides, my house is paid for.*

He realized that the real reason he was slightly infatuated with the Dawson property was because he had always been here with Wendi. Although it was a nice house, it wasn't the house he liked so much as the immediate company. Jimmy felt he could be happy anywhere as long as he was with her.

Many of the trees they saw had lost their leaves in preparation for the impending Southern version of winter. Thanksgiving was at the end of the week, and Christmas was only a month away.

"Do you remember what I said to you when this whole business with the Dawsons started, Jimmy?" Wendi asked, leaning against a leafless sweetgum tree.

Jimmy shook his head. He hoped this wasn't a trap to see if he had been paying attention.

"It was after the hurricane, and we'd been awake for two days without sleep. We had come over here to help Carolyn, and you met Aleesha, Hank, and Carolyn. We also found two severed hands that I think were primarily meant to scare you off or at least throw us off the trail. We went back to your house and looked at pictures of the first severed hand enlarged on your 5K monitor, searching for clues and their relevance to anything. I was getting ready to go back to my condo, and I said, 'I can't do this.' Remember? You said I scared you because you thought I was talking about us, but I was talking about staying up without sleep for days, eating poorly, not showering, and wearing the same clothes for multiple days in a row. I know you haven't forgotten."

Sheepishly, Jimmy nodded. Pepé gave him a gentle smack on the back of the head, but at least he didn't say anything to make Jimmy more embarrassed.

"Do you remember sending Pepé a selfie of us on the couch? I'm sure Pepé can pull it up on his phone if you don't."

"No need," Jimmy answered, taking a playful swipe at Pepé as he started to wave his cell phone toward Jimmy.

"I told you I wanted to help you solve cases, unravel their mysteries, piece together the puzzles they often are. I've been thinking about what I said…"

Jimmy held his breath. He couldn't help it. Despite what she had told him that morning on his couch, he still thought their relationship was too good to be true. It was always in the back of his mind that she would come to her senses and leave him.

"… and I still want to do it. But I want to do it more officially. I think we should form a business – you, me, and Pepé. We'll call it Blue Bridge Investigations. I can take care of the paperwork to incorporate the business, and you guys can take care of adding another line to your business cards. You guys work together a lot of times, so why not make it official?"

"Wait. So you weren't just kidding around when you said you wanted to help me solve cases? Does that include insurance work and vetting people for job applications?"

"No, Jimmy. Like I told you that morning, it won't be on every job. I still have to work at Lyst Publishing, and you and Pepé have your own gigs that you do—like job application vetting. But sometimes you get something juicier, a case with some real meat, and the three of us can all bring our special talents to bear on the job."

"I like it," Pepé said. "And you're right, Jimmy and I *do* work together a lot, but not on every job. And with our individual licenses, we can continue to work together in our licensed areas. Several times, Gwynn has wanted me to have a partner for backup. This would take care of that. I'm in. And I know Gwynn is, too."

"I'm in, but that was kind of a foregone conclusion since it was my idea," Wendi said. "However, you should know that Hillary said he wouldn't mind being pressed into service on occasion as well. I think his words were, 'It keeps a man from rusting.' It's down to you, Jimmy. In or out?"

Jimmy looked at the two people he trusted the most in the entire world. *Who needs to think about it?* He thrust his hand out into the open circle between them.

"I'm in."

Jimmy waited for the others to stack their hands on top of his like athletes do in a huddle. Instead, Wendi hugged Pepé, who gave Jimmy a light slap on the back.

We'll work on it, Jimmy thought, shrugging internally.

Chapter 25

THE NEW BLUE Bridge Investigations team walked away from the marsh and headed back toward the house. Jimmy's phone buzzed with a text. He guessed it was Aleesha, wondering where they were. He knew she had probably made a light supper for the group.

He guessed wrong.

> I hope the funeral was pleasant. But it doesn't change anything. The old lady's death doesn't balance anything. We're still coming for her son.

Jimmy read the text to his new partners.

"Do I reply?"

"To try and accomplish what?" Pepé asked. "To make him mad? To try and talk him out of it? From what I've seen, you can't reason with him."

Wendi threw the 'boys' a curve. "How does he respond to the truth?"

Jimmy and Pepé stared at her, trying to figure out where she was going with this line of reasoning.

She continued. "If Abaddon is so big on matching an eye-for-an-eye, he needs to know that Kaycie may have caused the crash, not David. On the other hand, it may make him madder, which can also play into our hands."

"Play into our hands?" Jimmy asked. "How does making a psychopath more angry work to our advantage?"

"The truth will set you free," Pepé answered before Wendi could say anything.

"Excuse me?"

"The truth will set you free. John 8:32 – 'Then you will know the truth, and the truth will set you free.' He's emotionally trapped by losing a daughter forty years ago. His desire for revenge keeps him in chains because he feels she was taken from him. But that's not the truth. The truth is, she probably caused the accident. David didn't take her away from him; she did it herself. That little bit of truth could make the difference. It may set him free."

"But the coroner and the sheriff all said they couldn't find any cause. David was healthy and died as a result of the crash. The plane had no issues, so it shouldn't have happened on a regular flight," Wendi responded.

"Humanical," Jimmy said.

Wendi looked at him like he was speaking a foreign language, but Pepé smiled, nodded, and repeated Jimmy's strange word.

"Humanical."

"Explain, please, Jimmy," Wendi said, turning to face Jimmy so he knew she was reaching the end of her patience.

"It's a ... um ... new word. Pepé coined it the other day to answer what happened to the plane. It wasn't a *mechanical* failure; it was a *human*ical failure. It was the human factor that caused the crash. Except it wasn't David with feet of clay and a weakness for young ladies."

"Not like King David in the Old Testament with Bathsheba," Pepé offered. "More like the other way around ..." Wendi looked at him, puzzled for a second, then returned to Jimmy's explanation.

"We automatically think men initiate sexual liaisons, especially in the case of an older man and a younger woman. But it ain't necessarily so," Jimmy defended. "It was something Hank said to me that got me thinking. He said Kaycie liked going out with him because she felt like she had a 'night off.' He thought she meant a reprieve from fighting off the testosterone-fueled high school seniors she usually dated. That's what I thought at first, too. But the more I thought about it, the more I thought it sounded like a night off from *work*. Could she have been making the boys pay to play? It's easy money ... or so I've heard," Jimmy finished, and Pepé stepped in to take over.

"When I was on the Charleston police force, the hookers used to say the young guys were good customers because they still connected sex with love, not like the older clientele who equated sex with power. Young guys didn't usually cause any trouble for the girls, genuinely trying to show them a good time. I mean, they got what they were paying for, but ... you know ... Help me out here, Jimmy. I feel like I'm digging myself a hole," Pepé said, a look of desperation on his face.

"Yes, Jimmy. Help him make the hole big enough for both of you," Wendi answered, giving him a little smile so Jimmy knew she wasn't upset. She was enjoying watching their discomfort.

"Okay, just hold on," Jimmy said. "I visited the Jacksonville Sheriff's Office holding cells about five years ago. And before you ask, it was part of a job; I was trying to find someone. The JSO thought they might have picked him up and called me to come check. Wrong guy. But in the process of waiting for the JSO to find the guy in their system, I had a conversation with a …um 'working girl.' She told me that she started having sex for money to pay for her student loans."

"You fell for that?" Wendi asked. "Seriously?"

"As the proverbial heart attack," Jimmy replied. "She said she was in a bar and got hit on by an older guy and declined his advances. She told him, 'Look, I'm not interested, so unless you're offering to pay my student loans,' and he said, 'Well … how much?' After that, she said, 'he paid for stuff.' He gave her money to help out with her living expenses. She called it 'sugaring.' I guess she meant like having a sugar daddy, you know? Here's the thing: she said more and more girls in their late teens and early twenties are getting into the sex trade for school expenses, to pay the rent, and that kind of stuff. They don't have a pimp, and they're not into drugs. They don't work every night – just often enough to pay for what they want," Jimmy recalled.

"I still remember something she asked me. She said, 'Do you like everyone at your job? Yet you still work with them, right? That's how it is with sex work—it's a job. I get paid for it. I do it for the money. What do you do for the money?' I think that's what Kaycie was doing. And I think she misread the signs from Hank's dad. I think she thought she was going for a plane ride for a completely different reason than he was," Jimmy concluded.

"And that's the truth that will set The Man free?" Wendi asked Pepé. "You're going to tell him his daughter was a hooker?"

"I hope we could word it a lot more delicately than that, but that is the truth as I see it. From what Hank told us about her and the fact that her pullover shirt was off when they brought up her body, I don't come to any other conclusion. And to answer your unspoken question, David Dawson was fully clothed. Hank told us not even his belt was unbuckled," Pepé explained.

"All right. How do we winnow that much information down into a text? From what we've seen up to this point, the guy doesn't do lunch dates," Wendi replied.

"Do you think he would understand a counteroffer?" Jimmy asked.

"Such as…?" Wendi responded. Pepé stared at Jimmy like he hoped a window would open in Jimmy's head so he could read his mind.

"Such as, 'We have new information about the crash that shows Kaycie caused it.' With Hillary's connections with newspapers, it wouldn't be difficult to get them to do a story on an unsolved case like that. I doubt even The Man wants his late daughter's name dragged through the mud," Jimmy answered.

Pepé nodded his agreement and added another point. "Plus, if he's trying to reconcile with Aleesha, he has to be aware that the media will easily connect the dots between Kaycie and Aleesha. He wouldn't make any points with her that way."

Wendi thought it over for a minute before announcing her decision.

"Do it," she said. "But let Pepé and I see the texts before you send them. And let us see The Man's responses when you get them."

"Aye, Cap'n," Jimmy answered. Wendi rolled her eyes in response.

Jimmy was tapping away on his phone. *This is worse than writing an essay for school,* he thought. He held the phone out for Wendi's approval of his message.

```
Thank  you   for  asking  about  Miss
Carolyn's   funeral.   Yes,   it   was
comforting, pleasant, and it was well-
attended.
```

"Comforting? Well-attended?" Wendi asked.

"I'm trying to be the good guy. What do you want me to do, challenge him to a duel? Threaten him? I'm getting ready to tell him his daughter was trying to break into the pros, and I don't mean a sports league. Haven't you ever heard of a compliment sandwich?"

Wendi and Pepé looked ready to say something but closed their mouths before chastising Jimmy. It was part of the give-and-take partners had to learn.

"Basically," Jimmy explained to his new associates, "it's where you compliment somebody, give them some critical feedback, and then close with another compliment. It's usually a business management tool, letting management get the criticism in there without making the employee feel so bad they decide to quit. But you can use it whenever you're dealing with people, not just business. I just don't know if it's appropriate for this situation."

"You mean like this: your goons looked sharp in black. Your dead daughter was a tramp. Sorry we destroyed your car," Pepé threw into the conversation. "I dunno, dude. Not sure it'll fly for this."

"Then someone else should write something. It's not easy!" Jimmy said gruffly.

Wendi put her hand on Jimmy's arm.

"You can do this. I believe in you," she said firmly.

Jimmy took a deep breath and deleted the message he had composed.

```
I was sorry to find out Kaycie was your
daughter. That's  hard  -  losing  a
child, even one who's almost grown.
You should be proud of Aleesha.
```

"Yeah?" Jimmy held out his phone for his partners to read.

"Send it," Wendi replied.

Jimmy pressed the return key. A second later, the message had a little 'Delivered' note and checkmark by it. He looked at Wendi and Pepé, shrugged his shoulders, and said, "What next?"

"We wait for his response."

They didn't have to wait very long. It dinged in as Wendi was answering Jimmy.

```
Aleesha is weak.
```

"He's such a warm, fuzzy, family-oriented guy, isn't he?" Pepé asked as he read the reply.

"Let me," Wendi said, commandeering Jimmy's phone.

> She's stronger than you know. She had to be, growing up without a father and losing her mother when she was twelve, just when she needed a mother's guidance the most.
>
> > Not strong enough. She always tries to please other people instead of going after what she wants.
>
> It takes great strength to have a servant's heart, to devote your life to helping others rather than trying to accumulate physical wealth.
>
> > I've been rich, and I've been poor.
> > Rich is better.

"Should we try some truth talk?" Pepé asked.

"We can try," Wendi replied, handing Jimmy's phone back to him.

> There's been some new information uncovered about the plane crash that took your daughter's life.

This time there was no immediate response. Jimmy took that as a sign that The Man was waiting for more.

> Are you aware that Kaycie's top was off when they brought her body up?

Again, no response.

One more try.

> David Dawson was fully dressed. He was just there to give her a flying lesson.
>
> > Says who?

> Says the sixteen-year-old boy who
> watched as their bodies were brought
> up.

Jimmy waited. His phone didn't buzz. He sent another text.

> Hank didn't know how important that
> fact was, but talking about it made
> him remember everything he saw that
> day. He could see things differently
> as a grown man. He finally understood
> what he saw.

No response. Jimmy sent another.

> He was trying to protect his mom all
> these years, but it turned out it was
> his dad who needed protecting.

Nothing. Jimmy tried one more.

> Can we at least agree your vendetta
> has no legs? Hasn't everyone lost
> enough?

Jimmy pressed return and waited. It said 'Delivered,' but there was no answer. They waited a few moments, but there was no reply from The Man.

"I'm going to take that as a positive sign," Jimmy told his partners. He slipped his cell phone into his pocket.

When the trio got back in the house, Aleesha had a simple sandwich supper laid out. Hillary – who had not been outside for their meeting – already had a plate and a cup of hot tea in front of him.

Jimmy checked to see if there was banana pudding. Luckily for his stomach, there was not.

Chapter 26

AFTER ENJOYING ALEESHA'S supper, the group split up for the evening. Pepé decided to follow Hillary down to Fernandina Beach for a nickel tour of Lyst Publishing. Jimmy and Wendi left to drive down to her condo and take a leisurely sunset stroll on the beach. Hank and Aleesha were already home, where they planned to stay after their long day. There were a lot of sympathy cards from the funeral they needed to go through.

On the way to the condo, Wendi decided to swing by her office for a minute. Jimmy had no objections. He was glad the day was over so he could finally relax. He had been stressed out for over a week dealing with everything, starting with a hurricane. Next up on his social calendar: he was scheduled to celebrate an authentic American Thanksgiving with Wendi and Hillary in a few days. All he knew about Thanksgiving American-style was napping after eating and watching football through his eyelids. It sounded delightful.

Wendi pulled into the parking lot near the Staples store a few doors from Lyst Publishing. The first time Jimmy tried to find the little publishing company, Wendi told him to go to Staples and turn right. Even with such *precise* directions, he had to ask an employee from Staples where Lyst Publishing was. He discovered it was almost completely hidden between two buildings next to Staples. There was just a small entrance door, and then a narrow hallway led back to Hillary and Wendi's offices.

That was then. Now, Jimmy could find the office in his sleep.

They exited Wendi's car and walked toward the buildings. It was quiet, like evenings here usually were. Most people were at home, eating dinner. Very few cars were in the parking lot, and no one was on the sidewalk in front of the stores. Jimmy looked to his left and thought about steering Wendi toward the little Peterbrook Chocolatiers shop but decided to wait until another time. Turning back to his right, he noticed a black SUV suddenly stop in the driving lane. Jimmy assumed it was letting them cross, but he couldn't see the driver through the darkly-tinted windows. Jimmy cheerfully waved nonetheless.

The SUV's doors flew open, and The Man's three-person goon squad piled out from inside. They rushed toward Jimmy and Wendi, and they didn't look friendly or cheerful. From within the SUV came The Man's electronically disguised voice.

"I'm going to let Hank off the hook, but you and I need to have one more dance, Mr. Favreaux. I'm getting very tired of your meddling."

Jimmy hurried Wendi across the lane toward the office door, hoping to get inside and avoid a confrontation, but the hoods arrived quicker. It was obvious they weren't looking for conversation, so Jimmy tossed his cell phone to Wendi and said, "Call 9-1-1."

She caught it one-handed, tossed it back, and said, "*You* call 9-1-1, and while you're at it, call Merry Maids to come and take out the garbage."

Jimmy was caught off-guard but caught his phone without bobbling it and slid it back into his pocket. Everything from that moment on seemed to occur in slow motion.

As Dimebag rushed Wendi, she took a couple of quick steps and met him halfway, threw her purse in his face, and followed it up with a kick to his knee that bent his leg backward, forcing his head down involuntarily. She brought her knee up to meet his chin as he doubled over. His teeth cracked loudly as his jaws crashed together, and his head snapped straight up and back as he went down.

Reacting to what was happening, Wheels rushed over and made the same mistake Jimmy had made three weeks before, grabbing Wendi's arm from behind. She whipped around, shot her arms straight up in the air to dislodge his grip, and stepped *closer* to the thug. Jimmy saw her fingers become as stiff and rigid as a solid wooden stake, then strike her opponent's Adam's apple perfectly, just as she had done to Jimmy.

Watching it happen was different than being on the receiving end. Jimmy noticed that as she lashed out with her deadly fingers, she simultaneously gave a little shout. He had read once that martial artists gave a little yell to concentrate the power into their kick or strike. It intimidates their opponent, removes air from their diaphragms, and gives their attacks more speed and power. All Jimmy knew was that it worked.

Wheels went down the same way Jimmy had, his hands grasping in vain at his throat to pry it open and get air flowing into his lungs again. Jimmy almost felt the blow in his own throat again as he watched. Wheels looked pale and like he was about to pass out, just like Jimmy had when Wendi struck him the same way.

Dimebag was struggling to get back up and had reached his hands and knees. Wendi turned toward him and, with a form that would make an NFL field-goal kicker jealous, used Dimebag's head as a football. After her perfect kick, he was sprawled out on the sidewalk, the second man to go down for the count.

Suddenly Jimmy heard a roar and, from out of the corner of his eye, saw Kingpin charge toward him just before the gargantuan man scooped Jimmy up the way a normal-sized person would scoop up a toddler. Kingpin hoisted Jimmy over his head as easily as he would a throw pillow and, with both hands, hurled him against the side of the building. Jimmy's head hit first with a sickening sound, and he blacked out, sliding down the wall and pooling into a motionless heap.

Wendi screamed angrily and ran full speed at the giant gangster. She launched herself into the air, hoping to wrap her legs around his head and use the strength of her legs to get the giant off-balance and throw him to the ground or at least get him down on one knee. If that failed, Wendi hoped to let her momentum slingshot her behind his head and up onto his shoulders. From there, she could smash the heels of her palms against his temples, clap his ears, and try to pop his eardrums, hopefully cutting him down to her size. The behemoth was just too big to take on one-on-one.

As Wendi flew through the air, Kingpin swung one massive arm out like he was playing handball and swatted her to the ground, knocking all the air from her lungs. He grabbed the front of her shirt and pants, hoisted her about four feet off the ground as effortlessly as lifting a toy doll, then body-slammed her back to the concrete sidewalk. Wendi landed hard on her back, unable to brace herself. The back of her head bounced once on the sidewalk, and she groaned, then lay still.

Kingpin stomped over to Jimmy, grabbed him by the hair, hoisted him to a semi-standing position, shoved him against the building wall, then sat him down hard against the building, facing Wendi. He slapped Jimmy roughly across the face several times. Jimmy's head rolled down against his chest, and he slumped over. His cheek landed hard on the concrete sidewalk, scraping his cheek, and leaving skin and blood behind.

"Wakey, wakey, Jimmy!"

The oversized beast reached into his coat pocket and pulled out a handgun. It looked like a toy in his massive fist.

"I'm going to eliminate you, Favreaux. But first, I'm going to get rid of your cute little girlfriend, so open your eyes."

Jimmy tried to do as he was told. His head felt like it was splitting in two. He forced one eye open partway. The other eye wouldn't respond. Through a haze, he saw Kingpin turn toward Wendi and point the handgun down at her still form.

"Are you watching, Favreaux? Because it's going to be good."

Jimmy was powerless to do anything, not to stop Kingpin, sit up, or even watch. One eye fluttered open and shut several times, but things were growing dim, and a smoky gray mist covered what little he could see. As his good eye lost its ability to stay open, Jimmy heard several loud gunshots, but he couldn't force his eye open to see what had happened. He was powerless to open his eyes, not even a slit. The sides of his head were throbbing, and his forehead felt like someone was holding a hot frying pan against it. The top of his skull felt like it was about to come off. Time had slowed to a crawl. There was only pain.

Just as everything was nearly black, Jimmy heard one more gunshot. It sounded distant and incredibly close simultaneously, and the sound echoed like someone had too much reverb turned up on their guitar amp.

His head! It was pounding continuously, and his eyes felt like they were about to pop out of their sockets. As he heard the last gunshot, time seemed to slow to almost a complete stop. Jimmy's world momentarily turned bright white, then changed to black with no fade out, as quickly and efficiently as if a light switch had been flipped.

Unlike people with near-death experiences who reported seeing a bright tunnel, Jimmy experienced no sounds, lights, or bodily sensations – except his head, which felt like it was about to burst.

Then, there was nothing.

Epilogue

HE FELT LIKE he had been run over by a steamroller. In the back of his mind, he wondered if he looked as flat as Wile E. Coyote always did after being run over by an Acme steamroller in the Roadrunner cartoons.

He tried to open his eyes, but there was something wrapped around his head. Reflexively, he reached one hand up to determine what it was.

Gauze.

It was wrapped around his head so many times he figured his head looked like a bowling ball under the Christmas tree.

Okay, so they don't want me to see anything. I can deal with that.

He brought his hand down *and rested it on the bed by his side.* He felt the crispness of the sheets, starched and smooth. His pillows, one behind his back and one behind his head, crinkled when he moved. He didn't know if it was from extra starch or if the pillows were encased in plastic inside the pillowcases.

He inhaled through his nose. Despite the gauze wrapping, his nose was assaulted by the antiseptic scent of a hospital, a mixture of Lysol, betadine, and bleach.

He listened carefully and heard soft voices. Were they actually soft, or were they distant? It was hard to distinguish. Every once in a while, he would hear a squeak; it was a familiar noise, but he couldn't quite place it. It finally came to him: the soft rubber soles nurses wore and the shiny, well-waxed floors they walked back and forth on each shift. He was positive if he woke up in the night, he would hear the hum and click of a floor buffer, shining the soft wax to a high gloss.

He realized something was missing as he listened to the sounds around him: no beep from a machine keeping track of his vitals. He took that as a good sign. He wiggled all his fingers and determined there was no pulse-ox monitor on his index finger. He squeezed his fingers and hands into fists, held them for a moment, and then let them relax. There was no stinging sensation in the back of his hand or his forearm, so there was no IV, another good sign, although somewhat surprising.

He leaned back, relaxing against the crinkly pillows. The clean smell of the hospital was comforting. The quiet was peaceful. Even the lack of beeping and alarms was soothing. He tried to reach the bed controls but couldn't find the remote for them. No matter.

He had no idea how long he had been here. Hours? Days? Had he possibly been here longer than a few days? He could have been here months, and he wouldn't know it.

But at least his head didn't hurt anymore.

Wait. Why did my head hurt?

He tried to remember, but the effort created an aching feeling behind his eyes. The more he thought about it, the more the ache spread.

He tried to relax and turn off his brain. Thinking made his head hurt, and the minor exertion exhausted him. The gauze wrapped around his head kept his world pitch black, but even so, he intentionally tried to close his eyes. He tried to determine if he was successful, but thinking hurt.

So tired.

In less than thirty seconds, he was asleep.

*

The next time he woke up, the gauze seemed thinner, like someone had unwound some of it. Tiny little stars of light were shining through it in the thinnest areas.

He immediately thought of the Twilight Zone episode with the beautiful girl who was classified as ugly by the people of her planet, who all had misshapen faces. He remembered the scene when they took her gauze wrapping off to see if the plastic surgery was successful.

"No change. No change at all!"

Remembering the old TV show made him chuckle.

"Well, someone's feeling better, aren't they?"

A woman's voice. Soft and melodic.

He was about to say something in response when a smooth hand with cool skin took his wrist and felt his pulse.

"Good. Strong and even. Open your mouth and put this under your tongue."

Something about her voice was familiar, and he did as he was told.

After a couple of minutes, the woman – a nurse obviously – took the thermometer from his mouth and announced, "98-point-4. That's very good."

He felt satisfaction about his near-perfect temperature. He didn't know why. Maybe it was her tone. It was like she was singing when she spoke. It was …nice. He thought she sounded like a brunette.

"I'm going to wash your arms now. Hold out your right arm, please."

Again, the smooth, cool hands took ahold of his arm, and a warm, sudsy washcloth was rubbed up and down from shoulder to fingertips, followed by a slightly rough towel to dry off. His left arm received identical treatment.

"Now you lie still and rest. The doctor will be in to see you in just a few minutes."

And she was gone.

True to her word, a man came into his room and stood beside the bed.

"Are you ready to get those bandages off, young man?"

Young man? Has he seen me without this turban?

"Yes," he answered simply. His tongue felt thick, like he hadn't spoken in a while, and he swallowed.

"All right. I'm going to turn the lights off so your eyes don't get overwhelmed by too much brightness when the bandages are removed. Now, young man, keep your eyes closed."

Several minutes of careful unwinding followed.

There must have been more gauze around my head than I guessed.

No change, no change at all!

A giggle escaped his lips.

"Something funny, son?"

"No, not really. Just a show I was remembering."

"Oh. Okay." There was a brief pause, and the doctor spoke absently as he worked.

"There. Good. Now hold still. Okay. Here goes the last of it. Keep your eyes closed."

He could see the light through his eyelids and wanted to open them wide, but he did as he was told.

"Okay, now slowly open your eyes. If it's too bright, go ahead and close them."

He slowly opened his eyes, allowing just a little light in at a time, allowing them to adjust. Then after a moment, he realized they were open normally. The room was dark and subdued.

"I'm going to turn on the lights now," the doctor said.

The room blazed, and everything turned white for a second, and there was a tickle of an ache behind his eyes, but then they settled down, and the hurt dissipated.

The sudden flash of white …

Something about the sudden total whiteness sparked a memory, but it was gone as quickly as it came. He couldn't hold onto it.

He turned his head and looked at the doctor. He wore a white doctor's coat with a stethoscope hanging around his neck. He was wearing dark slacks and a white shirt and tie.

He thought, *Like someone else I know,* but the thought drifted away before he could examine it.

The doctor had heavy black-framed glasses, and the coke-bottle lenses made him look bug-eyed. His dark hair was combed to one side, and he had a thin, dark mustache.

He looks like Floyd, the barber from Mayberry.

The doctor leaned over the bed and said, "I'm going to look in your eyes with this little light."

He sounds like Floyd, too. And I swear I smell Barbasol on him.

"Your eyes look fine. How's your head?"

"Good, I guess."

"Excellent. One more question. Do you suppose you could tell me your name?"

My name? he thought. *I've been in here for Lord knows how long, and you guys haven't even figured out who I am?*

"It's Jimmy. Jimmy —"

Nothing came.

"It's Jimmy ... Well, that's just stupid. I should know my own name. It's Jimmy—" He was starting to get agitated and angry, and his head was beginning to ache again.

"That's all right, son. Don't you worry about it. I'm sure it'll come to you soon."

"What do you mean don't worry about it? Where I come from, if I can't remember my name, that's something to worry about."

"Where do you think you come from?"

"What? That's just an expression. Besides, I come from —," but he couldn't complete the sentence, which made him more exasperated.

"Now, don't get yourself all riled up, young man. That'll just make things worse."

The doctor had turned around and was getting something from a little table on wheels next to the bed. He turned back around and quickly injected something into Jimmy's arm from a syringe.

Ow!

"We'll talk again later, Jimmy. At least you know your first name. That's a good start. You take a nap now, Jimmy, and I'll be back to see you soon."

Great. I'm in Mayberry with Floyd, the barber, for my doctor. But what's my name? Jimmy what? Jimmy —.

Everything whirled and twirled, and Jimmy felt the too-familiar fog envelop him as he drifted off to sleep.

*

The next time the doctor came back, Jimmy was ready for his questions.

"Can you tell me your name, son?"

"It's Jimmy. Jimmy Marlowe. I'm a private eye. I do a lot of work for insurance companies."

"Oh, that's very good. Pleased to make your acquaintance, Mr. Marlowe."

"Thank you, doctor. Can you tell me how I ended up in here?"

"Oh, my. No one told you? You had a severe concussion. It looked like someone used your head for a battering ram," Dr. Floyd said. "They dented your head and cracked your skull. It was bad."

"But I'm fine now?"

"Oh, yes. You're much better. And since you remember your name, I don't see any reason to hold you here. But I need to ask you, do you know your home address?"

"Of course. 1313 Mockingbird Lane."

"Hmm. I'm not sure where that's at, but you answered so quickly and with such assurance that it must be right. You wait here a few minutes, and I'll discharge you."

"What about my clothes?"

"Yes, that's a good question. Let me just look in this closet ... There you are. Neat and crisp, freshly laundered and ironed. We do have wonderful support services here, don't we?"

Dr. Floyd shook Jimmy's hand and shuffled out, closing the door behind him.

He even walks like Floyd.

Jimmy scrambled out of the bed and went to the closet. He pulled a pair of khaki pants off the hanger and pulled them on. They fit, so they must be his. The shirt came next. It was a Hawaiian shirt with palm trees, grass huts on little islands, and a sky-blue background. *Whatever!* As he was buttoning it up, he heard the door open.

A beautiful blonde head peeked around the door and said, "I guess this means no more sponge baths for you."

The beautiful brunette voice he had heard had beautiful blonde hair, but it worked.

Ain't that a kick in the head ...

At the thought of an actual kick in the head, his head responded with a twinge of pain. He ignored the sudden ache and concentrated on the scene unfolding before him.

The blonde nurse opened the door all the way and stood in the doorway, her arms folded across her chest, one leg pulled up partway and bent at the knee. Jimmy stopped buttoning his shirt and looked at her. There was something familiar about her, but he couldn't say what. There was also something very <u>un</u>-familiar about her, and he knew what.

Instead of the usual hospital scrubs he was expecting, she wore a crisp, white dress that fell just below her knees, white shoes, and white nylons on shapely legs. The top of her head was adorned with a little white cap. It was either Throwback Thursday or this was a very old-fashioned hospital. But he wasn't sticking around long enough to find out which. He resumed buttoning his shirt.

"You never know," Jimmy answered his Florence Nightingale. "I could get hit by a car as soon as I walk out of here. Then I'd be right back in here, and you'd be back in the geisha business, baby."

Baby? Geisha business …?

"The doctor said you remembered your name. Is that true?"

Jimmy offered his hand, saying, "I'm Jimmy. Jimmy Marlowe, private eye."

She took his hand in hers. Her skin was smooth and cool.

"Well, Jimmy, I, for one, will be sad to see you go. Maybe we can get together outside the hospital for a drink or dinner. Or both."

"You never know what fate will throw your way, do you, sweetheart?"

Sweetheart? What the …? And the nurse didn't seem surprised by his choice of words.

Jimmy slipped his shoes on, tan wingtips with pink shoelaces, and gave her a wink and a smile before he strolled out of his room. He followed the signs to the exit, his pace increasing the closer he came to freedom.

Pushing through the exit door, he noticed the sun was shining, the sky was blue and clear, and the birds were singing merrily in the trees.

He took a few steps down the street and stopped to sit down on a bench conveniently located outside the hospital's entrance. His head had begun throbbing again, and he felt dizzy and nauseous. It was probably the bright sunshine. He decided to try and 'walk it off,' like his Little League baseball coach always said.

The sunshine and blue skies were too bright for Jimmy's eyes, and he held a hand up like a visor over his eyes. For a moment, everything went white again. Jimmy closed his eyes to the brightness for a few seconds and opened his eyes again. He wasn't sure how, but he wasn't where he thought he should be. Somewhere in his brain, he knew that the hospital was behind the funeral home off Atlantic Avenue. And he had been there. He had! But now he was somehow downtown, blocks away from where he should be.

His surroundings looked like an old movie set. All the cars appeared to be from the late forties or older. The old downtown looked similar to TV's Mayberry, except even older. The main street looked wider than he remembered, and it was brick or cobblestone. Most of the buildings lining the street were two-story brick constructions, and the one on the corner proclaimed Thompson Sundries. A large mural or billboard on one side of the Thompson building advertised a Luncheonette inside. A few doors down from Thompson Sundries, Jimmy saw a Western Union sign. At the end of the street, the long concrete fishing pier on the Amelia River was missing; there was just a squat white building that said US Coast Guard on the roof.

The men Jimmy saw walking among the business establishments were all wearing suits, complete with hats like his grandpa used to wear. Jimmy started to feel out of place in his Hawaiian shirt and khaki slacks. Most of the men were accompanying women, all wearing brightly-colored dresses that hung below the knee. Almost all of the women Jimmy saw had shoulder-length hair, and some wore scarves tied over their hairdos while others had large, wide-brimmed hats. A few carried brown paper bags that Jimmy decided held groceries for the evening meal or 'sundries' from Thompsons.

He had no idea what was going on. Maybe someone was shooting a motion picture, and he had wandered onto the set. But right now, Jimmy's first order of business was to sit down before he fell down. He reached a bench next to one of the brick storefronts and flopped down hard, panting. His head was throbbing, and he felt like he might throw up.

*

"Whatever it takes, Doc, you do it. This is my best friend in the whole world. Put his bill on my insurance if you need to. I've got military insurance. Give him private nurses around the clock if necessary. You do whatever you need to make him better."

"I wish we could move people on and off other insurance policies that easily, but that's not how things work. I assure you, Mr. Perez, we're doing everything possible. Mr. Favreaux has suffered a traumatic brain injury. The neurosurgeon said Mr. Favreaux's brain was injured significantly when he was thrown against that building. His skull was cracked. If you've heard the term depressed skull fracture, well … now you've seen one. He is in ICU, where we have intubated him, placed him on a ventilator, and put him in an induced coma to reduce the swelling of his brain. Shutting down many of his brain functions can give it time to heal. We're helping his brain and body to do what they normally do independently. Mostly, he's going to need time."

"Okay, I got it. How's Mrs. Lyst – Wendi?"

"She's doing fine. We're going to hold her overnight for observation. She sustained a concussion, but it's very mild. The overnight hold is just to make sure nothing crops up. She may have mild amnesia about some recent events or not. We just can't say for sure. But you can see her tomorrow. We have her lightly sedated right now. She's resting comfortably, I assure you."

After the doctor left, Hillary walked into the waiting area and straight to Pepé.

"How did it go with the cops?" Pepé asked.

Hillary shrugged and looked down the hospital hall before answering.

"The police are going to need to see you. In-person, I'm afraid. They're only giving you some leniency because they know Jimmy, Wendi, and me. They already have our guns, but they explicitly said they needed to see you personally within the next twelve to twenty-four hours. I also took the liberty of informing them that you were a former Charleston police officer and Naval watch commander, and, like Jimmy, you are a private investigator. Telling them those things may not have helped, but they didn't hurt. I don't foresee any difficulties, Pepé, but remember, we did just kill a man."

"It was a righteous shoot," Pepé said when Lyst finished. "We did what we had to. That giant ape was about to kill Jimmy and Wendi. We put four shots in his center mass—two from each of us—and he was still moving. He was still trying to take a shot at Wendi. I had no choice except to try a headshot. I cut Pinocchio's strings, and he finally went down."

"And you did it perfectly, right behind the earlobe like they teach you in marksman school. Wendi is alive because you took the shot, and so is Jimmy. Now tell me about Jimmy's condition."

"Jimmy is in an induced coma. Traumatic Brain Injury, the Doc said. A depressed skull fracture. The neurosurgeon says the coma is best for him. He couldn't talk right now anyway – they have a tube down his throat. I guess he's on a ventilator, too. And Wendi has a slight concussion, so they're going to hold her overnight. After that, we'll just have to wait and see how they do."

"To sleep, perchance to dream. Ay, there's the rub."

Pepé looked at Hillary and raised his eyebrows. He didn't have to say the words. His new friend knew what he was asking.

"Hamlet, Act Three, Scene One," Lyst explained. "I wonder what adventures our sleeping colleague might be experiencing."

Loose Threads

So MANY THINGS to tidy up. But that's what this section is for: explaining some of those questions that are bothering you. Did they...? Was it...? That really happened? So let's get to it.

Yes, there are still people in iron lungs. But that number is down to two or even one or none, depending on when you are reading this.

Paul Alexander and Martha Lillard are the last known Americans still using giant metal tubes to help them breathe. The last person in the United Kingdom to use an iron lung died in 2017.

Paul Alexander of Dallas, Texas, dubbed 'Polio Paul,' has lived inside the lung ventilator longer than anyone else in the world – ever since he contracted the deadly disease in 1952 when he was only six.

Doctors told his parents they didn't expect him to survive. Though never able to leave the iron lung behind him, he did more than merely survive. Paul has lived a full life inside the iron lung for the past seven decades.

Paul graduated high school and college and attended law school, becoming a successful attorney. He taught himself to be able to breathe on his own for limited amounts of time and even argued cases in court from his wheelchair. In college, he lived in the dorms inside his iron lung. He was forty when he passed the bar exam. He wrote a memoir – *Three Minutes for a Dog* – which took eight years to finish, as he had to use a plastic stick placed in his mouth to type.

When Paul was younger, he spent most of his days outside the iron lung while sleeping in it at night. However, now in his late 70s, he spends most of his time lying in the machine.

Martha Lillard was five years old when she woke up with a sore throat and pain in her neck. After being diagnosed with polio, she was hospitalized for six months and put inside an iron lung to help her breathe.

Martha still sleeps in her iron lung every night but is able to be out of the machine during the daytime. And though her life has been limited due to her disability, she enjoys painting, taking care of her dogs, watching movies, and spending time with her childhood friend, who has taught her to "appreciate small things."

There was a third person who depended on an iron lung for survival. Mona Randolph contracted polio when she was twenty and lived using the iron lung until 2019, when she died from long-term complications of the disease. Mona was an advocate for independent living for people with severe disabilities and was able to live alone in her home with the help of caregivers.

Carolyn Dawson is a composite of all three polio survivors, but I primarily borrowed from Martha and Mona's stories to create her. Rather than painting like Martha, Carolyn became an author, like Paul, but on a much larger scale than Paul. Unlike Paul, Carolyn could type at a computer, whereas Paul uses his mouth and a pointer stick.

The Cutter's Labs incident is true. The demotion of Bernice Eddy after discovering the bad batch of vaccines is true. The country's reaction to the disease and vaccine is true.

Polio is caused by a virus called poliovirus. The virus enters the body through the mouth or nose, getting into the digestive and respiratory (breathing) systems. It develops in the throat and intestines. From there, it can enter the bloodstream and attack the nervous system.

There are three strains of poliovirus: types one, two, and three. Types two and three have been eliminated, but type one still affects people in a few countries. Although there is no cure, there is a safe and effective vaccine, thanks to Dr. Jonas Salk.

The two types of vaccines used are an inactivated poliovirus given by injection and a weakened poliovirus given by mouth. Vaccination means polio is now very rare in most parts of the world. It's mainly found in two countries: Afghanistan and Pakistan.

Despite the rarity, a polio case was officially confirmed in New York on July 21, 2022. In June of that year, the disease was also found lurking in London sewage, suggesting it may be spreading in that city – although no cases have been officially detected.

Hillary Lyst's recollections of the end of the Vietnam War are all true events. I have known more than a few members of the armed forces from that era, including relatives who served, and to each, I say, Welcome Home and thank you for your service. All gave some, and some gave all.

Old Chester Cemetery is a real place, and the Chester Church of God is right across the road from it. Yes, the church is yellow. The descriptions of the church and cemetery are accurate. To the best of my knowledge, though, there have been no gunfights in front of either.

I did deliver newspapers to Young's Hut when I filled in on a paper route in the summer. It was a metal Quonset hut that had been turned into a café on the east end of town in Redwood Falls, Minnesota. It's no longer there, and the east end of town has moved much further east with the town's growth.

Although not specifically named, the funeral home in the story is based on the Oxley-Heard Funeral Home. The description Jimmy reads from the brochure is on their website. The funeral home's interior in the story is a composite of other funeral homes I have been in.

Hurricane Nicole did come close to Florida's First Coast in November of 2022. I attempted to stay true to the actual chain of events and impact on the Amelia Island area. The storm was much more brutal to the coast, where it made landfall 250 miles south of Fernandina Beach. According to the National Weather Service, Nicole impacted areas that were still recovering from Hurricane Ian's wrath in

September and contributed to major beach erosion along the East Coast. Nicole caused over $1 billion in damage and was responsible for five direct fatalities. It was a tropical storm as it went past Fernandina Beach on its way north.

Jimmy's Traumatic Brain Injury (TBI) treatment is consistent with current treatment. A nurse in Jacksonville said a person in Jimmy's condition would be in ICU, intubated, and on a ventilator. At a minimum, he would be assigned a Neurosurgeon for the neuro part and an Intensivist as his ICU doctor. The hospital has an Observation Unit whose job is to specifically monitor everyone under observation.

The hospital where Jimmy thinks he has woken up is fictional but based on the old Nassau General Hospital, which was behind the funeral home. Nassau General is no longer there.

I thought it might be fun to have Floyd from Mayberry play the doctor. Actor Howard McNear can be heard in many, many radio dramas from the 1940s and 50s with his instantly recognizable voice, decades before Mayberry was created. He was the original voice of Doc Adams in the radio version of Gunsmoke. He also played robbers, murderers, cops, doctors, essentially any role the radio script called for, but it always sounded like Floyd. He played Floyd from 1961 to 1967. Many people – myself included – didn't know McNear suffered a debilitating stroke in 1963 and played Floyd for three more years despite being unable to use the right side of his body. Many scenes were shot with him sitting on a bench outside the barber shop, as opposed to his pre-stroke scenes showing him inside the shop trimming hair. In most of his post-stroke scenes, McNear's left hand would be holding a newspaper or resting in his lap while he moved his right arm and hand as he spoke his lines. Howard McNear passed away in Los Angeles in 1969 at age 63.

I have tried to be true to the late 1940s-era landmarks in downtown Fernandina Beach, Florida. You can find internet pictures of the 'old' downtown and see the cobblestone street, Thompson Sundries, the mural on the store's exterior wall advertising their Luncheonette, and the Western Union sign a few doors away.

Web surfing will also reveal pictures of the Palace Saloon at the end of the main thoroughfare. Originally constructed as a haberdashery in 1878, Louis G. Hirth bought the Prescott building in 1903, replaced shoes with booze, and named it the Palace Saloon.

According to local lore, it was the last bar in Florida to close on the eve of Prohibition. A shrewd businessman, owner Louis G. Hirth stored up for a last hurrah selling till midnight and grossing $60,000 in a single day. Another first for the Palace, it was the first hard liquor bar to begin serving Coca-Cola around 1905 and allegedly the first to serve rum and Coke. The Palace survived the Prohibition years by selling Texaco gasoline, ice cream, special wines, 3 percent near beer, and cigars.

Between nurses from the hospital, Thompson's Luncheonette, the Palace Saloon, and characters we've met before, Jimmy's days and nights should keep him busy in book #4, *Perchance 2 Dream*.

About the Author

Mike Zimmerli is an author, ghostwriter, and editor whose fingerprints can be found in over three dozen books, usually intentionally. Although most of his previous work has been as an editor, he is now writing and publishing his own series, *The Blue Bridge Mysteries*, featuring Jimmy Favreaux. He continues to work as a freelance editor.

A Minnesota native, he has lived in several places between the northern and southern borders of the Gopher State. In 2004, Mike and his beautiful bride, Mary, abandoned their empty nest, sold everything, and moved to St. Marys, Georgia – as far south as you can go without stepping into Florida and as far east as you can go without getting your feet wet in the Atlantic. From 2004 through 2020, Mike was in church ministry, and for the last twelve years at First

Baptist Church of St. Marys, GA, serving as the director of music and senior adults.

After a lifetime of writing words for others – through radio, newspaper, blogs, and full-time ministry, Mike – prompted in part by the pandemic – became a freelance writer and editor in 2021. That year, he published his dad's memoirs, *One Soldier's Story* by Jacob Wesley Zimmerli, which recounts his experiences in the Pacific Theater of War in 1944-45. That same year, Mike started freelance editing full-time.

Two years later, after editing or ghostwriting over two dozen books for others, it was time for Mike to write under his own name, and Jimmy Favreaux was "born." *Zamboni Is Not A Pasta* became the first installment of The Blue Bridge Mysteries, and *Wanted: Dead or Alive (Again)* continued where *Zamboni* left off. *To the Last Breath* marks book number three in the series, and there's more fun to come!